Praise for
Felicity George

'An evocative romance with a delightfully unconventional
heroine and a hero I fell in love with'
VIRGINIA HEATH

'The perfect mix of dramatic, sexy, emotional
and deliciously romantic'
CRESSIDA McLAUGHLIN

'This is Felicity George's best book so far. A powerful
exploration of the dark reality of women's lives in the Regency,
as well as a gripping and deeply satisfying love story. I couldn't
put it down and when I finally did it was with a happy sigh'
EMMA ORCHARD

'Oh what fun! It's a treat!'
JANE DUNN

'A gorgeous, captivating Regency romance'
SOPHIE IRWIN

'A smart story, compelling writing and a big
smile on any reader's face when they finish'
JODI ELLEN MALPAS

'A scorching romance combined with a very
satisfying mystery. Readers are in for a treat'
JESSICA BULL

Felicity George is a writer and teacher from Toronto, where she lives with her husband, her two teenage children, a large cat, and a tiny dog. A lifelong devotee of Jane Austen and Georgette Heyer, Felicity adores a happily-ever-after.

Connect with Felicity

X Felicity George @FGeorgeRomance
🦋 @felicitygeorge.bsky.social
f Felicity George, Author @FelicityGeorgeRegencyRomance
📷 @felicitygeorge_romance

Also by Felicity George

THE GENTLEMEN OF LONDON

A Lady's Risk
A Courtesan's Worth
A Debutante's Desire

A Lady's Guide to Murder

FELICITY GEORGE

ORION

An Orion paperback

First published in Great Britain in 2025
by Orion Fiction, an imprint of The Orion Publishing Group Ltd,
Carmelite House, 50 Victoria Embankment
London EC4Y 0DZ

An Hachette UK company

1 3 5 7 9 10 8 6 4 2

The authorised representative in the EEA is Hachette Ireland,
8 Castlecourt Centre, Dublin 15, D15 XTP3,
Ireland (email: info@hbgi.ie)

A CIP catalogue record for this book
is available from the British Library.

ISBN (Paperback) 978 1 3987 2222 4
ISBN (eBook) 978 1 3987 1049 8

Typeset at The Spartan Press Ltd,
Lymington, Hants

Printed and bound in Great Britain by Clays Ltd,
Elcograf S.p.A.

www.orionbooks.co.uk

For Tim, the hero of my real-life romance

DRAMATIS PERSONAE

Henrietta Percy, née Matlock, Duchess of Severn: our protagonist.

Theodore Hawke: a despicable gossip-slinging journalist and constant thorn in Henrietta's side.

Edmund Meredith Percy, seventh Duke of Severn: Henrietta's much older husband; a reformist in the Upper House.

Lord Marlow (Viscount Marlow): Edmund's second cousin on the maternal side and his chief antagonist in Parliament; an infamous rake.

James Beaucastle: the squire of Kennetford Manor and Edmund's dearest friend.

Perceval Percy: Edmund's paternal first cousin and heir presumptive; more interested in pleasure than responsibility.

Désirée du Pont: an opera dancer and Perceval's mistress.

Jane Babcock: Perceval's fiancée; daughter of Bishop and Mrs Babcock; dedicated to social reform.

Lord and Lady Lockington (the Marquess and Marchioness of Lockington): Henrietta's loving but financially constrained parents.

George Matlock, Lord Deancombe: Henrietta's eldest brother amongst five.

Libby Forman: one of many servants working in the Duke of Severn's London household.

Thomas: the duke's principal footman; indisposed on a crucial afternoon.

Sir Robert Baker: Chief Metropolitan Magistrate of the Bow Street Magistrates' Court.

Eliza King: a controversial radical leader revered by many but loathed by the aristocracy.

Mr Quigley: the Duke of Severn's solemn solicitor.

Mrs Ford: Theo Hawke's landlady, with a heart of gold to compensate for her wandering hands.

Jim King: a respected villager from Surrey.

Sam Walker: a disgruntled radical.

Haggett: an incorruptible Bow Street Runner who spells trouble for our protagonist.

PROLOGUE

The gardens of Severn House, Park Lane, Mayfair

Late July 1815

The man leaning towards Henrietta Percy in the twilit garden niche wasn't her husband, but she closed her eyes and pretended he was.

His arm encircled her waist as he drew her against his chest. The plunging neckline of her elegant evening gown met the fine silk of his waistcoat, setting her heart aflutter.

Over the scent of garden roses, a whiff of starch mingled with a hint of tobacco. Henrietta told herself a tale. *It is Edmund's snuff you smell. Your husband's arm clasps you. He is about to kiss you so passionately it will knock the breath from your lungs.* She parted her lips, ready to receive her first romantic kiss from the imaginary Edmund. Her body quivered in anticipation. Almighty God, she needed this. Her pent-up passion was desperate for release.

But the moment the man's mouth captured hers, the illusion

shattered. Surely Edmund's cool lips, which he'd only ever pressed to her hand or cheek, would never be this slobbery. Nor would they taste of sour port and cheese.

Her mind reeled – *this* was what a man's kiss felt like? The open-mouth kissing she'd practised on her pillow had been infinitely better, even if it had ended with a mouthful of lint! When she'd touched her breasts in her lonely, cold bed or had slipped a hand between her legs, she'd made herself shiver with delight, so, naturally, she'd expected new heights of pleasure from a real kiss. But this? Well, if this sloppy mess was representative of the sexual experience for a woman, it was a wonder babies existed.

Just then, the firework show began, the timing too absurdly coincidental not to make Henrietta giggle, even as her companion's sluglike tongue probed her mouth. The cracks and sizzles of the rockets were met by distant, polite exclamations from the guests enjoying the evening rout. Everyone's mood was elevated after Waterloo, so celebrations abounded – and this happened to be the new Duchess of Severn's hosting debut, a mere two months after her wedding.

Henrietta was missing her own party and for a man she'd never liked, whose kiss was nothing short of repulsive.

She disengaged. 'Enough, Lord Marlow.' After all, she'd never intended to finalise an arrangement tonight. Only to test the waters – and they were decidedly foul! 'We must return or others will mark our absence.'

'This won't take me long, Duchess.' Marlow lifted her skirts with one hand and grabbed the fall of his breeches with the other.

His presumption was so appalling, Henrietta gasped outright, which seemed to increase his ardour. He responded by clawing at her petticoats. Disgusting. Yet since she was now a duchess and no longer the impetuous wildling of her childhood, she'd provide Marlow one last chance to behave like a gentleman before shoving him to the ground. 'My lord, cease your groping before you crumple my gown! For my husband's sake, I must be discreet.'

Marlow chuckled deep, his fingers digging into the flesh of her thigh. 'I don't care one whit if Severn knows he's a cuckold. Dry old men oughtn't take wild young beauties to wife if they don't intend to share.'

Now utterly furious, Henrietta planted her hands on Marlow's chest and pushed. The scoundrel stumbled back but managed to keep his feet. 'Do not disrespect my husband, and be not so careless with my reputation, sir.' She mustered all the aristocratic authority of the daughter of a marquess, and the wife of a duke. Frankly, a viscount should quake in her presence.

Marlow didn't quake, but he did readjust his breeches and smooth his waistcoat as he grumbled. 'You're a poor sport to play coy now, but, very well, we won't tonight.'

Henrietta set about repairing her crushed skirts with a scowl. What a disastrous beginning she'd made. She'd only ever intended to initiate a mild flirtation with Marlow at this soirée, for she must acclimatise herself to her task. She certainly didn't relish the thought of conducting an affair.

In fact, in order to make a start at all, she'd had to fortify her nerves with two – or was it three? – glasses of champagne. That was where she'd erred. When she'd cut her eyes invitingly towards Marlow, he'd responded immediately with a bold lift of his brow and purse of his lips, as if blowing a kiss. The viscount was a handsome, practised rake, and, frankly, his attention had gone straight to Henrietta's tipsy head, leading her to accept his arm when he suggested a stroll through her lantern-lit gardens. But she'd expected him to play his part appropriately, with the proper standards of discretion and deference; since he hadn't, he was clearly no gentleman.

Henrietta decided she'd never tryst with him again.

Marlow clasped her hand before she could duck out of the niche. 'I shall call upon you tomorrow, Henrietta.'

'You most certainly will *not*, my lord,' she said firmly. 'And as I did not give you leave to call me by my Christian name, refrain from such familiarity in the future.'

His lips curled into a smile. 'What an enchanting minx you are, ma'am. Do not put me off again. For weeks, you've cast me languishing looks—'

'I've done no such thing!' She was properly incensed now.

He covered her lips with two fingers. 'No need to protest for the sake of decorum, my jewel. I shall call tomorrow.'

Then he bowed, lifting her hand to his mouth, and, despite his vileness, Henrietta's silly heart fluttered. Marlow was Edmund's second cousin on the maternal side – the men bore a striking physical resemblance, from their blonde hair to their tall build – and when she could see only the top of Marlow's head, she couldn't help but imagine he was Edmund.

Oh, how she longed to hear words of ardent desire from her husband, but theirs was a marriage of convenience. He had his role; she had hers. She'd accepted these terms before she'd wed him and she'd been grateful for them, as her marriage fulfilled her destiny, her life purpose. From birth, she'd been raised to marry title and fortune combined; her father, the Marquess of Lockington, couldn't afford to endow her with a large portion, for he'd spent his lifetime repairing the ruinous excesses of the previous marquess. The Matlock family was not yet free of debt and Henrietta's brothers also required provision.

In turn, she was beautiful, young and well-bred, a visual testament to Edmund's virility, lest anyone doubt it as he slipped into middle age. With such a wife, no one would dare accuse him of being too dry and dispassionate to lead the fractionated Whigs into unification at last.

By the standards of her class, she and Edmund had formed a perfect union. And Henrietta counted herself fortunate. Or mostly fortunate. Usually. After all, she hadn't been raised to expect a love match – and a kind, temperate, generous husband was more than many ladies received.

The trouble was, she'd never been lonelier in her life.

After Marlow had departed, Henrietta paused once more to assess her appearance by feel, wanting to return to her husband looking flawless. She gingerly adjusted her flaxen curls, straightened her diadem and confirmed the presence of both ten-carat teardrop earrings, two of the Percy diamonds.

Everything being in order, she emerged from the niche, plastering a stately smile upon her face, ready to face her guests as the elegant young Duchess of Severn.

'If you wish to hide the evidence of your sport, Your Grace,' said a masculine voice behind her shoulder, emanating from the niche she'd vacated and causing Henrietta to very nearly jump out of her skin, 'then you might want this.'

Horrified, Henrietta gathered her thoughts before facing this unexpected threat. Not that the man's tone was menacing, for he sounded more disappointed than anything else, but if he'd witnessed her interaction with Marlow – and he *must* have done so, given what he'd said – that was not only quite thoroughly sordid, but also a potential catastrophe.

Naturally, a gentleman would most definitely think twice before causing her trouble, no matter what he'd seen (if for no other reason than that he wouldn't want to be twenty paces from a pistol held by her husband, her father or any of her five elder brothers), yet, based on the speaker's faint Cockney accent, he wasn't gently bred. Who was he then? One of the footmen? A gardener? If so, why was his voice unfamiliar?

Oh, turn and get your answers, Henrietta told herself, *and don't be a weakling about it.* She swished about on her heel, confidence abounding. After all, she could manage men. Her brothers had ensured she'd had a well-rounded education in all manner of self-defence, physical and otherwise. It was nothing to put a peeping Tom in his place.

Yet her resolve faltered when she saw him amongst the roses, his back to the brick garden wall, her garter ribbon dangling from his fingers. The shadow of his hat hid the details of his upper face, but he was a decidedly tall, broad-shouldered man. And confident, standing as he was, with his feet firmly planted in the exact spot where Marlow had kissed her. His rough woollen tailcoat, dark neckcloth and sturdy boots fitted his frame rather breathtakingly well, but they weren't bespoke items from the exclusive shops of Bond Street and St James's, confirming that he wasn't of the *ton*. Henrietta's wariness grew. He certainly wasn't one of her servants, so why was he in her private walled garden?

He spoke again. 'Or perhaps you *do* wish to reappear at your fête with your stocking rumpled round your ankles?' A bit of mocking now, but there was still a note of disappointment in his voice. Or sadness, perhaps. Similar to Mama's tone on those many occasions when young Henrietta had accidentally torn yet another new frock by climbing a tree or scrapping with one of her brothers.

Her garter's silver embroidery glinted as more fireworks burst overhead.

As their light briefly illuminated the man's entire face, a memory stirred in her mind. He wasn't unfamiliar – those eyes had pierced into her before, not so long ago, when she'd been standing amidst a crowd. Where had it been? She racked her brain for details, recalling that when she'd returned his gaze over a sea of heads, she'd been momentarily captivated. Not merely because of his features – firm chin and jawline, straight dark brows, all strong angles pleasingly offset by surprisingly tender and full lips – but because something about his thoughtful, observant expression had reminded her of Edmund. Henrietta gave her head a little shake, irritated at her fanciful mind, always torturing her with thoughts of her unrequited love.

Quite suddenly, she recalled where she'd encountered the man before. 'You were standing in Hanover Square, after my wedding in May.'

Another firework burst, allowing her to witness the glimmer of surprise that crossed his face before shadow fell again. 'Please accept my compliments on Your Grace's performance that day.' Now there was most *definitely* a mocking air about him and no trace of sadness. Perhaps she'd imagined it before. 'You acted so convincingly like a bride devoted to her husband that you fooled me entirely until tonight. But I should not be surprised. Once again, I am reminded your class doesn't concern itself with trifling nonsense like morality.'

Indignation swelled Henrietta's breast, but she maintained a composed demeanour. 'While appearances can indeed deceive, you've misconstrued where the deception lies.'

He pushed his hat back, revealing a cynically lifted brow. 'There's only one interpretation of what transpired between you and Marlow, who is a rakehell and reprobate and outright piece of filth. Two months married and you choose to cuckold your admirable husband with the very man who thwarts him politically at every turn? Explain to me why?'

Henrietta narrowed her eyes. So, this bold intruder was choosing to be antagonistic. To what purpose, she didn't know, but she intended to find out. 'I have no obligation to explain myself to a stranger. Tell me, what is your name?' Stepping closer, she studied his features intently, in case she needed to describe them to the Runners later. He was very tall – she rarely had to lift her chin to look a man in the eyes – and quite young, surely not much older than her own three-and-twenty years. 'What reason have you for trespassing in my garden? Do you intend to steal my garter?'

'Not in the least.' He tossed her the ribbon and, as she caught it, he bowed, doffing his hat to reveal dark, wavy hair. He threw out his arms, again in a decidedly mocking manner. 'Theodore Hawke of the *Mayfair Examiner*, regrettably not at *your* service, Your Grace, but dedicated to serving the British public, who deserve to know the truth about the people who live so grandly off the fat of this land.' He replaced his hat with a flourish. 'Therefore, on Wednesday, said public will read about your tryst with Marlow over their morning toast.'

Terror gripped Henrietta. She was in the presence of none other than London's most notorious reporter, a man whose weekly gossip column was gleefully devoured by half the kingdom. A man who possessed the power to unleash scandal from which she might never recover. A man who held nothing and no one sacred.

Except Henrietta's husband.

It was an established fact that Hawke, like many commoners, possessed a soft spot for Edmund, the reforming 'People's Duke', and Henrietta decided to use that to her advantage as she appealed for the reporter's silence. She lost all trace of haughtiness. 'Please, don't reveal what you witnessed, Mr Hawke. It would do my husband great harm.'

'Ah, but I have never yet picked and chosen from the bad behaviour I witness. To do so lacks integrity.'

Angry at her instant failure, Henrietta clenched her fists. '*Integrity* from a gossip-slinger? You delude yourself, Mr Hawke.'

He held up a finger. 'Tsk, tsk. You are in no position to insult me, madam.'

Henrietta considered planting him a facer and only rejected the notion with reluctance, as it was unlikely to help her cause, and extremely likely to leave her knuckles swollen, given Hawke's enviable facial bone structure. 'Then what will you take in exchange for your silence? Name the sum and I shall pay.'

Hawke assumed an air of insincere pity. 'I'm dreadfully sorry, but you cannot alter my resolve.'

Desperation replaced Henrietta's anger. This *couldn't* be published, for there might be no end to the terrible repercussions. Never mind the scandal she'd face – it was far more dreadful to think what people would say of Edmund. They'd mock him as an old cuckold who couldn't satisfy or control his young bride, and Henrietta couldn't bear that.

With a few rushed steps, she was before the reporter, clutching his forearm. 'Please don't. I am willing to do anything.'

Hawke glanced at her hands on his arm, his eyes darkening in a way Henrietta couldn't quite interpret. 'Ah. Anything, is it?' His voice was deeper, huskier than before. 'Forgive my dullness, but what *precisely* do you mean to suggest?'

She'd intended patronage, support, access to other information, perhaps. Whatever a man like Hawke valued and needed. But the change in his demeanour gave her another idea altogether.

Men considered her desirable, or so she understood. Before her marriage, many had tried to kiss her, with passion flaring in their eyes and slurred love words on their lips; many had offered for her hand and had only been rejected because they weren't Edmund. Perhaps Hawke also found her attractive.

Besides, nothing ventured, nothing gained. Henrietta's palms prickled as she attempted a seductive tone. 'I am prepared to offer you a kiss, Mr Hawke.'

For a moment it appeared he might accept and she grew surprisingly excited, her pulse rising as his smouldering gaze moved from hands to bosom, lingered there, and then trailed to her lips. She leant closer, softening her mouth in invitation,

hoping the handsome Hawke's kiss would erase the foul memory
of Marlow.

But when the journalist's eyes once again met hers, a storm
brewed in their dark depths. 'I admit your proposition appeals to
my basest desires. You possess the face of an angel and the body
of a goddess.' His voice was throaty but icy, devoid of mocking or
sorrow. 'Yet neither tempts me enough to forget my respect for
your husband.'

Henrietta's desperation mounted. 'Mr Hawke, you do not
understand. Exposing me as an adulteress will not serve my
husband as you think it will. If you proceed with your report, you
will inflict tremendous harm—'

'In real life, such as *most* of us live, people pay a price for
their actions. Your husband is beloved – by others, if not by you.
People across the kingdom rejoiced at your wedding. Celebrations
abounded. Why? Because it gave them joy and hope to see the
People's Duke take such a lovely young bride, sure to breed
another generation of reformers. I can't expect you to understand,
but joy and hope are precious to those of us who weren't born
with silver spoons in our mouths. Meanwhile, your class has
everything, takes everything, flaunts everything – and yet often
evades accountability, thinking yourselves above morality, above
even the law. Therefore, *I* provide the accountability you receive
nowhere else.'

'Perhaps *some* amongst my class abuse their station.' Henrietta
kept her voice calm, sensing the depth of Hawke's emotion. They
were standing as close as two lovers, with her fingers still curved
over his forearm, and the fervour of his speech reverberated inside
her. 'Perhaps indeed someone has wronged *you* in this manner,
Mr Hawke. But that doesn't mean all of us disregard decency
and honour. Be not judge and jury against me, for nothing in
this world is so simple as black or white. What I did, I did for
reasons—'

Abruptly, Hawke shook off her hands. 'I am not the one to whom you should justify your actions, madam. Explain to your husband. If anyone is your judge and jury, as you say, it is he. Meanwhile, I shall report what I see. This has ever been my way and so it will continue.'

He grabbed the top of the garden wall, hoisted himself up and straddled it.

If he slipped away, all would be lost. 'Mr Hawke, *please*. If you write about this, society is my judge and there is no harsher one.'

He looked down, his dark eyes intense. 'I assure you, there are harsher judges.'

'Why are you set upon my destruction?' she asked in despair.

'I shall merely report your actions. If they lead to your destruction, as you say, it is a consequence of your own choices.'

Henrietta stomped her foot, not caring if her behaviour wasn't that of a duchess. 'Then you are a despicable, wretched, loathsome *beast*.'

'You are certainly entitled to your opinion, Your Grace, but if you read my weekly column, you will come to see I write the truth.' He paused then, and, in the gleam of another firework, Henrietta again read sorrow in his expression. Her hopes rose that she might yet succeed and she extended her arm, intending to touch the side of his leather boot. But he moved his leg out of her reach, swinging it to the top of the wall. With a quick, 'Good evening, madam,' he vanished over the other side.

Henrietta pressed anguished hands to her mouth. For only two months, she'd been married to the man she respected and loved above all others, and to whom she owed her obedience, yet she'd already failed him completely. How she'd extract herself from this catastrophe was a mystery, but one thing was crystal clear.

She'd hate Theodore Hawke until the day she died.

The Hawke's Eye

CONTAINING A Weekly Report of Society's Affairs

After half a decade of tirelessly pursuing hidden truths, rare indeed are the intrigues that elicit genuine astonishment from The Hawke's Eye, yet this week offered one such occasion: at the Duchess of S–n's rout two nights past, this reporter beheld Her Grace the Hostess en flagrante, pressed against a garden wall by none other than her husband's most ardent political adversary – and all this not two months after the kingdom raised a toast to her union with the People's Duke. Be assured, dear Readers, that The Hawke's Eye will keep a vigilant watch on H–a P–y's future affairs...

CHAPTER 1

A Murderous Headache

Five years of (nearly) perfect behaviour later...

Severn House

June 1820

Henrietta reclined on her favourite chaise in her husband's library, engrossed in the day's newspapers as a gentle breeze rustled their pages. Half an hour earlier in this same room, she and Edmund had hosted three afternoon callers she'd much rather not have seen, but, thankfully, those men had now departed, leaving her to enjoy a few precious minutes of quiet camaraderie with the duke.

She didn't typically peruse the broadsheets this late in the day – she preferred to devour them when the smell of ink was still fresh on their pages, snatching each one the moment Edmund laid it aside during breakfast. But she'd ignored the news this morning. *This* morning, she'd been preoccupied with contemplating the meaning of an event from the previous night – namely, that Edmund had kissed her before she'd slipped between her sheets. In a manner quite unlike anything he'd done before. He'd held her tenderly against him. Had trailed one hand down her back until it had rested on the curve of her bottom. And his lips had lingered upon her own.

Following the kiss, he'd said, 'My dear, I've only lately realised how remarkable your steadfast loyalty is – pray, forgive me for the times I've resented it,' and Henrietta's heart had taken flight, for, despite her failure to secure him an heir in five years of marriage, he'd finally recognised her devotion.

He'd spent his weekly night in her bed lying so close his soft snores caressed her shoulder, rendering her own sleep nearly impossible. She'd waited in breathless anticipation for touches that never came, leaving her preoccupied and tired at breakfast.

But the demands of the day had since settled her mind. Whatever Edmund's unexpected intimacy had meant, he'd resumed his typical kind but aloof demeanour ever since his grey eyes had fluttered open on the pillow beside her own.

That kind aloofness had been ever-present in her marriage, both before and after the dreadful scandal of five years earlier. Though his brow had creased when she'd tearfully confessed everything on the night of the soirée, he'd stood resolutely beside her when the news broke, never allowing anyone to disparage her name. That and the staunch support of her loving family had repressed the tide of scandal, albeit with a tenuous hold, like a seawall strained almost to bursting by violent waves.

A stronger gust of wind now drew Henrietta's attention from the article she'd just finished, an anonymously published political treatise advocating for universal suffrage. It had left her mind churning, wondering anew if indeed all British men – *and women* – might one day have a representative voice in Parliament. She gazed through the tall windows, admiring the clouds dotting the sky above Hyde Park, and yearned suddenly to be outside. The breeze was the perfect degree of crisp; in her life prior to becoming a duchess, she and her brothers would have spent a day like this sea-bathing or sailing at their father's estate of Deancombe Manor, which overlooked the Channel not five miles from Brighton.

Henrietta's limbs ached with desire for movement – and nothing was better than exercise to help process her thoughts on the political treatise and consider discreet ways to support its cause without troubling Edmund. While her husband was a progressive Whig leader, he must avoid *radical* issues during these turbulent times. Advocating for more men to have the vote was already considered extreme; broaching topics like property rights and suffrage for women could incite violent reactions. Yet if Henrietta could discover who wrote these independently published articles, several of which had intrigued her in the past, she might aid the author financially so he or she could publish more regularly. But how did one go about investigating an anonymous author's identity?

Thus, her need to think. 'Shall we go for a ride in the park, Edmund?'

Seated in a nearby armchair, the duke flipped a page in his book. 'Not I, my dear, for I have a murderous headache. But you may certainly do as you desire.'

Henrietta's brow furrowed. Edmund never complained of illness and he rarely passed on an opportunity to ride when at leisure. 'I shall stay and care for you,' she said, for there was no question of leaving his side if he felt poorly and she rarely went in public without him anyway. 'Should I send for headache powders? Or the doctor, even?'

He responded without lifting his gaze. 'No need.'

Henrietta considered. 'Tea, then.' She rang her small silver bell on the table alongside the newspapers.

The door opened promptly, but it was the new housemaid, Libby, rather than the principal footman who entered.

'Why! Is Thomas still indisposed?' Henrietta asked of the mousey young woman, for it wasn't Libby's task to wait outside doors and yet, earlier also, the maid had assisted due to Thomas's absence. 'If so, why has the second footman not replaced him?'

'Don't know, Your Grace.' Libby twisted a strand of her unruly brown hair, which seemed incapable of staying confined inside her mobcap. Her gaze darted to the duke, as it often did in his presence, and a spark lit up her unusual eyes – one blue, one green. 'S'pose they might *all* be indisposed.'

'Well, please find a footman or send the butler, Libby.' Henrietta did not want to encourage the young woman's infatuation by having her serve tea to Edmund. 'That'll be all.'

With a lingering glance at the oblivious duke, Libby bobbed a curtsy and turned, knocking her toe on the door as she departed.

'What an odd afternoon,' Henrietta said. '*You* have a headache and the footmen aren't at their posts. I wonder if they are unwell, too? Perhaps I should summon the doctor for the household.'

The corners of Edmund's lips quirked. 'I can't speak for the footmen, but my headache will soon pass. It's merely the consequence of spending an afternoon in Marlow's company.'

Henrietta forced a smile, for Edmund was making a jest. Personally, she despised Marlow – not only because of what had occurred between them, but also because he was always seeking to thwart the good her husband tried to do in Parliament.

Edmund had been closeted alone in the library with the viscount for an hour before the other two visitors – his heir presumptive, Perceval Percy, and Edmund's reclusive friend, James Beaucastle – had unexpectedly arrived, both claiming an urgent need to speak to the duke. It had been then that Henrietta had joined the men, anticipating that her presence as hostess would ease any potential tension amongst such a diverse group of guests. And it had. After exchanges of pleasantries all around, Edmund had conversed quietly with each of the new visitors while Henrietta had forced herself to speak primarily to horrid Marlow, who she knew hated her with that unparalleled vitriol that only an arrogant and powerful man, spurned, could produce. But, as always, she and Marlow had produced a passable show of amiability until Edmund had ordered a particular bottle of wine 'to drink to Britain's glory'. Libby had served, due to Thomas's absence; everyone had enjoyed a glass or two, and the three men had left with no further ado.

'Was your meeting with Marlow productive?' Henrietta was extremely curious to hear about it, if Edmund was willing to tell her.

'Surprisingly so. I've discovered something Marlow desires enough to back me as party leader.'

As the daughter and wife of devout Whigs, Henrietta pursed her lips doubtfully. 'I fail to comprehend how Marlow calls himself a Whig when his views align more closely with the Tories. He doesn't support *any* reform measures.'

'Family tradition, Henrietta – and because he and our King are old carousing mates, which is what makes Marlow's support so crucial. Even if my fellow party members choose me to lead before the next election, becoming prime minister hinges on His Majesty's appointment.'

'But will Marlow also assist you in bringing about a repeal of the Six Acts?' Henrietta ventured the question though she knew Edmund didn't like her asking about political reform. He regarded her ideas on female property and voting rights as dangerously radical – not to mention incompatible with the role of women in society. Since her father shared that opinion, Henrietta was accustomed to being told not to bother her mind with the matters of men.

Edmund glanced up from his book then, his grey eyes unusually dark. Though two-and-twenty years her senior, he was a striking man, his thinning blonde hair turning a glorious shade of silver, his figure still trim and upright, and, deep inside, Henrietta's old passions flared. While she'd mostly learnt to repress such feelings, his bedtime kiss the night before had evidently stoked some embers of desire.

'No, my dear girl.' Edmund spoke in a gratingly paternal manner that served to temper Henrietta's unwelcome ardour very well indeed. 'But that was not my objective. Now, no more political talk from my wife, if you please.'

But now that the topic had been broached, she couldn't let it go. She'd always struggled to hold her tongue when she yearned so desperately to be part of the change. 'Edmund, the Six Acts repress the freedoms of press and of speech, which are necessary for the success of long-due reforms. And while some reformers go too far by veering into radicalism, to punish all people by restricting meetings and stifling ideologies—'

'Enough, Henrietta.' He spoke quietly but severely. 'Kindly remember that I took my place in the Upper House before you were born.'

A wave of mortification flushed over her. As accustomed as she was to disappointing him, she still hated inciting his displeasure. Besides, her wish to be heard was an impossible dream. 'Forgive me, Edmund. I should've held my tongue. I am sorry I angered you.'

He softened. 'Sweet, beautiful girl, I'm not cross. As I've explained countless times, I simply wish to protect you. Conversations like this pose risks. Although I have long striven for parliamentary reform – advocating for the abolishment of rotten boroughs and expanding voter eligibility, as you are aware – it *is* a Tory government. Additionally, Cato Street instilled tremendous fear in my peers.'

'But the Cato Street conspirators were traitors, not reformers,' Henrietta said hesitatingly. 'True reformers would never conspire to assassinate the prime minister and the cabinet.'

Edmund inclined his head. 'There is a fine line between reform and radicalism, and a finer one yet between radicalism and treason. I urge you to be careful – these delicate distinctions are the cause of my present political difficulties. If I do not proceed cautiously in my support of the people's causes, I shall make powerful enemies who will hinder what progress I've made to date. Now, my dear, my home is a respite from these distressing matters and you are the mistress of my respite, so let this topic be. *Please.*'

'Of course,' Henrietta replied, and then said no more. Edmund meant well. He was noble and honourable, through and through, but, naturally, they viewed matters from different perspectives.

She harboured no resentment. She understood Edmund's expectations of his duchess: a society leader, a hostess, a household manager and a vessel for carrying his heir, at whatever cost. As the daughter of a reformist marquess and his fecund lady, Henrietta was well qualified for the role; she'd entered it eagerly and although all those tasks had proven much more difficult than she'd anticipated, she had no regrets. She loved Edmund, and being the Duchess of Severn was no small matter. It allowed her a tremendous reach of influence within the spheres of women.

Or it would, if she could ever overcome those whiffs of scandal that *still* hovered about her despite Edmund's support, all because of that bloody journalist, Theodore Hawke…

If one could call the lurid filth that dribbled from his quill 'journalism'.

Which reminded Henrietta that *somewhere* in the pile of newspapers beside her would be that rag Hawke wrote for, the *Mayfair Examiner*, because it was a Wednesday, its weekly publication day. She sifted through the papers until she found it. Gingerly pinching it between her fingers, she skimmed past the advertisements and a sensationalist article claiming the fugitive conspirator, Eliza King, had been spotted in London, to the column that dominated the third page: *The Hawke's Eye. All-Seeing Observer of Society's*

Affairs, as he was evidently calling himself this week. Other times, he bestowed ridiculous titles upon himself such as *Truth-Seeker of Mayfair* and *Dutiful Reporter of Dastardly Deeds*. She curled her lip. If Parliament felt the need to control the press, why had they not repressed gossip rags along with political radicalism?

After five years of reading Hawke's weekly column – and watching him closely, on the frequent occasions when Henrietta had had the misfortune of encountering him on the prowl – she'd accepted that the man wrote what he deemed to be the truth, but his dichotomous thinking frustrated her. It was a waste of the talents she begrudgingly realised he possessed.

She scanned the densely printed lines of this week's column, searching for the familiar 'S–n' ('Severn' thinly disguised), to see if Hawke had generated poison about her this week. Her heart positively stopped when she spotted it in the third paragraph – but it resumed beating when she realised it was a piece on her husband's cousin.

> Mr P–l P–y, the Duke of S–n's heir presumptive (and likely to remain so, since Her Grace has yet to produce what is euphemistically termed 'a token of affection' for her husband)...

Ah, so there was a dig at Henrietta after all, and *she* knew what that beastly Theodore Hawke wished to imply – not so much that she was barren, but that she didn't love Edmund.

Henrietta ground her teeth. Vile, hateful man. He understood nothing. *Nothing.* The next time she saw him lurking, she'd glare at him even more venomously than usual and she *wouldn't* be affected by the bold wink with which he often countered. For that was what their interactions had become – an exchange of accusatory expressions only they understood. Her cold condemnation declared: *You waste your talents by refusing to see shades of grey*, and his cocky assurance countered with: *No, you refuse to acknowledge my consistent lack of bias as journalistic integrity*. She knew as much, because on the few occasions when they'd edged close enough to each other to hiss words under their breath without drawing attention, they'd said some variation of the same.

Well, except for *one* time, on *that* day – that exceedingly odd day – when she'd been shopping with her mother. She and Mama had been progressing along Bond Street, approaching a wagon delivering beer to a tavern, when a quarter-tun hogshead barrel had rolled off its skids, heading straight for Mama. Realising the danger, Henrietta had sidestepped to swiftly shield her parent; at the same moment, Hawke had suddenly appeared (well, no doubt he'd been trailing them) and had thrown himself between Henrietta and the barrel. The force of the impact had bowled him over. He'd fallen to the ground with a grunt – Lord, who wouldn't have, with five hundred pounds chucked at them? – but he'd got back to his feet and had steadied the barrel. Henrietta and her mother, and the crowd of pedestrians who'd been frozen in terror, had watched as he'd then helped the delivery men carry the hogshead down the stairwell into the basement of the public. Despite her mother urging her to walk on, so as not to be seen interacting with the man, Henrietta had waited until Hawke had crested the stairs again. His surprise at seeing her still there had been immediately evident, for his cheeks had coloured slightly and he'd replaced his customary cockiness with a warily lifted brow.

He'd made as if to move on without a word, but she'd inserted herself in his path and had held out her hand. 'Mr Hawke, stay a moment. In gratitude for your ... your service to ... to my mother, may I please arrange for my physician to call upon you at your residence? You received a dreadful blow and though you appear unharmed, you might have internal injuries.'

For a moment, she thought he wouldn't take her hand, much less answer her enquiry. But then he looked between her white kid glove and his ink-stained hand, wiped his palm on his breeches, and took only the tips of her fingers between his. His touch was gentle but firm – causing her heart to skip a beat for some un-accountable reason – and he bowed handsomely as he responded. 'I am quite well, thank you, Your Grace. But I intended no service beyond what I would do for anyone in danger. Neither you nor her ladyship owe me anything.'

And then he released her to continue on his way, leaving Henrietta with an odd longing for less hostility between them. However, that longing passed as soon as she recalled what he had done, and, now, as a rule, Henrietta tried not to think of the Bond Street encounter, for it didn't absolve Hawke of his prior actions.

She returned to reading about her husband's heir, curious what had landed Perceval in the gossip rag. He'd been in their library with the other guests, not half an hour past, and he'd cast nervous glances at Edmund all the while.

> ... recently announced his impending union with the ravish-ing Miss B–k, rightfully crowned this Season's Incomparable, for she possesses wealth and beauty, and – what is of more critical need to Mr P–y – intelligence to boot. But this reporter wonders if there will be a wedding once Miss B–k's papa, the bishop, learns his prospective son-in-law was seen tying a necklace around a certain opera dancer's swanlike neck in the shady refuge of a Hyde Park elm last Sunday morning, when he really ought to have been in church.

Anger flared as Henrietta thought of sweet, brilliant Jane Babcock. During the girl's first afternoon call after the engage-ment, Henrietta had learnt Jane harboured opinions that aligned with her own on matters of social and political reforms, and they'd fallen into a delightful tête-à-tête that far surpassed the customary twenty minutes and had necessitated the consumption of *three* pots of tea and a *second* tray of cake and fruit.

Perceval's ability to win the heart of such a worthy young lady had impressed Henrietta. Now, she was incensed on Jane's behalf.

'Perceval still keeps his mistress?' she asked Edmund. 'If so, 'tis no wonder he looked fit for the gallows this afternoon. Is Jane to cry off the wedding?'

Edmund looked up from his book, his eyes positively black. 'My dear, you know better than to lend credence to Theodore Hawke's column.'

Henrietta's cheeks warmed. Again, she ought to have held her tongue. There was an unspoken agreement amongst the beau monde to pretend Hawke's column was meritless. Although *The Hawke's Eye* had been the initial source of revealing the Charitable Relief Scandal, which had ultimately exposed a network of corruption and embezzlement by government officials, no one had ever publicly credited Hawke with uncovering that abuse of power. Nor had they acknowledged he'd been the reason public attention had been at last drawn to a dreadful case of domestic cruelty by a prominent parliamentarian. Even as intervention had been imposed, forcing the MP to relinquish his wife and children to the safety of her family, no one had credited Hawke's role. It was best to *pretend* his column was worthless, for, at some point, nearly everyone fell under his ruthless pen in one way or the other.

As Henrietta contemplated Hawke's column, she observed her husband and her thoughts of gossip and its merits began to vanish, replaced by concern for Edmund. He had returned to his book, but he rubbed his temples as he read. His face was flushed and he shifted in his seat, as if uncomfortable or uneasy.

What could the matter be?

'Edmund, did Perceval upset you when he called today?' she asked gently.

Edmund shook his head, although his colour belied the action.

He was becoming purplish, the way some men looked when suppressing anger, although never Edmund, whose manner was always unimpeachable.

Despite his appearance, he delivered his response with his customary composure. 'Perceval called to inform me that despite the implications in Hawke's column, his relationship with his former mistress ended before his engagement. According to him, she continues to make troublesome demands, but he claims to have spoken to both Miss Babcock and her father about the matter.'

'That *greatly* relieves me,' Henrietta said sincerely. 'That he ended the relationship and that he's spoken to Jane, I mean. Not that he continues to be harassed by his former mistress.' She didn't like to think badly of Perceval. If the worst happened and Edmund died before she managed to bring herself to produce a son, she'd be dependent upon Perceval's generosity. Her meagre dowry alone would keep her only in genteel poverty.

'You are hot and cold, my dear – too quick to jump to conclusions. Regardless of whether Perceval has shed his mistress, Hawke's column will bring trouble and precisely at the time when it is most imperative Perceval's character be unblemished.'

'But why? If Jane and her father forgive him, what matters anyone else's opinion?'

Edmund skirted her question. 'It remains to be seen if Perceval's newfound maturity can weather this storm.' Although he spoke calmly, his voice was becoming rather thick, as if affected by emotion, which was again unusual. He stuck two fingers under his cravat and tugged, loosening its hold. 'At any rate, I caution you strongly against optimism.'

Henrietta pleaded Perceval's case. 'I believe he is changing his ways for Jane. He loves her and she is a sensible, clever girl. With her influence, he will continue to embrace duty.'

Edmund's gaze was intense. 'I know why you wish to believe

that,' he said firmly. 'But it is still best for the dukedom if you give me the son you promised, my wife.'

Five years of guilt washed over Henrietta. She had promised, it was true, but she'd promised rashly, before she'd understood the impossibility of bedding one man, when one was married to another. She'd tried – that one time, she *had* tried – but the whole encounter turned her stomach when she thought of it. Not merely because of Hawke's interference, but because she knew disloyalty went against the very fibre of her being. She'd made a sacred vow of faithfulness and though faithfulness meant different things to her and to Edmund, the one scrap of individuality she had as a married woman in her society was to hold to her values and principles. If she discarded them, she discarded her autonomy entirely. And she hadn't yet been able to bring herself to do that, despite her love for Edmund.

Or perhaps because of it. Because if her role was 'wife', was it not up to her how to interpret that role? Just as it was Edmund's prerogative to determine his roles of 'husband', 'duke', and 'politician'?

So, despite what he said, of course Edmund was cross at her for what he considered to be misguided stubbornness rather than the actions of an obedient wife. In fact, he was so upset he was becoming physically ill. He was dabbing his forehead with a pristine handkerchief – he who never sweated without physical exertion, he whose skin was always as cool and smooth as marble.

Henrietta cast aside the silly gossip rag. 'Forgive me, Edmund. My disloyalty has made you unwell.'

'What nonsense, child. As I told you last night, you are excessively loyal, but let us not speak of that now.' His eyes darted to the window, his fingers picking at his collar again. 'It's rather warm in here, is it not?'

Henrietta considered. True, the sky was bright, but no afternoon sun streamed into the room and the breeze was pleasant. No, there was something troubling Edmund and if it wasn't Marlow, Perceval or Henrietta, it must be…

Her mouth went dry. She was about to trespass on forbidden grounds, but, as a wife, she had a right to be worried about her husband. 'Then was it Mr Beaucastle who upset you?' She named Edmund's reclusive friend, the third gentleman who had been in the library half an hour earlier.

'James?' he said, too quickly. 'Nonsense again, Henrietta! I told you I'm not upset.'

She didn't believe it. Edmund was putting her off, like he always did if she spoke of Beaucastle. 'He did so! He did something to upset you, Edmund. I know he did, because I know you argued dreadfully with him yesterday over *something* and today he returned, and I do think he meant to continue the quarrel had not Perceval and Marlow been with you as well.'

'Nothing of the sort,' Edmund said testily. 'It's merely that it's a devilish warm day. I'm overheated.' His words were slurred and Henrietta wondered if he'd had more wine than the two glasses she'd thought he'd consumed – but that couldn't be, for Edmund was never in his cups. 'This blasted library is as hot as hellfire. I must remove my coat.'

He rose abruptly, his book clattering to the floor, and staggered, clutching the arm of his chair with such force his nails dug into the upholstery, his knuckles whitening, his knees giving way.

And then he vomited violently on the carpet.

Henrietta sprang to her feet, overturning the newspapers, and rushed to support him, for he was swaying dangerously, on the verge of collapsing to the floor. He must be having a seizure from illness, she realised – he'd once told her he'd suffered one during a feverish ailment in his youth, terrifying his mother, though he'd come out of it soon enough.

Henrietta understood his late mother's distress, for Edmund's seizure was horrible to behold. Only a sliver of grey surrounded his vast black pupils, he'd turned a ghastly shade of puce, and his tongue and lips were swelling.

'Oh, how do I help, Edmund?'

Gurgling, he put both hands to his collar, frantically clawing at his neck, gouging his skin with his nails. His breath, his clothes, stank of vomit and wine. And of something else. Something unfamiliar. Something sweet, but putrid.

The full weight of his body now rested in Henrietta's arms and she collapsed under him when he fell to the floor. His torso pinned down her legs; otherwise, she would have run to pull the bell or open the door, screaming for assistance. But then again, perhaps she could not have done so, even if she weren't holding him, for she couldn't leave him when he was in so much pain.

Making what use she had of one hand, she tugged at his cravat. 'I shall loosen this knot and you will breathe easier, my beloved.'

Edmund gripped her wrist with both of his hands, staying her progress. 'My dear...' He gasped. 'My dear...'

'How do I help?'

'No, *my dear*...'

'I'm here, Edmund, I'm here.'

'*My dear... ah.*' He struggled to form the words and cried out in frustration as his convulsions intensified. 'My dear... ah... sweet... killed me.'

Then Edmund inhaled a terrible, rasping breath and, on the exhale, his body softened and he whispered one word – '*James*' – as his hands released her wrists and fell like rocks to his chest.

A scream filled the room. Long, shrill. It wasn't stopping, it wasn't going away...

And it wasn't until a second later when the library door burst open and Thomas the footman entered, his face twisting as he beheld her cradling Edmund's lifeless body, her hand at his throat, that she realised it was her own cries piercing her ears.

Screaming bloody murder.

CHAPTER 2

Mourning at Twilight

As the sixth child and only daughter of the Marchioness of Lockington, Henrietta had been raised by a great lady, to be a great lady, capable of navigating life with grace and composure; moreover, one didn't grow up with five elder brothers and not learn how to hold one's own. Therefore, the second she realised *she* was the one screaming, she fell silent, though her emotions raced frantic and afraid.

After a moment, she regained the ability to think. 'The doctor,' she said to Thomas, hoping above all else that Edmund yet lived. 'At once, for heaven's sake. *At once!*'

She pressed her ear to her husband's chest, listening for a heartbeat. She touched his wrist, feeling for a pulse. When these measures produced nothing, she shook him in her desperation, her eyes stinging and her voice breaking as she repeated, 'Breathe, Edmund, breathe.'

The butler, Wallington, approached, placed a silver spoon under

Edmund's nose and then gently removed Henrietta's clinging hands from her husband's coat. 'His Grace is gone, Your Grace.'

Henrietta sat back on her heels, absorbing the enormity of Wallington's declaration. Her husband was dead and this abrupt cessation to his existence – as quick as a snip of a thread – also extinguished her own identity. Her purpose in life, even. At eight-and-twenty, she was a widow. A *childless*, widowed duchess, which was an unenviable condition amongst the nobility, as it meant her status was expensive and necessary to uphold for the sake of appearances, but useful to no one. Her youth was a drain, not an asset. Furthermore, she was a childless widowed duchess who, without Edmund's steadfast support, reeked of scandal. And unless he'd provided for her in his will, she was all that and poor to boot, dependent upon a man she'd just been cautioned against.

She descended into a nightmarish realm of muted sound and blurred movement, her thoughts creeping like a snail through a fog while she knelt at her husband's side, holding his dead hand in hers, stroking it as if she could still comfort him.

In time, Dr Davies arrived and conducted the same pulse checks she'd performed earlier. 'Were you present at the time of his passing, Your Grace?'

'Yes,' she answered flatly, still utterly unable to absorb the enormity of what had happened.

The doctor peered from beneath prominent steel-grey eyebrows. 'Anyone else in the room? A servant, perhaps?'

She shook her head. 'We were reading together.'

Dr Davies' gaze lingered on Edmund's eyes. 'What was the last substance His Grace ingested, ma'am?'

'A glass of wine.'

He inspected the toffee-coloured vomit on the rug, then dipped a finger into the substance, sniffed, and muttered. 'Makes no sense.'

His comment was so odd it sparked a curiosity that over-powered Henrietta's dullness. 'What makes no sense, Doctor?'

she asked, leaning over Edmund's body in order to observe the vomit herself.

'It ought to have colour.' The medical man mused more to himself than to her.

The response was frustratingly unclear. 'Do you mean the *wine* ought to have colour?' she asked. 'It was a fortified wine. Madeira, of an amber hue.'

Dr Davies didn't reply on the matter. Instead, he pointed to the clawlike streaks upon Edmund's jaw and neck. 'And these marks?'

'His cravat was too tight.'

Dr Davies' gaze fell to her hands. He seemed to take special note of her long nails and then put a shaking hand to the knot of his own cravat. 'I see,' he said, and cleared his throat.

'Was it a seizure?' she asked. 'He had a seizure once, in child-hood.'

The doctor was still grimacing at her hands. 'A seizure?' He took a moment, blinked, and then examined Edmund's eyes again. 'A possibility, I suppose…'

She elaborated. 'He was complaining of a headache—'

He whipped his head around, eyes blazing. 'A headache? Well, and if His Grace complained of a headache, why did you not summon me, Your Grace?'

'B-because he didn't want me to.' Henrietta's throat tightened. Would Edmund still be alive if she'd defied his wishes and sent for Dr Davies? The notion was agonising and she pressed Edmund's hand against her cheek. 'Oh, how I wish I had.'

The doctor's stern gaze softened slightly.

'So it was a seizure?' she asked again.

He grasped Edmund's armchair, hoisting himself up with a grunt. 'That I cannot ascertain, Your Grace. I must send for a colleague.'

He dispatched Thomas on the errand, then conferred with Wallington in a corner of the library, their gazes steady upon

Henrietta and Edmund. Though uncomfortable under the scrutiny, she remained at her husband's side. As long as his body lay in the library, she knew her place. Drawing in a deep breath to stave off tears, she leant forward to close his eyes.

'Don't, Your Grace!' Dr Davies' abrupt command startled her. 'Do not touch the duke's eyes.'

'But I must close them before much longer.' Her mother had taught her how to tend to the dead, for a lady showed that respect to her servants and to her tenants when her assistance was desired or required. 'Within the first hour or the lids will stiffen.'

Dr Davies shook his head. 'My colleague will close them in due course, but they must remain open now. Otherwise, Dr Grimsley may not be able to determine the cause of death. If it was, indeed, a seizure.'

Reluctantly, Henrietta acquiesced, although Edmund's open-eyed gaze unsettled her. His eyes were too black and staring, as if he weren't at peace. As if his spirit lingered in disquiet, unable to ascend to the eternal reward he deserved for a lifetime of faithful service to his country and countrymen.

Eventually, Dr Grimsley arrived, a tall and thin man with waxy skin and a cold manner. He steadfastly ignored Henrietta's questions, as if she wasn't present, but at least he closed Edmund's eyes after his examination concluded. Wallington placed a gold guinea on each lid.

'Call Pinkerton to assist me in cleaning and dressing the duke,' Henrietta said to the butler. That, too, must be concluded before the body stiffened, or they'd have to wait for the resoftening.

He eyed her keenly. 'His Grace's valet is indisposed, Your Grace.'

Her frustration mounted. 'Why are all the servants indisposed today?'

The men exchanged heavy looks before Wallington answered. 'Your Grace, Mr Pinkerton is overwhelmed with grief.'

'Which is quite understandable, under these violently abrupt circumstances,' Dr Grimsley added, addressing Henrietta for the first time. His voice was hushed but scratchy, reminiscent of wind through reeds. 'The duke was no doubt as kind a master as he was a temperate and considerate political leader. It's natural for those close to him to express grief upon his passing.'

His implication took Henrietta aback. 'I do not weep in the presence of others, Doctor.' But he shrugged his thin shoulders in an insolent manner and she realised she'd receive no answers about Edmund's death from the doctors, who both seemed intent on hostility. She needed allies. *Male* allies, for such was the way of her world. 'Wallington, please send for my father and my eldest brother immediately.' With Lord Lockington and Lord Deancombe present, the doctors would think twice about their disdain.

The butler set off to fulfil her orders, but, before her family arrived, three unfamiliar men entered: a portly specimen around sixty years of age with grey side whiskers, accompanied by two dark-suited individuals, who proceeded to stomp all over the library, jotting notes. When Henrietta enquired, the whiskered man introduced himself as Sir Robert Baker, Chief Metropolitan Magistrate of the Bow Street Magistrates' Court.

'And why have you invaded my home and my privacy, Sir Robert?' she asked.

'Never mind, daughter.' Her father's stately voice intervened from the doorway. 'I shall handle matters now.'

As the distinguished, steel-haired marquess engaged in an animated discussion with the magistrate, Henrietta's brother George awkwardly patted her shoulder. 'A bad business, this,' he replied when she asked what was happening.

She bristled at his non-response. So often, men she loved brushed off her questions. 'Yes, but why has the magistrate come? Does he suspect a crime?'

George dismissed her concerns with a wave of his hand. 'Nothing to trouble yourself about, old girl. Pater'll set it to rights.'

Further queries were equally fruitless, but George's prediction proved correct, for not ten minutes later, Sir Robert and his men withdrew to another room, offering her their apologies for the intrusion. The physicians followed and then Thomas draped Edmund with a sheet, leaving Henrietta desolate until her senses filled with her mother's orange-blossom scent and she found herself embraced by the most comforting arms in all the world. 'Oh, Mama, Mama.' She sobbed into Lady Lockington's shoulder. 'Take me to my bedchamber, for I cannot bear to cry here.'

Her mother led her upstairs and undressed her while Henrietta wept, staring out of the window as the golds and reds of the sunset swirled like watercolours in the rain. When Mama offered a spoonful of laudanum, Henrietta swallowed the bitter tincture like a baby bird, hoping it would bring oblivion.

Her mother drew the drapes, extinguished the lights, and Henrietta slipped between her sheets clad in a nightgown of the softest fine cotton. Drowsiness washed over her until the moment she closed her eyes, when horrific visions of Edmund's black pupils and protruding tongue caused her to sit up, clutching the sheets to her breast. 'Mama, his face, his face!'

'Shh, dearest girl.' Lady Lockington cooed as she offered another spoonful of laudanum. 'Rest now.'

With the second dose, sleep overtook Henrietta.

It was dusk when she awoke to the sound of mournful singing, but, judging by the heaviness of her head and limbs, she'd slept for hours, not minutes. Her mother stood at the window, parting the drapes to reveal a sliver of grey-blue twilight. She wore a black bombazine mourning gown.

Memories of Edmund's death flooded back. Henrietta faltered, unsure if she could bear to confront her dreadful new reality, before summoning her courage with a steadying breath. 'How long have I slept, Mama?'

Lady Lockington turned, her face weary and her eyes swollen. 'Just over four-and-twenty hours.' She let the drapes fall and approached the bedside. 'How are you, dear child?'

'I hardly know…' As Henrietta sat up, her head throbbed from the effects of the laudanum. 'Edmund had a headache,' she said. 'Was it a seizure?'

'I'm not certain.' Lady Lockington placed a cool hand to Henrietta's forehead, giving some relief. 'That odd physician, Dr Grimsley, refused to speak to your father. He converses only with… well, with the duke.'

'The du—?' Cold realisation hit Henrietta. 'Why! Is Perceval here already?'

Mama twisted her hands, her gaze flickering towards the door connecting the duchess's suite to that of the duke. 'He arrived yesterday evening, while I assisted you to bed – but he slept in a guest chamber, not in Edmund's rooms, dearest.'

Heir or not, it seemed presumptuous for a cousin to intrude on a widow's grief before the body had grown cold. If the heir was a son, that would be one thing…

But the thought of a son – of the son who would now never be – filled Henrietta with such intense sorrow, she redirected her mind. 'Why did Perceval not wait until after burial?' she asked, worried Edmund's predictions about his heir's senselessness to duty might yet prove to be true. 'Does he seem grieved, at least?'

'In a way, I suppose… but he is not showing as much feeling towards you as one would wish.' Lady Lockington extracted a handkerchief from under her sleeve and dabbed her eyes. 'Oh, Henrietta – would but God had answered my prayers and given you a son.'

Short of a miracle, there was little God could've done about the matter, but there was no point now in explaining that which

Henrietta had never discussed with her mother. So, with nothing to reply, she merely sighed, hoping that would sufficiently discourage a continuance of the topic.

But Lady Lockington burst into tears, her sobs mingling with the muted singing. 'Forgive me, Henrietta. I shouldn't have said such a thing. I know you did all you could to provide Edmund with an heir.'

'Please let us not speak of that which will only bring more sorrow.' Henrietta wanted to banish thoughts of the child she never bore. 'However we might wish for matters to be different, Perceval is the duke now and I rely upon his generosity. The dower house at Highfield, perhaps, though Shropshire is so dreadfully distant. Or the townhouse in Bath; he mightn't mind lending that. Bath isn't as fashionable as it once was.'

Her mother frowned. 'What a strange way to speak, Henrietta. You have a home with your father and me until you marry again.'

After years of being mistress of her own households, the idea of relinquishing her independence depressed Henrietta's spirits even further. Besides, her parents already lived as sparingly as possible for a marquess and marchioness in order to replenish the family coffers and provide for their sons and grandchildren. They didn't need the expense of supporting a widowed duchess daughter, as well.

'Thank you, but hopefully Perceval will provide me a home of my own.' Henrietta rose from her bed to stretch the heaviness from her limbs. The sudden elevation caused her head to spin, but she steadied herself on the bedpost. 'What is that singing, Mama?'

'A protest of sorts, I believe,' her mother replied. 'Perceval said they've marched from Westminster, but they've been outside Severn House for a half an hour at least. Go and see for yourself, if you wish.' She offered Henrietta the black banyan she'd worn during national mourning for the king.

After she slid her arms into the dressing gown and fastened the buttons over her bosom, Henrietta gingerly pulled aside the drapes and peered down upon Park Lane. A few hundred people were gathered there. Some were poor and downtrodden, huddled in faded black clothes or the tattered uniforms of former soldiers left to fend for themselves after Waterloo. But a significant component appeared to be tradesmen and labourers, straight-backed, strong men, standing proudly as they sang, their deep voices resonating.

'I don't believe it's a protest.' Henrietta pressed her forehead to the cool glass, both for headache relief and to see the crowd more clearly. 'They are mourning Edmund. Or, rather, mourning what they lose with his death – a voice in the Upper House advocating for parliamentary reform.'

'Do you know the song they sing?' her mother asked. 'It's unfamiliar to me.'

Henrietta tilted her head, uncertain until a familiar phrase caught her attention:

> *A treas'ry is our common land.*
> *United all we make our stand*
> *And join together hand in hand*
> *For ev'ry child and ev'ry man*
> *Corruption will not win the day*
> *With votes for all we'll have our say . . .*

'It's Eliza King's song.' She hadn't recognised it immediately because the crowd sang it like a dirge, rather than a rousing march.

Mama recoiled. 'Why would they sing that radical anthem for our dear duke?'

'The song's sentiments express a need for reform, not radicalism.' Henrietta's heart brimmed with love and pride. 'Edmund was a symbol of hope for reformers. A nobleman who believed even the poorest people deserve a voice, a vote and proper representation.'

'Well, Eliza King is a radical,' Mama said, and Henrietta didn't argue. Eliza King was rumoured to have been involved with the Cato Street conspiracy to assassinate the prime minister, although she'd never been caught nor formally charged – perhaps due to her popularity with the people.

When the song ended, a faction of mourners began to call out and point upwards, and Henrietta realised they'd spotted her. As more and more faces turned, she pressed her fingers to her lips, and then to the glass, silently conveying her gratitude for their singing.

A new song began and although Henrietta didn't recognise the tune, she knew the lyrics.

'Psalm Twenty-Three.' Her breath misted the glass. '*Yea, though I walk through death's dark vale, yet will I fear none ill.* They want to comfort me.' Moved by their kindness, she spoke over her shoulder. 'Mama, I shall walk amongst them.'

Her mother was aghast. '*Henrietta.*'

But Henrietta was determined. She must find a new purpose now, mustn't she? She was no longer Edmund's wife, she wasn't loved by the *ton* and she might be dependent upon Perceval's charity forevermore ... *but* she could serve as a reminder of Edmund, and, in so doing, keep hope alive for his devotees.

'Call my lady's maid to dress me in mourning,' she said firmly.

'If you insist upon this, I know better than to try to dissuade you – but I shall assist you myself.' Lady Lockington walked towards Henrietta's dressing room. 'Many of the servants are indisposed.'

'Illness?' Henrietta asked, concerned that whatever ailment had incited Edmund's seizure might be contagious in nature.

Her mother returned bearing a black silk gown. 'Grief.'

'Ah.' Henrietta's fingertips were still on the glass, her eyes fixed on the sea of upturned faces. 'They all loved Edmund so.'

CHAPTER 3

Hope for the People

After following the reformers from Westminster, Theo Hawke leant against the Hyde Park railing, notebook and pencil in hand. A streetlamp provided sufficient illumination to scribble down his thoughts as dusk turned to night. What he wrote wasn't salacious enough for his gossip column – no one perused *The Hawke's Eye* to read about commoners mourning the People's Duke – but it would provide material for the articles he published anonymously.

He attempted to capture the appearance of the crowd. The tear-streaked faces of a cluster of women wearing black. The brave Waterloo soldiers who now leant upon makeshift crutches, their uniforms in tatters, too wounded to work. Even the young labourers singing in powerful bass tones were careworn. Their wary eyes darted to the circling Hussars, likely wondering if the cavalry would charge and slaughter them as had happened to the peaceful protesters at St Peter's Field in Manchester. Tensions were high and hope scarce.

Indeed, what was there to give the people hope in these dark times? Certainly not the ascension of an extravagant buffoon to the throne. Nor the high unemployment, the insufficient and corrupt poor relief, or the brutal Tory Corn Laws that benefitted landowners at the cost of a starving populace. And definitely not Parliament's recent enactment of the Six Acts, which suppressed fundamental freedoms so that people feared for their lives when they protested peaceably.

Now, on top of everything else, the loss of Severn dealt a devastating blow to hopes for parliamentary reform. The People's Duke had been sympathetic to the reformers' causes. He'd served as a bridge between two worlds, representing hope that the upper classes, who held all the wealth and influence, might one day genuinely address the common people's desire for fair representation.

The people desperately need – Theo wrote – *something, or someone, to rekindle their hope.*

He tapped his pencil to his chin. He must wield his pen to this purpose, as he had in the past through his independently published treatises. Not that those articles found their way into many readers' hands, but surely every bit helped at times like these... though that thought didn't take the sting from the knowledge he could do so much more, if *only* he could catch the attention of a reputable newspaper. He despised his job at the *Examiner* – yet a nobody like Theo, who'd scrambled from birth just to stay alive, much less make anything of himself, knew better than to take any legal employment for granted.

While the mourners transitioned from Eliza King's march into a series of dissenter hymns, Theo jotted notes. Ideas formulated rapidly and he sketched a plan for a series of articles intended to propose a path forward after the duke's death. A strategy to align other aristocrats to the people's causes.

His thoughts flowed as fast as he could write, but, after a time, the sounds of wailing drew his attention. He stashed his notebook and pencil in his pocket, concerned that altercations had erupted between the mourners and the cavalry, who were no doubt waiting for any pretext to break up the crowd.

Pushing back his hat, he peered over the sea of heads. Theo hadn't named his column *The Hawke's Eye* merely as a pun on his surname; he was, in fact, blessed with exceptional eyesight, a tremendous advantage in his line of work. Within a split second, he spotted the cause of the crowd's unrest standing in the open doorway of her London residence, bathed in a rectangle of golden light.

The Duchess of Severn herself.

Young, beautiful and wearing widow's weeds. A poignant sight even from Theo's jaded perspective. No wonder the old women wailed.

Knowing he wouldn't regain his train of thought about his articles while *she* was present, he crossed his arms over his chest and studied Henrietta Percy, wishing for the thousandth time that he could take her measure. Her true character eluded him, and, for some inexplicable reason, he found that as frustrating as the very devil.

Without doubt, her public manner was flawless. Reserved, but not timid. Beautiful, but never attention seeking. In truth, less like a living woman and more of a Greek goddess carved from marble, lovely but unapproachable, even by her own kind, as she appeared to have no friends beyond her family. Apart from the evening in the Severn gardens, Theo had never seen her without either her husband or her mother at her side, until now.

However, the memory of the night when she had rutted with that swine Marlow and then propositioned Theo in exchange for his silence was as fresh in his mind as if the interaction had transpired the week before. Then she hadn't been made of marble; she'd been very much a living woman. A temptress – and a nearly

successful one, at that. He hadn't forgotten how close he'd come
to capitulation, despite his respect for her husband. Half a decade
later and he *still* remembered the feel of her hand on his forearm
when she'd offered that kiss. In fact, the damned memory plagued
him all too often, because her soft, parted, inviting lips had a way
of bursting unbidden into his mind's eye whenever he found sleep
elusive.

And yet, as the duchess mingled with her husband's mourners,
Theo struggled (as he often had over the last five years) to
reconcile the temptress in the Severn gardens with the lady who
strode fearlessly into throngs of impoverished and desperate souls.
She certainly wasn't aloof with them. She shook labourers' hands,
she touched the cheeks of wounded soldiers, she let the weeping
women kiss her fingers...

She was giving them the hope they needed.

The door to Severn House opened again and Perceval Percy
emerged, flanked by liveried footmen. Theo focused his keen gaze
to better assess the new duke's expression. Percy was regarding his
late cousin's widow with undisguised abhorrence.

That piqued Theo's curiosity. What could have instilled such
animosity in Percy towards the duchess, especially now that he
held the title of Duke of Severn far sooner than anyone had
anticipated? Sensing the potential for something salacious, Theo
readied his notebook and pencil. He needed material for his
weekly column.

As Percy approached the duchess, some mourners grew agit-
ated, and one man cupped a hand over his mouth and called
out indistinguishable words. Percy ignored that. He gripped the
duchess's arm and whispered in her ear; whatever he was saying
to her, he certainly didn't want overheard. He tugged her arm...
she seemed to resist him, long enough for a decided unrest to
break out amongst the onlookers... and then she abruptly ceased

struggling, slipped her hand into the crook of Percy's elbow and walked into the house as obediently as a puppy.

But she was *furious*.

Theo doubted anyone else would realise, so subtly had she tightened the corners of her mouth and drawn her pretty brows, but *he* knew, because after five years of having every iteration of anger and loathing the duchess's lovely features could produce directed firmly at him, he could read her face. Theo half smiled wistfully – oh, yes, if looks could kill, he would've been long dead, murdered by one of her acrimonious glares. Which might mean that she detested Perceval Percy with a similar degree of loathing.

Theo flipped to a fresh page in his notebook and hastily penned notes:

1. Investigate relationship between duchess and the new duke
2. If enemies, why?

He tapped his chin and then added another note.

3. While at it, find out more about late duke's death

He closed the notebook over his pencil and dropped them in his pocket. Witnessing the interaction between the new duke and the widowed duchess had given rise to a bothersome sensation that something was amiss.

He intended to get to the bottom of it.

In the midst of the crowd before Severn House, Henrietta was comforting an elderly woman when her upper arm was clasped and her husband's cousin hissed in her ear. 'Come inside *immediately*. I did not grant you leave to mingle amongst these … these *radicals*.'

Astonished by his fierce manner, she faced Perceval. Edmund had favoured his mother's family, so there was little resemblance between the cousins. Whereas Henrietta knew many ladies found Perceval handsome, he'd always reminded her of a spoilt boy about to throw a tantrum, with his round face, pursed lips and copious soft brown curls.

'They are reformers, not radicals,' she said patiently, as if he were indeed a naughty child. 'Edmund would have wanted me to comfort them.'

Perceval stuck his nose in the air, no doubt attempting to appear imposing. 'As the Duke of Severn, it is my duty to manage all Percy family concerns, so I insist you return indoors. Your presence here will only attract more ruffians, and these numbers are dangerous already.'

'They are paying tribute to Edmund and so I wish to stay.' She tried to use a respectful tone, but she stood her ground, both figuratively and literally. Her physical resistance must've been obvious because a disgruntled ripple ran through the crowd.

A nearby man shouted, 'Release her, Percy, you poxy pup. You ain't fit to lick the dust off Her Grace's shoe.'

'If you force me inside, there might be a riot,' she said gently. 'They don't like how you're treating Edmund's widow.'

Perceval scowled, looking more than ever like a cross child, with cheeks as pink as a piglet. 'If a riot breaks out, the resulting deaths will be on *your* hands, not mine. Come inside *now*.'

It went against Henrietta's principles to abandon duty but the truth was, the crowd and the surrounding cavalry *were* ominously reminiscent of the Peterloo Massacre, and she didn't want anyone injured. Besides, until she knew what provision Edmund had made specifically for her, outside her meagre marriage portion, it was only wise to appease Perceval, as much as it chafed.

So, she took the old woman's worn hand in hers and gently pressed it in farewell before going obediently with Perceval towards Severn House, though her jaw was clenched and her cheeks flamed. Once the footman closed the door behind them, she attempted to reclaim her arm, intending to mount the grand central staircase to return to her bedchamber, but Perceval drew her aside none too gently and subjected her to more indignity. 'You are to remain in this house unless I give you leave to depart, Henrietta. You are *not* to encourage the crowds in any way. It is far too dangerous.'

Perceval was behaving like an overbearing ass, yet if whip-smart Jane Babcock had accepted his hand he must have redeeming qualities. 'They only want to show their respect. When I go amongst them, it comforts them and it comforts *me*. Do not forbid it – join me, instead. Edmund would wish it of us. For you, it could be a first step towards continuing his legacy. You can encourage more lords to consider reform measures.'

Inches from her own, Perceval's eyes flashed. '*I* am the Duke of Severn, Henrietta.' Evidently, he enjoyed reminding her of that fact; it was the second time within five minutes he'd mentioned it. 'The decisions I make will be my own and I don't care a snap of my fingers for your opinions. You aren't *my* duchess and you never should have been Edmund's, which is something I shall hold against you for ever.'

She recoiled, shocked at his obvious abhorrence. Had Edmund been correct about Perceval? Was he untrustworthy? Was he perhaps even … cruel? Why otherwise would he treat her with such indignity? 'Perceval,' she said carefully, her voice tempered. 'Whatever can you mean?'

He curled his lip. 'I know what you were willing to do for him, Henrietta, and I shall call it what it was: thievery of what is *mine* by right! While he lived, he controlled my purse strings and I could say nothing, but I have resented you both for years.'

Henrietta's heart leapt to her throat. 'Perceval, I depend upon

your kindness. Please recognise that I didn't take anything that
is yours—'

'You failed, yes, but not for lack of trying. And so now I shall
show you the same kindness you showed me with your conspiring.
Your time here is limited. Soon, there will be a new Duchess of
Severn, and your presence will be neither needed nor wanted. You
will leave my protection with nothing but what you brought into
your sham marriage. No Percy will speak your name. Your portraits
will be removed from my residences. I shall personally verify that
you return every Percy jewel in your possession. Oh, how eagerly
I await the day a deserving duchess replaces the whore before
me now, who was never worthy of the title my cousin bestowed
upon her.'

Having delivered this cruel speech, Perceval turned his shoulder
and stalked away, his footsteps reverberating in the high-ceilinged
hall, leaving Henrietta trembling in the shadows of what was
once her home and was now a prison. If Edmund hadn't made
irreversible provision for her in his will, her future was desolate,
for not only would Perceval take her financial stability, but he
would destroy both her reputation and Edmund's if he revealed
the truth of their marriage.

She would have no money. No friends. Be accepted nowhere.
Her life would effectively be over. The harm done by Theodore
Hawke's column would pale in comparison to the utter destruction
Perceval could wreak if he chose to do so.

And this time, there was no Edmund to protect her.

CHAPTER 4

War

In the days following, Henrietta was outwardly subservient to Perceval, solemnly fulfilling her official duties so Edmund could be laid to rest with the dignity he deserved. But the moment the coffin was interred at Westminster Abbey, she grew impatient for the will reading.

All she wanted was a comfortable provision so she could retain her independence, but if Edmund had failed to provide it – perhaps assuming his death was a distant event or that she would have borne his promised heir before his passing – she faced the prospect of retiring to her family's country estate, to live dependently and in quiet seclusion, so as not to incite Perceval's retribution. Nor was a remarriage likely. With no fortune and a reputation for both infertility and infidelity, she faced a bleak and loveless future.

Exactly two weeks to the day after Edmund's death, a small company assembled in the library for the will reading. Henrietta's anxiety overpowered her grief as she perched on a sofa in her widow's weeds, nervously clasping her hands. The vomit stain on the carpet, she noted with a strange sorrow, had been removed. Traces of Edmund were being erased all over the house – for example, the wine set from his desk was also absent – and she deeply felt their loss.

Henrietta's mother sat beside her. Her steel-haired father spread himself in a nearby armchair, and her eldest brother, George, sat upright in another, studying the ivory handle of his walking stick. Only the salting of George's thick, cinnamon-coloured locks revealed that he was well past his fortieth birthday. Otherwise, like all of Henrietta's handsome brothers, he was as trim-figured and well dressed as a young dandy.

Perceval sat adjacent to Henrietta, bouncing his knee as he played with the signet ring he must've taken from Edmund's body. Beside him was his prospective father-in-law, Bishop Babcock, who possessed ponderous jowls and a shiny forehead, and beside *him* sat Mrs Babcock, a handsome lady around George's age, from whom Perceval's fiancée derived the good looks that had made her the Season's Incomparable, despite her bookish ways. Jane Babcock was not present.

Perching on another sofa was Edmund's solicitor, Mr Quigley, a thin man wearing spectacles that enlarged his eyes to owl-like proportions. Beside him, an assistant withdrew a folded document from a leather case.

Quigley nodded to each of the company in turn. 'Your Grace and Your Grace, my Lord Lockington, my Lady Lockington, my Lord Deancombe, my Lord Bishop, and Mrs Babcock, this afternoon I shall read the last will and testament of Edmund Meredith Percy, His Grace the seventh Duke of Severn.'

'Get on with it, man,' Perceval said, scowling. 'I haven't got all afternoon to listen to a list of who gets which of Edmund's pocket handkerchiefs, when we all know Percy family property goes to the heir.'

If Quigley was quelled to be so admonished by a duke, he didn't show it. As his enormous eyes fixed on Perceval unblinkingly, the room fell silent but for the tick of a longcase clock. At last, Perceval cleared his throat and took up a glass of brandy resting on a table beside his chair.

Only then did Quigley answer. 'As it happens, Your Grace, I find myself perplexed by the matter of His Grace's recent passing, in light of the recent rumours, and—'

'The rumours are nonsense.' Henrietta's father spoke in a resonant voice.

This was the first Henrietta had heard of any rumours; since the dreadful day of Edmund's death, she had interacted only with her family and servants. Nor had she brought herself to read the papers, for the mere *thought* of seeing the fact of Edmund's death in cold black and white caused her eyes to sting and her vision to blur. It was impossible to consider reading; she would burst into tears. Best to avoid anything that would render her inconsolable until she had completed her public duties as a widow and could retreat to a place of privacy. Which she could hopefully do after this will reading *if* Edmund had provided her an independent income and a home for her own use.

But naturally, she was curious. 'What rumours, Papa?'

Lord Lockington glared first at Quigley and then at Perceval. 'I believe *everyone* in this room can agree that anything printed in the *Mayfair Examiner* isn't worth discussing.'

Ah, so Theodore Hawke was at the root of this, which was no surprise. Henrietta peeked at Perceval. He was studiously avoiding meeting his prospective parents-in-law's eyes, but he nodded a curt acknowledgement of her father's words, likely remembering that a report of his indiscretion with his mistress was printed the day of Edmund's death.

'A good horsewhipping,' George said enthusiastically. 'That's what that Theodore Hawke wants. Man is a scoundrel.'

Hawke was a scoundrel, but that was nothing to the point at hand. 'What are the rumours?' Henrietta asked again, not wishing to be put off.

Perceval swallowed a mouthful of brandy. 'Your father is correct, Henrietta. Hawke writes nonsense. You *especially* ought to leave it at that.'

'Now see here, Severn.' George sprang to his feet. 'Careful what you imply about my sister, sir!'

'Sit down, George,' Mama said, quietly but firmly.

George promptly complied and the masculine tension in the room eased somewhat.

Henrietta was destined to remain dissatisfied, for the time. Naturally, she could read Hawke's column later and discover for herself what the journalist had written, but she wished the men in her life would simply answer her damn questions. She'd grown accustomed to this treatment from her father, husband, and eldest brother, but that didn't mean she liked it.

'Get on with the reading, Quigley,' Perceval growled. 'And let's have no more mention of gossip.'

'As I was saying,' the solicitor said, 'I find myself perplexed by His Grace's passing, not only because of the aforementioned reason, but because His Grace rewrote his will the afternoon before his death, with the assistance of myself and Mr Pidgeon here.'

Perceval stiffened. 'I say, what?'

Henrietta was equally shocked. 'The afternoon before, Mr Quigley? That seems an extraordinary coincidence.'

Quigley turned his magnified eyes upon her. 'Perhaps it is, as Your Grace says, a most extraordinary coincidence. Or perhaps His Grace had a premonition of his passing? I have heard tale of such sentiments. At any rate, Your Grace' – he was still addressing

Henrietta – 'may have cause to … consider yourself fortunate, if such a word might be employed on such an occasion.'

Henrietta drew her brows together, disliking the man's tone.

Meanwhile, Perceval's boyish features twisted with rage. 'I call this *extremely* suspicious, Quigley! Where is the old will?'

'Destroyed by His late Grace in my presence, Your Grace,' the solicitor replied. 'He wished for his wife to be honoured properly upon his death. "Honoured properly for her unimpeachable loyalty" – those were his exact words and Pidgeon can attest to the truth of my story.'

Pidgeon nodded eagerly and for the first time in two weeks, Henrietta's hopes lifted.

'But what about my *birthright*?' Spittle projected from Perceval's mouth.

'Anything bound to the title is protected by law, naturally.' Quigley studied Perceval with a keen glimmer in his eyes. 'Does Your Grace object to provision for a helpless widow? Extraordinary, if so.'

Papa spoke. 'Enough of this. Mr Quigley, I advise you to read my son-in-law's will at once and refrain from any speculation regarding the sentiments of his widow or his heir.' He nodded munificently at Perceval, as if wishing to show he was on his side as well, but Perceval rose and paced to the mantelpiece, a furious scowl knotting his brow.

Quigley bowed his head. 'As your lordship wishes.'

Slowly, the solicitor broke Edmund's seal and unfolded the document. When the paper rested on his thin thighs and pointed knees, he removed his spectacles, held them towards the window, and squinted through them. Then he blew heavily on each lens and extracted a handkerchief to clean them.

Perceval stopped in his tracks. 'For the love of God, man, *get on with it*. Did I not already tell you that I have other business to which I must attend?'

Henrietta glanced at Bishop and Mrs Babcock. If they disliked their future son-in-law's impatient irritability, their impassive expressions didn't show it. Had Henrietta misjudged the family's rationality? Were Jane and her parents willing to accept all sorts of boorishness in exchange for a duchess's coronet? In fact, had Perceval *actually* given up his mistress as he'd told Edmund? Was everything she'd hoped about Perceval and Jane a fantastical construction? Wishful thinking, so she needn't bring herself to do the thing she hadn't wanted to do?

Quigley returned his spectacles to the tip of his nose and read in a monotone:

'*I, Edmund Meredith Percy, the seventh Duke of Severn, being of sound body and mind, imprimis do bequeath to the next male heir of the first Duke of Severn all properties held through entailment to the Dukedom of Severn, and all books, art, jewels, furnishings, linens, and plate not purchased by me during my lifetime, an inventory of which can be found…*'

Perceval leant against the marble mantel, smiling with relief as the lengthy list of bequests to the heir continued. He even received the best hunters in Edmund's stables, which Henrietta thought would have gone to Edmund's friend, James Beaucastle. As Quigley then detailed the monetary distributions to the servants, Henrietta began to wonder what the solicitor had meant by saying she had cause to feel fortunate. Apart from Edmund granting her ownership of the horses and carriages he'd purchased for her use, the will hadn't mentioned her name. Without an income, she wouldn't even be able to keep a stable.

But then it came:

'*To my steadfastly loyal wife, Henrietta Percy, in addition to the restitution of her dowry of five thousand pounds, I charge my heir to bestow upon her annually, for the duration of her natural life, and regardless of any subsequent marriages she may enter into, the dower's portion of the Dukedom's estates, encompassing one-third of the revenue derived from every property held within the dominion of said Dukedom.'*

'I say!' Perceval straightened like an arrow, his body shaking. 'The entirety of her life, even if she weds again? Why! Then it will be the rest of my life! She's barely older than I am.'

'That *is* the traditional arrangement for the Dowager Duchess of Severn, Your Grace.' Quigley's massive eyes lifted to Perceval. 'That the widow is so young is simply a consequence of your cousin having married later in life, and then dying before his time, *some* might say.' The solicitor's gaze returned to the document. '*This* is the part of the will in which His late Grace shows his marked favour for Her Grace.

'*Additionally, I bestow upon her the remainder of my own personal fortune after all prior bequests, which will amount to two hundred thousand pounds, held in investments managed by Mr John Tyrold. Furthermore, I hereby grant her complete and irrevocable ownership of all unentailed properties in my possession, by which act she will discern that I always held her opinion in regard, even in those instances where our sentiments diverged ...'*

Henrietta gasped, clasping her hands to her mouth. She fought back astonished tears. Edmund had *listened* to her. He hadn't discounted her feelings about women owning property, even if he hadn't championed the cause in Parliament.

He had been the dearest, kindest and best of men, and it grieved her he'd never know the extent of her gratitude.

Quigley continued reading without pause – though his eyes flickered to Henrietta for a moment – and her astonishment only grew. Edmund's will granted her immense wealth and freedom. Two hundred thousand pounds, plus the return of her dowry, in addition to thirty per cent of the dukedom's income, and the list went on. The house in Bath. A shooting box in Wales. And the darling estate of Grenham Park in Berkshire, worth two or three thousand a year. Calculating rapidly in her head, she estimated her annual income would exceed twenty thousand, making her one of the richest women in the land.

At the mantel, Perceval ground his teeth. No doubt he considered himself entitled to Edmund's personal fortune and unentailed estates.

Quigley's next words proved to be the most astonishing yet.

'*In reference to my wife and to the heir to the Dukedom of Severn, so steadfast is my faith in Henrietta's virtue and fidelity, I do hereby declare that any child born to her within twelve months of my demise will be the child of my own body, as I was myself more than eleven months in the womb, according to my late mother; therefore if said child is a firstborn son, he will succeed as the next male line heir to the first Duke of Severn. In the event that my wife has not yet borne my son by the time of my death, until one year elapses without the birth of a son by Henrietta, or until she declares herself not with child, my title and entailed estates shall be held in abeyance, to be administered by the office of my solicitor. This I declare as my last will and testament...*'

A palpable tension filled the room. Henrietta's nerves now failed her; she could not bring herself to meet the gazes of Bishop and Mrs Babcock, although she sensed their eyes fixed on her.

Perceval advanced upon the solicitor. '*What?*'

Quigley blinked. 'Does Your Grace – or rather, Your Grace as may be determined in a year's time or as Her Grace sees fit – wish for me to read the will again?'

Perceval didn't answer. He was livid, his jaw clenched, his hands forming fists. 'What is this absurdity?' He gazed at everyone in turn. 'My cousin and his widow seek to steal what is rightfully mine! He grants her twelve months to produce an heir, yet he never touched her.'

Papa and George straightened in their chairs, on alert, but Henrietta didn't want or need their assistance. She was now a wealthy woman, entirely independent from Perceval, so the time for submission was over, and she *wouldn't* allow him to besmirch

Edmund's name. 'I assure you, Perceval, your cousin touched me every day of our marriage.'

'But you are not with child.' Again, Perceval searched the faces of the assembled company and this time Henrietta followed his gaze. Bishop Babcock now stared resolutely at the floor, his forehead glistening more than usual. Her mother and Mrs Babcock both looked genuinely baffled, but her father and brother shot poisonous glares at Perceval, who persisted in his defamation. 'I am not alone in knowing that she is *not with child*. Not by my cousin at least. I'd wager he never consummated the marriage.'

Henrietta's annoyance turned to fury, though she couldn't immediately think of a defence that wouldn't be a lie.

Lady Lockington's face drained of colour as she pressed against her daughter's side. 'Has he gone utterly mad, dearest?'

But Mama's scandalised whisper fell on unresponsive ears; it was Henrietta's turn to ignore a question, for the tension in the room crackled and she was wary of speaking.

Bishop Babcock attempted to restore peace. 'Er, Perceval, I'm *certain* you cannot mean to imply your cousin never performed his marital duties.' He spoke pointedly. Too pointedly. 'A virile man like the duke, possessed of such a comely young wife? You must admit it is *quite impossible*.'

Did the bishop *know*?

Perceval worked his jaw. 'Don't make me say more, Henrietta. Simply admit you aren't with child by Edmund and we shall never speak of this again.'

Both for the sake of Edmund's posthumous reputation and so that there could never be doubts about the validity of her status as the Duchess of Severn, Henrietta had to defend her marriage and there was a way to do so without lying. Edmund had frequently slept in her bed, mostly to keep up appearances for the servants — but sometimes because either she or he needed to pass the night beside a comforting presence. Perhaps they hadn't been lovers, but she and Edmund *had* been partners, and that made their union valid, in her opinion.

She met Perceval's gaze steadily. 'Your cousin lay with me at least once a week throughout our marriage and he lay with me last on the night before he died.'

She paused. Everything she'd said so far was true, but now she faced a choice. She knew she wasn't with child. And therefore, of course, she couldn't possibly, ever, give birth to Edmund's baby. Yet Edmund had clearly wanted her to try to fulfil her old promise, even in the event of his death. He had provided her one last chance to protect the dukedom from Perceval, whom he'd never trusted as an heir – and now that Edmund was dead ... well, perhaps *now* she could do it. She wasn't married any more. So it wouldn't feel like disloyalty, would it? It would, in fact, be the greatest act of loyalty she could perform for her husband.

Strictly speaking, it wasn't impossible to become pregnant with three months of trying. Having never given herself the chance to get with child, Henrietta had no idea how readily it might happen for her, but, if her mother's fecundity was anything to go by, the odds weren't terrible. George had been born exactly nine months to the day after her parents' wedding, and Mama had produced four more sons and a daughter at regular intervals after that.

Henrietta realised what she must do. For Edmund's sake, she must try to get with child, but to carry such a plan through to fruition, she would have to lie. Not just now, but every day for the rest of her life, for *if* she managed to get pregnant, she could never tell the truth of her child's parentage.

She might as well start now. 'And' – she focused boldly on Perceval and lied to his face – 'I have not had my monthly courses since Edmund's death.'

Her mother gasped, no doubt because she knew Henrietta had just finished bleeding, but of course she didn't betray her daughter. 'Are you *quite* satisfied now, sir?' Mama asked Perceval. 'Do you consider it gentlemanly behaviour to treat your cousin's widow in such a way? To make a *duchess* speak before her father and brother and men of business about matters so very private? You should be ashamed of yourself.'

Perceval didn't look ashamed in the least. He was staring at Henrietta with unconcealed hatred.

'Perceval,' Bishop Babcock said solemnly. 'You would do well to accept this with good humour. After all, it *is* quite essential to ensure a young widow is not carrying the heir before estates and titles are transitioned, and I am certain we can rely on the duchess to inform us when or if she has the, er … necessary confirmation, so this matter can be resolved as soon as may be. Likely less than a fortnight hence.'

The anger peeled away from Perceval's face. 'Why, yes!' His eyes brightened. 'Yes, indeed. You are perfectly correct, Bishop. My dear Henrietta,' he said, extending his hand, although his smile was cold. 'Let there be no hard feelings between us. I have not been myself with shock and with grief.'

Henrietta shook the offered hand, but she served tit for tat, matching his icy smile with a flinty glare. 'I have no doubt you experienced unprecedented shock and grief *this afternoon*, Perceval. As for how much you've felt in the past fortnight, I shall refrain from speculating.' She rose and the men in the room did likewise. 'If you will all excuse me, I intend to rest for the remainder of the afternoon.'

She declined her mother's offer to accompany her upstairs. She needed solitude, to decide *how* to go about fulfilling Edmund's last request. Resting wasn't her preferred accompaniment to contemplation; she longed to go for a ride instead, to let vigorous exercise organise her thoughts and soothe her emotions, but it wouldn't be seemly for the recently widowed Duchess of Severn to gallop through Hyde Park (especially not if she was supposed to be with child) and there was nowhere else in London where she could enjoy a truly good run.

As she mounted the stairs, she determined to leave town in the morning. She'd think better in the country – and she'd have more *privacy* there. For riding her horses ... and, well, for riding something else, since there was but one way to get with child. Certainly there were more men to choose from in London, but there were always eyes upon Henrietta in town, especially Theodore Hawke's – and now Perceval's, as well.

She'd journey to Grenham in Berkshire, the estate Edmund had so generously bestowed upon her. The rose-covered brick manor house and picturesque parkland were less than a three-hour carriage ride from London, mostly along the Bath Road. It had been a favoured retreat for Edmund during breaks in the Parliamentary season.

The fact that James Beaucastle lived only fifteen miles from Grenham had never diminished Henrietta's love for the estate. She'd known about their friendship before she'd married Edmund, she'd never been resentful, and the beauty of Grenham had been sufficient to take her mind off her loneliness, even when Edmund and James had ignored her for days on end.

In truth, Henrietta was surprised Edmund had willed Grenham to her, as he'd seemed to associate it more with James. Certainly, she'd always assumed he'd purchased it in his youth because of its proximity to James's estate, so the knowledge that he'd given it to *her* instead warmed Henrietta's heart. He'd remembered how much she enjoyed Grenham, which meant she *had* mattered to him. He *had* loved her.

But it also served as a poignant reminder that Edmund was gone. She would never retreat to Grenham *with* him, ever again. She would never share another moment with her beloved husband, and she could never express her gratitude for the financial security and independence he'd given her.

Except by fulfilling his final request.

Which was somehow an intimidating prospect. So much so that by the time she entered her bedchamber, her head ached. She lay down on her bed, intending to rest briefly before beginning preparations for her departure on the morrow.

Possibly an hour later, she was roused from a deep sleep by the familiar sound of the door between her room and Edmund's sweeping open over the carpet, and her spirits soared. It *had* all been a dream. Edmund was walking through his door right now. He was there, alive, and she could tell him about her dreadful nightmare, and they could laugh and cry over it together...

She sat up in bed, heart pounding.

Bright afternoon sunlight streamed through the windows, but it was Perceval, not Edmund, who was now closing the door from the duke's suite, and it was suddenly all Henrietta could do to contain a wretched sob.

She chose disdain instead. 'It would be decent of you not to occupy Edmund's rooms until you've kicked me out of mine,' she said, hoping Perceval didn't perceive the sorrow in her tone. Not wanting to be reclining on a bed while he was present, she rose and crossed her room to sit at her dressing table. 'Which, I might add, you have no authority to do while the title is in abeyance.'

Keeping her eye on Perceval in the looking glass, she began to remove the countless pins holding up her thick blonde locks, hoping to ease her throbbing headache.

He didn't speak as he closed the distance between them, but his gaze never left hers in the mirror. And although Henrietta didn't lack for courage, his eyes were so hateful, and his stance so menacing, that a chill ran down her back.

She picked up her brush. 'I'm not frightened of you, Perceval. And even if I were, I have a bell pull here, beside me. One tug and a footman will arrive instantly, so you can cease this villainous act.'

'Is that your plan, then?' Perceval's voice was cold as he neared her dressing table. 'Do you intend to call upon your footman's services nightly now?'

She narrowed her eyes at his reflection. 'I won't honour such a vile accusation with a response.' She tugged her brush through her hair. As she'd hoped, the release of her coiffure and the rhythmic movements soothed her head.

Perceval stopped at her shoulder. Leaning forward, he placed a fist on her dressing table, his eyes following the movements of her left hand, where a three-hundred-year-old sapphire ring sparkled. 'That is a Percy jewel. It belongs to *me*.'

'This is my wedding ring,' she replied. 'What my husband gave me, you cannot take away.'

He leant so close his breath crawled against her skin. 'You and I both know Edmund never consummated your marriage. I would have a doctor examine you to prove my claim, but I know other men – perhaps *many* other men – have done what he would not. You are not intact, but you are also not with child, because you've had five years to get a bastard to usurp me, which is the only reason Edmund married you, and you haven't yet succeeded.'

Henrietta disguised her inner fury. 'If all that is true,' she said calmly, 'you must be confident your inheritance is secure.'

'Nonsense. You might attempt to pass a foundling off as your own.'

She smiled broadly as she placed down her brush. 'Why! That hadn't occurred to me. Rather clever idea, Perceval.'

His eyes flashed. 'I shan't give you the chance. Soon, you will have your monthly courses and I shall know when you do because starting tonight, you will reside with Bishop Babcock and his family. You will sleep every night in the same bed as Jane, and either she or Mrs Babcock will never leave your side until you bleed.'

Henrietta scoffed. 'You cannot imprison me.'

'Oh, but I can, and I shall, if you drive me to it. Your family has left, returned to Lockington House. Bishop and Mrs Babcock await you downstairs, ready to take you to their home immediately, where you *will* remain until your monthly courses come – or, if you do not like that option, you may admit right now, in front of Bishop and Mrs Babcock and Quigley, who is also still here, that you aren't with child. Admit it, and you are free to do whatever you want. If you cooperate, I won't detain you, and I won't contest Edmund's will, even if I could. You are a wealthy woman now, with the freedom of widowhood and the privilege of a great title. Choose wisely, Henrietta. Don't make an enemy of me.'

If she was angry earlier, it paled in comparison to her fury now. The indignity with which Perceval treated her was far too much to be borne. It spoke to the vileness of his character and reinforced why she *must* attempt to grant Edmund's last request.

She stood, edging close to Perceval until they were toe to toe. She was a hair taller than the weasel, which gave her such great satisfaction that she lifted her chin to further the impression she looked down her nose at him.

'No, Perceval. It's you who oughtn't make an enemy of me. Your threats don't frighten me, and I shall not, I *will* not, be treated like a prisoner by a man who has neither the authority of blood nor the authority of station over me, for you are *not yet* the Duke of Severn, and I shall do everything in my power to ensure you never are.'

She shouldered past, heading swiftly for the door, intending to depart immediately for her estate. She wouldn't pass another moment under the same roof as Perceval Percy.

Of course, the weasel lunged for her, but she had been expecting that. The attack didn't frighten her. A girl didn't grow up with five older brothers and not learn how to defend herself.

She seized the arm that attempted to restrain her, twisted it sharply, and forced it backwards over its elbow until he yelped and crumpled to his knees.

After releasing him, Henrietta delivered a solid kick to his groin.

'There,' she said, as he writhed on the carpet. 'That might even keep you faithful to poor Jane, at least for tonight. I suggest you call for some ice and have a nice lie down.'

He squeaked, both hands clutched between his legs. 'I shall destroy you, Henrietta.'

'Not if I destroy you first, Perceval.'

She marched out of her room. As she swept down the stairs, she called out to the servants to notify her personal driver to prepare her travelling carriage for immediate departure to Grenham. She wouldn't even take a change of clothes. Everything she needed could be found at her estate and she would arrive there in a few hours.

Once at Grenham, she'd begin her war against Perceval.

She just needed to find a man.

CHAPTER 5

Rabble-Rousing Rubbish

That same afternoon, in a very different part of London . . .

Theo leant back, propping his wooden chair on two legs, and adopted an air of innocence as his editor's face turned an alarming shade of red.

'You look overheated, Mr Scripp,' he said lazily. Since both windows of Scripp's cluttered office were already open to the dingy court, he added, 'As I cannot bring in more fresh air, shall I fetch you a pint from the Angel, instead?'

'I'm overheated because of *this*, you rogue.' Scripp frantically waved a copy of that morning's *Examiner*. 'What in the name of God's bollocks inspired you to write . . . to write this *rabble-rousing rubbish*?'

'It's not rubbish,' Theo replied calmly. 'The Duke of Severn was likely assassinated.'

'*Shh!*' Scripp's gaze shifted to his half-open door. Beyond it, a spacious room bustled with noise and activity as typesetters readied hundreds of plates. Within this knot of buildings near Newgate, dozens of periodicals were printed and bundled for distribution throughout the kingdom. 'Dammit, Theo, do you wish to provoke riots?'

'No. I simply wish to discover the truth. If the duke was murdered, the people deserve to know.'

'And what makes you think he was murdered?'

Theo shrugged. 'Call it a hunch.'

Mr Scripp slammed his beefy fist on his desk. 'Parliament may well consider the publication of this article a criminal act, and you tell me it was based on a *hunch*?'

Theo tilted his chair back further and thrust his hands into his pockets. 'In what way criminal?'

'Your column could be in defiance of the Six Acts, especially if it incites violence against the government in a misguided attempt to avenge someone who by all accounts *wasn't* murdered.'

'By what accounts?' Theo asked. 'I've not heard any official report of Severn's death, and he looked fit as a fiddle when I saw him leave Westminster in company with Viscount Marlow hours before he died.'

Scripp drew his bushy brows together. 'Are you implying Marlow had a hand in the duke's death?'

'Marlow hated Severn, but if I had any grounds to believe he murdered him I would have said so in my column. I'm not exactly known for holding back.'

Scripp huffed. 'You have yet to mention any of the grounds for your belief that the duke was murdered.'

Theo placed all four chair legs on the floor. 'Very well. I'll explain. Two weeks ago, I observed a palpable animosity between Perceval Percy, the new Duke of Severn, and the Duchess—'

'Ah, we come to it already.' Scripp rolled his eyes. 'I should

have known this has something to do with your obsession with
that lady.'

Theo bristled. 'I am not obsessed with the Duchess of Severn.'

Scripp snorted with a decidedly derisive air.

'I'm *not*,' Theo said. 'I admit I find her somewhat more enigmatic than most aristocrats, which intrigues me—'

'Somewhat more *enigmatic*?' Scripp chuckled. 'Which *intrigues*
you? Ha! What you mean to say is that you find the cuckolding
duchess ravishing and you wish she'd consider a Newgate-born
journalist for her next fuck.'

Theo curled his fingers so tightly around his seat that his nails
dug into the wood. It took all his self-control not to grab his
editor by his limp cravat and shake him until his teeth rattled.
Whatever one thought of Henrietta Percy, no man should speak
of a woman in such a foul manner.

Scripp was despicably coarse and a bloody fool to boot. If Theo
had felt that way about the duchess, he would have accepted her
offer of a kiss five years ago and he would have given her *such* a
kiss. At first gentle – but not *too* gentle, so that she could sense
the passion of which he was capable – and then, if she'd responded
with encouraging warmth, he would have incrementally increased
the ardency until she flamed with desire.

But he *didn't*. Because he didn't fancy the woman.

He cast his editor a scathing glare. 'If you can control your
vulgar mind, old man, perhaps I might explain why I believe
Severn was assassinated?'

That made Scripp sober down. 'Yes, yes, get on with it.'

Theo resumed his interrupted story. 'I investigated, primarily
seeking to ascertain why the duchess and the new duke despise
each other, but I soon discovered that everyone is suspiciously
closed mouth – and obviously nervous – about Severn's death. The
chief magistrate is investigating, but only his two most trusted
men are permitted to assist him. Even my most forthcoming

sources at Bow Street reveal nothing other than that the servants have been extensively questioned, that Sir Robert Baker is acting peculiarly, and that the coroner is involved.'

He paused to observe Scripp. Gratified to see the editor was hanging on to his every word, he disclosed his most damning discovery. 'Within hours of Severn's death, his body was autopsied, which is highly unusual, given his rank and status.' Then Theo leant forward and emphasised each word dramatically as he continued, the better to captivate Scripp's thirst for sensationalism. Taking a salacious angle was the only way he'd ever got the man to print anything of importance. 'Furthermore, this autopsy was performed by none other than the esteemed Dr Grimsley, Britain's foremost expert on *forensic medicine*. And lastly' – Theo pointed a triumphant finger at Scripp – 'you know damned well that my hunches are seldom, if ever, wrong.'

'And what the devil is forensic medicine?' Scripp scowled.

Theo should have known better than to use big words. 'The application of medical science to provide evidence in criminal trials.' Since his adolescence, he'd followed cases at the Old Bailey.

'By God.' Scripp's eyes gleamed at last. 'But why then no coroner's inquest? Why no declaration of cause of death?'

Theo lifted his hands, palms up. 'The coroner must not yet be ready for public disclosure. Perhaps he waited for the duke to be laid to rest? Perhaps there are political reasons why he refrains? Or perhaps' – he added more dramatic flair, giving his voice an eerie edge – 'or perhaps the magistrate hopes the assassin or murderer will grow careless, thinking he has succeeded in concealing his crime, make a mistake, and reveal himself?'

Scripp shuddered in delight. 'If so, your article could ruin the magistrate's plans. It may well force him into action.'

Theo winked. 'Precisely, Mr Scripp. Precisely.'

But then Scripp's enthusiasm waned and he looked at the

crumpled paper with stooped shoulders. 'Hang it, Theo, even if all you say is correct—'

'Which it is.'

Scripp held up a hand. 'Even if all you say is correct, this sort of devilry is dangerous to print. You should've asked first.'

Theo cocked an eyebrow. 'One *might* say that as editor, you should have read it before sending it to press.'

Scripp tugged at his collar. 'You know I haven't the time to read everything that crosses my desk. It hurts me to my core that you would abuse my trust in this way, when you know how dearly I care for you.'

'Leave off, old man.' Theo laughed, accustomed as he was to his editor's wheedling ways. At one time, he *had* owed Scripp for discovering him when he was a wiry but strong eight-year-old crossing-sweeper, and first giving him a job in the packing rooms, bundling papers and tossing them into delivery carts alongside grown men, and then later offering him the opportunity to use his wiles and cunning to spy on the elite. But Theo had repaid his debts with years of servitude – often thirteen, fifteen hours a day, doing whatever Scripp asked of him. There was no tenderness on the editor's part. 'You care about me as a tool. A particularly useful one, since I am the only writer you employ who is also willing to work the packing rooms.'

Theo packed newspapers many mornings, sometimes arriving directly from observing late-night society events to join the packers in the early hours before dawn, when the papers rolled fresh off the printing press. In fact, ink currently tinged his close-clipped fingernails and smudged his forearms below his rolled-up shirtsleeves because he'd been bundling and loading papers since four in the morning, though in today's case he'd done so as an excuse to ensure that Scripp hadn't changed a word of his column before the *Mayfair Examiner* had been carted out.

'I never thought to see the day when Theo Hawke turned into

an ungrateful scoundrel.' Scripp put a hand to his heart, as if mortally wounded. 'But that is what you are, young man. You know I cannot afford to draw the attention of the law. No one cares when we print salacious little rumours ... who cuckolds whom ... who wagered too heavily at the card table ... that sort of thing, carefully worded, with names obscured – *that* I can print. But *this* ... this could destroy me. A hefty fine, or worse. *Prison*, even, Theo. And if I go down, everyone who works for me will lose their livelihood. What have you to say to that?'

Theo tapped his foot and considered. His editor was *probably* playing him, but Theo had once been a half-starved orphan, making his way in the streets, and some things, like memories of the gnawing pains of poverty, never left a person. He certainly wouldn't want to be the cause of someone else's hunger, however indirectly.

Nonetheless, he stood by his theory. 'I won't write a retraction, but, since you're this concerned about criminal repercussions, I'll investigate until I uncover irrefutable evidence.'

Scripp sat back heavily in his chair, folding his thick hands over his thick middle. 'Be quick with it, Theo,' he said, all traces of his mortal wound vanished. 'And I still expect your regular column for next week.'

Theo rose, retrieving the coat he'd discarded earlier and extracting a folded paper from its pocket. He tossed the paper on Scripp's desk. 'How about this instead?'

As Scripp scanned the neatly written lines, his scarlet face turned purple. 'This is more radical politics!'

'It's not.' Theo defended the article he'd laboured over for days. 'It's a path forward in turbulent times. A call for the people to unify behind the vision of a less exclusive Britain, presented in a way that hopefully will allow some aristocrats to come alongside.'

Scripp ripped the paper down the middle. 'No one wants to read political opinions from a gossip columnist.'

Theo ground his teeth as his editor crumpled up the torn scraps. He wasn't surprised, for it wasn't the first time Scripp had dismissed his serious journalism, but he was annoyed, both by the insult and by the destruction of his article. Thankfully, he'd written out a second copy, safely on his desk at his lodgings, but it was the *principle* of the matter. For many years, he'd worked tirelessly for Scripp – would the editor truly *never* take him seriously?

'In dark times, people don't want to think about the state of the world, my boy.' There was a consolatory note in Scripp's voice. 'They want to read about their neighbours' intrigues and follies, and no one is better than you at sniffing out filth. So, once you find that proof, keep politics out of your work.'

But Theo wasn't about to give up on his ambitions. He bolstered his confidence as he left the newspaper offices and headed towards his lodgings at Newgate Market. Hooking his coat over his shoulder due to the warmth of the June day, he passed under the shadow of the prison where he'd first entered the world and reminded himself that he'd been successfully fighting adversity from the moment of his birth. He wouldn't stop now. One day, he'd make a valuable contribution to the betterment of Britain, but he'd need to work for a more reputable newspaper than the *Mayfair Examiner* to make that happen. The trouble was, better newspapers didn't hire street-urchins-cum-journalists, no matter how much they'd scrambled and toiled to learn to read, write and make something of themselves.

He needed to write something big. An article that would score such a success against rival newspapers that *everyone* would take notice of Theodore Hawke, not as a gossipmongering nuisance, but as a serious journalist.

Perhaps investigating the murder of Severn was his chance.

Newgate Market, one of London's biggest meat markets, was bustling with activity when Theo entered. In the mid-afternoon, the vendors sold the last of the day's stock at a discounted rate to kerchiefed goodwives and serving women. Despite the flies attracted to the sun-warmed carcasses, Theo's stomach growled as he passed the stalls. He hadn't eaten anything other than a bit of sausage and bread shortly after dawn, hastily grabbed between packing and loading papers.

The first thing he'd do upon arriving at home, he decided, would be to charm his landlady into giving him a hearty dinner. That was easily enough done, for Mrs Ford had a soft spot for him. She claimed he was like the son she never had, but Theo doubted mothers usually found so very many opportunities to pat their grown sons' bottoms. Fortunately, Mrs Ford's cooking and cleaning compensated for her wandering hands.

Halfway across the market square, he reached into his pocket, grasped his keys, and planned the remainder of his day. After his meal, he'd wash and change into one of his good suits of clothes. Then he'd dedicate the evening and night to scouring for information on the Duke of Severn's death, starting with yet another visit to the public house frequented by the Bow Street Runners, amongst whom Theo had several mates. Hardly bosom friends, but burly men who were good for a laugh over pints, who on occasion scratched Theo's back in return for his scratching theirs. A wily spy was useful to a thief-taker and on Theo's part, he liked to know the *true* intricacies of Bow Street and the Old Bailey.

As he approached the brick terrace where he leased two rooms, Mrs Ford appeared at an open upstairs window, leaning so far forward that her mountainous bosom spilled over the ledge. Theo raised a hand in greeting, but she didn't throw her customary kisses in return.

Instead, she gestured frantically towards a slender gentleman standing below her, just outside the front door. Clad in expensive clothes with his gloved hands behind his back, the man's head was lowered, concealing his features beneath a tall-crowned hat. 'Look, look,' the landlady silently mouthed to Theo. 'Look who is here!'

The visitor glanced up then, revealing the haughty, pink face of the new Duke of Severn, a man for whom Theo held no good opinion. Some years ago, Perceval Percy had belonged to a riotous band of wealthy scions called the Scourers, who'd smashed windows and gas lamps, picked fights with vagrants, tormented flower girls, stole from street merchants, and in general had made themselves a nuisance because they'd had nothing better to do. Although Percy had distanced himself from those troublemakers perhaps five years earlier, he remained an idle, frivolous peacock, prone to lavish spending on horses and a succession of exceptionally crass mistresses.

Nevertheless, Theo was intrigued – there must be the very devil of a reason for a newly minted duke to call upon a gossip journalist. Was Percy objecting to the fortnight-old report about his encounter with his opera dancer? Or today's column about the late Severn? Was there to be parliamentary action against Theo?

Percy greeted him with a supercilious sneer. 'Mr Hawke of the *Mayfair Examiner*, I presume?'

Meeting arrogance with arrogance, Theo cracked a grin. 'What an unexpected pleasure, Your Grace. Allow me to extend my condolences upon your loss ... or, rather, my congratulations upon your gains. I suppose now that the lovely Miss Babcock gets a coronet, she'll be more willing to share your favours with Désirée du Pont? Or perhaps now that you're a duke, you've set your sights higher than a rich bishop's daughter?'

Percy deepened his sneer. 'In some sunlit field, Mr Hawke, there's hemp growing tall and strong, destined to become a fine necklace for you.'

That made Theo laugh heartily, for it wasn't the first time a swell had told him he was heading for a hanging. They appeared to think the idea should terrify him into some sort of deference, perhaps accompanied by tugging his forelock, but the gallows had loomed over Theo's entire life and he didn't fear it any more than he feared any death. The grave was inevitable and no one knew that like a London street brat. In Theo's opinion, there was nothing for it but to embrace every day one got, and to try to leave the world a better place.

'Is that what you came to say?' he asked, wiping away a tear of laughter. 'Because if so, now that you've said it, shift your stuck-up arse out of my sight before I do it for you.'

Percy looked appalled, then drew his shoulders up, as if attempting to regain his authority. 'Mr Hawke, I happen to believe that somewhere under your boorish and ill-bred crust, there's a man of some intelligence. And a man who, despite obvious disdain for his betters, admired my late cousin. In ten years, you never printed an ill word about him – which leads me to suspect you'd want swift justice brought to the murderer of the People's Duke.'

That sobered Theo instantly, but the definite confirmation that his hunch was correct brought him no satisfaction. The late Duke of Severn had been more than just a good man. He'd been a brilliant strategist, a caring politician and a beacon of hope. Many Britons had believed that if ever the Whigs regained control of Parliament, it would be with Severn as prime minister, and of late he'd certainly seemed to be gathering support and building his leadership platform, one of parliamentary reform, male suffrage and amendment of the Corn Laws.

Someone had stolen that from the people by killing the man before he'd even reached his prime. Death might be inevitable, but murder was still the most heinous of crimes.

'Who did it?' Theo spat out the words, narrowing his gaze to meet Percy's icy blue stare, and wondering if he were looking into the eyes of a murderer. The new duke was a scoundrel, after all. 'What blackhearted villain deprived the world of Severn?' he asked, curious how Percy would reply. 'I will use my pen to destroy the man.'

'As it happens, Mr Hawke,' Percy replied slowly, 'it might be that the villain isn't a man at all.'

Theo's breath caught short. What game was Percy playing? Why had the man come to *him* with this tale? And if the killer were a woman, who could he possibly mean? There was only one woman whose name was ever connected with the late Duke of Severn, and that was …

… the duchess.

Into Theo's mind flashed a vision of Henrietta Percy's stately figure in widow weeds, silhouetted in a golden rectangle of light before a crowd mourning the death of her husband.

His blood ran cold. 'What do you mean, the villain mightn't be a man?'

The new duke's lips curved into a frigid smile. 'Invite me in and we can talk.'

CHAPTER 6

In Pursuit

Fifteen minutes later, Theo had difficulty concealing his horror as he stared at Perceval Percy, who stood before the fireless hearth, having declined to sit or to drink.

The chief magistrate believed the Duchess of Severn had had a hand in killing her own husband.

Theo strode to his desk, poured himself a gin and swallowed it in one gulp. Could it be true? The duchess was enigmatic, but was she a *murderess*? Theo's hand shook as he placed his empty glass on his desk beside the copy of his political article.

He inhaled deeply, hoping to conceal how the tale had affected him. 'Do *you* believe the duchess capable of such a heinous act, Your Grace?'

Percy walked slowly across the room. 'The evidence is certainly damning,' he said, peering down from Theo's window to the back court. 'She was alone with my cousin at the time of his death and his corpse bore marks of violence upon the neck. The duchess is by no means a weak woman; physically, she could strangle a man, especially one she'd already enfeebled by poison, as Dr Grimsley believes.'

Theo retrieved his glass and the bottle. He needed another bloody drink. 'Tell me again the *exact* last words the footman overheard the late duke utter before he opened the door of the library?'

'"My dear sweet killed me",' Percy replied.

'My dear sweet.' Theo poured himself a healthy draught of gin. 'Was this a term of endearment the duke frequently employed for the duchess?'

'My dear or my sweet.' Percy shrugged his shoulders. 'Such were the terms he used, yes.'

Theo sipped his gin. The wording of 'My dear sweet killed me,' seemed too awkward for accuracy. Surely the duke would have said, 'You've killed me,' to his wife, if they were in the room alone together? But he concealed his doubts to Percy. 'Has Sir Robert Baker questioned the duchess, if he believes her guilty?'

'As you can imagine, it is a delicate matter.' Percy drummed his fingers on the window ledge. 'Her father has some inkling of the magistrate's suspicions, but naturally he protests that she is innocent and too fragile in her grief to be questioned. She doesn't seem fragile to *me*; however, the magistrate doesn't like to go against Lord Lockington before he is *quite* certain.'

'You made it seem as if he is already certain.'

Percy returned to the hearth, twisting his signet ring as he strolled. 'I see I must be candid with you, Mr Hawke. Unless the duchess is publicly exposed as the killer, I worry she will never be tried, much less hanged. An innocent may die in her stead.'

Theo lifted his brows. 'Who?' he asked, wondering if this visit was somehow part of a ploy on Percy's part to save his own guilty skin.

'There is a maid – a clumsy, half-witted sort of girl – who Sir

Robert holds under lock and key. She is just the sort of hapless nobody who could be blamed and hanged in the name of serving justice; nobody would think twice about the matter and no powerful enemies would be made.'

Bile rose from Theo's stomach so violently he almost retched his gin. Percy's reply had taken him by surprise, although it oughtn't, for if what the duke said was true, it wouldn't be the first time a working-class girl had hanged for the crimes of the 'Quality'. Theo's own mother had been such a victim, having been executed shortly after his birth for supposedly stealing a valuable necklace. But based on Theo's investigation into court records, it was far more likely that the lady of the house had framed Deborah Hawke for the crime, seeking to punish the young chambermaid who'd engaged her husband's attentions.

Pleading her belly had given Deborah a few extra months, but it hadn't spared her life. Nor had it brought Theo's father to her side, for that man had drowned while boating, just before his widow had brought the claims against Deborah. In truth, the whole affair smacked of foul play, but, despite considerable effort, Theo had never found any evidence that his father's death had been anything other than an accident.

He stared into his gin, trying not to let his sentiments overpower his reason. 'What evidence do they have against the girl?'

'None that I am aware of,' Percy replied. 'But public reaction to your column this morning has forced the magistrate's hand. Just this afternoon, I learnt there is to be a coroner's inquest in which Dr Grimsley will announce the official cause of death. Not as poisoning *and* strangulation, as he once hinted, but poisoning alone. I, for one, worry this might be Lord Lockington's influence. Since the duchess and my cousin were alone together when he died, strangulation declares her guilt. I believe Sir Robert's intention is to charge the girl instead – who better to take the blame for a poisoning than a friendless maid? Which leads me to wonder how you'll feel if your column is responsible for bringing about the death of an innocent?'

Percy was taunting him. 'You didn't answer my earlier question,' Theo said, refusing to rise to the bait. 'Do you or do you not believe Henrietta Percy capable of murdering her husband?'

'Until the will reading today, I thought it impossible,' Percy replied after a moment's pause. 'Now I'm less confident. How else to explain the coincidence of the will alteration *the afternoon before my cousin's poisoning*? Not to mention these ridiculous terms that allow her twelve months to deliver an heir to supplant me?'

Theo rubbed his chin. That term of the will, which Percy had also explained, was confusing. *If* the duchess had killed her husband – and he emphasised that *if*, even in his thoughts – why had she not waited until she had already given birth to a son, if her intention was to assume control over all the lands and wealth of the dukedom?

Still, *someone* had killed the duke and the single fact that the duchess had been alone with him at the time of his death was damning evidence. Yet … 'The duke's generosity in his new will seems to suggest that he trusted his wife.'

'*Trusted her?*' Percy's voice rose an octave. 'Yes, as one trusts the devil because one is taken in by his beauty. The duchess is a demon, Hawke.'

Theo recoiled, surprised at the fervency of the duke's loathing, although he'd seen evidence of it outside Severn House two weeks earlier. 'Indeed?'

Percy closed his eyes, as if attempting to control his emotions. 'Forgive my outburst,' he said at last. 'The duchess has long been a point of contention between me and my late cousin. All I can say is, she is not a woman to be trusted, nor a woman to be underestimated. She is beautiful, with all the outward appearance of goodness. *That*, of course, captivated my poor cousin, as it would any man. But from the onset, she tricked him.' Percy stared intently at Theo. 'Five years ago, when you published your column on the duchess and Marlow, what did you think my cousin would do, once he knew his bride to be unfaithful?'

Theo lifted his shoulders. 'I did not presume to guess.'

Percy snarled. '*I* told him to divorce her. He forgave her instead.'

'That upset you?'

'Would it not upset any man if a bastard usurped his rightful title?'

Theo drank the rest of his gin in silence. While he didn't trust Percy's motives, the elusive nature of the duchess's true character *had* always baffled Theo. Now these new details added to his confusion. The late duke's generosity with his will and his tolerance of the duchess's infidelity seemed to suggest that he sincerely loved her. So had Severn been duped by his beautiful bride, as Percy claimed? Had the duke been controlled by a vicious and violent wife? Was Henrietta Percy a veritable Lady Macbeth? And, in the end, for reasons Theo couldn't yet fathom, had she killed the duke, even before getting herself with child?

Whatever the answers, Theo knew he wanted them – for the sake of the truth, for justice for the duke, to safeguard an innocent life, and because he owed it to Scripp's workers to ensure the *Examiner* wasn't shut down by Parliament. Besides, this was exactly the type of story he needed to write to draw attention to himself as a serious journalist. And it would be immensely satisfying to close the book on the enigma of Henrietta Percy, at long last.

Yet he was wary of Percy. 'Why have you come to *me* with this tale?' he asked. 'What do you think I can do about it?'

Percy regarded him steadily. 'This afternoon, the duchess departed for her estate of Grenham Park in Berkshire. I want you to follow her. Watch her, and when you have proof that she's taken a lover, then reveal her to be the murdering, adulterous thief she is.'

A suspiciously simple request. 'And why do you ask *me* to do this? Surely you have some underling who could perform the task?'

'I don't want to send an underling. I want to know the truth – and all the specific details of that truth – and you aren't scared of truth. I'll say this for you, Hawke – you have been a trial to me many times over the years, but you're an audacious bastard whom I can't help but respect. Nor am I alone in that sentiment. People read what you write, and people believe you, however much they pretend otherwise.'

The duke was employing flattery to get what he wanted, but Theo wasn't completely immune. 'If she's left town, I'll require funds.'

'I anticipated you.' Percy withdrew a purse from his pocket. 'Twenty pounds in coin to cover the expense of travel. Furthermore, my groom stands in the market square with one of the best horses from my stable, saddled and ready. The duchess took her carriage; on my horse, you can travel at twice her speed and reach Grenham before she does. And as for remuneration, once you publish your article exposing her as an adulteress attempting to pass off a bastard in my stead, then I shall personally give you—'

'I don't accept blood money.'

'I shall personally give you,' the duke said again, more slowly, 'one thousand pounds. Which' – he scanned Theo's spartan chamber – 'would change your life, I imagine.'

Yes, dammit, a thousand pounds *would* change Theo's life. With such a fortune, he could start his own newspaper. A real one, with a substantial reach.

'We shall see,' Theo said finally. 'But I won't print lies, no matter what you offer. I write the truth and the truth alone. If there is evidence the duchess committed murder, I shall print that, and the law must then deal with her accordingly. But if there is not, then I shan't write a word about her in relation to this foul business.'

Percy placed the coin purse in Theo's hand. 'Mr Hawke, while even I cannot fully bring myself to imagine Henrietta as a murder-ess, no matter what the evidence suggests, I know with utmost certainty that she is a thief and a liar, attempting to get herself with child to deprive me of what is rightfully mine. But, please, don't take my word for it – follow her, discover for yourself. You might even find yourself a target to a woman of her appetite. And remember, I don't care who lies with her – I just want the truth exposed before she attempts to pass that child off as my cousin's.'

Theo took in Percy's appalling meaning. Ah, perhaps at last the new duke was revealing his sordid purpose. 'You suggest I seduce the duchess in order to ascertain her goal?'

Percy's lips spread into a wide smile. 'No doubt you're too principled to stoop to such a level, although she is undeniably a beauty.'

Theo didn't hide his disgust. He would *never* interfere in any manner designed to fabricate evidence. Scowling at Percy like the loathsome insect he was, he pointed to the door. 'Show yourself out at once, unless you wish me to dismiss the entirety of your offer as *vehemently* as I dismiss that suggestion.'

Percy's smile didn't waver. 'Gladly shall I take my leave, Mr Hawke.'

Theo didn't waste time after the duke departed. In a matter of moments, he washed and changed his clothes, donning leather breeches and a brown tailcoat over a clean shirt and linen waist-coat, packed some essentials, took up the purse and went in search of the horse. Although his stomach growled, he didn't stop for food. The two glasses of gin would have to suffice as dinner, for the time being.

Right now, he must pursue a duchess.

One who might very well be a murderer.

CHAPTER 7

Truth

Perceval's villainy had two positive effects on Henrietta. Firstly, it forced her to shrug off a lethargic melancholia which had shrouded her since Edmund's death. As her carriage travelled the Bath Road, she rested against the velvet squabs and watched woods, estates and villages pass by, and her mood lifted. Her life choices rested in her own hands as they'd never done before. She could shape her destiny – once she decided what destiny she wanted.

The second positive effect was that her appetite, which had been in abeyance for two weeks, returned with a vengeance. Feeling ravenous – and knowing her unexpected arrival at Grenham would cause the servants trouble enough without having to produce a dinner – she instructed her coachman to stop at the George and Dragon in Wargrave, which she'd frequented several times with Edmund.

The landlord made a show of ushering her into the best private parlour, no doubt so he could alert as many customers as possible to the fact that a duchess was patronising his establishment. He'd been more discreet when Edmund was alive and Henrietta was not in the mood for display. Wanting to continue her ruminations in private as she dined, she ordered something of everything on offer and then dismissed the servants.

When the dishes arrived soon after, she eagerly rubbed her palms together under the table. She would eat until bursting, as slowly or as quickly as she wished, because, for the first time in her life, there was no one to please but herself. As she removed the covers after the servants once again departed, her mouth watered at the savoury and sweet aromas. Pigeon stewed with clove and mushrooms. Oyster soup. Trout with horseradish. February parsnips swimming in butter. Creamy artichoke fricassee. Roast hare doused in currant sauce. Lemon cheesecake and green gooseberry pie with custard.

It was forty delicious minutes later before she dabbed the corners of her mouth and rang for tea, feeling calm and content for the first time in ages. The tension of the past fortnight had rolled away like the retreating tide. It would return, yes, but for now, she'd relish this moment of precious peace.

Dishes cleared and tray brought, Henrietta again requested privacy. As she sipped her tea, a breeze blew in off the Thames. Cup in hand, she strode to the window to watch the fishing boats float by in the gold-washed early evening light.

Though grief still lay heavy over her heart, there was something appealing about not having to answer to father or husband. It was a rare thing indeed for a woman and Henrietta would be damned if she'd answer to a weaselly libertine in their stead.

Liking the way that sounded, she repeated it aloud, speaking to the boats. 'I'll be *damned* before I'll answer to you, Perceval Percy. You or any man, now that Edmund is dead.'

'Yet you must answer to the law,' said a vaguely familiar masculine voice from outside the window.

Henrietta was so startled she *nearly* dropped her tea. But since duchesses didn't *actually* drop their tea, she regained her composure with barely a spill in the saucer. She placed her cup upon the table behind her, wondering if she ought to ring for a servant before discarding the idea in favour of investigating the eavesdropper herself. In case he proved dangerous, she slipped her hand into her pocket and curled her fingers around her tiny silver pistol. 'Who spoke? Show yourself.'

And of all the possible people, it was the beastliest man in the world who popped his head over the window ledge. No, on second thought, Theodore Hawke was now the *second* most beastly. Perceval had recently taken top spot.

So much for her moment of peace.

The tide had rushed back in with a vengeance.

'*You!*' Henrietta's blood boiled, but she hid her fury behind disdain. 'The pestilent Hawke himself.'

'And a good evening to you too, Your Grace.' He gave her an appallingly cheeky grin and it was all Henrietta could do not to aim a solid kick at his teeth.

She removed her hand from her pocket. Hawke was dangerous, but he wasn't there to rob her. The question was why he was there at all, but she wouldn't yet give him the satisfaction of enquiring. She'd torture him a little instead, for pure enjoyment. After years of acrimonious interaction, she'd grown to realise Hawke was a proud man, in his way. He wouldn't like her baiting him, but he deserved it for invading her privacy.

She returned his smirk. 'No need to ask why you are here. The answer has been obvious for years. You're obsessed with me.' Her purpose was achieved, for Hawke's handsome face tightened into a scowl, and she triumphed. 'Well, and so you've had the great pleasure of seeing me, but now you must be gone, for I do not share your obsession. Fly away like a good hawk or I shall send my footman for a magistrate.'

Rather than relieving her of his foul presence, he hoisted himself up and over the ledge *into* her private parlour. After his dusty boots landed with a thud on the carpeted floor, he slowly extended himself to his regrettably impressive height and rolled his broad shoulders, watching her all the while. 'It's *you* who have need to avoid a magistrate, not I.'

That forced her laughter. 'Indeed?' Oh, how she hated that she had to tilt her head up to meet his gaze. 'Tell me, Mr Hawke, why should *I* avoid a magistrate, when *you* are the one invading my privacy in a threatening manner?'

'Threatening?' He took a seat on the window ledge, stretched out his long legs and pushed his hat to the back of his head, which allowed the evening light to highlight his cheekbones and chiselled jaw in a most disconcerting manner. He blinked innocently; the man had impossibly long lashes. 'In what way do you find me threatening, madam?'

At the moment, the most threatening thing about the scoundrel was how her traitorous body warmed to him. Nor was it the first time. She loathed him – truly, she did – but even as they'd exchanged glares over the years, she could never loathe him so much that she failed to notice his good looks.

Feeling her danger, she changed the subject. 'I understand you wrote more vitriol about me, or about my late husband, in your column this morning. You'll forgive me for not knowing the particulars. I haven't had the chance to peruse your vile lies today.'

'Not lies, Your Grace. And even vile truths deserve to be spoken.'

'Truth!' Henrietta rolled her eyes. 'And what is truth, Mr Hawke? I believe we established some years ago that you and I subscribe to different accounts on this matter. I prefer an informed version of the truth and you prefer to believe whatever your sordid imagination thinks you saw.'

'Some truths may depend upon interpretation, yes. But others are absolute,' he replied coolly. 'By the by, perhaps it would be more fitting if you quoted Judas rather than Pilate.'

Henrietta tapped her foot and stared at the man, wondering how he always succeeded in frustrating her when she'd managed to ignore the scorn of people many times his consequence over the years. 'So, you persist in believing me a traitor to my husband.'

His reply was as sombre as a Good Friday sermon. 'As of today, I have more reason than ever to believe you a traitor.'

She sighed, resigned. 'I already know it's useless to ask you not to print what you overheard me say about Perceval Percy – which was a private thought spoken aloud only to give myself strength, not that you care.' A faint line appeared between Hawke's straight dark brows before quickly disappearing. 'But why are you here, Mr Hawke? Tell me and perhaps I shall give you what you wish, just so I can get on with my life and grieve in private, which is all I want.'

'Grieve?' he asked. 'Do you grieve for him?'

She steadied herself with a deep breath. 'Yes, Mr Hawke, I do. But you will never believe that, so I shall ask again. What do you want from me?'

'The truth, Your Grace.'

Henrietta lifted her hands in exasperation. 'For heaven's sake, *what* truth?'

'The truth about your husband's murder.'

Because he said the words as matter-of-factly as one might mention the weather, it took a moment for her to absorb them. But when she did, they hit her gut with the force of a thousand horses. These must be the rumours to which her parents and Mr Quigley had referred.

'His … his …' She couldn't bring herself to say the word *murder*.

It stuck in her throat, a filthy word, an evil word. Edmund *murdered*? No one, *no one*, could wish to end the life of someone so wholly honourable.

Rage overtook her and she didn't attempt to contain it. She clenched her fists, shaking, and addressed Hawke with vehemence. 'How *dare* you? How dare you besmirch my husband's memory with your horrid lies?' She hated that her composure was crumbling. She hated that her voice was cracking. She hated that she was falling apart in front of the man who had sought to ruin her for years. But at the same time, she didn't fight it. She wanted Theodore Hawke to understand – for once, to understand – that he didn't have the *right* to hurt Edmund any more. 'My husband died of a seizure, in great pain, and yet even now you cannot let him rest in peace? You seek to soil his name, to bring about rumours and speculation that will do nothing but incite hate and fear, and for what? Tell me, for *what*?'

'For the truth,' Hawke replied, cool as a cucumber.

'The truth is no one killed my husband. He died alone with *me*, in *my* arms.'

'Yes, that is supported by witnesses. As are his dying words, overheard by your footman. "My dear sweet killed me."'

Henrietta stared in disbelief. '*That* is the basis for your preposterous theory? His having uttered the phrase "killed me"? Edmund's last words were senseless, a disconnected jumble. He was struggling to speak. And besides, his very last word was something altogether different.'

James. The last word Edmund had uttered in his earthly existence.

Hawke dismissed her protest with an unconcerned shrug. 'The statement your footman overheard is not the sole reason I – and others – know your husband was murdered. He was most certainly poisoned—'

Henrietta choked on her own breath. 'Poisoned!'

Hawke's eyes narrowed, as if scrutinising her reaction. '*And* his body bore evidence of strangulation. The magistrate may simply be waiting for you to make a blunder before arresting you – and your flight from London on the very day my speculations regarding the murder were printed could be perceived as confirmation of your guilt. If the Runners have learnt of your flight, it's possible they will arrive at Grenham soon and you could find yourself escorted back to London by the chief magistrate himself.'

Henrietta's hands flew to her cheeks as she grasped his meaning. 'You think *I* killed my husband?'

'*Some* people think you killed him,' he replied calmly. 'I've not yet decided if I agree.'

It was all she could do not to slap his face. 'And do you think that if I did this despicable thing, I would simply confess so that you can write about it in your filthy rag? Is that why you followed me?'

He regarded her with steely focus. 'I already said I haven't decided if you are so wholly evil, Your Grace. But I'm not letting you out of my sight until I discover the truth.'

Indignation rose in Henrietta.

If Theodore Hawke thought he could keep his eye on *her*, he needed to think again.

CHAPTER 8

In Pursuit Again

On his ninety-minute ride from London, Theo had thought over matters. By the time he'd spotted the duchess's blue-and-silver carriage outside the inn in Wargrave, he'd determined the evidence was likely too damning for Henrietta Percy to be entirely innocent, if not wholly and completely guilty.

1. She was alone with the duke at his violent death.
2. His body bore evidence of strangulation.
3. Severn changed his will in her favour the day before his death.
4. He seemingly named her as his killer.
5. How could she be innocent?

And yet, perhaps because her angelic beauty always seemed to affect him so damnably, Theo couldn't bring himself to believe she'd acted without an accomplice.

If so, who was her accomplice? The maid? He thought it unlikely, as the girl would have nothing to gain and everything to lose. A lover was much more plausible. Together, they perhaps intended to assume control of the dukedom – or, at least, the man hoped to marry her and take her newfound wealth into his possession. Perhaps the duchess was already with child, and she and her lover hoped for a boy. Perhaps they knew of desperate, pregnant women – easily found – and stood ready to take the first male baby born from amongst them.

The possibilities were endless and Theo intended to discover the answers. He believed that by frightening the duchess, she might run to her partner for assistance. Then, wherever she went, whatever she did, he would follow.

He watched her now, searching for any hint of her intentions, but she'd grown as still as a statue after his declaration that he would follow her. She merely gazed through the other window, towards the river, her face illuminated by the soft evening light. Theo settled back against the window frame, ready to watch her all night, if necessary.

In truth, watching her was no hardship. Today, she wore her hair loose and it fell in thick waves down her back. Endless shades of honey and flax and wheat mingled together to form an exquisite gold.

Theo *wasn't* obsessed, no matter what anyone said, but one needn't be obsessed with the Duchess of Severn to appreciate that she was lovely to look upon. Devilishly kissable lips. A bloody fine figure. Eyes that were large, finely shaped and as blue as forget-me-nots.

Which was an apt comparison, for Theo hadn't forgotten them, not from the first moment of their locking with his across Hanover Square, when she'd been an ivory-lace bride emerging from the church to the roar of the crowds and the pealing of bells.

Beautiful beyond compare.

On that day, he'd decided the Duke of Severn was the world's most fortunate man. Two months later, after seeing the duchess with Marlow, he'd reversed that opinion. But now, Theo was gutted. No one deserved Severn's fate, but least of all a man as noble as the duke. A man who had once altered the course of Theo's life, merely out of the goodness of his heart.

Theo folded his arms across his chest. Was the duchess physically capable of strangling her husband? She was certainly statuesque. And tall. Theo was considerably taller than most men and she wasn't more than three inches shorter.

Yes, he decided. The duchess possessed the physical strength to kill a man. She was a strong, hearty woman; Theo recalled how her arms looked when bared in evening gowns – she possessed the lean, sculpted muscles of a woman who engaged in vigorous exercise regularly. And he'd seen her canter on magnificent beasts in Hyde Park, her body rising and falling with perfect control to the rhythm of her horse's gait.

But the memory of that sight bothered Theo while he was near enough to smell her expensive perfume. Adjusting his seat, he turned his head towards the boats, where a fisherman had pulled up to a dock and was handing a basket of spotted pikes to two maids. It would be foolish to grow lax around a potential murderess, but if he stared more he might find himself under her spell.

A rustle of silk made him whip his head back towards the duchess.

She was staring directly at him.

Ice crept up his spine. She'd been watching him for a while, he realised, like a cat observing its prey before it pounced. Tense muscles; piercing cerulean gaze.

He flashed the arrogant grin he often employed around her, to show he wasn't intimidated. 'You wish to tell me the truth about what happened, Your Grace?'

'I already have,' she said calmly. 'And as I have nothing to hide from the magistrate, I shall continue my journey to Grenham. *You* are not welcome at my estate, Mr Hawke.'

'Ah, but sadly for you, even a duchess can't keep a man off public roads and bridle paths. I'll go where I must, in search of the truth.'

'Please yourself, but I won't make it easy for you.'

With a swish of her skirts, she walked out of the room.

He rose as she exited, intending to follow at once, but before he'd made his way to the door, the lock clicked from the outside. In and of itself, being locked in was only the mildest inconvenience, as he could leave the same way he'd entered, but the sound of the lock gave him a skin-prickling *sense* – his innate hunch, so invaluable in his line of work – that the duchess had no intention whatsoever of returning to Grenham.

He threw himself into the pursuit by leaping out of the window, his boots landing hard on the paving stones outside. Directly in front of him was the riverbank, the maids now returning with their basket held between them; to the right was the length of the inn and around the far corner was the court, where carriages were loaded and unloaded. There he ran at full speed.

Only to barge forcefully into the broad form of an ostler rounding the corner with a bucket of grain.

This man took great offence to the accidental assault, which had caused him to spill the feed, and many minutes passed before Theo succeeded in assuring the ostler that he wasn't, in fact, begging for a beating, but instead in such urgent need of passing through the court that he'd foolishly not looked where he was going.

By the time he'd appeased the ostler and helped return the grain to the bucket, Theo reckoned the duchess's carriage would be long gone. So he crossed the court to the stables, tossed a coin to the boy who'd taken charge of the fine mount Perceval Percy had supplied, hitched himself into the saddle and gave the horse the reins.

When he exited onto Wargrave's high street, he looked both ways past the half-timber buildings, hoping for a sight of the duchess's carriage.

And, indeed, a glimmer of blue and silver caught his eye, not upon the road, but *behind* him. Theo turned his head. Yes, there still stood the very thing that had alerted him to Henrietta Percy's presence at this inn: her travelling carriage, with her coroneted arms emblazoned on the side and her footman and driver sitting upon a nearby bench, munching sandwiches and drinking from tankards.

No horses were hitched to the carriage and judging by the relaxed state of her servants, she hadn't ordered her team. Which meant the duchess *couldn't* have returned to her carriage.

He scanned the road in front of the inn for a black gown and golden waves of hair, but the duchess was nowhere to be seen, which meant she was either hiding inside or ...

He spurred his horse and returned to the stables.

His ostler friend was tossing hay into a stall with a pitchfork. 'Back for that beating after all, are you?'

Theo ignored him and peered into every stall until he found three perfectly matched, high-bred greys, clearly the horses to pull the elegant carriage outside.

But there were only *three* of them.

He located the boy who'd cared for his horse earlier. 'Where did she go?' he asked. 'The beautiful lady dressed in black on one of her grey horses?'

The boy's gaze darted about furtively. 'My master wouldn't like me telling on her. She's a *duchess*.'

Theo reached into his pocket and extracted a half a crown.

Grubby fingers grasped the coin in a flash. 'Back south, towards Twyford. Round right and out the back in front of your nose she went, while you was fighting with the ostler. Astride and saddleless like a farmer, but by gad, can she ride.'

Theo pulled his horse's reins, turning the beast, and rode out the back of the inn. He rose in his stirrups, looking south along the riverbanks.

His remarkable eyesight didn't fail him. Beside the silver Thames, he spotted a distant figure riding hellbent towards Twyford.

He spurred his horse, his sights set, his energy high, and the thrill of the successful chase coursing hot blood through his veins. 'I have you now, Your Grace.'

He wouldn't lose her again.

CHAPTER 9

A Fugitive Duchess

Bareback and astride, Henrietta galloped along the riverbank towards Twyford, her hair blowing behind her, her skirts whipping around her legs. For a fortnight, she'd yearned for a ride and she didn't enjoy the gallop any less simply because it was a fugitive's flight. There was nothing like exercise for organising her thoughts and there had never been a time in her life when her mind had been in more desperate need of organising.

In the moments when Hawke had stared at her in the parlour, before he'd turned to look at the river, she'd accepted the truth. Edmund *had* been poisoned. Her father and brother had been concealing that from her, and if she hadn't been living in a fog of grief and anxiety she would have realised it sooner.

She also realised exactly what Edmund had been trying to say just before he died. Not 'my dear sweet killed me', as Hawke thought, but also not a disconnected jumble, as she'd assumed.

Edmund had been trying to tell her he had ingested poison in his wine. At last, she understood.

But who would have killed him? And why? And how to uncover such a truth, when all the circumstantial evidence was stacked against *her*?

By going on the run she would appear even guiltier, but the stakes were too high for passivity. She *must* discover the real killer. She would *not* climb the gallows for the crime of another.

Her thoughts flew as fast as her horse's hooves. It was Edmund's *glass* of wine – not the bottle – that had been poisoned. The bottle had been opened in the library by Edmund himself. He hadn't drunk any wine or eaten anything after their visitors had left. Which meant that the killer was one of the three men in the library.

Perceval certainly had motive. Marlow might have. In both of those cases, Henrietta could believe she might even have been framed, for neither would shed a tear if she were hanged in his stead. And what about James Beaucastle? She couldn't dismiss any possibilities.

She composed a mental list of suspects and motives as she approached the Bath Road, and turned back towards London.

There was Perceval, Edmund's heir, ever in need of money, who hated both her and Edmund, and who clearly believed he'd gain immense wealth and power from Edmund's death. Moreover, he'd been so very shocked and furious about the contents of the will ...

Then there was Lord Marlow, Edmund's political rival. Perhaps the viscount hadn't been as pleased with the private meeting as Edmund had thought. Furthermore, Marlow had despised Henrietta ever since the day after the garden tryst, when he'd arrived at Severn House expecting bedsport, only to be dismissed instead. Powerful men didn't like being spurned. They didn't forget it, either.

And then there was James Beaucastle, whose name Edmund

had uttered immediately after mentioning the poison. There was no love lost between Henrietta and James, and he and Edmund had quarrelled dreadfully the day before Edmund's death.

After a moment's more reflection, she decided to start her investigation with James, since his estate was an easy distance. But first, she must disguise herself.

On the edge of the Maidenhead Thicket, two miles back towards London along the Bath Road, stood a respectable but shabby hostelry catering to labourers and farmers. Three years earlier, a torrential downpour had forced Henrietta and Edmund to spend the night under its roof. The innkeeper and his wife had been so overcome by the presence of a duke and duchess at their establishment, they'd outdone themselves to make Edmund and Henrietta comfortable, despite reassurances that warm food and dry sheets alone would be adequate. The next day, Edmund had repaid them so generously they'd wept over his hands and on two or three occasions afterwards, he and Henrietta had stopped for a cup of tea, much to the delight of the innkeeper, his wife and their grown daughter, who was around Henrietta's age.

This was the inn to which she now fled, knowing the innkeeper would aid her. Once she was effectively disguised in the daughter's clothes, with her wedding ring on a string round her neck and tucked into her bodice to conceal her identity, and her carriage horse exchanged for a sturdy cob and saddle from the innkeeper's stables, she'd travel along the Bath Road towards the lowering sun. There would be no need to rush, since she wanted it to be well past dark before she arrived at the home of James Beaucastle. And in disguise, neither magistrate nor that horrid journalist would ever find her.

From a thicket of trees, Theo watched Henrietta Percy reemerge from the small stone inn about a half an hour after she'd entered it.

He raised his eyebrows at the sight he beheld, for the duchess had transformed herself into a country maiden. A straw bonnet topped her long blonde waves, still loose down her back. Her silk mourning gown was gone; in its place she wore a cornflower-blue frock with embroidered daisies along its scooped neckline. Its hem was some inches too short, displaying her elegant black half-boots. She hadn't changed them, but as she walked towards the stable she stepped in mud and muck, possibly to disguise the fine workmanship of her footwear.

Theo shook his head in reluctant admiration. Henrietta Percy was a clever one, he'd give her that. *He* would have recognised her anywhere, of course, but he doubted it would enter anyone else's imagination that this golden-haired girl was the Duchess of Severn.

But gone was any shred of his sympathy for the woman. It seemed all too likely that she was a villainess, out to save her own beautiful skin rather than face the consequences of what she had done.

As she vanished into the stable, he took a deep breath. He couldn't allow his assumptions to dull his attentiveness. He must be alert. What did the duchess intend to do next? Run to an accomplice, perhaps? Bolt to a lover? Flee to France or America?

Whatever her plan, he would be there to witness it.

By the time she exited the stable astride a stout brown horse, now with a saddle, he was back on his own mount, reins gathered and ready to follow wherever she went. He let her get a solid lead down the Bath Road, to the west, because, thanks to his hawkish eye, he needn't follow too closely.

She'd never know he was there until he chose to reveal himself.

CHAPTER 10

A Tussle in the Dark

It was almost eleven when the manor house at Kennetford loomed into Henrietta's view across sloping parkland, its wisteria-laced stone façade pale grey in the light of the waxing moon.

As she walked her horse into a woodland edging the demesne, an owl swooped from a tree, startling her. She took a moment to steady her nerves. It wouldn't do to be jittery when she was about to confront a potential murderer.

Just inside the woodland, she extracted her horse's bit and tied him loosely to allow him to graze. Then she removed her bonnet, tied it to a tree branch, and checked the pistol she'd put into the pocket of the borrowed frock. After ensuring it was properly loaded with wadding, gunpowder and a ball, she stuck it into her scooped bodice, between her breasts.

Leaving her horse, she paused at the edge of the woodland, surveying the house across the rolling hills of the demesne. She knew James's bedchamber was on the front right corner of the first floor. Her eye had lingered there often on previous visits to Kennetford, especially during the lonely garden walks she'd take to pass long evenings when Edmund and James had neither wanted nor needed her company after obligatory, stilted dinners.

As expected, no candlelight shone from the windows at this time of night, for James was a gentleman farmer, early to bed, early to rise. So far, all was as she'd hoped – she'd wanted to sneak into a sleeping house, so none of James's servants saw her disguise. After running from the beastly Hawke, she was a fugitive. Assuming James *wasn't* the murderer, she'd still be on the run tomorrow and still the top suspect. With only a handful of small coins for the tolls given to her by the innkeeper, Henrietta wouldn't easily be able to acquire a second disguise.

And if James *was* the killer, well, Henrietta wasn't quite certain how she'd apprehend him, but that's why she had the pistol. She'd never shoot to kill, but her brothers had once told her to aim for the thigh in a desperate situation. It would cause enough pain and blood loss for her to gain the advantage.

With her eyes focused on those darkened windows, she exited the wooded area, keeping alert to the possibility of a grounds-keeper or watchdogs. She walked slowly into the open. One step. Then another, looking sharp all the while.

A twig snapped behind her, a man's quick curse sounded and Henrietta flew into action, grabbing her pistol as she spun, turning upon a sixpence.

Or rather, she *began to*. Someone large and *very* strong grasped her, entrapping her in a pair of constricting arms, with her back pinned against an exceedingly hard chest.

'Running to your lover, Your Grace?' The voice was instantly recognisable and proved *yet again* that Theodore Hawke was the bane of her existence. 'I meant to catch you in the act, but I'm unaccustomed to trailing someone in the woods – curse these twigs and roots – and certainly I can't have you waving that pistol about. Drop it and let's talk, eh?'

She didn't waste her breath answering back. She *fought* back, kicking up a heel, twisting it around his leg and hitting his knee from behind. When his leg buckled, she jutted her bottom directly into his pelvis, causing him to fold over with a grunt and creating enough room for her to duck down and slip out of his arms. It was the work of one second more to shove her pistol against his neck.

His eyes widened then. Clearly, he hadn't expected her proficiency as a fighter. She pressed her free hand to his upper chest and backed him into a tree, and he complied without resisting.

Once he was pinned, she cocked the hammer. 'Move again and I shall shoot.' He was in no real danger, for it was a modern percussion pistol not yet fitted with the cap that would spark the gunpowder; even if he fought back and caused her finger to pull the trigger, the gun wouldn't discharge. But *he* couldn't know that, because with the barrel under that firm jaw of his, he couldn't possibly see it was capless.

Defiance flared across his face. 'I shan't let you succeed with this.'

She rolled her eyes. 'Admirable bluster, but you are entirely at my mercy, of course. Now, explain how you managed to follow me from Wargrave without my hearing.' Henrietta prided herself on her hunting skills and as slowly as she'd been travelling, she couldn't imagine how she'd missed the sound of a following horse.

His lips curled into that familiar smirk. 'I'm not merely a hand-some face and a witty pen. My talents are endless.'

'You mistake sensationalism for wit, but I'm not unimpressed with your tracking skills, Mr Hawke.' She also admired his gump-tion, displaying cheekiness in the face of what he thought was mortal danger.

'Impressed enough to put away your pistol?'

She scoffed. 'Of course not.'

'I noticed you didn't deny my handsomeness; would it not be a shame to destroy such good looks?'

Henrietta hid her amusement by casting him a scathing glare. 'I'm sure I've never given a single thought to your appearance,' she said, lying.

Perhaps he thought he'd distracted her sufficiently with his silly conversation, for he suddenly attempted to push off from the tree and strongarm the gun away, but Henrietta wasn't so easily overwhelmed. She fought back, pinning his right side harder against the trunk by digging her shoulder against his large biceps and her hip into his groin. With the elbow of her gun arm, she pinned his left side and dug the pistol sharper under his jaw.

'Really, Mr Hawke,' she started to say, only to find that she was quite out of breath. He was pushing back against her and since he had the stability of the tree as an aid, it was only a matter of time before he'd overpower her. Even now, her boot was slipping against the soil and she couldn't risk moving her foot to feel for an anchoring root or rock.

She had to speak fast.

'Really, Mr Hawke,' she said again as he pressed his chin against her forehead, using every available part of his body to fight her. 'You are a constant thorn in my side, but I've never underestimated your intelligence, so stop fighting me and *think*. If I were indeed a cold-blooded killer, I would have blown out your brains the moment I pinned you against this tree. But I didn't! And why haven't I, even though I despise you? Because I'm *not evil*. Because I'm *not a murderess*. I didn't kill my husband and I won't kill you. For God's sake, stay still so we can speak rationally!' She raised her voice for he was resisting more effectively than ever.

'I might believe you,' he said, his voice laboured and his breath hot in her hair. 'If not for your suspicious behaviour. Why would an innocent lady of means and station – a *duchess* of this land, no less – flee in the manner you did, swapping gown and horse with an innkeeper's daughter and travelling the countryside in shadow? If you are innocent, why not seek assistance from your father and brothers? Your actions imply guilt, madam, and I shall find proof of it soon enough.'

She clenched her teeth, allowing her frustration to bring her more physical strength as she pushed back. 'Mr Hawke, you have always deliberately misunderstood me and now you're permitting your prejudice to narrow your reasoning so it arrives only at the vilest possible conclusion, rather than considering I might have other reasons for behaving as I have. You pride yourself on your truth-seeking, so hear this truth, Mr Hawke: I *loved* my husband. I would never, ever have harmed him.'

He started to protest, but Henrietta cut him off.

'Oh, hush!' she said, exasperated. '*Hush* and listen. If I could get rid of you, make you stop following me, I would, but I can't, because, as I've already said, I'm *not* a murderess. I am innocent of my husband's death. And despite what you have persistently assumed, I was a loyal wife who always had my husband's best interests at heart.'

'You admit to being alone with him when he died.' Hawke strained against her. 'And there were marks of violence on his body.'

'Yes, I know,' she replied, holding her grip though her muscles shook from the exertion and a fine sweat dampened her upper lip. 'Scratches on his cheek and on his neck. Edmund himself did that, when he was choking to death, from what I believed until this evening was a seizure. But once my initial shock wore off after you told me he was poisoned, I realised you were correct. What's even more significant is that *Edmund* knew he'd been poisoned. His last sentence wasn't "my dear sweet killed me". His last sentence, which he struggled to form, I *now* realise was to tell me that the *Madeira* – the wine – was poisoned. *Ma-deer-ah-sweet-killed-me.* That is what he said.'

Hawke's body tensed and stilled, doubt flickering in his eyes.

Perhaps she was finally convincing him. 'He drank two glasses of wine – of a very special Madeira he had acquired – about an hour before his death. When he drank his first glass, he was disappointed in the taste. He thought it too *sweet*. But I told him mine was lovely, so he poured himself a second glass and said it was perfect. Neither he nor I thought much of it *then* – but now I know he realised, as he was dying, why the taste was off with the first glass.'

At last, Hawke stopped resisting her. He softened against the tree trunk, and, in her relief, Henrietta slumped against him as her shaking muscles relaxed. His coat smelled of newspaper ink.

'Edmund knew wines,' she said, her forehead on Hawke's shoulder because she didn't yet have the strength to stand on her own. She eased her grip on her pistol as she let her hand rest on his chest. 'He was trying to explain before he died, but I was frightened and I didn't understand. And then he was gone.'

For a moment, all was still but for Hawke's breath against her cheek.

Then he pounced, grabbing her gun and clasping both her wrists in one hand. She didn't even attempt to resist. As he held her hands captive, he disengaged the hammer of the pistol and pocketed it.

She sighed. 'Well done. You have overpowered me with your superior size and strength, an accident of your birth, because you are a tall, strong man, and, although I am a tall, strong woman, I am not as tall and strong as you.'

'Now, come!' he said, obviously annoyed. 'Don't make me feel like a churl, when you were the one thrusting a gun under my jaw a moment ago.'

'That was simply my natural reaction to being grabbed from behind by a man, Mr Hawke. But tell me, now that you have me helpless, with my only weapon in your pocket, what will you do? Throw me over your horse and take me to London? Hand me to Sir Robert Baker and his Runners? Incite hate against me through your pen – you can do it, you know you can, because you did it once before – and then gloat as the crowds jeer during my hanging? Or do you want to consider, just for a second, that you *might be wrong about me*? That perhaps you were always wrong about me? Because I can prove that you were – and I can prove it tonight. And if you are half the truth-seeker you profess to be, you will at last see some shades of grey in your black-and-white world.'

He looked at her, lips flattened, and then sighed heavily. 'I am no doubt a fool, but fine. Speak and I will listen. What can you prove to me tonight? Do you know who murdered your husband?'

'No, but there were only three men who *could* have slipped poison into Edmund's drink and every one of them had *some* type of disagreement with him before his death. I further know that the very last word Edmund uttered was the name of one of those three men: James Beaucastle.'

Hawke frowned. 'Never heard of him.'

'No, you wouldn't have. He's no one, particularly.' She nodded to the house. 'This is his estate and he prefers a country life, but he was a dear friend of Edmund's for many years. And while I have a hard time believing James capable of murder, I do know that he and Edmund were angry at each other at the time of Edmund's death – that James had come to London, which he despises, for the express purpose of speaking to Edmund, and then they quarrelled dreadfully. Since Edmund uttered his name last, I decided to begin my investigation here. If you release me, Mr Hawke, I shall allow you to accompany me inside – after all, I certainly can't let you out of my sight to run back to London with tales of my flight and my disguise.'

'Perhaps you want me to accompany you inside so your lover can kill me.'

'Ugh!' She stamped her foot. 'You and I both know I could have killed you already if I wanted to. In fact . . .'

She threw herself forward, pushing his shoulders, causing him to fall hard on his bottom. She then pounced and straddled him, pinning him fully to the ground with her hands on his wrists and her knee at his groin. He struggled, but she pushed him down forcefully.

'Don't tempt me to cause you significant pain, Mr Hawke.' She positioned her knee against the soft bulk at the apex of his legs and waggled her eyebrows as she leant forward. 'I think you know what I mean.' He went perfectly still and she smiled, her hair curtaining their faces. 'There now – *that's* better. You know, you really must stop underestimating me. I grew up with the five most boisterous elder brothers any girl ever had, and they taught me to fight as soon as I could stand. Will you *now* admit that if I intended to kill you, I would've done so twice over already – if not more?'

He met her gaze, still defiant. 'I could regain the upper hand if I wished.'

'You're delirious. Yet I'm tempted to let you try, because it's been many years since I've enjoyed a good tussle.' His brows shot up, his expression as shocked as a dowager watching a waltz. Henrietta couldn't help but laugh. 'It's not *seemly* for a duchess to fight,' she said. 'Even if it *is* good fun.'

He appeared to be pointedly avoiding letting his gaze drop, perhaps because her breasts were all but nestled against his neck. 'I agree we should stop tussling, as you term it. Immediately.'

Only then did Henrietta realise that the area her knee pressed against wasn't as soft as it had been before.

It wasn't soft *at all*.

Mortified, she leapt to her feet and retreated into the shadow of a nearby tree as he rose. With no better way to fill the awkward silence, she attempted to compose herself by running her fingers through her long hair while Hawke dusted off his clothing, with his back to her.

But startling thoughts popped into her head. *Aren't you seeking a man to father a son for Edmund, Henrietta Percy? Well, Theodore Hawke is not unattractive. Quite the opposite. He's a stubborn ass, but he's intelligent and resourceful – and he certainly seems endowed with plenty of the necessary equipment and stamina.*

Equally repelled and fascinated by the turn of her mind, she raked her fingers through her hair more frantically than before. Was Hawke attracted to her? If she initiated a kiss, would he respond? Her only point of comparison was Marlow, but the thought of Hawke excited her far more than the viscount ever had. She suspected the journalist's tongue would *not* be a slimy slug in her mouth, like Marlow's had been, but what *would* a kiss from Hawke feel like?

When he turned, sudden shyness overcame her, and she returned his gaze from the corner of her eye. The play of moonlight and shadow accentuated his jawline, the slight cleft of his chin, the ridge of his nose and the length and thickness of his dark lashes. Yes, Hawke was no hardship to look at, even though she hated him.

But of course she couldn't *actually* take him as a lover.

He'd never keep quiet about the affair.

Or would he?

'Here,' he said, returning her pistol. 'Thank you for not shooting me.'

She tucked it into her bodice. 'You were never in any danger. It's a percussion primer, not a flintlock. Perfectly safe until I fit a cap on the nipple.'

His gaze trailed to the pistol. 'Fit a cap on the what, now?'

'The nipple.' She pointed to the small metal projection near the gun's hammer, which rested at the cleft of her breasts. 'Here. This bit that looks like ...'

She stopped, suddenly realising *exactly* why the projection was called a nipple.

But then she caught Hawke's eyes and found it quite impossible to repress a bubble of laughter, and he flashed a grin in turn. 'Please don't cease your explanation *now*, Your Grace. Better yet, show me a comparison.'

His boldness spiked Henrietta's pulse, but she couldn't let *him* know that. 'Your brain really does take the wildest flights of fancy, does it not, Mr Hawke?'

His eyes sparkled. '*You* chose to speak of nipples, madam. Far be it from me not to indulge the conversational whims of a duchess.'

Feeling the danger of continuing on a path that edged far too close to flirtation, Henrietta lifted a cool chin. 'The only conversation for which I have time is one with Mr Beaucastle, not this nonsense with you, Mr Hawke.' Tossing her hair out of her way, she marched towards the house and his long strides soon caught her up. Her skin felt overwarm and sensitive with him so close.

There was nothing for it but to change the subject to one that couldn't possibly lead them astray. Easily enough done, considering they were engaged upon a grim task. 'Mr Hawke, do you believe the laws in this nation are fair?' she asked, speaking over her shoulder.

He took a moment before replying. 'That's a complex question, the answer to which could be intelligently debated for days on end. At the risk of a gross oversimplification, I shall respond thusly: the criminal code is brutally harsh and desperately in need of reform, but *if* justice were applied equally to all people, regardless of class, and if all people had the same access to defence, there would be a *sort* of fairness. Currently, that doesn't exist in Britain.'

'You told me before that my class believes itself to be above the law.'

'Some of you do. Some of you get away with murder.'

Henrietta prepared herself to admit that which she'd never told another person. He had to know, if he was coming along with her – and she wasn't about to let him out of her sight to run back to London with what he surely must consider gossip gold. 'Mr Hawke, according to the law, my husband was a criminal, merely because he acted in accordance with his good and honourable nature. That is why I say no truth is absolute.'

'You persist in believing me incapable of seeing the world as anything other than black and white, but I assure you, no one who has lived the life I have could feel that way.' He gave her an odd look, a bit pitying, a bit mystified. 'You appear to possess a peculiar *naïveté* not in accordance with your stage and station in life, and I've not yet determined if it is an act, or if you genuinely don't realise you've revealed your husband's secret already?'

She came to a sudden halt, her heart thundering. 'What do you mean?'

He stopped beside her, moonlight reflected in his eyes. 'Mr Beaucastle was your husband's lover, of course.'

Her jaw slackened. 'But … but … how did you know?'

'I've inferred it from your conversation tonight,' he replied, gazing at her with wary disbelief. 'As nearly anyone would.'

'But how have you heard of such a thing?' she asked, more confused than ever.

He tilted his head. 'I should think most people have heard of this type of love between men.'

'You act as if it were … commonplace?'

He considered. 'I really can't speak to that. I should imagine it happens often enough, but with the consequences what they are, naturally, it's not spoken of openly. But I can say that there are known brothels catering exclusively to the trade, ignored by the Runners, and public opinion is growing increasingly intolerant of punishing the practice.'

'So you would never judge two men for engaging in sexual love together?' she asked. 'You would never report their actions in *The Hawke's Eye*, knowing they might be pilloried or hanged?' And when he replied that her conclusion was correct, she crossed her arms under her bosom. 'I admire your generosity of heart, Mr Hawke, for I am of a like mind, but this does beg the question of why you did not apply that same kindness to me? You knew a report of adultery could've destroyed me – perhaps less absolutely than a noose, but certainly more thoroughly than an afternoon in a pillory? Had not my husband chosen to support me, I might've ended up destitute. No home, no family, no friends – and no legal recourse. So tell me, how do you justify what you did to me?'

There was a very long pause, broken only by the sound of the nighttime breeze shifting the trees' leaves and the distant hoot of an owl.

'I cannot,' he replied at last, his manner subdued. 'I cannot at all, Your Grace. And I am so terribly sorry for how I wronged you.'

CHAPTER 11

Aiding and Abetting

The duchess responded to Theo's apology with a scathing glare before resuming her march towards the manor house. He followed with a heavy tread.

The sudden, dreadful realisation of his despicable guilt had hit with terrible force when she'd demanded his justification. Now he knew he'd deserved every one of her hostile glares over the years. On that fateful night in her garden, he'd let personal feelings cloud his judgement, and, while he could certainly guess why he'd done so, he'd been in the wrong.

Yet caution still prevented him from fully lowering his guard. Not only did it remain highly suspicious for a duchess to skulk about the countryside in disguise, Theo hesitated to relinquish his part of their antagonism. That mutual animosity had been strangely gratifying over the years – certainly far better than her ignoring him entirely, the only alternative he could imagine. If he relinquished five years of contentious feelings towards the Duchess of Severn, what would fill the void?

Her whispered voice drew him from these reflections as they neared the house. 'We'll enter through there.' She pointed to an open window on the first floor. 'It's the room next to Mr Beaucastle's chamber, which I know to be an unused bedroom. The one intended for the mistress of the house.'

The plan was as ridiculous as it was suspicious. 'Tell me, please, why we are entering through a window when knocking upon a door is the more accepted way to pay a call? Surely you are aware that breaking into this man's house makes you appear extremely guilty?'

'It's not breaking if the window is open,' she replied pertly. 'But since you asked, I have two reasons for my actions. Firstly, I wish to use the element of surprise to my advantage when I confront James. Secondly, I can't trust his servants not to inform on me, once it becomes known that I am on the run, for I cannot afford a new disguise.' She cast him a triumphant grin, as if she'd made her point so effectively there was no room for further argument. 'I suggest we scale the wall using the wisteria to support ourselves.'

The wisteria was ancient, its gnarled vines as thick as small tree branches, but Theo was doubtful. 'It's unlikely to support my weight.'

She studied the plant with her hands on her hips. 'I shall climb first, fashion a rope from the linens or dustcovers in the bedchamber, and then assist you up.'

He cocked an eyebrow. 'What a convenient way to pass off my murder as an accident, if you release your hold when I near the top.'

She waved away his concerns as if they were of little value. 'We established that if I'd intended to kill you, you'd already be dead. Besides, you'd do no more than break an arm falling from such a piddling height.'

'Piddling height?' He gazed up to the window. 'It's near twenty feet to the ledge, if not more.'

'The children's bedrooms at Deancombe were higher yet, and my brothers taught me to scale the downspout when I was seven.'

Theo frowned. 'For what possible purpose?'

'Why, for *fun*, of course,' she replied, as if his question were ridiculous, which provided unnecessary proof that their childhoods couldn't have been more dissimilar. Theo's young existence had been primarily focused on avoiding danger, not courting it for fun.

She grabbed the wisteria and hoisted herself, establishing her first foothold in the ground-floor window well. When she reached for a higher branch, the vine shook precariously and she hesitated. 'Rather than standing about useless,' she hissed at Theo. 'You *could* give me a boost, or, at the very least, stand *under* me and catch me if I fall.'

'How will a boost help?' he asked, sceptical.

'There's a stronger branch that would be within my reach if I stood on your shoulders. Then I could pull my feet to the top of this window.'

'Utter madness,' he murmured with a despairing shake of his head. 'Yet I suppose as I'm in this far with aiding and abetting you, I might as well assist further. You realise I'll have to reach under your skirts?'

'Under the circumstances, I have no objection,' she answered primly.

He lifted layers of cotton petticoats and took a firm hold of her shapely calves. 'Keep steady now.' One leg in each hand, he bent his knees and, with the strength gained from two decades of tossing heavy bundles of newspapers, he hefted her up. Fortunately, she did her part, for though Theo couldn't see once her petticoats covered his face, he could feel her efforts, the strain of her muscles, the relief in his own when she managed to support herself more securely. All the same, he gritted his teeth to stabilise her as she placed her feet onto his shoulders and found her balance. She wasn't a featherweight – she was a solid and extremely well-formed woman.

'That was beautifully done, Mr Hawke,' she whispered down. 'I can reach the upper ledge now.'

A second later, she kicked off and began to scurry up the wisteria. Theo remained below her, rubbing his shoulders, and was rewarded with a decidedly pleasant view of her stockinged legs, complete with a glimpse of lace-edged drawers as she swung herself over the sill.

After she vanished inside, he waited, arms crossed over his chest, but it wasn't long before her blonde head popped over the ledge. She dropped a makeshift rope of knotted bed linens and gestured frantically for him to take it. 'It's quite secure,' she said, mouthing the words clearly although she spoke quietly. 'I tied it at this end.'

Perhaps he was a fool for trusting her, but Theo's curiosity was piqued. He grabbed the rope and pulled himself up the wall until he was at her level.

Her eyes gleamed as she helped him over the ledge and into a dark bedchamber. 'My brother George wants to horsewhip you, Mr Hawke. But I'd wager you'd lick him first. George has grown soft. *You* most certainly aren't soft.'

Theo nearly choked, but a quick glance at her face revealed the same innocence she'd displayed when they'd 'tussled', so he refrained from replying that he was softer now than when she'd straddled him. Besides, soon that statement might not be true, judging by the state of matters in his breeches.

He shoved a hand in his pocket and adjusted the situation discreetly. 'Why does Lord Deancombe want to horsewhip me? I've never written a negative word about him.' The duchess's eldest brother presented himself as a devoted husband and adoring father to his numerous offspring, and he never appeared to engage in excesses outside his tailor's establishment, which was neither salacious nor unusual enough for Theo's column.

She looked at him as if he were a fool. 'My family despises you for what you did to me. Wouldn't you, had it been your sister?'

'Don't have a sister,' he replied matter-of-factly. Of course, he was widely disliked by the *ton* – that had never troubled him – but for some unfathomable reason, hearing that the Matlock family hated him stirred an uncomfortable feeling in his chest. For the second time that night.

'I shall leave the rope for a quick escape if needed.' The duchess pointed to a door. 'James's bedchamber is through there.'

'How do you propose we confront him?'

She retrieved the pistol from her bodice and fitted a metal disk to what she'd called the nipple. 'You will wait at the open door once I enter. Listen to our conversation but keep your presence secret unless I choose to reveal you. If it turns out he *is* the killer, and he *somehow* gains the advantage, don't try to save me – not that you'd want to, anyway. Instead, escape through the window as he's murdering me—'

Theo grimaced. 'Good Lord – as if I would!'

She stopped fiddling with her pistol and met his gaze. 'You'll do as I say, Mr Hawke.' She sounded every inch a duchess. 'Leave him to kill me and ride back to London. Tell everyone that James Beaucastle murdered both the Duke and the Duchess of Severn. Get justice for Edmund and clear my name. I can die in peace, knowing that will happen.'

Theo started to protest, but she pressed her fingertips gently to his lips, an act so intimate it startled him into silence.

'I won't die.' She aimed her pistol towards the ceiling, cocked its hammer, and grinned. '*Now* this is loaded and dangerous.'

An ice-cold chill ran down Theo's spine. What the *devil* did the duchess intend to do?

But she had opened the door and vanished into the shadows of the other room.

Henrietta tiptoed across the moonlit chamber. The open drapes admitted a cool breeze. The bedcurtains were also open, but no one slept on the bed.

She lowered her pistol. It hadn't occurred to her James Beaucastle mightn't be home.

'*Henrietta?*' A tentative voice spoke from the depths of the room. 'Can that be you?'

It was a night for being startled and Henrietta felt her foolishness as she pivoted towards James, pistol at the ready. She'd been careless, for if he'd wanted to attack her, he would have succeeded. She must exercise greater vigilance if she intended to track down murderers without being killed herself.

He was seated in a shadowy armchair, a bottle and glass at his side.

'Good evening, James,' she said, steadying her aim.

James Beaucastle was a giant of a man, about five-and-forty years of age. Had not Henrietta always borne an intense (though unfair) jealousy towards him, she would have liked him for his gentle demeanour alone. He was soft-spoken and seemingly kind-hearted, handsome and well formed, with greying brown hair, intelligent eyes, and skin tanned by years spent outside.

His weathered brow furrowed. 'Am I imagining you?' His voice was worn and tired, his words cracking as if he wept. 'Are you conjured by this damned brandy – the only thing that helps me pass the nights? If so, why have I envisioned you with a pistol?'

Henrietta's heart softened. James was grieving. Of course he was. If she hadn't been so preoccupied with Perceval's cruelty for the last fortnight, she would have thought of that sooner. Regret washed over her for not reaching out to him immediately. She should have written, sent something of Edmund's, such as a lock of his hair. Although James probably already had a lock of Edmund's hair, didn't he?

She uncocked her pistol and slipped it into her pocket. 'I'm real, James.' She approached with outstretched arms. 'Forgive me for the pistol. I was confused.'

He tentatively touched her arm, then drew in a rasping breath and pulled her close, until she was beside him on the armchair, half in his lap, and wept upon her shoulder.

Henrietta comforted him. There was no fear. She knew instinctively that she was not in the presence of her husband's killer. Her heart recognised his heart's agony.

'Oh, Henrietta, Henrietta,' James was saying, his fingers in her hair, his tears on her skin. 'The grief rips me apart, and, now, when I thought nothing could torture me more than what I've already experienced, today's *Examiner* printed the most nightmarish drivel, and I am destroyed all over again.'

'Not drivel.' Hawke emerged from the shadows and James recoiled with a horrified gasp. 'I'm extremely sorry for your loss, Mr Beaucastle. But what you read was most definitely *not* drivel.'

Henrietta got to her feet. 'I *told* you to stay hidden, you pestilence.'

Hawke looked unconcerned. 'Trouble is, I'm not your servant.'

'Sir,' James said, sounding justifiably outraged. 'May I enquire as to your identity, given that I find you in my bedchamber in the middle of the night?'

'He's Theodore Hawke,' Henrietta said. 'Self-professed truth-seeker and the scourge of Mayfair. As you likely know, he writes that drivel in the *Examiner*.'

'Not drivel,' Hawke repeated, lifting a finger. 'I really must insist you choose a different descriptor, as I never write drivel.'

Henrietta didn't even attempt to repress her eye-roll. 'Make yourself useful by lighting the candle by Mr Beaucastle's bed, so we needn't speak in darkness.'

This time, Hawke did as he was told.

James glanced between them. 'Why have you brought that man to my home, Henrietta?'

She braced herself to deliver the devastating news. 'Because *some* of what Mr Hawke wrote in today's *Examiner* is true.'

James visibly paled in the candlelight and shook his head slowly, as if the controlled movement would negate the facts. 'For God's sake, no. Henrietta, don't tell me that Edmund was ... that Edmund was ...'

A lump formed in her throat. She understood. A loved one's murder was a horror nearly impossible to grasp.

Hawke replied instead. 'Mr Beaucastle, I regret to inform you that the Duke of Severn was indeed murdered.'

James crumpled forward, burying his face in his arms and muffling ragged sobs. As Henrietta fought tears of her own, she sat in an armchair across from her husband's lover and indicated for Hawke to do the same.

Whoever killed Edmund, it wasn't the man before her, who wept as if his heart had been shredded. The reason Edmund's last word had been 'James' was because Mr Beaucastle, not Henrietta, had been the love of his life.

Of course, she'd always known that.

CHAPTER 12

An Unlikely Partnership

When James's sobs subsided, he asked the question Henrietta continuously asked herself. 'Who would have killed Edmund?'

'I don't yet know,' she replied. 'I am conducting an investigation and it would be tremendously helpful if you could answer a few questions.'

'In front of *that man*?' James indicated Hawke.

'I have faith in his abilities,' she said, hardly believing that she was defending her enemy. But then, she had a worse enemy now. 'Recall how he uncovered the Charitable Relief Scandal?'

James looked sceptical. 'Was that not a reporter from *The Times*?'

'That reporter rewrote Hawke's article and then received all the credit.'

'I'm astonished you noticed,' Hawke said, sounding as if he meant it. 'Not even my editor credited my role,' he added quietly.

Henrietta shot him a scowl. 'If you hadn't made yourself my enemy, *I* might have credited your role publicly. And if I hadn't been unfairly disgraced, the Duchess of Severn's opinion might've actually accounted for something, as well.' Turning to James, she gathered a breath. 'Now, James, why did you come to London? Why did you and Edmund argue the day before his death? And why did you return to our house the next afternoon?'

James stared at his hands. 'I asked Edmund to travel with me to Italy. For an extended time. Something we dreamt of many years ago that never happened.'

'Why would you make such a request *now*?' she asked, confused. 'He couldn't have left while building support for party leadership.'

'There just *was* a general election. He had *years* still to gather support.'

Henrietta frowned. 'These things take time. The Whigs' leadership is a disaster, and the King fell out with Earl Grey—'

'Spare me, Henrietta,' James said heavily. 'With Edmund gone, I don't care if I never hear another word about politics for the rest of my life. And I wish not to be lectured to by *you* – the person to whom, in the end, he gave his loyalty, as if his years with me had been nothing.'

James's words startled her. 'What do you mean?'

'He refused to leave *you*, even for a few months. After all I'd given him, he could not do that one thing for me. For five-and-twenty years I've loved him as no other has—'

'I loved him as well,' Henrietta said quietly. 'You don't get the monopoly on that.'

'You do not understand,' James told her. 'You are a child, in his life for a mere five years. You did not love him – *could not have loved him* – as I did.'

Henrietta fought back an urge to cry. 'You mayn't say my love wasn't valid. Maybe I didn't have his body, but I gave him my heart and he gave me his . . .' But the last of her protestations deflated. Her argument was unjust. 'Oh, forgive me, James,' she said, putting her hand upon his knee and hoping he believed her sincerity. 'I should not have spoken as I did. I'm not being fair because I've always been jealous. At most, I only ever had a sliver of Edmund's heart. You had the rest of it. If he cited me as the reason he couldn't go to Italy, it was for the sake of appearances. It was your name he uttered last. *You* were his last thought.'

James's eyes glistened anew with tears, but he shook his head. 'Even if I was his last thought, I also only ever had a piece of his heart. It was his work he truly loved. His reforms were a thousand times more important than anything else. Though it pains me to say it, even more so now that he's gone, the truth is both you and I gave more love than we received.'

'He gave himself first to duty,' Henrietta said, with an odd mixture of pride and intense sorrow. 'But, James, did Edmund become so very angry simply because you asked him to travel to Italy?'

'No. He grew angry because I told him our friendship was over.'

'Over? After all this time?'

'All *what* time? What did he give me of himself in those five-and-twenty years?'

'Why, everything he could.'

'Two days here then, months later, perhaps a week, and growing less frequent with every passing year. Henrietta, I hadn't seen him since *November*.'

'With the King's death, and then the election, and the new Parliament, and with Cato Street, how could it be otherwise?'

'Naturally, it couldn't,' James replied. 'Not when Edmund put his work and service first, which he has always done. I was tired. Tired of being an afterthought in his life. Tired of feeling jealous of your sharing every day with him.' His shoulders sagged. 'But there's more. I made matters worse. I told him I'd met someone else. Someone who could love me back.'

Henrietta gasped. She hadn't expected *that*. 'Have you?'

James lifted his hands, palms up. 'There is someone who cares for me. Naturally, my own sentiments could never progress beyond fondness while I was still bound to Edmund, but recently … that person had asked me to … become closer friends, and I … realised how lonely I am, waiting and waiting on snatches of time with Edmund. As I grow older, I yearn for daily companionship. That was the reason I had to ask Edmund to do this one thing – to go with me to Italy, to share a few months. To take the time to decide together what the rest of our lives might look like. I'd never asked *anything* before and yet he refused.'

Her heart ached, for she understood his feelings. 'Edmund *did* love you dearly,' she said, hoping the words might help.

'You are young yet. Your years still stretch ahead of you, but when more have passed than are yet to come, you may find yourself assessing your life. Thinking about your hopes and dreams. And those that mean something to you, you will want to chase wholeheartedly, for there is no time to waste. I want something more than what Edmund was willing – or able – to give. I want to fall into the rhythms of daily life with someone I love. I faced a choice: be first in the heart of someone with whom I can share every day, or second or third in Edmund's heart, seeing him but a few times a year. What could I do but let him go, so I might give my new friend a chance?'

'But then why did you return to Severn House the next day – the day Edmund died?' Henrietta asked. 'Did you change your mind?'

'No. I knew everything was irrefutably and forever over between Edmund and me, but I couldn't end matters as we'd left them the day before, with vicious and cruel words. I returned to apologise and thank God I did, because I don't think I could have lived with the grief if that dreadful argument had been our last words ever.'

'Did he forgive you?'

James knotted his forehead. 'Perhaps it is too much to say he forgave me, but our conversation was amicable. He was as ashamed of his vehemence the day before as I was ashamed of my harsh accusations. He said soon after I'd left, he'd begun to feel grateful that I'd been so decisive, because he'd been caught between two personal loyalties – his friendship with me and his marriage to you – and that it hadn't been fair to either you or me. My decision, he said, would allow him to be a true husband to you.'

'A *true* husband?' Henrietta asked, confused.

'The timing was fortuitous, he claimed. Something to do with Perceval.'

As realisation struck like a bolt of lightning, Henrietta jumped to her feet. '*Now* everything begins to make sense, at last ...'

Theo had been absorbed in the conversation, watching it as intently as a play in the theatre. Yet when the duchess exclaimed that everything began to make sense, he felt he must've missed a key point. What had she concluded? Did she know the killer?

Her gaze met his before returning to Beaucastle. 'James, forgive tonight's intrusion and *thank you* for your assistance. I must take my leave.'

Beaucastle's brows drew together, concerned. 'Henrietta, it's the middle of the night. Stay until morning—'

'I cannot. I am in hiding because the magistrate thinks I killed Edmund.'

'You? But why in heavens?' Beaucastle looked aghast. Theo took it as further evidence in support of the duchess, if her husband's lover believed her innocent.

'It's a long story,' she replied. 'Keep my visit secret and I shall bring our dear Edmund's killer to justice, if it's the last thing I do.' With that declaration, she fled from the room, leaving Theo to bid Beaucastle an awkward good night before he followed.

By the time Theo reached the window, she was nearly down the wisteria. He used the makeshift rope to lower himself to a safe distance and then jumped.

She was crossing the lawn with determined strides when he

caught up. 'I hope *now* you understand what you witnessed five years ago, you beastly man,' she said, tossing the words over her shoulder.

Theo suspected he did, but best to hear it from her. 'Why don't you explain it to me?'

Her shoulders softened though her pace didn't slacken. 'Well, when Edmund proposed, he explained he'd never *fully* be a husband to me, but he needed heirs. He asked me to find suitable fathers and conduct discreet affairs. He promised to love my children as if they were of his body.'

'Why would you agree to such terms?' Theo asked, appalled.

She stopped walking and stood bathed in moonlight, gazing into the distance, as if seeing ghosts of the past rather than the silver-washed parkland. 'I would have agreed to anything,' she said, so quietly. 'I loved him. As my father's friend, he'd always been a presence in my life, a frequent visitor to Deancombe for my mother's house parties, and when I was but a tiny child, I made him my romantic ideal. He was as handsome and kind and courtly as a storybook prince. Perfection, in my eyes.'

'If you felt that way about him, it must have been challenging to take other lovers.'

'Yes, but I was too hopelessly naïve to realise that.'

'*He* was not naïve,' Theo replied. 'Therefore, he shouldn't have asked it of you.'

'He's blameless,' she said softly. 'He always wanted me to find love – he encouraged me to take lovers not only for procreation, but to enjoy companionship like he had with James. Prior to our marriage, he'd had no idea that I'd created a narrative that he loved me back. Based merely on his kindness to me, at fifteen years of age, I told myself he'd remained a bachelor because he was waiting for me to grow up. I had an active, romantic imagination as a child – I truly believed the tale I spun. That is the reason I refused to participate in London Seasons once I was of marriageable age, much to my mother's chagrin, and why I rejected every offer my father received for my hand, much to his annoyance. No one but Edmund would do.'

'Ah, that's why I never saw you before your wedding day,' Theo said. 'So how *did* you get your proposal in the end?'

'When Edmund visited my father's estate the summer before I turned three-and-twenty – when I'd been out for five seasons – he and I spent a great deal of time riding and sailing together. My mother invented opportunities for us to do so, for she was as eager for the marriage as I was – and he seemed … different. Kinder than ever. Almost fascinated by me, I suppose. One day, he asked why I had rejected all offers of marriage I had received, for by then, I'd had a bit of a reputation for it. I realised later that he was wondering if I was … if I was like him, but in the way a woman can be like him …'

'A sapphist?'

She nodded. 'But at the time, I didn't know of such matters. I thought … well, I thought he was flirting with me, so I replied that I hadn't yet received an offer I couldn't refuse. He asked, "Because you have not yet fallen in love?" Again, I thought he was flirting, so I said that since my father insisted I must marry for title and fortune rather than love, I was determined to outrank him through my marriage, and no duke had yet proposed. Edmund found that amusing and I suppose that's when the germ of the idea began to sprout in his head. He took me at my word, you see – that I had no illusions to a great love.'

'So he proposed?'

'Not yet. The autumn following that summer, my father said he couldn't continue refusing the offers of respectable and honourable men – the sons of his friends – without reason, and that I was becoming known as a flirt and a tease …' Her face turned fierce. 'That was a wholly unfair reputation, for I never encouraged anyone but Edmund. Oh, of course, I accepted dances here and there, but that's simply what one does to be polite. I meant nothing by it. Sometimes gentlemen talked to me of love, but it's not my fault a man who wants to hear his own voice won't be hushed. Some of the more daring ones would try and kiss me, and when I didn't allow it, they called it "teasing".'

Theo believed her. 'Flirt and tease are the types of words weak men employ when they are unwilling to accept that a woman simply doesn't want them.'

Her eyes gleamed fiercely. 'Just so! But my father didn't see it that way. He said soon no respectable man would ask, so I must take a husband within the year or he'd choose for me. I was furious, but no one within my family would support me against him. After all, none of my brothers wanted the expense of a spinster sister falling to their lot one day. So when Edmund joined us for my mother's Christmas house party, I decided to tell him of my father's ultimatum, if for no other reason than it made me feel better to speak with him about distressing matters. He was wise and kind, and might offer advice on how to approach my father about removing the ultimatum.'

'But he had a different suggestion?'

'Not immediately,' she said. 'In fact, his immediate response puzzled me exceedingly. He was quiet as he listened, said very little, and to my dismay, he abruptly left the house party after-wards.' Her gaze travelled back to Beaucastle's house. 'I found out later he'd travelled *here*, to explain matters to James and ask his permission. I suspect that visit was terribly hard on James.'

'Yes, it would be.'

'But I knew none of that until later,' she continued. 'And though I was dejected by his departure, he returned within days, arriving unexpectedly at my father's house after all the other guests had left, and asking my parents for an audience with *me* before he'd even changed his travelling clothes, which naturally threw the house aflutter. Everyone understood the significance of such a request and as I tied on my bonnet – for he took me on a walk – I knew I must return engaged.'

'For your sake or your family's?' Theo asked, still appalled.

'Why, for both,' she replied. 'I knew my duty as the only daughter of the Marquess of Lockington. I knew it from childhood, which is why I'd set my mind on the most eligible match within my father's circles. Though the Matlock fortune suffered in the last generation, mine is a noble line, Mr Hawke. Far be it from me to disregard that. Don't imagine that even when I fell in love with Edmund as a child, I didn't realise fully that my marriage to the Duke of Severn would elevate my entire family, as well as create a formidable political alliance for my father and brothers.'

Theo pressed his lips together to avoid saying what he wanted to, namely that her tale didn't convince him she knew anything about romantic love. But then again, what did *he* know of it? What she described sounded as dry as day-old bread, but that didn't mean it wasn't valid for her. It simply further illuminated the gulf – nay, the ocean – between her life experiences and his.

She continued. 'On our walk, Edmund explained *everything*. Told me I was the first person he'd ever trusted to know the truth. Told me I was the first lady he'd ever dared to ask for help in such a way. I was heartbroken at first, but then his words went to my head and I fabricated a new meaning for them. He told me he loved James, he told me he'd never consummate our marriage, he explained what he wanted me to do – and I heard only that he cared for me differently than he'd ever cared for any woman, and so I told myself my dreams had come true. I would be his wife and *surely* he'd learn to desire me.'

She looked down at her hands. 'So you see, I entered our marriage with secret hopes, despite what he had told me, which was very, *very* wrong of me. On my wedding night, I approached him attired in a nightdress my mother had chosen, put his hands on my body and asked him for a kiss. A romantic kiss, I mean. And it wasn't a … proper nightdress.'

Theo cringed, guessing how the story would end, and genuinely feeling for both her and Severn.

'Edmund was kind,' she said. 'But stern. He explained it was utterly impossible to set aside his love and commitment to James, and bed another person, even for the sake of the dukedom. He said he thought he'd made that perfectly clear when he proposed.' She shuddered. 'He was so terribly disappointed in me for breaking his trust. His expression showed that he thought our marriage a dreadful mistake. I apologised profusely, changed into sensible nightclothes, and I never asked again. I loved him far too well, I would *never* have been the cause of his discomfort.' She gathered a breath. 'But I'd rashly promised him an heir before we were married and so I knew what I must do. I would take a lover to prove I'd dismissed my childish fantasies. The sooner, the better.'

'But why *Marlow*, of all men?' Theo asked. 'Not only is he a despicable human, but his sole purpose in Parliament has always seemed to be to thwart your husband. Why choose a rat when any man would want to bed you?'

As soon as he said the words, he realised what they revealed about himself. Her gaze pierced him and Theo swallowed a nervous knot in his throat. 'Or so I would assume,' he added awkwardly.

'It is not my experience that it is so easy to find lovers,' she said in reply. 'But I agree, Marlow was a mistake. I was not thinking beyond his willingness and his appearance. He is my husband's second cousin on the maternal side and has something of Edmund's build and colouring. The height, the blonde hair. Shape and colour of their eyes. Do you not agree?'

He nodded reluctantly. 'I *suppose* there's a resemblance. Similar to how a rat's fur might be the same shade as a horse.'

She looked at him for a moment and then a bubble of laughter escaped her lips, and Theo gave her a half-smile in return. 'I think the resemblance is a *little* closer than that.' She grew serious again, looking down at her hands and twisting them together. 'And I thought... well, I wanted a child whose appearance resembled Edmund, so no one would suspect.'

'But Marlow would have known?' Theo said. 'And no doubt used it against you?'

The duchess lifted her shoulders. 'If a husband accepts a child his wife bears, then he is the legal father. Certainly, any lovers I took *might* have guessed there was a possibility they'd fathered my child, but naturally they would've assumed Edmund was also bedding me. And, anyway, in the end it came to nothing with Marlow. He wasn't considerate during our single, ill-fated tryst; I realised I'd made a bad beginning and that's why I finished things before they'd even begun.' Her eyes narrowed. 'Which you can attest to, Mr Hawke, since you were there, watching us all the while.'

A twinge of embarrassment hit Theo. 'No doubt you found someone more suitable the next time. I'm very sorry that no baby came of it, if that is what you wished.'

She didn't respond, but turned and continued her progress across the parkland. By the time they reached her horse, she seemed so set on silence, Theo changed the subject.

'At the end of your conversation with Beaucastle, you said something made "sense". What did you mean?'

She eased the bit into her horse's mouth. 'The night before he died, Edmund slept in my bed. Chastely, of course. That by itself wasn't unusual, but he also *kissed* me, and his manner was... different. More intimate than ever before, but also odd, as if he were trying to come to terms with something.'

Theo considered. 'You think he intended to consummate your marriage?'

She stroked her horse's neck. 'I've always hated that term, as if that act alone makes a marriage valid. But, yes, I now think he was considering it, although he didn't act on it *that* night.' She drew her lips into a line, paused, and then gathered up her reins. 'Perceval and the Babcocks dined with us the night before Edmund died. As best as I can construe, Edmund must have rewritten his will soon after his argument with James – he was in his library for the remainder of that afternoon, according to the servants. I was busy with household tasks and took some afternoon calls – Edmund's solicitor arrived and left while I was otherwise occupied, and others might have done so as well. At seven, Edmund came upstairs with me and changed for dinner, and we were together for the rest of the evening and throughout the night, *except* for when the gentlemen remained in the dining room after I withdrew with the ladies. That night, they stayed behind for an hour and a half – an extraordinary amount of time. Edmund might have discussed anything with the bishop and Perceval then. Perhaps he revealed something of his intentions towards me. His intentions to father a child.'

'Ah,' Theo said. 'So you suspect Perceval ended his cousin's life, rather than take the chance of losing his place as heir?'

'It's possible,' she said. 'And if it's true, my life is in grave danger.'

'How so?' Theo asked. *He* knew the answer, though. She referred to the terms of the duke's will, which allowed her a year to deliver a possible heir. But the duchess didn't know he knew that Perceval had shared that information, so he tested her, to see if she would reveal her plans. 'How can your life pose any threat to him now? Perceval is already the Duke of Severn.'

Her eyes cut to his. She hesitated, lips parted. Then she shook her head, looking annoyed. 'Never mind, Mr Hawke. I'm not even certain why I'm sharing *any* of this with you. I despise you for what you did to me years ago.'

Ah, so she wasn't revealing her intentions, whatever they were. Well, if she was keeping secrets, he would too. He wouldn't tell her he knew the terms of the will.

'I already apologised for my failings that night,' he said instead. 'Yes, I erred, but I *was* doing my job.'

Her eyes flashed. 'Your job is despicable.'

'It serves its purpose. And believe it or not, Your Grace, most people in this land must make our livings however we can.'

His rebuke subdued her manner only a very little. 'But why not make a living as a *respectable* journalist, writing thoughtful and informative articles?'

'Because respectable newspapers don't hire someone like me.'

'Why not?' she asked. 'You're not unintelligent.'

Theo laughed. 'I'm extremely clever. And had I been born, say, a tradesman's legitimate son, I might've had a chance at a respectable life. But I am an unclaimed bastard, born on a filthy pallet in Newgate Prison to a condemned woman who was hanged after my birth, at which point my life became rather worse yet. It may be challenging for the daughter of a marquess to understand, but, with such a past, I'm damned grateful to be where I am, even if I'm unlikely *ever* to have an opportunity to work for a respectable journal.'

Her face was an unreadable mask as he revealed the circumstances of his birth, so that Theo didn't know if it had made any impression at all. 'But perhaps you would be taken seriously if you were the first journalist to expose the killer of the Duke of Severn,' she said slowly, after a moment's pause. 'If you partner with me to solve this murder, you may print the whole story – except what you just learnt about Edmund and James.'

Theo raised his eyebrows, taken aback. 'A partnership between *us*? Am I not your sworn enemy, Your Grace?'

She lowered her gaze, appearing so lovely in the moonlight, with her long blonde tresses framing her face, that Theo felt something akin to tenderness. 'I am scared, Mr Hawke.' And for the first time, she sounded it. 'I need help. The sort of help you can give. The sneaking about and finding things out. You're an expert at that.'

Though her appeal seemed sincere, she also needed him for another reason. One she'd revealed earlier. 'That and you don't have money, so you require a travelling companion who does, eh?'

She glared. 'I shall reimburse you the expenses, so the monetary outlay will be but a temporary inconvenience, far outweighed by the long-term advantages. Are we in agreement or not?'

He shrugged, pretending an indifference he didn't feel, for he was eager to start the hunt. 'Might as well.'

'Excellent.' She glanced towards the horizon. The moon had dipped behind the trees. 'Once the moon sets, further travel tonight will be impossible. Come, let us find your horse and a place to sleep.' Together, they began to walk to the other end of the woodland, where Theo had tied his horse. 'Oh, and Mr Hawke?'

'Your Grace?'

'I'm terribly sorry about your mother.'

Ah, so she had been listening. 'Thank you,' he replied, and he meant it, for he'd missed the mother he'd never known every day of his life.

Her soft footfalls fell into rhythm with his. 'If I am to travel in disguise,' she said after a time, 'you mustn't call me Your Grace. You know my Christian name and I give you leave to address me by it.'

He concealed his surprise, reminding himself she had suggested the intimacy for a practical reason rather than a personal one. 'Then I'm Theo, Your Gr ... Henrietta.'

She laughed softly. It was a sweet, musical sound. 'I like it when you call me Henrietta. You always managed to sound sarcastic when you said, "Your Grace".'

They walked onwards in companionable silence, but, oddly, after years of animosity with the duchess, Theo was beginning to think 'Your Grace' epitomised Henrietta Percy surprisingly well indeed.

CHAPTER 13

A Matter of Life or Death

The remnants of a winter haystack provided Henrietta's mattress for the night, and she awoke to the sight of sheep-dotted pasture-land bathed in clear morning light. The sun had only recently crested the horizon. Since these were the long days approaching midsummer, she estimated the time to be around five or six in the morning.

She yawned away her exhaustion, rolled her shoulders and stretched her legs, wiggling her toes inside her boots. Her body was stiff and damp. Though she rested partially upon her saddle blanket, the thin wool hadn't protected her from the dew.

But a warm garment covered her, smelling pleasantly of ink and man.

A vague memory surfaced. In the depths of the night, Theo had tucked his coat around her. Cringing, she recalled that she *might have* produced a sound rather like a purr when it happened – and

God forbid, she might've even nuzzled her cheek against his fingers like a cat showing affection.

She grimaced. Yes, her feelings towards the journalist had undeniably softened *a lot* the evening before – between his sincere apology and his story about his mother, how could she possibly still hate the man – but *if* she'd rubbed herself on his hand, that was beyond mortifying. *Definitely* best to pretend it hadn't happened.

She sat up, intending to freshen herself before Theo awoke.

'Morning,' said a deep voice behind her.

So much for tidying up.

Henrietta peeped over her shoulder, wishing her hair weren't so dishevelled and stuck through with bits of hay, and that her damp gown didn't cling quite so tightly to her bosom.

Theo was reclining in scattered hay some three yards distant, looking as merry as a cricket. Bright eyes, cheeky grin, relaxed limbs, as if he had slept upon feathers and silk. How he could look so handsome with his head propped on his saddle, his sleeves rolled to his elbows and his cheeks shadowed with stubble baffled Henrietta, but he did. She'd never seen him without a hat in the daytime before, let alone in the morning sun; his hair was lighter than she'd previously supposed. A medium brown, glimmering with gold in the sunlight. Nor were his eyes dark brown, but hazel with deep golden flecks, like the mottling of a hawk's feathers.

'Did the duchess sleep well in the haystack?' he said teasingly.

Henrietta pulled a face. 'Naturally, I would have preferred a feather mattress, but I daresay any sensible person would, so if you are attempting to provoke me, you haven't succeeded. But,' she continued, holding out his coat, 'it was extremely kind of you to wrap this about me.'

Surprise flickered across his face. 'Aw, keep it, if you like.' He glanced at her short sleeves. 'My shirt and waistcoat provide more warmth than your frock.'

'Thank you again.' She tucked herself into the garment's folds as if it were a blanket. It was much too big, but it warmed her chilled arms. She looked at the sun, which was now well over the horizon, a white orb in a cloudless sky. Already, the day carried a promise of heat. 'I doubt I'll need it for long.'

Indeed, by the time she'd readied her horse, she was warm enough to return the coat to Theo. He was kneeling by his saddle, gathering his belongings, and shoved the coat into his leather satchel, evidently intending to ride about the countryside in his rolled-up shirtsleeves. Henrietta lifted a shocked brow, but his forearms' corded muscles flexed so admirably when he buckled his satchel closed, her appreciation made her rather warmer yet.

As she dabbed her damp upper lip, the juxtaposition of the well-oiled but worn satchel and the smoothly finished, full-grain leather of Theo's exceptionally fine saddle stilled her hand. She frowned. Why did a city journalist who went about Mayfair on foot have a Corinthian's sport saddle, designed for long hours on the hunt and ease of jumping? Any saddle Theo owned (in the unlikely event that he owned one at all) should have been more like the one she'd borrowed from the innkeeper: a practical, hard-working, high-pommel-and-cantle affair.

Perplexed, she turned to his horse, a magnificent black beast with perfectly matched white leg markings and a star high on his forehead. She knew that gorgeous gelding – she'd seen him before on a number of occasions, most recently at the Christmas hunt on the Percy estate.

He was one of Perceval's horses.

Which meant *Hawke had been outfitted by Perceval.*

Henrietta's hands flew to her mouth, too late to conceal a horrified gasp. Theo wasn't in a partnership with *her* – he was in a partnership with her enemy. And to make matters worse she'd asked him to put her pistol in his satchel the night before, so he was in possession of her only weapon. For all she knew, he had it in his pocket now. If she didn't take him by surprise and overpower him, he might kill her.

Theo looked up from his task securing his satchel, his traitorous face the picture of worry. 'What is the matter?'

The element of surprise would be lost if she hesitated, so she launched herself forward, aiming to wind him with a solid thrust to the abdomen...

The moment she moved, Theo responded, jumping to his feet, catching her in midair and twisting her around so her back was to his chest. With her arms pinned between their bodies, he squeezed her torso, rendering her effectively immobile. She could kick her legs, but her feet were an inch or two off the ground, so she gained no traction and her heels merely pummelled his boots. She squirmed, but her struggles were futile against his iron grip.

'Why are we doing this again?' He growled the words, his chin on her shoulder, the side of his mouth touching her cheek. She could feel the movement of his lips, the scratch of his stubble, the warmth of his breath. 'Stop wriggling and tell me – am I to expect you to pounce on me several times a day, as if you were a cat and I a mouse?'

'You're a *rat*, not a mouse, Theodore Hawke.' Her squirming was making her breathless. 'Here I was, *trusting* you like a fool, when you are Perceval's man! Well, I won't let you succeed in turning me in or killing me or whatever it is you plan. I'll get my pistol and I'll... I'll...'

'You'll what, Henrietta?' His breath against her cheek did odd, tingly things to her body. The thrill was further enhanced by his muscular arms under her breasts, and his impossibly hard and broad chest against her back. Good Lord, she was responding to his overpowering her like he had responded to her tussle the night before; her bosom was heaving with each short and shallow breath, and that wasn't exactly an unpleasant sensation. 'We already established you aren't going to kill me. So what do you propose doing with that pistol?'

'Force you to submit,' she replied breathily. 'Then I'll tie you to a tree and leave you.'

'You'll tie me up?' He deepened his growl. His vocal cords vibrated against the side of her neck, and the warmth of his body and his intoxicating scent made her close her eyes and let her head fall against his shoulder, her fight gone. It didn't make sense that Theo was her enemy, she realised. His voice and manner were not the least bit threatening – despite his grasp having rendered her immobile – and if he'd intended to hurt her, he would have done it already. He could have done *anything* as she'd slept helpless in the hay, yet he'd only covered her tenderly with his coat. 'How will you manage to tie me?' he said, his lips on her cheek. 'You haven't any rope.'

He was ... sort of *playing* with her, was he not?

She thought he was. And she ... *liked* it.

Enough to want to play back.

She drew in a deep breath and responded slowly, tantalisingly. 'I'll tie you with my stockings.'

This time the growl was wrenched from his throat. 'Oh, sweet Jesus,' he said, burrowing his face into her neck and speaking into her hair. Through her skirts, Henrietta felt his manhood harden between the crack of her bottom – if she stretched out her fingers squished between their bodies, she could have touched it through his leather breeches – and between her legs, her body throbbed a deep, silent response.

Her head swirled and she exhaled softly, her cheek against his. 'Theo, why do you have Perceval's horse?'

He answered gently, his words a reassuring caress. 'Percy sent me after you because he thought I'd be eager to expose you as a murderess. But my only interest is in reporting the *truth*. You know that about me, Henrietta – whatever mistakes I've made, you know my goal is truth. I am under no obligation to Perceval Percy. If he is the murderer, I swear on my poor mother's soul, that is what I shall report. Now, you really *must* stop attacking me or I shall be forced to teach you a lesson we might both regret.'

He lowered her feet to the ground and eased open his arms, releasing her, and the absence of his embrace left Henrietta longing. She peeked over her shoulder. He was staring at her, his gold-flecked eyes dark, his lids heavy, looking very much as if it might not be difficult for her to encourage him to take her in his arms again.

A thrilling thought.

'You swear on your mother's soul that you won't betray me?' she asked, to confirm.

'If I'd intended to betray you, I would've taken you to a magistrate in the night. Unlike you, I do *have* rope.' He jerked his head to the side. 'There, in my satchel.'

She nodded, satisfied. 'Very well. Our partnership still stands.'

He raked his eyes over her body, released a slow breath, and then met her gaze. 'So. Should I saddle my horse and we'll be on our way?'

He sounded as if there might be other things he'd prefer to do.

Henrietta hesitated, more than half tempted to pounce again with an altogether different objective. But the potential repercussions of her desire, and how this electric connection with Theo fitted into Edmund's last request for an heir, demanded extensive consideration before action.

And nothing helped her think like fresh air and exercise.

'Likely best we start our journey, yes.'

Nevertheless, as Theo bent to pick up his saddle, her gaze lingered on the contours of his firm backside, admirably displayed under his taut leather breeches. *Any man would want to bed you*, he'd said the night before. He'd been embarrassed afterwards. Tried to conceal what he'd accidentally revealed about himself.

Henrietta might not have much experience, but she knew one thing.

Sure as could be, Theo Hawke wanted her.

And God help her, she wanted him back.

But the last time she'd acted impulsively with a man, it hadn't turned out well, so the only sensible action was to wait.

For now.

She tied her bonnet under her chin and let Theo boost her onto her horse. Her skirts bunched, displaying most of her stockinged calves, and she longed for her side-saddle. Having ridden since early childhood, she could stay on a horse for hours, galloping across fields and flying over hedges, but she was unaccustomed to riding astride. Her inner thighs ached from yesterday's journey; the prospect of another, lengthier day in the saddle concerned her.

Yet travel they must, so she steeled herself to endure it. At least her sore muscles provided distraction from her desire for Theo.

'Where are we bound next?' he asked, throwing his leg over his saddle.

'Back to London, though not by way of the Bath Road, where Perceval or a magistrate might seek me out. Let's venture into Hampshire and Surrey, and return to town from the south.'

As they travelled on the Basingstoke Road past vistas of hilly pastures dotted with thatch-roofed cottages, Henrietta related her thoughts on Edmund's murder. 'If he was correct that his wine was poisoned, there are only two other people who could have murdered him. Marlow or Perceval.'

She described the fateful afternoon – how Perceval and James had arrived while Marlow had been closeted with Edmund in the library, both desperate to speak to him. Henrietta hadn't wanted to interrupt a political session, but as she'd stood in the entrance hall, encouraging the men to accompany her to a drawing room to wait, Edmund had popped his head around the library door, asking Thomas, who'd stood at his usual post outside any room Edmund occupied, to bring a certain bottle of Madeira from the cellar. A bottle Henrietta knew he'd been saving for a special occasion.

'His meeting with Marlow was successful,' she said to Theo. 'Both were pleased, which makes me suspect Marlow less than Perceval. Yes, he and Edmund were always at odds politically, to the point where it often seemed Marlow had a personal animosity towards Edmund, even before I rejected his advances, but they'd arrived at an agreement that pleased them both; I could tell by Edmund's expression when he asked for the wine that he was happy. He himself reiterated this shortly before he died, when I asked him about the meeting. I can further attest that when Perceval, James and I entered the library at that point, at Edmund's urging, Marlow also seemed content. As we awaited the bottle of wine, which took some time in coming, I spoke with Marlow so that Edmund could converse with James and with Perceval, and Marlow – who normally despises me – was pleasant.'

'Why does Marlow despise you?' Theo asked.

Henrietta lifted a brow. 'As you know all too well, I allowed him to kiss me once. The day after our interaction in the garden, he called upon me, expecting … more. When I refused him *then*, his ardour turned to hatred.'

Theo made a sound very much like a growl. 'What a vile villain, to blame *you* for his own intemperance.'

'I concur.' Henrietta peeked at Theo from the corner of her eye, unexpectedly moved. Edmund and her family had been supportive after the disastrous scandal, but no one had called Marlow a villain. No one had uttered a word about *his* behaviour, even Edmund, who'd known the truth. All gently murmured reprimands had been directed at Henrietta – *she* must take care, for a lady's reputation was as delicate as Brussels lace, et cetera, et cetera. 'Nevertheless,' she continued, somewhat shakily, 'on *that* afternoon, Marlow was amiable. In due course, the maid, Libby – the poor girl who you say is being held – arrived with the wine. Libby is quite timid and her shyness was worse that afternoon, but no wonder, for it's not her responsibility to serve wine to men. Marlow cast his debauched eye over her and naturally that made her even more nervous, but she was determined to be helpful.'

'If it is not her job to serve wine, why *did* she?'

'That was a bit odd,' Henrietta said after a moment's thought. 'But she said Thomas was indisposed and she'd wanted to help by bringing the wine in herself. She is eager to please, especially when the task benefitted Edmund.'

'Could she be the murderer?'

Henrietta scrunched her face. 'I can't see it. Why on earth *would* she? She had no motive. Besides, she held Edmund in awe, either because of who he is ... I mean, who he was ... or because she was in love with him.'

'Perhaps he rejected her advances and she was bitter?'

Henrietta considered, but then shook her head. 'Even if Libby *had* approached him amorously – and I'm quite certain he would have told me, if she had – Edmund would have said no in the gentlest possible way. Remember, I speak from personal experience. He would have been so kind that it could not possibly be motive for murder, Theo. Besides, were she guilty, would she not have fled my house the moment he ingested the wine? She must've known servants would be scrutinised closely in a suspected poisoning?'

'I should imagine, yes. And naturally, my sympathy is very much with the girl. I considered her guilt unlikely myself, but one must explore all possibilities, especially if she poured the wine.'

'But she didn't,' Henrietta said. 'Edmund poured the wine himself. Libby brought him the sealed bottle, he uncorked it, smelled it and poured it out.'

'Who served it?'

'Libby did, though not immediately. Edmund said it must breathe after pouring, so the glasses sat on his desk.'

'For how long? And who approached the wine during that time?'

'As for time, perhaps fifteen minutes. But as for who approached it, I can't say. It could have been anyone. None of us remained seated. After I spoke to Marlow, even I walked about the room, conversing briefly with Perceval, James, Edmund and even Libby. However I'm quite certain no one entered or left the library during that time, so it *must have* been someone in the room.'

'And you suspect Perceval did the deed?'

'Did he not stand to gain the most? Especially if he believed, as James led me to understand, that Edmund intended to get me with child. Moreover, he seems eager to lay the guilt on me, does he not? He supplied you with horse and equipment, and sent you in pursuit, well aware of the enmity between us.'

Theo agreed it seemed plausible.

'No doubt Perceval thought he would gain everything by Edmund's death,' she continued. 'Until the will reading, when he realised I shall be a financial millstone as long as I am alive. Now, whether I face the noose or utter disgrace, Perceval will benefit greatly. My dower rights would revert to him and perhaps Edmund's full fortune as well, though I confess I'm ignorant of the legal particulars of such matters.'

Theo made a sympathetic noise and they travelled on in silence past more rolling hills. Since the morning was progressing into a reasonable hour, farmers were at work in the fields, walking amongst the vibrant green grain. In pastures, shepherds herded flocks, darting collies yipping at the bleating ewes and lambs.

The day was warming rapidly and when they approached a brook, Theo suggested they let the horses drink. When Henrietta made ready to dismount, he told her to remain in the saddle, that he would lead her horse.

'Thank you,' she said, meaning it. Her thighs and bottom felt shaky; to her secret shame, she doubted her ability to dismount gracefully.

Theo brought her water as well, served in a tin cup from his satchel, and when she drained that, he served her another. Only then did he drink. Her breath hitched when his lips touched the rim where hers had just been. He leant his head back to drink his fill, his eyes closed and his throat exposed.

Then he knelt by the bank and splashed water over his face. Rivulets ran down his cheeks and jaw to dampen his collar, and Henrietta's mouth went dry again. As if he sensed her renewed thirst, he brought her another cupful with a smile that made her heart flip in a most worrisome manner.

The gossip-slinging scoundrel she'd despised for years was proving a surprisingly pleasant travel companion, but Henrietta took herself to task for the tendre she was developing. Lust was one thing, but her heart mustn't make a habit of flopping about. Perhaps Theo wasn't completely horrid, but he *had* ruined her life five years ago. And even if – no, *especially if* – she took him to bed to give her a child, she simply *couldn't* develop lasting feelings for him. If he were the father of a baby she was passing off as Edmund's, Theo Hawke and her child could never be near each other, lest others suspect the parentage.

Shortly after they resumed their southerly progression, he returned to their previous subject. 'Was Perceval aware of your husband's inclinations?' he asked. 'Towards men, I mean?'

'Yes.' She sighed. 'Although I didn't learn of this until fairly recently. Two years before my marriage, Perceval walked in on Edmund and James together. Perceval was about twenty at the time. Evidently, he made a horrid – but *private* – stink, threatening all sorts of nastiness if Edmund didn't do first this and then this. From that moment, Edmund told me, Perceval never lifted a finger to advance himself of his own accord. His adult life has been one of waiting.'

'Waiting on a healthy man to die is an exceptionally poor life plan.'

'Yes, so you can understand Edmund's frustration with his heir. Edmund proposed to me not so very long after the incident, thinking our marriage would solve everything. His possession of a young wife would have made Perceval's claims significantly less believable, had he made good on his threats of exposure. Also, Edmund hoped I'd bear a son to replace Perceval as heir.'

'Perceval knew your marriage to be unconsummated?'

'I learnt at the will reading that he certainly suspected it, but that was a complete surprise.'

'And do you think Perceval capable of murdering his cousin?'

Henrietta gazed towards the horizon, shaking her head. 'Truly, Theo, I wouldn't have thought *anyone* capable of killing Edmund. My husband was a kind man. Oh, he could be cool, distant, absorbed in his own thoughts for days and weeks on end, but that was due to the weight of his responsibilities, not unkindness. Though Perceval disappointed him time and again, he was never cruel, never unreasonable. He simply wanted Perceval to understand that being the Duke of Severn is so much more than wealth and social prominence, that with the title comes tremendous obligations. I thought Perceval more fool than evil until the day the will was read. Now, I can't help but think he *must* have killed him.'

'And how,' Theo said slowly, 'do you propose we find proof?'

Henrietta's shoulders sagged. Confronting Perceval would be no easy task, certainly not while still hiding her identity. 'That's something I haven't yet determined. But I will.'

It was a matter of life – or death.

Her death.

Henrietta shuddered.

CHAPTER 14

A Half-Crown

Breakfast was boiled suet pudding stuffed with bacon and onion, purchased from a cookshop in the town of Alton. With the hearty fare filling her stomach, Henrietta's energy was refreshed and they made good time for the rest of the morning.

But as the day progressed into the afternoon, her riding difficulties grew more bothersome. It took considerable effort to find her point of balance and an effective seat, and while her drawers protected her thighs from chafing, her half-boots didn't prevent the stirrup leathers from nipping into her calves. Additionally, the heat caused her to sweat and she disliked her increasingly sour smell.

Meanwhile, Theo looked relaxed and comfortable in the saddle. He gazed about the countryside with shining eyes, for all the world as if he were enjoying a sightseeing holiday. He'd pushed his hat back on his head and his arms and face were growing tanned, whereas Henrietta's skin was overly pink. Just past Guildford, he began a jaunty rendition of Sheridan's 'Let the Toast Pass', which made Henrietta smile.

When he finished the last refrain – '*let the toast pass, drink to the lass, I'll warrant she'll prove an excuse for the glass*' – he gave her a teasing wink. Wondering if it was his way of praising *her* as a woman well worth his toast (he *had* emphasised the line '*here's to the girl with a pair of blue eyes*', hadn't he?), Henrietta grew flustered.

Rather pleasantly flustered.

She asked an abrupt, unrelated question before she could dwell too long on her inconvenient feelings. 'Where did you learn to ride, Theo?'

'I delivered the newspapers when I was a whelp,' was his merry response. 'Learnt to ride the cart horses round London twenty years ago.'

'*Twenty* years?' she asked, uncertain if she'd misheard.

'Indeed.'

She frowned. 'But you couldn't have been more than ten?'

He met her gaze, his eyes sparkling in the sunlight. 'I was eight.'

'You started to work when you were eight?' she asked, aghast. When she was eight, she'd started school, but her life until that point had been one of freedom, play and fresh air. Nor had Miss Shirley's Seminary in Brighton been overly strenuous. The girls had attained only as much feminine-appropriate learning as they'd felt inclined towards, and Henrietta had concentrated on riding and sport. To this day, she had no skill at all with singing or instruments, and despised anything requiring a needle. She could draw and dance because she possessed some natural ability with both, but she only spoke French because she'd had a French nurse-maid and learnt the language in her infancy, along with English.

Theo looked at her with something between pity and amusement. 'Delivering newspapers wasn't my first job. When I was about two, I was deemed hearty enough to begin work, so I was transferred from an infant asylum to St Sepulchres workhouse – the one by the burying grounds off Chick Lane, near Smithfield, if you know it, though I was raised in the old building before it was rebuilt some years ago. From the earliest days of my recollection, I – like almost everyone there – spent ten hours a day picking oakrum.'

'Rigging?' Henrietta asked, knowing the term from her experience with boats.

'Yes, it's also called rope picking. Tearing apart the fibres of worn rigging, so it may be reused to waterproof ships.'

Henrietta scrunched her nose. 'Is that … unpleasant work?'

Again, Theo gave her that oddly pitying glance. Then he used his teeth to remove a glove and edged his horse closer, displaying his left hand, which was large and calloused, the long fingers marked with webs of fine scars. It was the hand of a man who'd performed physical labour all his life. A hand that told a hard story but spoke of survival as well.

'Grown soft, they 'ave.' Theo emphasised his accent with a laugh after catching her gaze. 'There was a time when my callouses would've sanded wood. That happens when hemp rips apart your flesh when you're naught but a childling.'

'Oh, Theo, I'm sorry,' Henrietta said, pressing her lips together and blinking so rapidly at the hedgerow her vision blurred. Her earliest memories were of her French nursemaid rubbing scented lotions into her rosy flesh after extracting her from warm baths, and then enveloping her in the softest towels, fresh from airing in the sea-salt breezes.

'Now, now, Henrietta.' Theo's voice was tender. 'I didn't show my ugly hand because I want your pity. We all have our scars, eh? Some inside us, some outside. They're old pains now healed, there to remind us of what we overcame.'

Henrietta swallowed the ache in her throat but couldn't bring herself to look at those gold-flecked eyes. 'What about when you went to school?' she asked, hoping Theo had pleasant childhood memories as well.

He laughed. 'Never went to school.'

That didn't make sense, for he was most certainly well educated. 'But who taught you to read? To write?' *And write well* – though she'd never admit to him that she *sometimes* admired his column's wit.

He tapped his temple. 'Told you I'm clever.'

'But you can't have picked up a book and simply started to read? Someone taught you your letters.'

'In a way, yes. Sunday mornings at St Sepulchres. We littles were given Bible verses to memorise. If we didn't remember them from one week to the next, we got a lashing, but I had no trouble with the task. In fact, I'd remember the older children's verses too, and, one Sunday, the curate gifted me a collection of Bible quotes. It was the cheapest sort of publication, close-printed pages stitched between pasteboard covers, but it was the first new thing I'd ever possessed of my very own and I felt as fine as a gentleman with my little book. I kept it with me day and night, flipping through the pages during breakfast, dinner and supper. At first, the words meant nothing to me, but the curate would point to the phrase that I'd been set to learn that week, and, little by little, I came to identify that the letters had sound. In time, the workhouse master noticed my diligence and took to teaching me some of the trickier words, even releasing me from my work on occasion to spend an hour or so with him.'

'That was kind,' Henrietta said, glad to hear a happy part to the story.

As a speedy curricle raced past, Theo's eyes cut to hers, but he only spoke once the dust cleared and the sound of pounding hooves receded. 'One of the first lessons an impoverished orphan learns is that kindness almost always comes with a cost.

The workhouse master's fee eventually became more than I was willing to pay.'

'What do you mean?'

He paused, but then shook his head. 'Never mind that. 'Tis one of those inside scars I spoke of, but it's healed, long ago. The main point of my story is, that's how I learnt to read. The secondary point is that when I was six years old, I knew I needed to get out of the workhouse – which brings us to an incident of my childhood you *will* like.'

She inclined her head. 'Yes?'

'One day, a charitable organisation visited St Sepulchres – this was by now 1798, when the parish first began to raise funds for the rebuilding of the workhouse. We'd had to clean for days – they wanted to show the crumbling state of the building, but they didn't want the rich folk offended by squalor or foul smells – and the most infirm were tucked out of sight, for the master wanted the charity to believe that the inhabitants were hale folk, making a valuable contribution to society. The master wasn't well pleased with me by then, but I'd defied the odds against me – I was a hearty, well-formed chap, and I could read to boot, so he paraded me out to the fine folks, all scrubbed up with my first pair of new shoes. Told everyone my story, how I was the bastard of a whorish thief who'd hanged after I'd entered the world, but I'd been at the workhouse since infancy, and look what a fine, clever lad I'd become with hard work and rigorous study – barely six years old, but with the body and mind of a boy two, three years older. He told me to read from my little book and then I received praise from all those rich folks – except one fine gentleman, who remained aloof, watching me. I was offered money and sweets, but the master was there all the while, pinching my neck, and so, as much as I wanted to claim the money for my own, I had to answer as I'd been taught: "God and Mr Wessel" – for such was the master's name – "provide for my needs. If you wish to contribute financially, please let it be to the workhouse, so all may benefit."'

'I don't like this story very much,' Henrietta said, being honest. 'Mr Wessell sounds dreadful.'

'Ah, but I haven't got to the good part yet.' Theo laughed. 'Before the end of the visit, the gentleman who lingered approached Mr Wessell and I noticed then that everyone present was deferential to him. Mr Wessell bowed so low I thought he'd topple forward. "I wish to speak to the boy alone," the man said, and Mr Wessell didn't dare argue, though he gave me a look indicating he'd flay my bare bottom if I said anything amiss. But I decided to throw caution to the wind, for I sensed this great man was an opportunity, like learning the verses had been.' Theo looked at her. 'Can you guess who he was?'

Her breath caught. 'Edmund?'

He nodded. 'I didn't know it at the time, for he didn't give me his name. He took me aside – Mr Wessell watched all the while – and asked me a series of questions, to which I replied truthfully. When he asked me if Mr Wessell was a good master, I said, "Both good and bad. He taught me my letters, but he stopped when I refused to do something he asked of me." He enquired what that something was and when I told him, his eyes turned steely. "Soon, Mr Wessell will no longer be master here. Thank you for your honesty." And then he turned away, but something dropped, landing right at the toe of my new boot. I looked down and I could see it was a gold coin, the likes of which I'd never laid eyes on. "Sir," said I – for I did not know to call him *Your Grace* – "You dropped this," and I handed it up to him. He knelt but closed my hand over it. "That was for you. Something you needn't give to Mr Wessell, though now I suspect you must, for he has seen it. Why did you not take it, if you thought I'd dropped it without knowing?" And I answered him truthfully. "Because a boy like me would be hanged if found in possession of such a thing. If it had been a half-crown, I might have pocketed it. But I would've thanked you in my heart.'"

Henrietta laughed outright. It didn't surprise her that boy Theo had been a cheeky imp, since grown Theo was, as well. Though perhaps rather too large to be called an imp...

Theo's eyes sparkled. 'Yes, your husband found my response amusing as well. He smiled then, for the first time. He was still holding my hand over the coin, then he slipped his other hand into his pocket and slid another coin between my fingers. "There," he said. "A half-crown for you. Tell me, what will you do with it?" I replied without hesitation, for I'd already planned my venture, if given a bit of coin. "Buy a broom," I replied. "A good sturdy one, for sweeping the crossings." He wished me the best of luck with my endeavours and I didn't spend another night under the workhouse roof. I handed the guinea to Mr Wessell – for that was what the coin was, I later learnt – and pocketed my half-crown. The next chance I got, I climbed over the workhouse wall and I was free. Spent the first night in an alley; the next morning, I was sweeping the crossing near the Sessions House before the sun rose. I did that for two years. One day, the editor of the *Examiner*, Mr Scripp, was crossing when a draught horse passed by and released a massive, steaming shit. I scurried forward, scooped it with a shovel I'd acquired by then, and flung it aside. Mr Scripp was so heartily impressed by my show of strength that he offered me my third job, packing and loading and delivering the papers.'

'Is that half-crown the reason you never disparaged my husband?'

'No,' Theo replied. 'I never disparaged your husband because I never found fault with any of his actions. I told you, I don't pick and choose.'

'Did Edmund know who you were?' Henrietta asked, intensely curious. 'Later, I mean. After you began writing *The Hawke's Eye*.

Did he know Theodore Hawke was the workhouse boy to whom he gave a half-crown?'

Theo's lips turned down. 'For the longest time, I didn't think so. But shortly after the Charitable Relief Scandal, I happened to pass him on the street when, much to my surprise, he stopped and spoke to me.'

'Saying what?'

'As close as I can recall, that the Charitable Relief exposé was a much better application of my talents than exposing illicit affairs.'

'And so it was.' Henrietta heartily agreed.

'Well, I nearly lost my job with Scripp over it. Which is why, when your husband then told me he was "pleased his half-crown wasn't wasted", I was annoyed. Oh, I was astonished to learn he remembered me, naturally, but I was *also* irritated. I told him I've done the best I could to make my way in the world. He responded, "You can do better," and he seemed so dreadfully disappointed that I was devastated; it is one of the reasons I want to solve his murder. Let him see from heaven that his half-crown wasn't wasted.'

Henrietta was deeply moved. 'My life experience is so vastly different from yours that I can relate to little of what you say. However, I *do* understand how affecting Edmund's disappointment could be. One gentle glance of disapproval from him would distress *me* more than all the scolds my father ever delivered.'

'Your father scolded you?' Theo sounded sceptical. 'Always thought you'd been ... but never mind.'

'Cosseted?' she said. 'Spoilt? Treated like a little princess?'

His lips twitched, but he held back the laughter dancing in his eyes. 'All I'll say is, my observations have led me to believe your parents think the sun rises and sets with you.'

Henrietta laughed. 'They were so immensely pleased when I became the Duchess of Severn, they forgot every last one of my youthful transgressions. Please don't misunderstand, my parents are lovely, but they had their hands full with their children. I was an exceedingly naughty, headstrong girl – as wild as the waves, ever striving to keep up with my brothers, who were imps, every one. So, yes, I was frequently scolded for not behaving like a young lady.'

'After suffering three of your vicious attacks, I can verify that you are still a wild imp. Yet you manage your public duties elegantly, so you must have applied yourself to learning how to behave like a fine lady at some point?'

'I did,' she said. 'Yet my motivation arose not from my father's scolds, but because there was someone I wanted to impress.'

'Your future husband?'

She nodded. 'It seems he impacted both our childhoods.'

Theo winked. 'Aye, we have that in common.'

Henrietta grew rather breathless while his gold-flecked eyes gazed back. Embarrassed, she looked away and they travelled on in silence.

But after a time, she stole another glance, wondering at her growing attachment to the man. She'd heard many heartbreaking tales over the years ... why did Theo's story affect her so deeply, as if it should have personal meaning to *her*?

After some time, she reasoned the oddity away. She was a grieving widow whose life had been upended. There was a huge hole in her existence where Edmund had been, and learning of his unexpected influence on Theo's life had shaken her.

Theo started to whistle. They continued without conversing and Henrietta was glad. She felt the danger of asking too many personal questions. Further fascination with Theo's past would only feed her growing, *terribly* inconvenient tendre.

CHAPTER 15

All at Once

As the miles progressed, Henrietta grew increasingly fatigued. Though she didn't complain, Theo stopped whistling and his gaze fell on her more and more often. After some time, he suggested they veer off the busy Portsmouth Road because of the dust and traffic.

Henrietta readily agreed, provided they were certain of the road's destination.

'I once travelled on that Old Millford Road.' He jerked his chin towards a shady country lane signposted Kingston upon Thames. 'Albeit coming from London, and I didn't travel down as far as this, but it was a pleasant, quiet route, well-enough maintained.'

Henrietta cocked her head. 'That sign is marked as Kingston, not Millford.'

'The *old* name is Millford Road. Read the other signpost.'

She squinted at a block of mossy stone, possibly a medieval signpost. If it had words, they were invisible to her. But it mattered little if Theo was mistaken, for travelling to Kingston would certainly bring them near London, and she'd much prefer a country lane to the Portsmouth Road, even if it were circuitous.

She decided. 'Very well, let's take it.'

They turned their horses off the high road. As she passed the mossy stone, the words *Millford, 10 miles* materialised through the lichen. How had Theo read them earlier? The question nagged at her until she recalled his ability to track her in the dark and from a distance the night before.

'Do you have exceptionally excellent vision, Theo?'

'A Hawke's eye,' he said over his shoulder.

She cringed. 'That's a *dreadful* pun.' But laughter bubbled up despite her best efforts.

He glanced back, flashing a grin. 'If it's so dreadful, why are you laughing, darling?'

No doubt the presumptuous term of endearment had rolled off his tongue without thought – she'd overheard labourers and shopkeepers calling both known and unknown women of their class 'love' and 'darling' often enough to realise it was a customary practice and meant nothing – but it nevertheless struck Henrietta silent. She followed Theo's horse, her cheeks burning like a schoolgirl.

The new route provided a pleasant respite from the heat. It was a narrow lane, winding its way north through hedgerows and canopied passages. Leaves cast dappled shadows on the ground. Yet Henrietta remained in considerable pain, for the stirrup leathers sliced into her raw calves. She repeatedly readjusted her legs, but nothing offered relief.

About five miles after they'd parted ways with the Portsmouth Road, they came to a narrow break in the hedgerow, revealing a pond tucked into a dip in the land not more than two hundred yards off the laneway. Its banks were dotted with a few gnarled oaks and a copse of lanky beeches, and the whole effect was shady and welcoming. Not only was it imperative to stop and fashion bandages for her calves, but Henrietta also longed to wash away the grit on her clammy body.

'We shall rest a while at the pond to our left,' she said, and, before Theo could turn towards her, for he was riding slightly ahead, she manoeuvred her horse through the break in the hedge and cantered across the field.

She had dismounted by the time Theo joined her.

He watched her remove her horse's bit. 'Is this to be an extended rest?'

'An hour or so.' She patted her mount's neck as he lowered his head to graze. 'There's plenty of daylight remaining. Even with a rest, we can reach London before dark.'

Theo looked back towards the hedgerow. 'I thought we'd press on. Stop in Kingston for a hearty meal. And perhaps a pint?' he added hopefully.

She put her hands on her hips. 'I'm hot and I *stink*, Theo. I want to bathe.'

His brows shot up. 'Bathe? *Here?*'

She glanced at the pond, its sparkling surface dotted with waterlilies. Her skin tingled, anticipating diving into the cool depths. 'Oh, yes, indeed,' she said with conviction. 'Now turn your back until you hear me *in* the water.'

His face registered mild disbelief, but he complied.

Under the overarching branches of an oak, she undressed fully since she didn't have a change of clothes. Then, with the afternoon breeze teasing her naked skin, she neared the pond, skirting the banks to judge the water's depth. The outer ring wasn't deep enough to dive from the shore.

'I have to wade in,' she said over her shoulder. 'Don't turn around until I say you may.'

'You can swim, can't you?' he asked, and Henrietta thought she detected a note of genuine concern.

'I grew up by the sea.' She pushed into the water until it was as deep as her thighs. 'I swim like a fish.'

'Be careful all the same. Even those who swim well can drown.'

'I'm touched by your concern,' she replied glibly, and then she dived.

Her body sliced into the water, washing away the heat, the grime, the sweat and the aches, all in one deliciously icy moment. Not knowing the pond, she swam open-eyed amongst the reeds and fishes, her hair reaching out like seaweed, then she kicked upwards until she crested the surface. 'I'm quite decent now,' she called to Theo.

As she trod water, he nudged his horse around and gave her a smouldering stare. 'Well, thank God for that.'

He was being sarcastic. Or possibly teasing her. Or maybe flirting? Whichever it was, she took too long to think of a suitable reply, and he appeared to lose interest in her, dismounting and tending to his horse instead.

Somewhat flustered, she dived underwater again and lost herself in the swim. When she surfaced, Theo stood half turned away under the oak tree, all his clothes save his breeches folded upon the ground, his hands fiddling with his waistband.

Henrietta froze, utterly unable to draw her eyes from the magnificent sight before her.

The forearms that had plagued her thoughts throughout the day now led to muscled biceps, flexing as he unbuttoned his breeches. His back spread broad and strong, as if he could have borne the world upon his shoulders, and his partially visible chest was sculpted and dusted with dark curls, tapering into a flat abdomen. Then he released one last button and his breeches crumpled at his ankles, exposing a stunningly firm bottom...

She gasped. He turned, his startled gaze shooting to hers. Horrified realisation slammed into Henrietta – she was behaving like one of the lecherous gentlemen who let their wandering eyes travel all over her. She hadn't *meant* to stare at Theo while he undressed, but his beauty was so captivating, she had done it without thinking. Her mouth dried, an apology stuck in her throat – then, to her shame, she made everything worse by dropping her gaze ...

And *that* sight jolted Henrietta into action. She dived underwater, cooling her scalding cheeks, but the split-second glance of heavy, thick male genitals hanging prominently between a pair of muscular thighs had left her trembling.

She swam deep into the pond. Again, she was behaving like a silly schoolgirl, not like an eight-and-twenty-year-old woman. She had been married. Theo believed she'd had lovers. He would think she had seen men's parts before in real life and not just on statues and in paintings, where they appeared significantly ... smaller than what she'd just witnessed. Her behaviour was both immature and suspicious. She needed to face what she'd done like an adult.

She crested the surface, gasping to feed her stinging lungs with oxygen.

Theo stood waist-deep in the water. 'You dived under in a hurry.' He laughed. 'I'm trying not to let it affect my pride.'

She met his gaze steadily, as if the image of his naked body wasn't branded upon her brain, and as if she weren't the least bit tempted to stare at his chest again. 'I apologise. I emerged from the water at an unfortunate moment and in my surprise, I didn't turn my back as swiftly as I should have.'

He lifted his broad shoulders in a shrug. 'I have no objection to a beautiful woman ogling me, provided she likes what she sees.'

Then he winked. Bold, cocky man.

Even cooled from her swim, Henrietta's cheeks flamed. To salvage her dignity, she changed the subject. 'The water is so refreshing, is it not?'

Her voice was too high. Almost squeaky.

Theo grimaced. 'That's one way to describe it.'

'Can you swim?' she asked, mirroring his question. 'Or is it that you find the water too cold?'

His eyes met hers. 'I'm acclimatising.'

'It's best to jump in all at once.'

He didn't reply, but continued to inch his way forward, and Henrietta, remembering how her brothers had taught *her* to overcome hesitation about entering cold water, ducked under the surface again. A bit of playfulness was exactly what was needed to put that awkward episode behind them...

She swam forward until she saw his legs. Determining *not* to look higher than his knees, she grabbed his ankles and pulled, dragging him under as she swam towards the bottom again. He tried to kick her away, but she held firm until she guessed he was fully submerged. Then she released, just as her brothers had done to her many years earlier.

She surfaced, grinning. 'There, isn't that better?'

Theo was sputtering as he swiped dripping hair from his forehead – and he looked *furious*, not refreshed. 'I told you to stop attacking me, woman!'

But even angry, he didn't frighten Henrietta. The situation was too amusing. It reminded her of summer days playing with her brothers and her childhood friend Georgiana, and so she laughed merrily until his face softened and he was laughing too – or, rather, trying but failing to suppress his laughter.

'Come, you must admit it *is* refreshing, isn't it?' She flashed what she hoped was an irresistibly charming smile.

The fury in his eyes faded, replaced by a dark, mischievous gleam. He drew closer, the waters swirling around them as he trod. 'But I warned you if you attacked again, I'd have to teach you a lesson.'

His voice had changed. It was thicker. Throatier.

Henrietta's heart pounded in response. She managed to say,

'I'm not concerned about your idle threats,' but her breathlessness belied her words.

'That's just it, though.' His eyes were planted on her mouth. 'I can't have you believing my serious warning was an idle threat. You were cautioned, you chose to attack anyway and now you must take your punishment.'

Under the water, his fingertips grazed her forearm, and Henrietta's body moved closer of its own accord, like a magnet to iron. 'If you attack me in punishment, I shall fight back.'

He cupped the nape of her neck and brought her so close his breath caressed her cheek. 'We aren't going to fight, darling. That wouldn't be a punishment; you enjoy it too much.'

'What will you do instead, Theodore?' Now her silly voice was emerging as a purr.

'It's not what *I* will do.' He trailed his fingertips along her neck. 'It's what *you* will do. Namely, give me the kiss you offered five years ago.'

'That is quite impossible.' Their treading movements brought them together and her nose brushed against his. Her toes curled under the water. 'I offered the kiss as incentive for your silence. The offer was revoked the moment you wrote that beastly column.'

He pulled her closer, her nipples grazing his chest. His jaw knotted, released, tightened again. 'Tell me you want my kiss, Henrietta.'

Her head spun. Her eyelids were growing too heavy to keep open and her arms reached around his torso of their own accord. His skin against hers was heavenly, his hard body intoxicating. Gone were her thoughts about avoiding impulse, gone were all thoughts entirely other than that Theo wanted her. Badly. And she reciprocated his desire. Years of unquenched urges raged inside her and fulfilment might finally be within her grasp.

'If I want your kiss, how is it a punishment for me?' she said teasingly, pursing her lips the moment the words left her mouth.

'My kiss will make *you* want *me* as much as *I* want *you*. As much as I have always wanted you. That is your punishment. Now admit you want my bloody kiss.'

'I want your kiss,' she murmured.

His mouth was upon hers before she could take another breath.

He groaned as their lips touched, as if the contact pained him, but it couldn't possibly hurt, for he was gentle.

So gentle.

His kiss was honey, his mouth caressing, catching, playing, teasing, nipping. But he was too gentle, going too slowly, and Henrietta whimpered, wanting more. She tentatively sought the join of his mouth with the tip of her tongue, and he opened for her, letting her explore the shape of his lips, the feel of his teeth.

After her second, more frustrated whimper, Theo took control, cradling her head securely with his hand and guiding her body towards his until his hard length jutted into her abdomen.

His tongue entered her like molten satin, stroking her masterfully. Her back arched and she melted in his arms, heat coursing through her body.

Against his chest, her nipples grew hard and painful; between her legs she throbbed, swollen and sore. She mimicked his movements in kissing and he responded with a primal growl. His desire fuelled her confidence and their kiss grew hungrier until Henrietta had to break away, gasping for air.

Her head fell against his shoulder, and he cradled her tenderly. The scent of his wet skin ignited a deeper hunger. After years of yearning to explore these mysteries, Theo's kiss had left her coiled and tight inside. Without release, it would be torture. And no matter how it might appear, she wasn't a wanton woman – she had a *dutiful* reason for desiring this union. She owed Edmund an heir. Didn't she?

She lifted her head until her eyes met Theo's.

Her lust was mirrored in his gaze and she thrilled to be so wanted.

'Will you …' The words caught in her throat as terror suddenly gripped her. Could she disguise her inexperience or would he guess the mortifying fact that he would be her first?

But she *couldn't* falter now. Her body thrummed with desire for the man holding her. He was handsome and intelligent and resilient, and every new thing she learnt about him deepened her admiration. That was enough for now; they could cross future bridges if and when they encountered them.

She lifted her chin boldly. 'Theodore, will you … will you lie with me?'

CHAPTER 16

A Brewing Storm

Theo faced two cold, hard facts.

Firstly, that he had feelings for Henrietta Percy. He'd had feelings for her for five bloody years. Complicated feelings, but feelings all the same.

And, secondly, that in one thing at least, Perceval Percy had possibly been correct. The Duchess of Severn might be rooting for a mate, trying to get with child. Her offer of sex was at best impersonal lust and at worst a desire to use him for stud.

It would only wound him if he let himself believe otherwise.

These thoughts raced through his mind in a split second, during which time he cupped Henrietta's round arse and lifted her to his hips, so her cunny pressed against his aching cock when she wrapped her legs around him. He would never sire a child he couldn't be a father to, so he wouldn't finish in her, but he wasn't going to refuse her request, either.

'In the water or on the ground?' he asked.

Her body tensed and her blue eyes widened. Perhaps a note of anger had unintentionally seeped into his voice. If so, he was sorry. He might be frustrated with the circumstances of their union, but he needed to release his anger before he joined his body with hers. They were going to fuck, not make love, but hostility had no place in this action, ever.

He kissed her tenderly and she responded by softening into his embrace again, and Theo tempered his emotions. She was a duchess and he was a nobody. It wasn't her fault she thought nothing of his feelings, it was a result of the society they lived in, the one that had told her from birth that she was somehow better than the common person. In her defence, she was more egalitarian than most of her kind. Theo had recognised that quality as she'd greeted the crowds after her wedding. Her innate kindness had been the very origin of his complicated feelings.

He broke the kiss gently. 'Let's make you more comfortable, darling.' As much as he felt like he could thrust into her now, in the water, and yet manage to bring them both to fulfilment, even more, he wanted to see her in all her glory. If the Duchess of Severn was deigning to fuck him, he wanted her nakedness spread before him like an altar at which he could worship.

She nodded but remained silent. Fear flickered across her face, despite his carefully modulated voice and calm demeanour.

He kissed her cheek. 'Hold on to my neck, Henrietta. I will swim us to shore.'

She obeyed, still wide-eyed.

As he swam, his mind churned. What had altered her so radically, so suddenly after her proposition? *She'd* suggested they lie together, but anything more than kisses seemed to terrify her and now she clung to him like a frightened child.

Carrying a person out of the water gracefully was a difficult task and Henrietta didn't make it easier by helping him in any way. He stumbled up the silty bank with her clinging to his neck.

When he attempted to scoop her into his arms to carry her more comfortably, she pressed like a plank against him, as if she were hiding herself.

Perhaps that was her concern. 'Are you worried others might see us?' he asked.

Her eyes brightened. 'Yes, yes,' she said, very quickly. 'That's what I'm concerned about.'

The water lapped around Theo's knees as he stood, holding Henrietta's stiff body to his side, searching for a place where they'd be well hidden. 'There. That copse of beeches is perfect cover. We can lie down behind the overturned tree.' He jutted his chin towards a sizeable trunk that had long since fallen, and which formed a sort of natural bench along the shore. It looked like it would be a shady and soft area, well sheltered from the road and fields.

Henrietta nodded in agreement. She disengaged from his neck, folded her arms tightly over her breasts and scampered over to the copse. Theo raked his eyes over her backside. Her wet hair had darkened to amber and was plastered to her smooth back, trailing rivulets of water to her waist and over the luscious swell of her arse. The dappled sunlight played on her naked skin, and Theo's desire, which had ebbed because of her timidity, reached a fevered height again.

He ran his fingers through his own wet hair and then, without another moment's hesitation, grabbed his coat from the pile of clothes so he could lay her down on something dry, and joined her in the copse.

She was sitting on a stump, well into the shelter of the trees, curling forward over her legs while hugging herself.

Theo laid his coat on the ground and sat next to it. 'A blanket, of sorts.' He patted the garment. 'Come, lie down, darling.'

She nibbled her bottom lip, her gaze darting from Theo to the coat, and a decided flush rose over her neck and cheeks.

She was acting *nothing* like the experienced seductress Perceval had claimed she was.

'Are you having second thoughts?' he asked, very kindly. 'Please tell me, if so. I won't hold you to your offer.'

She hesitated, her eyes glistening with unshed tears. Then she shook her head back and forth. 'No.' She spoke adamantly, but her voice wavered. 'This is something I must – I mean, something I want to do.'

That was a bitter blow to Theo's pride. Not only was she *most certainly* using him for stud, but she didn't even desire him. Well, Theo had never lain with a reluctant woman and he wasn't about to start today. When he believed her eager and aroused, that was one thing. But he was not about to fuck someone who was going through the motions.

His cock agreed, albeit more reluctantly, and began its transition into a resigned slump.

'I see,' he replied, rather more shortly than he intended. Without looking at her, he gathered his coat and stood. 'Let's get back on the road, then.'

He returned to his horse. The sky was darkening, with storm clouds brewing, and he welcomed the cool relief of swelling breezes on his overheated skin. Although he'd done the right thing, it wasn't *easy* to walk away from a woman he'd long desired.

He was buttoning his breeches when she next appeared at his side, wearing her chemise and nothing else. Theo averted his eyes so they couldn't linger on the swell of her breasts under the thin fabric, or the peaks formed by the pert nipples he thought he'd be kissing by now.

'Forgive me, Theo. I was confused for a moment, so I misspoke. Will you kiss me again?'

'No, thank you,' he replied.

'Why not?' She spoke quietly. 'Don't you want me any more?'

Theo yanked on his stockings. 'Not like that, no.'

A sharp whimper escaped her lips, but Theo refused to engage. He thrust his feet into his boots.

After a time, she spoke again, her words laced with hurt. 'I *told* you it's not easy for me to find lovers.'

He hitched his braces over his shoulders. 'Well, if you routinely tell your lovers you *must* be with them, rather than want to be with them, I hope they all say no.'

She opened her mouth, as if to reply, but closed it quickly.

The sky was now darkening rapidly and Theo examined it with apprehension. 'A storm is coming,' he said, picking up his waistcoat.

'Yes,' she replied, her voice flat.

And then she walked away.

Her unhappiness tugged at him, but surely her sorrow extended far beyond his rejection. The past weeks had been tumultuous for her. Theo shouldn't judge her too harshly. He'd been guilty of that mistake before, to his shame. She deserved better.

After he finished dressing, he glanced her way. She sat on the ground in her blue frock, studying her bare legs with a furrowed brow. Gone was the untouchable grand lady; in her place sat a woman, alone and vulnerable, a fugitive travelling with an old enemy, stripped of all familiar comforts. At best, she faced an uncertain future. At worst, the gallows.

And to make matters even more heart-wrenching, vicious red welts scored both of her calves.

The hardness inside Theo dissipated like dandelion seeds in the wind. 'What happened to your legs?' he asked in his kindest tone.

'My boots are too short to protect me from the stirrup leathers.' She studied her injuries, which were red and inflamed, and raw at the centre. 'I need to fashion something to protect them, or they will only grow worse.'

'You need ointment too. We'll visit an apothecary in Millford, which should be no more than five miles distant. In the meantime…'

He located his clean shirts inside his satchel. Each shirt was a precious commodity, for linen was expensive, but he ripped one of them into wide strips and extended his offering. 'Here. It's clean, anyway. And it will provide extra layers over your wounds.'

Her lips turned down at the corners. 'Thank you.'

'I'll bandage one while you do the other.' As he wrapped the linen gently around her calf, he peeked at her face. No tears fell, but her eyes were red, and she sniffled from time to time. 'You've suffered a great deal lately, Henrietta. It can't have been easy.'

Her hands stilled over her calf. 'Yes, well.' She resumed wrapping the makeshift bandage. 'I'll manage.'

'You needn't be brave around me,' he said. 'I won't judge you for crying.'

She snorted. 'So you can write about how the Duchess of Severn lost control?'

'I would never mock grief.'

'As if I'd trust you with my feelings *now*,' she said bitterly.

That angered Theo, because she *still* didn't understand him. That he strove to do what was fair and decent. 'You won't trust me with your emotions, but you were willing to let me have your body?'

Inches from his own, her eyes grew cold. 'I hate you, Theodore Hawke.'

That was a punch straight to his gut.

Shouldn't be, but it was.

Theo pretended indifference. 'Well, that's nothing new.'

'It is, in a way.' She blinked rapidly, her forehead creased, and looked anywhere but at him. 'Because I hate you *again*, after starting to like you.'

Her injustice infuriated him. 'You hate me for acting honourably?'

'You lied. Lying isn't honourable.'

'When did I lie?'

'When you said any man would want to bed me.' She tied off her bandage. 'Yet *you* don't want to.'

Theo's fingers fumbled as he knotted the linen. So his rejection *had* cut her; her current sorrow had more to do with him than he'd realised. His arms ached to cradle and comfort her, but his feelings ran too deep. One tender embrace and he might surrender more than he was willing to give. And God forbid she cry in his arms – he'd have no defence against that.

Words would have to suffice.

'I did want to bed you, Henrietta. When I thought you wanted it *as well*. But then you seemed hesitant and that was reason enough to refrain. In truth, I shouldn't have agreed in the first place.'

She curled her arms around her legs. Her brow softened as she met his gaze again. 'But why? I don't understand.'

'Because there's …' He ran a hand through his hair, twisting his fingers in it before letting go. 'Well, goddammit, because there's a significant attraction between us. On my part, it's been present a long time and it's bloody intense.'

She tilted her head. 'Isn't that good reason *to* lie together, rather than refrain?'

Theo's gaze lingered on her gorgeous face. Soft red lips. Petal-pink cheeks. Wide blue eyes on the cusp of tears. For a moment, he allowed himself to imagine she really *was* the country girl her attire suggested. A fantasy unfolded before him. An honourable courtship in which he'd give her flowers and ribbons, and other pretty gifts, and they'd while away hours enjoying picnics in fields just like this one. In time – or maybe all too quickly – fondness would blossom into love. Then there would be a simple but joyous wedding. Thereafter, he'd work tirelessly to provide her with a home filled with warmth and comfort. Perhaps the laughter of children would follow one day.

Reality crashed back like a cold wave. That was a path he could *never* travel with the widowed Duchess of Severn. The gulf between them was too vast. There was no future in which they could be together.

He held out his hands, palms up. 'Remember this morning when I first teased you about that silly punishment? I said we'd both regret it, didn't I? That's because, as you know, *some* complicated feelings always arise once ... well, once intimacy develops.'

She blinked. 'They do?'

'Of course.' Her confusion puzzled him. 'Hasn't that been your experience as well? I know you loved your husband, but surely you developed sentiments for some of the men you took to bed?'

Tears pooled along her lower lashes. 'What men do you suppose there were, Theo? You are clever; think this through. After your column was printed, how could I have taken a lover? Everyone was watching me, searching for any hint of an indiscretion, so that I never dared smile at a man, much less flirt. I never went anywhere without my mother or husband. I never allowed a gentleman other than my father or brothers to call if Edmund was not at home. My behaviour had to be perfect. I couldn't have borne for Edmund to be mocked as a cuckold.'

Theo's jaw dropped. 'You mean ... no lovers? Never at *all*?'

'Precisely.' She narrowed her eyes. 'You stole that sort of companionship from me.'

'That's not fair.'

'I don't care if it's fair. Maybe one day, when I'm not hurting so much, I will care. But right now, I can only see every mistake I've ever made and everything I have lost. And the horrible, unbearable truth is that it's all my fault for agreeing to marry a man without disclosing my true feelings for him. And now he's dead and although I didn't do the deed, it's probably because of the *fact of me* that Perceval did it. Because I was the threat. So, Theo, the least you can do for me now is to let me blame you for never ever once in my life receiving the kind of physical companionship that I assure you I have very much wanted.'

A knot formed in Theo's throat. 'Very well, I can absorb that blame. Blame me. Hate me. If it eases your pain, I welcome it.'

She gave a single, ragged sob before collecting herself. 'I've said my bit and it helped, as much as anything could. I won't blame you any more. You were doing the job you were assigned to do; I was doing the same. It's merely an unfortunate circumstance that our jobs clashed, nothing more vindictive than that. I won't mention this again.'

She straightened her back, looking at the sky. Theo's heart tugged in a manner he didn't want but was helpless to resist.

He joined her in studying the brewing storm. 'We cannot reach Kingston before the rain comes. We can shelter in the village of Millford.' He found the prospect unappealing. He'd passed through the village once before, on an unsuccessful mission to confront a haunting part of his past – an emotional wound he doubted would ever heal into one of the scars he'd spoken of on the Portsmouth Road. 'There's a tavern there. I doubt it'll have much by way of food, but it has a roof.'

'A roof will be enough,' she said. 'Please boost me into my saddle?'

He complied and once she was settled, he laid his hand on her knee. 'Henrietta, do you still want my help finding the killer, once we are in London? Perhaps you'd rather have someone else's aid? A friend, perhaps? One of your brothers?'

'I don't really have friends any more,' she replied quietly. 'And my brothers would advise me to fight this through the courts, which I don't want, because I will be at every disadvantage.' She looked down, the steel-grey clouds contrasting with the lovely blonde waves of her hair. 'I want *your* help, Theo. We both have much to gain from solving this together. And besides,' she added, regaining some of the feistiness she typically employed when they sparred, 'I want you to become a reputable journalist. The sooner *The Hawke's Eye* is out of my life, the better.'

Clicking her tongue, she took off across the field and Theo was left pondering her meaning. Did she want *The Hawke's Eye*, the column, out of her life? Or its author as well?

Naturally, he knew the answer. She'd made no secret that she hated him. Thing was, whenever Theo encountered adversity, his courage rose. He had no future with her, but, nevertheless, he cared what the Duchess of Severn thought of him. When they parted at the end of this investigation, he wanted them to part as friends.

Which meant he had his work cut out for him.

But he had never been afraid of hard work.

CHAPTER 17

The Pickled Dog

Most of the day, Henrietta had walked her horse to keep it from exhaustion, but now she travelled as swiftly as the narrow country lane allowed. On top of the impending necessity for shelter, she needed exercise to sort her mind and emotions.

At first, tears prickled her eyes. She'd been frightened and unsure of the act itself, but she *had* wanted Theo. Now humiliation burned within her, mingling with frustrated desire. Moreover, if Theo didn't help her fulfil her last duty to Edmund, who would? As a fugitive with a limited time to get with child, where would she meet another man as handsome, intelligent and (generally) kind? Her current circumstances hardly offered a wealth of choice.

But the more distance she put between herself and the pond, the more her mind cleared, and she grew disappointed in her behaviour. She'd lashed out in hurt when he was acting nobly, and she hated that she'd done so. Contrary to her bitter words by the pond, she *did* like Theo. It was becoming ever clearer that she hadn't truly hated him for a long time. Perhaps ever since he'd saved her from the beer barrel, she'd developed, well, a bit of a soft spot for him.

As the first thatched cottages of Millford came into view, Henrietta's confusing feelings for Theo and Edmund's last task remained unresolved. The rights and wrongs of it still tangled in her mind, but further travel was impossible.

Storm clouds swirled overhead and the whipping wind carried the loamy scent of rain, so Henrietta looked about for the tavern Theo had mentioned. The hamlet consisted of buildings clustered around a small green, including an ancient mill straddling a sizeable Thames tributary, the likely source of the town's name. The tavern was the most prominent building and possessed small leaded windows, a sloping slate roof and a chequer-work façade of alternating white stone and dark flint.

All in all, Millford possessed some storybook charm, for it looked much as it would have four hundred years earlier. Yet poverty had struck hard at some point in its history. Exhausted cottages seemed ready to topple in the current strong wind. Their roofs were sway-backed, their painted doors weathered to grey. The mill wheel wobbled, in need of repair but still spinning in the fast-moving river. And over the smell of impending rain, another scent wafted from the mill's direction. Henrietta scrunched her nose. It was sweet, but with an acrid undertone, like souring fruit.

'That was once a fulling mill,' Theo said, arriving at her side, one hand on his hat to keep it from blowing away. If he was still upset over what had happened at the pond, it didn't show, and Henrietta admired his temperance. 'Until about two hundred years ago, this area of Surrey produced large quantities of woven woollen cloth and Millford was a place of some prosperity.'

'What is the mill used for now, to produce such an unpleasant smell?'

'Cloth dyeing. Millford produces a specific shade of pale purple known as Millford Blue. You see it all over this corner of Surrey. Amongst poor folks, anyway.'

Henrietta tilted her head. 'How in heavens do you know all this about a tiny village on a country lane?'

'Several years ago, investigative work led me to this area. I only passed through Millford, but I learnt bits and pieces of its history. Not that much, really, as local industry wasn't the focus of my research.' He nodded at the tavern. Its creaking sign displayed a mongrel holding a pewter tankard under the faded words *The Pickled Dog*. 'Shall we wait out the storm there?'

'I think it's best. Not only because of the storm,' Henrietta said ruefully, 'but also because I still don't have a plan for how to approach Perceval.'

Theo studied the tavern a moment longer. 'Best if I do the talking here,' he said firmly, and rode off towards the court as if it was not a matter for discussion.

Despite Henrietta's remorse about her behaviour at the pond, an old irritation flared. She scowled at Theo's back. She despised it when men dismissed her, saying they would take care of matters. Why! She could invent a false name and story as well as the next person.

The heavens unleashed their fury shortly after she relinquished her horse to a groom. Theo grabbed his satchel, hitching its strap over his shoulder, and threw his arm around her. Grudgingly, she felt gratitude for the gesture, which offered some shelter from the rain as they dashed towards the tavern door.

The entryway, a centuries-old affair with a typically low lintel, forced Henrietta to duck her head as she crossed the threshold into a dark vestibule. Conversation and fiddle music drifted from behind heavy wool drapes hanging over an interior doorway, accompanied by a powerful smell of smoke, tallow and ale.

Theo tugged at the main door, struggling to close it. 'Wait for me. The hinge is broken.'

Henrietta dismissed his orders. Rain lashed into the vestibule, soaking her thin frock and bare arms, causing her to shiver. Intending to request a private parlour with a roaring fire while Theo managed the door, she pushed aside the dusty drapes, nibbled at by moths and mice, and exposed the taproom. Thick beams crossed a low ceiling above a crowd of burly men who smoked and drank, many wearing at least one purplish-blue item of clothing. A fire burned in a wide hearth, around which hung political caricatures in the style of Cruikshank and Rowlandson. In a place of honour above the wooden mantelpiece hung a fine etching of Edmund, its frame draped in black cloth.

With her husband's portrait so prominently displayed, Henrietta grew hesitant about proceeding, but, just as she decided to return to Theo after all, the fiddle player dragged his bow to a halt, every man in the room looked boldly in her direction, and, for one horrifying second, she assumed she'd been recognised.

But then someone gave a low whistle and a general murmur of approval followed. The men were simply *surprised* by the appearance of a woman in their midst – and judging by their admiring gazes, they found her pretty. Perhaps it was silly, but after Theo's rejection their appreciation soothed her wounded pride. Yet she lingered in the door, now wary about approaching the bar counter alone with so many men calling out for her companionship.

An authoritative man with greying hair stood, straightened his waistcoat and cast a disapproving eye over the room until everyone fell silent. Pulling a vacant chair next to his, he addressed Henrietta. 'Women visit this tavern so rarely that these men forget themselves. Please, be seated, miss. Name's Jim King, and I'll bring you refreshment.'

A younger man with a puckering scar across his cheek and lip voiced his disapproval. 'She don't want to sit by an old man, Jim. You want to sit here with Sam, don't you, beauty?'

'She's with *me*,' Theo's voice said suddenly, and, with a rush of damp air, he pushed through the drapes to glare at Sam, Jim and every other man in turn.

Henrietta pulled a face. So *now* he claimed her? 'With *you*, am I?' she muttered. 'Yet at the pond—'

He threw his soggy arm around her shoulder and stopped further words by hissing through closed teeth, '*Don't speak.*'

Most of the men averted their eyes, evidently accepting his prior claim, but not the one who'd called himself Sam. He hooked his thumbs into the armholes of his purple waistcoat and looked Theo up and down. 'Seems to me she ain't with you, if she's entering taverns alone.'

Theo tugged her closer. 'Well, she has a mind of her own.'

Sam sucked his teeth. 'If you don't know how to keep your woman at your side, London boy, you'd best hand her over to someone who does.' He gave Henrietta a lusty look. 'I'll teach you to mind, love.'

'Hold your tongue, Sam Walker,' Jim snapped. 'A woman has a voice same as a man and if you don't understand that, you can tip your tankard elsewhere.'

Tired of being treated like a silent plaything to be fought over, Henrietta removed Theo's arm from her shoulder. 'Quite right, Mr King. I've always made my own decisions and so shall I continue.'

That wasn't strictly true of the Duchess of Severn, but the sentiment fit the feisty-country-girl persona Henrietta was adopting. She was so busy inventing a name for herself in case anyone asked – Etta Edwards, since Etta had been her brother Edward's pet name for her when they were little – that she didn't notice the tavern had again grown as silent as death.

By the time awareness dawned, everyone was staring at her with dark and suspicious eyes.

Sam spoke. 'How is it you talk like a gentry mort?'

Henrietta realised her dangerous mistake. Her accent had betrayed her. If rumours of the Duchess of Severn's flight had circulated, one of these men – who clearly admired Edmund enough to drape his portrait in black cloth – might make a lucky guess. She and Theo could never overpower this many adversaries, and the pouring rain forbade a mad dash to safety. All would end now and Edmund would never have justice.

So, Henrietta held her head high and spun what she hoped was a plausible story. 'I was in service. A chambermaid at a big house.'

The answer evidently satisfied most of the men. The tension eased; many returned to their conversations and the fiddler took up his instrument again, commencing a folk song, accompanied by a tuneful singer.

But Jim's eyes trailed her as she and Theo walked to the counter. While the barman pulled the tap for Theo's pint, the older man approached. 'Where were you a maid at, miss? Not up the hill at Enberry Abbey, I hope?'

Theo edged protectively close, his beer in one hand, his other hand coming to rest on the small of her back. 'Not there.'

'Let her speak for herself, boy,' Jim said, though not unkindly. He smiled encouragingly at Henrietta.

Enberry Abbey was a familiar name, but Henrietta couldn't place it and after her brush with danger she hoped to avoid giving any specifics. 'I worked elsewhere, like my friend said.'

The barman laughed, his lips stretching to reveal largely tooth-less gums. 'No girl as comely as her would still be a *maid* working for Marlow, with his wandering hands.'

Ah, yes! Enberry Abbey was *Marlow's* country seat. Over the years, Henrietta had sent her regrets to a handful of invitations to strawberry-picking excursions and the like. How telling of the viscount's character that local villagers despised him.

Jim grabbed a bottle from behind the counter, poured a small

glass of clear liquid and handed it to Henrietta. 'My treat, Miss…
Forgive me, I don't know your name, love.'

Theo tensed. 'You don't need to know—'

Henrietta placed a hand on his forearm and took the offered
drink, glad she'd prepared for this moment. 'My name is Etta
Edwards.'

'A name as lovely as you are,' Jim King said. 'D'ye know of Lord
Marlow, Etta Edwards?' When Henrietta shook her head in the
negative, he continued. 'Well, if you have a mind to stay in these
parts, keep clear of him. He's a damned dog, that's what he is. Up
in London still, but he'll be coming down for the summer soon
enough. Evisceration would be too good for the likes of him, yet
here he is, lord over us all, eh, men?'

He projected his last sentence to all the assembled company,
eliciting a chorus of grumbles.

'Cato Street would've ended him,' someone muttered darkly.

'Watch your tongue, Harry Skilton.' Jim peered closely at Theo.
'We don't know yet where our visitors' sympathies lie.'

Theo froze, his ale halfway to his mouth. 'Etta and I believe in
the people's right to a voice in Parliament, but we aren't traitors
and we aren't looking for trouble. Only food and shelter as we
wait out the rain.'

Jim tapped his fingers on the bar. 'Well, I reckon we can do
that, aright. Though more for this angel than for you.' He looked
kindly on Henrietta and she bestowed a smile in return, not
entirely untaken with the man. 'You make sure your London boy
treats you right, Etta Edwards. If not, remember the names Jim
King and the Pickled Dog, and come looking for me.'

The man turned away, and, looking over the company, held
out his hands. 'Let's greet our guests with a proper Pickled Dog
welcome, my friends.'

The men banged their fists on the tables. Henrietta's hand

found Theo's. They'd stumbled into a radical enclave and worry nagged at her. How dangerous were these men?

But the fiddler merely struck up Eliza King's march. As male voices rose in song, she and Theo wove their way to a small table in a far corner, distancing themselves from the other occupants.

Once settled in their seats, Henrietta lifted Jim King's offering to her nose. She recognised the piney scent of gin, a common-enough smell in certain London quarters. As Theo downed half his ale, she took a tentative sip. Fire scorched her mouth and throat. She struggled not to gag.

Once her eyes stopped stinging, she leant towards Theo. 'Do you suppose Jim King is any relation to Eliza?'

'Possible, but more likely a coincidence.' He nodded at her gin. 'Would you prefer to share my ale?'

'I'd prefer tea to either.'

He slid his tankard over the grooved wooden tabletop. 'You'd do better with ale at a place like this. If they have tea, it will be thrice-used leaves and taste of nothing but filthy water.'

Resigned, she brought the tankard to her mouth. The ale was bitter, but milder and more refreshing than the gin, which Theo drained in one swallow, turning his back to the room so Jim King couldn't see that Henrietta had rejected the offering.

'How can you drink that?' she asked, fascinated.

He grinned. 'Mother's milk to a Cockney like me.'

She grimaced. Knowing there were no other beverages to be had, she contented herself with a few more sips of Theo's ale as she again pondered the coincidence of the surname. 'Where is Eliza King from?'

Theo looked around the taproom. 'I don't know, but I imagine someone here could answer that question. These are radicals through and through.'

Henrietta studied the assembled company. The men had fallen back into conversation, but their discussion was quiet now, words muttered over their pints, far too low to decipher, and some of them cast dark glances her way. 'I dislike asking anything. They are suspicious of us.'

Theo agreed. 'Strictly speaking, I suspect this gathering is in defiance of the Six Acts. With your accent and looks, they know you aren't what you say you are.'

'They didn't believe me when I said I was a housemaid?'

He gave her that funny look, half amused, half pitying. 'Perhaps, but, all the same, they are no doubt speculating about you right now. Saying that no maid has hair like yours—'

'My hair?' She pulled a face. 'What can you mean? My hair is in such a state! Tangled, ragged—'

'And that no maid has skin like yours,' he continued, interrupting her interruption.

She laughed, putting a hand to her cheek. 'Now I know you jest, for I'm sunburnt.'

His eyes caressed her face. 'Naught but a hint of rose on fine porcelain.'

'You're ridiculous,' she said. But judging by the warmth of her cheeks, she'd gone a bit rosier yet.

His gaze rested on her hand, curled around the tankard. 'Take your hands, for example. Your nails, your fingers, exquisite ...' He traced one and the touch of his calloused fingertip sent chills down her arm. '*Not* the hands of a housemaid.'

'Well, then, what shall we do, if my disguise is so poor that they suspect me?' she asked, hiding his effect on her with a snappish tone. 'We are trapped by the weather; must we wait for the magistrate himself to appear?'

'Nay, darling. Don't trouble yourself on that account. Your true identity won't enter their imaginations. Perhaps one or two of the more suspicious men think we are the king's spies, but I suspect most are creating a more salacious backstory based on your beauty and my roughness.'

'What sort of backstory?' she asked, doubtful.

He took a swig of ale. 'Oh, I've no doubt we're providing plenty of fodder for their imaginations. Perhaps they suppose you to be an actress, or a fine gentleman's mistress, run off with the stable boy.'

He laughed and after a moment, Henrietta joined him, and soon they were laughing heartily, their hands clasped and heads close.

Minutes later, she was wiping tears from her eyes. 'How lovely to laugh,' she said, although the loveliest thing had been the warm companionship between them as they'd shared the laughter. She was glad the friction from the pond had dissipated and they'd returned to their newfound friendliness. 'I haven't had a proper laugh since before... well, you know.' She sobered somewhat, but thankfully her spirits remained light and she smiled at Theo. 'What was my fine gentleman thinking, keeping a stable boy as good-looking as you?'

His eyes glistened. 'Good-looking, am I? I thought you'd never given a single thought to my appearance. I feel quite certain you said those exact words yesterday.'

She glanced shyly through her lashes. 'Over the last few hours, it has occurred to me that you aren't painful to look upon.'

He flashed his cheeky grin but didn't reply because the inn-keeper arrived with two flat-bottomed bowls. Henrietta regretted the interruption. The flirtation had been fun and it gave her hope she might yet entice Theo into her bed.

The innkeeper plopped the bowls upon the table while the singer and fiddler began a lilting ballad about 'Bess the Black-Eyed Beauty'. Henrietta sipped Theo's ale, impressed by the singer's soaring tenor, but she couldn't quite follow the tale. It was something odd, about a woman who went about in many disguises but was identifiable by black, black eyes, which could fell her enemies with a glance.

With a shrug of her shoulders, she turned her attention to her meal. Swimming in the chipped earthenware was a watery substance with indecipherable pale chunks, poured over a thick slice of brown bread.

'Er, what is this, Theo?'

'Pottage.' He shovelled a sizeable bite into his mouth, chewed and swallowed. 'Chicken, barley and whatever the cook had to hand, I'd say.'

She sighed, remembering the fine meal she'd had at the George the night before, but she took up her spoon and sampled the broth. It was bland, cooked without salt or herbs. Further nibbles revealed that the meat was gristly, punctuated by shards of bone and the odd quill tip, but it was food and it soothed the hunger gnawing at Henrietta's stomach. Little by little, she swallowed, washing it down with sips of ale.

Theo finished first. He pushed away his empty bowl and ordered a second ale. Then he stretched out his long legs, crossing them at the ankles, and made pleasant conversation as she ate.

Until Sam Walker clanged an empty tankard against his chair leg. 'Men, it's time we discuss the rumours about the Duke of Severn's death.'

Henrietta's hand stilled, her spoon halfway to her mouth. Under their table, Theo's burly hand found hers. 'Keep eating,' he mouthed.

She did but swallowing nearly choked her.

Jim King stared. 'Now's not the time, Sam,' he said. 'Let our guests enjoy their supper.'

Sam's expression darkened. ''Tis the purpose of this meeting, Jim – and there's more news since yesterday, just come down from London with Harry Skilton.' He waved *The Times* in the air. 'Early this morning, the maid, Libby Forman, was formally indicted for the murder of Severn. She is imprisoned now at Newgate, await-ing trial.'

Henrietta's spoon fell from her hand, clattering upon the stone floor, and for the third time since she arrived, the room went quiet.

'What does this news mean to you, Etta Edwards?' Jim King asked, sitting back in his chair, his voice deceptively calm. 'Why does it affect you so?'

Henrietta frantically attempted to invent a plausible answer; the story of Theo's mother flashed to mind. 'Two fears haunt housemaids: the roaming hands of our masters and unmerited blame when something goes wrong in the household.'

'You think this Libby Forman is innocent, then?' Jim asked.

Henrietta lied. 'I don't know the particulars, but I fear for her, all the same.'

Jim tapped a foot against the floor. 'Who was it *you* worked for, Etta?'

Henrietta's mouth went dry. The names of acquaintances weren't safe to speak and she could think of no other.

Theo intervened, a warning in his voice. 'Etta's trials are her own. She fled that life. She needs peace now, not an inquisition.'

Jim's steely gaze shifted to Theo. 'I'd say it's time for you to be on your way, but the storm's not abating and I'm not one to turn a girl out in this weather. Best take your woman upstairs, young man, and give her that peace she craves.' He addressed the company. 'Men, cards out until our guests take their leave.'

'We've outstayed our welcome,' Theo said under his breath. 'And yet, with the storm raging and the roads surely swamped with mud, we can't continue our journey today. I'll secure rooms for the night, then visit an apothecary and purchase ointment for your legs.'

Henrietta grabbed his forearm. 'One room, Theo, and send someone for the ointment.' She looked round the tavern. 'Against a single gentleman, I can hold my own. But near this crowd of rough and suspicious men, please don't leave my side.'

Besides, she had a secondary motive for wanting him nearby.

CHAPTER 18

A Secondary Partnership

The storm rattled the tavern, but Henrietta sat cosy and warm before a crackling fire, brushing Theo's comb through her hair. Behind the wooden screen that portioned off a third of their bedchamber, clothes rustled. The thud of boots, the drop of a heavy coat, accompanied by Theo's whistling. Then splashes as he washed himself.

Under her rather soiled chemise, Henrietta's skin tingled, clean and refreshed, for Theo had ordered a tub of hot water and soap, and she'd borrowed his tooth powder. Her calves were medicated and bandaged in clean cotton. As she tugged his comb through a particularly difficult tangle, her gaze drifted to the bed nestled under the sloping ceiling. It was narrow, with a sagging mattress and thin quilt, but it would suffice.

She steadied her nerves. Bedding a man was a daily occurrence for many women. She, too, could manage it. Moreover, she *wanted* this. She longed to renew the sensations Theo's kiss had evoked and she was far more certain than she had been at the pond. There, her request had been one of impulse, driven by desire and duty. Now, she knew her mind.

The truth was, her desire for Theo had *never* stemmed from Edmund's will. She desired him because she was a passionate woman with long-repressed urges, and Theo frankly set her aflame. Furthermore, she didn't want to spend the rest of her life untouched, and, since Theo now knew her secret, he was the perfect man to rid her of her virginity.

Because one day she might wish to remarry. Or enjoy a discreet liaison with a bachelor of the *ton*, a privilege sometimes afforded to widows. And *that* gentleman, whoever he might be, would expect her to have been bedded by Edmund. He'd expect her to be knowledgeable. If she weren't, if she acted frightened and unsure as she had with Theo, it would betray her inexperience.

And she *couldn't* have that. Whispers must never arise about the Duchess of Severn's unconsummated marriage. Not only would it tarnish Edmund's reputation, but it might raise uncomfortable questions, like whether she *was* the Duchess of Severn at all. Whether she had dower rights. Whether Edmund's will was valid.

Her confusion over the matter of the heir and the will had not abated. At the pond, she'd used it to justify her impulsivity, but now that her mind was calmer, it turned her stomach to contemplate using Theo. If she chose that path – and that was a *very* big if, because it went against her nature to deceive anyone – she'd ask Theo first. And if a child happened to come from what they did tonight … well, that was a bridge to cross at a later time. Still, she wouldn't lie to Theo about it.

But her virginity was a problem she must solve. The sooner, the better.

She just needed to convince Theo.

With that in mind, she loosened her chemise's laces, allowing the neckline to fall open just as he emerged shirtless from behind the screen, rubbing his wet hair with a towel. His breeches hung low on his slim hips, his braces hanging at his side. His face was freshly shaven and he smelled of soap.

'Tired?' he asked, stretching the towel over the back of a chair so it could dry.

She *should* be tired, but anticipation had overridden her exhaustion.

'Relaxed is a better word.' She laid aside the comb. Her chemise slipped off one shoulder as she stood, allowing a generous view of the tops of her unbound breasts.

As she'd hoped, his gaze fell to her bosom, but his reaction left something to be desired. His jaw tightened, and, after a short, smouldering stare, he tore his eyes away and turned his back.

Henrietta drew upon her courage. There would never be a more perfect time to lose her virginity to a man she trusted – strange as it was that she *did* trust Theo Hawke after years of animosity. She couldn't let this opportunity pass. As he riffled through his satchel, she edged closer, her feet whispering on the floorboards, and placed her palm on the taut muscles of his bare back.

He froze.

She lay her cheek against his shoulder blade, relishing the warmth of his skin. 'Are *you* tired, Theodore?'

'Not very, when you press next to me, clad in that scrap of fabric.' His voice was strained. 'My thoughts aren't on sleep much.'

Her confidence swelled. Ah, so he *did* want her. She need only reassure away his reservations and he'd take her to bed. 'I've given some thought to what you said earlier,' she said, rubbing her cheek against him. 'That we should refrain from bedding together because we will later regret it.'

His gaze cut over his shoulder. 'Yes?'

She pressed her lips to his skin. 'It won't be the obstacle you imagine.'

'Ah, indeed?'

She slid a hand over his biceps, allowing her fingers to trace the hard curves. 'Our time together is limited to the duration of our investigative partnership. This is going to end one of two ways – with me hanging on the gallows or with my vindication. If the former, well, I don't particularly wish to die a virgin.' She paused, letting her words sink in, but he remained motionless, his face a mask. 'If the latter, you will write your article and we shall both continue with our separate lives, after wishing each other well. The only difference from before is that our animosity will be gone.'

'The only difference, eh?'

She trailed her fingers down the groove along the centre of his back, stopping at his waistband although she longed to stroke his bottom, so tight under his leather breeches. 'I need your assistance, Theo, so I'd like to propose a secondary partnership while we are fulfilling our primary partnership.'

And she explained to him why she couldn't remain a virgin.

'You want me to bed you so no one will realise your husband didn't?' he asked when she'd finished.

'Precisely.'

'And there is no other reason you wish me to bed you?' His gaze was piercing. 'No additional motive?'

Her breath caught, wondering if she should tell him about Edmund's will – but she didn't yet know how she felt about that, so she didn't want to think or talk on the subject now.

She tried fluttering her lashes. 'Only that I want you, Theo.'

'That's *it*? You want me?' When she tentatively answered in the affirmative, his gaze hardened. 'Dammit, woman.' He caught her in his arms, his rough grip unbearably exciting. She didn't understand why he was angry, but his fierceness titillated her. 'Tell me, what's in it for me with this secondary partnership?'

Her heart pounded, but only with excitement, for she wasn't scared, though his breathing was quick and ragged, and his grip crushingly tight. Was this play? A way to revive the tension of their years-long animosity, which, she *now* realised, had been fraught with sexual attraction? If so, she could play in return.

'You get me,' she said boldly. 'After years of obsession.'

He grabbed a fistful of her hair at the base of her neck. 'Witch,' he said. 'It's to my detriment that I want you like I do, but I cannot conquer it. As for your claims that I obsess over you, you're one to talk. Our attraction is mutual. It burns in you as it burns in me. That's why your eyes fell on me every time we met in public.'

He was correct, but she didn't have to admit that.

'How could I not look at you when I felt your hot stare boring into me?' she retorted.

'Bah! Deny all you want, but we both know I speak the truth. In my line of work, I must closely observe many ladies of the *ton*. You're not special in that way – other than that of those ladies, only *you* never failed to stare back.'

She was equally incensed and aroused by his aggression. 'I only stared because I hated you, Theodore.'

'Hated me?' He tightened his grip on her hair, pulling her head backwards so her neck arched towards him. Then he growled, devouring her with his eyes before kissing her taut skin. The searing heat of his lips jolted throughout her body, over her breasts, down to her throbbing sex. 'For a woman who hates me, you certainly throw yourself at me a great deal.' He trailed hot kisses over her neck and shoulders. 'Both literally and figuratively. Well, this time you are going to get some of what you want and don't blame me if you find you keep desiring it, long after our partnership has ended.'

He scooped her up and tossed her on the bed. She fell onto the creaking mattress, her limbs like jelly, her body aflame with yearning for the world of sensation he was about to introduce her to, at long last.

CHAPTER 19

An Unexpected Endearment

The village of Millford held nothing but negative connotations to Theo.

Odd that it should be the place where he would at last release his long-repressed desire for the Duchess of Severn. That such an action would eventually hurt him, and likely only make Millford an even more heartbreaking memory, troubled him little *for now*. Henrietta lay sprawled across the sagging bed in her thin chemise, her long hair like spun gold falling over the faded quilt, and he desired her with every fibre of his being.

Releasing his anger that she might be using him for stud without even being honest about it, he focused on her wonderful qualities – her bravery, her confidence, her sense of fun, her headstrong determination, and her love for and loyalty to her late husband.

She was acting upon a misguided sense of loyalty and duty now, he suspected. One in which – at best – she thought the state of her virginity wasn't a choice she got to make for herself, but one she must make for the sake of her husband's reputation. At worst, she'd determined that she owed her husband and the Dukedom of Severn her body for breeding.

Well, Theo would show her that her body was her own, a means by which she could receive pleasure without owing anyone anything. He'd whet her appetite and curiosity for more, but he wasn't about to give her everything she asked. He'd hold back *that thing*. It wasn't that he didn't want to give her the vigorous fuck she *definitely* needed, but he wouldn't give himself fully until she was honest about the will – and until she wanted to shed her virginity for *her* sake, not her husband's. At the pond, he'd impulsively considered it, but not any more. Not now that he knew the extent of her inexperience. Not now that they'd shared companionable laughter in the taproom, two partners against an antagonistic crowd. Not after he'd tenderly rubbed ointment over the wounds on her freshly bathed calves and wrapped them in bandages, just before washing himself. Not while her big blue eyes caused his heart to flip every damned time they met his.

Still, he'd enjoy the physical pleasure he'd derive from worshipping every square inch of her luscious body, and, with that goal in mind, he knelt by the side of the bed.

She gasped as he caught her foot in his hand and kissed the arch, her scent filling him. He kissed and sucked each beautiful toe until her body, stiff and hesitant at first, began first to soften, and then to writhe and twist, her breath increasing, her fingers tangling with the bedcovers and her hips instinctively rocking. His lips travelled up the right leg and he slid onto the mattress as he progressed. Above her knees, he began to inch up the hem of her chemise as he worked one thigh.

She whimpered.

He smiled against her leg. 'Feels good, does it?'

'No.' She shook her head, her eyes tightly closed. 'Or, yes, but also no. It feels good where your lips are, but everywhere else *aches*.'

'Aches how, darling?'

She touched her thighs. 'Here from riding.' Her hands moved to her bottom, which she lifted slightly. 'And here as well. I'm not accustomed to riding astride. But here …' She tentatively touched her chemise between her legs. 'This aches the most and that has nothing to do with riding at all.'

Theo's lips twitched. 'Let me see what I can do.'

He kneaded the muscles of her thighs with firm strokes while she whimpered that his fingers were exquisite torment. Then he flipped her over and worked her beautiful bottom with his hands and his kisses.

He tugged at her chemise. 'Take this off, darling.' His voice emerged husky and raw. 'I need you naked.'

She twisted to face him as she slid the garment over her head and tossed it aside, and he feasted on the sight before him. Magnificent breasts, nipples perky and rosy. Below them, a slim waist that curved into generous hips.

And then … the exposed tuft of dark blonde hair at the apex of her legs, which she parted slightly, a knowing glint in her eyes. His cock throbbed violently and he doubted his resolve. With her pretty cunny glistening, he wanted to rip open his fall and thrust until his bollocks hit her arse.

But he steeled himself. Lord, he was a man and not an animal. He could control himself, consider every facet of this interaction rather than succumb to pure lust. Besides, there were other parts of her body he'd secretly coveted for five years and this might be his only chance to explore them.

He dragged his gaze back to her face. 'You are beautiful.'

Her pretty lips softened into a smile. 'So are you.'

He leant over her until she fell back against the mattress. 'Indeed?' he asked, prodding his knees between hers until she spread wider. He pinned her forearms above her head, his hard cock pressed between her legs, only the leather of his breeches barring him from thrusting. 'Just how beautiful am I, darling?'

Her eyes travelled from his face to his torso and back again. 'Magnificent. Hard where I am soft, and when you rock your hips like that, and ... and your hardness rubs against me, it feels simply marvellous.'

His grinding was bringing her so much pleasure her eyes rolled up before her lids fluttered closed over them, and he considered giving her a dry bob to her completion, but dismissed the notion out of worry his breeches would chafe her. There were sweeter, gentler ways to satisfy a virgin.

He smothered kisses along her jaw, her fine neck; he slid his body and lips down until he came to her breasts. Breasts which – fuck him – he'd thought of far too often, ever since he'd first rejected her advances years ago. Many times, his eyes had traced their shape in her bosom-baring evening gowns, and on more than one occasion he'd imagined what they'd look like free from the constraints of her undergarments.

He now realised his imagination had fallen short, for their beauty surpassed his expectations.

And that's when the magnitude of what was happening sank in. The woman of his dreams was naked beneath him and moaning to his administrations, and the feelings he had for her were far more than mere lust or desire. They were sentiments so powerful they were searing his heart, leaving impressions he'd never eradicate. She had the power to destroy his contentment for ever, he realised. He should stop. Step away from this.

He didn't want to.

He applied himself properly to her breasts instead, possessing one with his hand and the other with kisses. As he licked around her nipple, she cried out, threading her fingers into his hair and pushing him closer. 'More.'

Oh, yes, he'd give her more. He'd spike her own desire, to supply her a sample of what she was doing to him. His fingers trailed her torso, slipped between her legs and glided into her slick folds.

'Oh!' She gasped. 'Oh,' she said again as he rubbed, his fingers deftly exploring the places he knew would be most pleasurable. She was dripping with readiness. 'That feels so much better than when I do it.'

Theo licked the hard tip of her nipple. 'You rub this sweet cunny, do you?'

She hitched her hips, grinding herself on his finger. 'I try.'

'And do you achieve fulfilment?'

She squirmed, twisted, released a sharp cry. 'Some pleasure.' Her voice was straining now, as if she found it difficult to speak through the sensations. 'A release. It never feels like enough.'

Theo thrilled, confident enough of his skills to suspect he could improve upon her solitary explorations. He rounded her nub with the pad of his thumb; at the same moment, he suckled her breast until she filled his mouth. She cried out, and loudly, and he relished it, not giving a damn who overheard. Let everyone know he was driving a goddess to distraction. He wanted her to scream with pleasure he'd incited, to writhe and shriek, for her exertions to thump the bed, rattling the floorboards while the unpleasant men downstairs were forced to listen.

His cock was painfully erect, a heavy weight between his legs, on the verge of exploding in his breeches; meanwhile, his hand was slick with her excitement. The time had come to give them both some satisfaction. On his part, he had five years of desire to release. He didn't know how long she had similarly wanted him, but he knew she'd been wanting sexual satisfaction for at least the same amount of time.

He kissed down her abdomen, slipping off the mattress to kneel on the floor. None too gently, he hefted her bottom to the edge of the bed and spread her legs to expose the coral shimmer of her engorged folds, her clitoris standing erect like a pink pearl, and he realised anew the shocking fact that the Duchess of Severn was offering *him* her virginity.

No doubt he'd regret his refusal for the rest of his life.

He slid a hand under her arse and lifted her to his mouth, drawing in her sweet smell. Starting with her enticing entrance, he raked his tongue through her slit until he found the centre of her pleasure.

Then she gasped and shuddered. 'More there, Theodore. Please, more.'

He buried his nose in her soft hair and took her fully into his mouth, the taste of her intensely, carnally satisfying, sending spirals of hot lust from his loins. She called out and tensed her abdomen, gripping his hair with both her hands, so he applied himself vigorously to his task. He sucked and licked as she squirmed, and when her cries grew more feverish, he teased her opening with the tip of his thumb. At first, her tightness barred his entrance, but he persisted gently. She was wet. So wet from her own essence and from his mouth, and at last he breached her with the upper joint of his thumb. She closed like a vice around him. God, but she was tight. He nudged forward until he found the aphrodisiacal area just inside and stroked that firmly, while still feasting.

She bucked her hips high.

Then she came.

Hard.

Her pulses were intense, squeezing his thumb, reverberating against his mouth. She cried out, grabbing his hair; he continued to suck and lick, the taste and smell of her so heady he wanted to draw it into himself. When he could tolerate no more torture, he reached under his waistband and he took his cock in hand, his throbbing, intense erection unbearable, and he gripped it so damn hard, tossing himself off with no quarter as he imagined taking her, having her, claiming her with repeated thrusts, until he came with such an explosive orgasm it tore a primal yell from his throat and he pumped his breeches full of his seed.

Then he slumped against the side of the bed, his head resting on her wet thigh.

She stroked gentle fingers though his hair. 'Why did you yell?'

'Because you destroy me.' He extracted his hand from his breeches, and, after bestowing a last kiss between her legs, stood and walked to the other side of the room where the water from their baths still sat in the copper basin. He unbuttoned his breeches and let them drop to the floor.

'What are you doing?' Her voice came from just behind him.

He looked over his shoulder. She was leaning against the wall, stark naked, and he dragged his eyes over her body. Her long legs, her full hips, and her breasts with those lush nipples, soft and pink now, begging for his tongue to make them hard again.

And he desired her as much as he ever had.

Nay, more.

As if the explosive release that had nearly torn his body in two hadn't even happened.

'Cleaning myself.' His voice was slurred.

She blinked. 'Are we ... finished?'

If his cock could have spoken, it would have screamed in the negative. It wasn't even a little bit soft. The truth was, Theo could have made love to her all night. Come a dozen times. He'd wanted her so long ... she was everything he yearned for, everything he desired ... and he knew he couldn't have her for ever, that she could never be his for more than a fleeting few moments and then she would be gone back to her own world, and he would be left to wish her well only from a distance, one of the admiring crowds and nothing more. Desire and logic both told him to have her repeatedly while he could. If only his cock and brain were making the decision, he'd carry her back to the bed.

But there was also his heart to consider. If he let himself get too close emotionally, if he joined his body with hers intimately, if he took the virginity she offered him, if she climaxed around his cock, breathing his name, he feared he'd fall irrevocably in love with this woman.

'Aye, we're finished for tonight, Henrietta.'

And before he could change his mind, he extracted the clean breeches from his satchel.

She watched him keenly as he tugged them on. 'But don't you have to go inside me to finish the deed?'

He tucked his hard cock into his fall and buttoned his waistband. 'To take your virginity, yes. But for us both to feel pleasure, no.'

She looked concerned. 'Did you feel pleasure from what we did?'

'Every moment,' he said honestly.

A furrow formed between her brows. 'But you don't ... want to be in me?'

Theo rubbed his hand through his hair. He'd have to explain. Give her *some* reason. Something truthful, but that didn't expose the vulnerability of his heart. 'Henrietta, I wanted to be inside you more than I've ever wanted anything. But I was so aroused, so hot to fuck you, I would've spilled my seed the moment my cock touched your cunny. That or accidentally thrust in you too hard, too forcibly. Neither would have been good. Not for your first time. Not ... never mind.'

Not if he wasn't going to permit himself to finish in her.

But she didn't let it go. 'Not what, Theo? Tell me.'

He decided to lay his cards on the table and see what she would admit. 'Not without taking the risk I might get you with child, which you can't possibly want.'

'Ah.' She pressed her lips together, hesitating, and Theo's hopes rose. He doubted he'd ever agree to father a child she likely didn't intend to let him raise, but he craved her honesty. If she'd simply ask, it would demonstrate that she respected him. Or at least that she recognised he was a person, with feelings. That she didn't simply view him as a means to achieving her goals.

But she disappointed him again. 'Just as well you stopped, because I'm tired anyway.'

He heard dissatisfaction in her voice. Ah, so neither of them reached a true fulfilment, in body or sentiment. The realisation depressed his spirits rather solidly. 'I shall sleep on the floor.'

'Please don't,' she said softly, sincerely. 'Please, lie beside me instead. I won't tempt you. Edmund shared my bed often, yet I never sought his touch. Since his death, my nights have been haunted by terrible dreams. Please, Theo. I ... I need a friend.'

His anger melted away. She'd suffered greatly in the last fortnight, and she was vulnerable and in peril.

'I can do better than lie beside you,' he said tenderly. 'I will hold you. Keep you safe and warm. Chase those dreams away, if they dare to come.'

Her blue eyes filled with tears and that was all the thanks he needed.

He led her to the bed and settled her on the side by the wall, where she'd be more secure. The bed creaked under his weight as he lay beside her. Taking her in his arms, he held her against his chest so that her bottom nestled into his groin and her legs curved around his.

He pinched the bedside candle's flame, extinguishing all light but the glow of the fire, and laid his head on the pillow. Her soap-fresh hair tickled his nose, her bare back was warm silk against his bare chest. It was heaven to lie beside her, though with his cock still a rod in his breeches, it would be a long time before he'd sleep.

'Good night, my l...' Theo caught himself, mortified that he'd almost revealed how deeply he was beginning to care for her. 'Darling.'

But Henrietta was already asleep, her breathing soft and rhythmic.

He released a heavy breath. He felt burdened with his complicated feelings not just for her, but for this part of Surrey, and the memories he'd rehashed earlier in the day talking about his past. How would Henrietta react if she knew about his father? Would her heart be moved with tenderness? Would she be appalled? Or would she simply not care, because Theo was nothing to her but a temporarily useful tool?

He held her more securely and her rhythmic breathing didn't alter. 'I'm sorry for all you've been through,' he whispered, because he knew she slept and couldn't hear. 'But I can't be sorry that you are in my arms tonight, love. I don't want to want you – I don't want to want your heart – but I do.' He kissed the back of her shoulder, yet she didn't stir, and he gathered his emotions to say something he'd never revealed to anyone. 'This area was the home of my paternal ancestors – my father drowned not a mile up the river from here several months before I was born. I thought I hated this place, but I can't hate it or you or anything about our situation when I am holding you.'

There was still no response from the sleeping duchess and Theo now found himself somewhat disappointed she hadn't awakened when he was baring his soul. But it was best that way.

He drifted into a light sleep. Sometime in the depth of night, when the fire had dwindled and the rain subsided, she cried out in distress, as she had done the previous night in the hay. Then, he'd covered her in his coat, and she'd instinctively sought comfort by clinging to his arm, nuzzling her cheek against his hand.

Tonight, he held her close, kissing her hair until her sobs subsided. 'There now, Henrietta, all will be well. I'm here.'

She turned her face, brushing her damp cheek against his nose. 'I thought you'd left me, sweetheart, and I couldn't bear it.'

She was mistaking him for her late husband. A pang of sorrow hit Theo, both at the heaviness of her grief and – selfishly – that he would never be to her what the duke had been. She might still be half asleep, but it was no kindness to let her continue in her misconception that Edmund was alive, for she'd have to face the truth again at some point.

Brushing her tears away with his thumb, he corrected her. 'Henrietta, I'm not Edmund.'

'You're Theo.' She sounded mollified, relaxed. Almost fully asleep again. 'And you're here after all. You never left me.'

'You dreamt you'd lost *me*?' He must have misunderstood. He couldn't let his hopes rise.

Yet unbelievably, she murmured her assent. 'Just a bad dream, because you are here.'

His heart thudded against his chest wall so hard she surely must feel it as well. 'Yes.' He hastened to assure her. 'A bad dream and nothing more, darling. I'm here. I'm here with you.'

'Please don't leave me?'

'I wouldn't.' He reeled with sudden realisation. With this small exchange, he'd become a hopeless cause, destined for heartbreak. 'I couldn't if I tried, darling. For as long as you need or want me, I shall stay.'

'So good to me,' she muttered, her words slurred with sleep. 'My Theo.'

'Your Theo, yes.' Oh, how his vulnerable heart soared, yet a question pressed there, too. 'Darling Henrietta, did you intend to call me sweetheart? Am I that to you?'

But she didn't answer, for she was fast asleep once more.

CHAPTER 20

A New Disguise

When Henrietta awoke the next morning, the first thing she noticed was how wonderful it was to be secured against Theo's body, with his arms encasing her. The second thing she noticed was the throbbing soreness of her calves. When Theo had applied the ointment the night before it had soothed her wounds, but the benefits weren't long term.

'There's an infection,' Theo said later, inspecting the injuries, his fingers gentle on her inflamed skin. 'Let us visit the apothecary before we return to London. Benzoin and new bandages ought to help.'

When they stepped outside the Pickled Dog, glad to leave the radical enclave behind, early morning mists were rising from the saturated ground, stretching tendrils towards a clear sky. The air was rich with the earthy smell of the country after a rain.

The apothecary shop was in a half-timber cottage near the mill. The medical man himself had just returned from a night call when they arrived, and he was in the process of handing his horse to his son when Theo enquired about benzoin and bandages.

He nodded towards the shop door. 'Wait in there while I attend to my necessaries.'

He lumbered off towards the privy, followed by a small, one-eared terrier.

The shop proved to be the front room of the cottage, crammed with jar-filled shelves and cabinets. Dust motes danced in the dim light cast by small leaded windows. These, combined with a pungent mixture of herbal, astringent and sulphuric scents, caused Henrietta's nose to twitch, and she stifled the sneeze that followed.

Theo handed her a purplish-blue handkerchief embroidered with bilberries from a folded pile on the apothecary's counter. 'Mice sneeze louder than you,' he said, laughing.

She dabbed the handkerchief to her nose. 'It's not ladylike to sneeze loudly, Theodore.'

He winked. 'Well, I like it when you're loud.'

He was referring to her exuberant sounds the night before, and she blushed as she tucked the handkerchief into her bodice. She'd never experienced going about daily life with the same person with whom one had recently entwined one's body intimately, and, though she liked it, she gave him a mild scold. 'You're not a gentleman to remind me.'

His cheeky grin made an appearance. 'I'm not a gentleman at all, darling.'

'You're more a gentleman than you realise,' she answered simply. And then, sensing emotions she wasn't prepared to acknowledge, she shifted her gaze from his handsome face and surveyed the shop. Her eyes settled on an upper shelf containing jars labelled with large black Xs, prompting her to edge closer for a better look. 'Did Dr Grimsley say which type of poison was used, Theo?'

'Not that I ever heard.' He came alongside her and tapped one of the labelled jars. 'I keep abreast of the more salacious trials, so

I can tell you that arsenic is used in, oh, nine out of ten deliberate poisonings. It's virtually undetectable. Odourless, colourless and tasteless. But you said your husband indicated his wine had a sweet flavour?'

'He definitely tasted something.' She read the other labels. *Female-bane*. *Opium*. *Mercury*. *Cyanide*. She took a jar labelled *Nux Vomica* off the shelf and opened it to expose a collection of guinea-sized, flat brown seeds. 'If we knew which it was, perhaps that would be a clue.'

The door opened and closed behind them. 'Trouble in the marriage, eh?' The apothecary smirked knowingly, his twinkle-eyed terrier panting at his side. 'Aye, that'll solve it. I'll mix a tincture, missus, and you serve it to him just before bed. You won't have no more problems.'

Horrified, Henrietta hastily recapped the jar. Was the apothecary implying this poison was a perfect way to kill a spouse? 'I … I … no, we simply need bandages and benzoin.'

The apothecary's gaze jumped between her and Theo. 'There's no cause for shame. Happens to many men, from time to time. My tincture will have Roger up and standing for an hour or more, like a soldier at drill.'

Henrietta was baffled, but Theo laughed heartily. 'Roger doesn't have any trouble standing, I assure you. We were merely curious about the various types of poisons.'

The apothecary closed the distance between them, took the jar from Henrietta's hands and returned it to its place on the dusty shelf. 'Taken in the wrong amounts, nux vomica is poisonous, missus, which is why you should never touch anything on an apothecary's shelves.' He waggled a finger, as if she were a naughty child, and then tapped the arsenic jar. 'If you have rats, this is what you want.'

'I don't have rats,' she replied, annoyed. 'My interest is of a scientific nature. What would you say are the most dangerous poisons?'

'Dangerous for what? A rat?'

'Something bigger than a rat,' she replied. 'An extremely large dog, say.'

The apothecary's eyebrows popped up like two jack-in-the-boxes. 'Here, what are you wanting to kill a dog for?'

'It's a hypothetical situation,' she said.

He looked at his terrier, who cocked its one ear. 'I don't like it all the same.'

She repressed an eye-roll. 'Let's say the large dog preys upon smaller dogs, like the size of your terrier there. What are the most effective poisons against such a beastly creature?'

Appalled, the man scooped his dog into his arms. 'Arsenic, opium or strychnine,' he said, supplying an answer at last. 'Very effective, strychnine is.'

'Does strychnine have a flavour?'

The apothecary peered over his dog's head. 'None at all, same as arsenic.'

'But opium does,' Henrietta said, recalling the laudanum her mother had given her. 'It's a bitter flavour, isn't it?'

'As laudanum, yes, but it depends upon the preparation, and there are endless methods.'

'So it could be made colourless and sweet?'

'I imagine,' the apothecary said, growing cagey.

So perhaps opium was the poison used. Memories of Edmund's dying moments, his pain, his face, now flooded back, shaking Henrietta to the core. Her knees weakened and she leant against Theo for support, which he instantly provided with an arm about her shoulders. 'And the . . . death? Would it be immediate or delayed?'

'Depends again upon the preparation. The strength of poison ingested.'

Her throat was dry, prickly, her stomach sick. 'Would it induce convulsions? Heated skin, like with a fever? Vomiting?'

'Vomiting, aye. Convulsions less likely. The effect would be similar to the effect of laudanum. The ... dog might suffer purging, but then he would experience drowsiness as the systems of his body slow. Weakened breath, slow movements, less and less energy, until he fell into death as one falls into sleep. Quite painless.'

Oh, yes – laudanum took *away* pain and put one to sleep. She had used it so infrequently in her life, she wasn't thinking. 'Of course. Not that, then,' she muttered, dismayed. 'What would produce a sweet-tasting poison with a delayed response, and induce headache, convulsions and vomiting before death?'

The apothecary returned his terrier to the floor. 'What we have in abundance in this part of England. Death's herb, of course.'

'Which is?' Henrietta asked.

'Dwale.' And when that received no response from her or Theo, he added, 'Deadly nightshade.'

Of course! Henrietta knew the berry-producing weed well enough – she'd been warned as a child never to touch or eat it, but she and her brothers had been curious, so warnings only served to stoke their interest. Once, she and her brother Edward had gathered some of the poisonous berries using their handkerchiefs. Edward had said they'd make a good pigment – even as a young child, he'd been an artist – so they'd smashed the berries into a purplish-black pulp. Edward had taken up a brush and used the substance to draw fantastical monsters in his sketchbook as she'd giggled over his shoulder. Years later, they'd gone through Edward's old drawing books, laughing over the memories; the nightshade monsters had faded somewhat, but even then, they'd had a distinctive purple cast.

'But nightshade isn't colourless?' she said. 'In a light-coloured wine, it would be discernible?'

The apothecary narrowed his eyes. 'What are you talking about wine for? I thought you needed to poison a dog. If you have a nefarious purpose in mind, I won't be aiding you.' His tone grew increasingly hostile and Henrietta's palms prickled. 'Now, do you intend to pay for that handkerchief at your breast? 'Cause it'll cost you fourpence. The girls make 'em at the charity school.'

Theo hastily removed his coin purse from his pocket. 'A groat for the handkerchief, my good man, and how much do I owe you for the benzoin and bandages?'

They left the apothecary shop soon after with more questions than answers.

The muddiness of the roads slowed their progress to London somewhat, but, due to their early start, they still managed to stable their horses off Newgate Street and arrive at Theo's lodgings just as the bells of St Paul's pealed the ten o'clock hour.

In London, Henrietta hid her face with her bonnet brim. Anyone might recognise her, even in her dirt-splattered clothes. Her fears proved justified at the lodgings when, despite Theo's attempt to shield her from prying eyes, his landlady took great offence to 'a filthy streetwalker' entering her house.

'She'll give you the clap or the French pox, my boy.' The woman yanked Henrietta's arm and shoved her towards the door. 'Or both of them together, like as not.'

Henrietta gave her assailant a scathing look. When the landlady saw her face, she gave an almighty gasp, turned a brilliant red and released her arm. Clasping her hands to a mountainous bosom, she fell upon the newel post.

''Pon my word! If I'd known it were Your Gr—'

'*Shh*, Mrs Ford,' Theo whispered. 'You cannot reveal her identity. She and I are investigating the murder together.'

The landlady burst into violent tears, declaring she wouldn't do anything to harm the widow of 'that blessed man'. Henrietta assured her repeatedly that she was not in the least offended by the misunderstanding.

Mrs Ford dabbed at her eyes with her apron. 'To think, you are in my house and more beautiful up close than all the times I viewed you from afar. But we must get you out of that muddy, tattered frock.'

From that moment, Henrietta found herself treated with the utmost care.

While Theo vanished on mysterious errands, Mrs Ford drew a hot bath, sprinkled with rosewater, in her own rooms. She insisted on attending, washing Henrietta's hair and brushing it dry over the fire until it shone like gold, and reapplying benzoin and fresh bandages to the much-improved wounds.

Theo returned with new clothes and then went upstairs to tidy himself. As planned during their ride from Millford, they would dress as a middle-class man and wife, to blend in while conducting their investigation.

The clothes he had purchased for Henrietta fitted surprisingly well. They included a serviceable chemise, wool stockings and pink garter ribbons. She wore her own stays, but added a new petticoat, followed by a dark-blue cotton dress with a smart spencer. After Mrs Ford arranged her hair in a simple chignon, Henrietta completed the ensemble with a wide-brimmed hat ornamented with a huge bow and a lace face veil.

'I purchased that hideous hat *only* because I hoped the veil would keep your identity hidden,' Theo said later, when she joined him in his parlour. He had shaved and bathed, and had clothed himself in a brown wool suit. The trousers and tailcoat hung beautifully on his broad frame; he wore a fresh shirt, smelling lightly of starch, an undyed linen waistcoat and a brown cotton cravat. His wavy hair was still damp, darkening the gold tones into a tawny-brown, and he was so devastatingly handsome it made Henrietta's heart ache. 'I hope the rest of the clothes are serviceable enough.'

'I love them.' And though they were the least lovely clothes she'd ever worn, she meant it wholeheartedly. They were clean, comfortable and serviceable – and Theo had chosen them for her.

He dismissed her assertion with a wave of his hand. 'You are being kind. Of course, they are nothing like you are accustomed to, but I can't afford to buy even a ribbon from one of the shops you frequent. Besides, we don't want you to look like the Duchess of Severn. This is a disguise.'

'A perfect disguise.' She observed herself in the looking glass over Theo's mantel. 'I look exactly like any regular woman, leading a normal life. No one will give me a second glance.'

'Your veil would have to be thicker for that to be true,' he replied with a laugh. 'And you'd need to cover your figure with a sackcloth. Now, if you'll excuse me a moment, I'll clean the mud from our boots.'

After he left with the footwear, Mrs Ford brought a tea tray and then Henrietta was alone in Theo's rooms. For the first five minutes, she contented herself with savouring a well-brewed cup after two days without tea, glancing down to the court behind the lodging house. Seeing little activity there other than Mrs Ford emptying the bathwater, Henrietta's eye wandered around the lodgings. Though reluctant to pry, she was curious about Theo's life.

His living quarters consisted of only two rooms. The plank-floored parlour she occupied was sparsely furnished with a sofa, two armchairs and a small dining table. A large desk dominated one corner, laden with stacks of papers, various writing implements, a half-empty bottle of gin and a nearly full French brandy.

The adjoining bedchamber was even more modest. A tidy bed with a downy quilt, a pine wardrobe, an undyed wool rug and a wash table with shaving basin and mirror were the only objects it contained, but the room was clean and neat, with the pleasant scent of shaving soap.

She closed the door to that room and glanced again around the parlour, struck this time by how impersonal it was. There were no books other than two or three on his desk. Theo was clearly a well-read man; she'd imagined he'd have shelves of books. How odd that he didn't.

Then she realised why. It was the same reason no art decorated the walls, no knick-knacks ornamented the mantel and why everything was serviceable but spartan. What sort of wages could Theo possibly earn, writing his gossip column and packing newspapers, as he'd told her he did on occasion? She looked down at the clothes he had purchased for her. However much he'd spent, it probably represented a greater sacrifice than her most lavish court dress or diamond necklace from Edmund, yet Theo hadn't even mentioned the cost.

A pang tugged at her heart. She'd tried so hard the day before to suppress her warm feelings for her old enemy. Today, the task seemed impossible. Was it as Theo had said, that once a certain intimacy was shared, sentiments would arise to complicate matters? And, if so, should she not be building up walls to protect herself, rather than letting him seep into her heart?

She should. She knew she should. But she didn't want to. She *liked* him. Not only because of all they'd shared the night before – both *that thing* and then sleeping in his arms – but also because he possessed a steadiness of character and a kindness that she found both extremely attractive and deeply comforting. For the five years of her marriage, she'd kept many secrets bottled up inside her – things she hadn't even told her mother – and it felt so good to have shared them with a friend.

Urged forward by a desire to know more about him, she walked to his desk to read the titles of the handful of books he did own, but before she could peruse the volumes, her eyes fell to an article lying atop the other papers: *On a Way Forward After the Death of Severn.*

She sat in the chair to read. Not even one paragraph in, she knew the voice – it was that of the political journalist who published anonymously, whose musings always gave her so much food for thought. Whose article on universal suffrage she'd been reading the afternoon of Edmund's death. The author she'd wanted to seek out, to offer financial support.

Of course it had been Theo all along. She'd read both the anonymous author and *The Hawke's Eye* for years – she must have unconsciously recognised some stylistic similarities. No doubt that had fed her weekly frustration with his beastly gossip column – because the *real* Theodore Hawke was a thoughtful and progressive journalist in search of meaningful truths. His anonymous articles represented his capabilities, if he only had the chance to earn a living outside of gossipmongering.

The door from the corridor opened and she swivelled in the chair to face Theo as he entered with their newly polished boots. A powerful wave of emotion washed over her. Impulsively, she closed the distance between them in a flash, threw her arms about his neck and offered her lips.

He dropped their boots, gathered her close, and then kissed her with wild, consuming passion. 'Please tell me what I did to deserve such a greeting,' he said when they stopped for breath. 'So that I can make a habit of it in the future.'

Henrietta replied by squeezing him until her heart ached, yet even that wasn't enough to convey the depth of her feelings. She yearned for something she couldn't even define.

A surprised squeak pierced the air; Theo pulled away and his absence left her so cold and bereft she embraced herself, rubbing her upper arms through her spencer.

Mrs Ford stood in the doorway, mouth agape, eyes darting between them, face reddening. 'I'm sure I wasn't meaning to interrupt anything, but I had an idea, Your Gr ... I mean, ma'am. For your disguise.' With a tentative smile, she held a small round squab cushion aloft. 'I thought to make you appear with child.'

In the ensuing awkwardness, Henrietta peeked at a stone-faced Theo, and she was utterly ashamed she'd *ever* considered using him to fulfil Edmund's wish. His admirable, endearing characteristics were the very things that would prevent him from siring a child without being a father.

One can never have things both ways. She'd had romantic feelings for two men: one eminently suitable for her station in life, but unable to offer the love she craved; the other, perhaps everything she'd ever desired from a romantic partner but despised by her family and her society.

With a heavy heart, she answered Mrs Ford. 'The cushion is an excellent idea.'

Because while Henrietta doubted she would ever hunt for a man to father a child for Edmund now that her feelings for Theo ran so deep, she was extremely keen to give Perceval the fright of his life.

CHAPTER 21

Désirée du Pont

After Mrs Ford left, Henrietta asked Theo's opinion on speaking first to Désirée du Pont, opera dancer, famed beauty and courtesan – and Perceval's mistress, perhaps former, perhaps current. Either way, most certainly the woman about whose neck Perceval had placed a diamond necklace three days before Edmund's death.

'The potential dissolution of his engagement might have been another impetus for Edmund's change of mindset regarding the, er, circumstances of our marriage,' she said. 'Edmund approved of Miss Babcock. He believed Perceval's proposal to such a sensible young lady was the only intelligent thing Perceval had ever done.'

Theo rubbed his chin. 'So once the betrothal faced dissolution, your husband wanted his own heir to replace Perceval more than ever?'

She lifted her hands. 'Possibly, yes. And if Perceval somehow knew, that might have been motive for murder.' She looked towards the window, considering the next move. 'I wonder how we could discover Miss du Pont's place of residence?'

'She lives in a flat on Jermyn Street. Number forty-seven, if I recall correctly. At any rate, I shall recognise it from the outside.'

'*Indeed?*' Henrietta raised her eyebrow pointedly. 'I see, then.'

His eyes sparkled. 'No, you don't. Not if you suppose I've had any *intimate* dealings with the woman. I know her direction because she's sought my attention on numerous occasions, in the hopes of a mention in *The Hawke's Eye*. In fact, I suspect she is the one who sent me the anonymous message telling me when she'd be at Hyde Park with Perceval that day. In *her* case, any attention, good or bad, improves her business.'

Henrietta pondered the truth of Theo's statement. She'd first encountered Désirée du Pont's name in his column, linked at the time to another gentleman. The next evening, at the opera with Edmund and Perceval, she'd asked which of the dancers was Miss du Pont. Perceval had pointed her out; not a year later, she was his mistress, and absorbing the bulk of Perceval's allowance, according to Edmund's assessment.

So, with their destination set on a flat on Jermyn Street, they began their walk to St James's. Less than an hour later, Miss du Pont's manservant ushered them into a bedchamber papered with floral print in garish colours. Crimson drapes hung at the windows.

Miss du Pont was propped up in an equally crimson bed, a breakfast tray spanning her lap, wearing a lace nightdress and a diamond necklace. Her black hair fell like silk about her pointed face. Her skin was ivory, her neck and bare arms long and thin, and she possessed sharp black eyes rimmed with inky lashes. Her smiling lips were blood red.

'Mr Hawke,' she said, trailing her fingertips suggestively over her diamond necklace. 'To what do I owe the pleasure of this early morning call?'

St James's Church had rung the one o'clock hour when they'd passed it, but Theo simply responded that they hoped to ask Miss du Pont some questions.

Black eyes examined Henrietta intently. 'Remove your veil first.' Her voice had lost the saccharine quality she'd used with Theo.

Henrietta lifted the lace and the intense stare turned into a knowing gleam.

'Oh, 'tis *you*.' Miss du Pont popped a grape in her mouth and unceremoniously spat the pips into a bowl. 'My dear Mr Hawke, are you helping your duchess escape justice? Foolish, if so. Everyone knows of your obsession, but she won't spare another thought for *you* once you've served your purpose, even if you swing for her.'

Henrietta's blood boiled. 'Don't speak to him like that. And I'm not escaping justice. I am *seeking* it.'

Miss du Pont selected another grape and chewed it slowly. 'There's a reward offered for your recovery, Madame Hoity-Toity.'

Odd, if that were true – she'd only been absent from London for two days and Libby had been arrested. Then Henrietta realised who must be Miss du Pont's source of information. 'I imagine your lover told you so. No doubt he's the one offering the reward.'

'And how would you know who my lover is, *sang bleu*?'

'Everyone knows of your arrangement with my late husband's cousin, Perceval Percy.'

'Perceval?' Miss du Pont laughed. 'That milksop hasn't been my lover since before Christmas when he met that insufferable bluestocking. What he sees in a woman like her, other than her fortune, I cannot tell, but she has him firmly tied to her apron strings, let me assure you.'

'Then why did you meet him in the park?' Henrietta asked.

She stroked her diamond necklace. 'He owed me a farewell present for my silence.'

'Silence over what?'

She grinned, popping another grape in her mouth. 'Well, that would be telling, wouldn't it? I'm far too fond of my diamonds to risk losing them.'

'Silence over his plans to murder his cousin?'

Miss du Pont's thin black brows jumped up. 'You think *Perceval* murdered your husband? Impossible. He is too nerveless and weak.'

Henrietta shook her head. 'It doesn't take nerves or strength to slip poison in a man's drink.'

'It takes either nerves or desperation to do anything that might make one face the gallows,' Miss du Pont said. 'Perceval hasn't got any nerve and he wasn't desperate once Miss Moneybags came along, so he's not the killer.'

'You are protecting him,' Henrietta said. 'By your own admission, you are concealing some pertinent information, in exchange for your necklace.'

Miss du Pont laughed again. 'What I'm concealing is not *that* condemnatory.'

'Tell me what it is, then. Perceval won't know you told me, because Mr Hawke won't write about it. You have my assurance.'

The dancer's eyes cut to Theo. 'Are you tied to apron strings, too, Mr Hawke? I wouldn't have thought you the type.'

'The duchess and I are investigative partners,' he replied curtly.

Miss du Pont sipped her chocolate. 'That's a euphemism I've not yet heard.' She jerked her head at the bump at Henrietta's abdomen. 'Are you the one who knocked that baby into her?'

'Never mind that,' Henrietta said. 'Explain why Perceval requires your silence and I shall buy you another diamond necklace if he demands the return of that one.'

'How casually Your Grace promises diamonds here and there,' Miss du Pont said, her voice laced with mockery. 'What it must be, to be a duchess. Very well, I shall tell you, but only if Hawke leaves. I question your influence over what he chooses to print.'

'I print the truth,' Theo said, but then his attention shifted to Henrietta and his manner softened. 'Rather, I aim to convey what I see or hear, which I admit is not always the complete story, and thus is, at times, only a partial truth.'

Henrietta smiled warmly, hoping it expressed her gratitude for his admission. 'Please wait outside?'

He hesitated, glancing between her and the opera dancer, but at last he nodded and exited the room amidst Miss du Pont's burbles about men ruled by pussies, which puzzled Henrietta exceedingly as she had no idea what cats had to do with anything.

After the door closed, she repeated her query about what Perceval had done to require her silence.

'It's not so much what *he* did as what he allowed *me* to do, when he called to inform me our affair had ended in favour of Miss Babcock. I don't take defeat well. I require a certain sense of victory and nothing gives me victory like seeing a man who claims to be in love with someone else come for me.' Miss du Pont made a gesture, curling her fingers into an o-shape and moving her hand back and forth in front of her open mouth.

Henrietta frowned. 'What do you mean?'

The dancer burst into peals of laughter so violent that she dabbed a pale purple handkerchief to the corner of her eyes. 'Good Lord, Madame Cuckold. Don't pretend you haven't had as many pricks down your throat as I have – and maybe more.'

Miss du Pont's conversation was utterly baffling.

'What down my throat?' Henrietta asked. 'Of what are you speaking?'

Miss du Pont's laugh turned derisive. 'You may fool your lovers when you act the ingénue, but Perceval spoke often of your true nature. You are fully aware a prick is a man's penis, and you've sucked plenty of them.'

Henrietta's first impulse was to recoil, until she considered the potential value of this information. If a woman put a man's penis in her mouth, it wasn't so different from the delicious things Theo had done to her the night before. It stood to reason that a man would enjoy the reciprocal action.

'Oh!' she said, pondering how Theo would react if she asked him if he'd like her to ... how had the dancer termed it? ... ah, yes: *put his prick down her throat*. But Miss du Pont was regarding her suspiciously, so Henrietta cleared her throat and resumed the interrogation. 'And when did this ... er ... event occur?'

'In early January.'

'Yet he didn't give you the necklace until June?'

Miss du Pont observed her nails. 'Well, I *intended* to be content with a private victory. I believed it would be enough for me to observe Miss Bluestocking prancing her conquest through the Season, while *I* secretly knew her dear Perceval came in my mouth after he'd professed to be in love with her.'

Henrietta's temper rose on Jane's behalf. 'That's a horrible thing to gloat about.'

'Men are horrible.' Miss du Pont tossed her handkerchief aside. It lay like a crumpled purple bird on her blood-red counterpane. 'Lying bastards, every one.'

Henrietta thought of Edmund and Theo, of her father and of her brothers. Yes, there were Marlows and Percevals out there as well, but she had to believe they were the exception and that the good men far outnumbered the bad. '*Most* men are honourable and honest,' she said, hoping her words comforted the dancer.

But Miss du Pont snarled, revealing her teeth like a vicious dog. 'You know *nothing*, stupid woman. My family was like yours before Madame Guillotine; my grandfather was a marquis until he lost his lands and his head. Though my parents escaped, they were pampered fools like all *aristocrates*, unprepared for the harsh reality of this world. I learnt for myself how to navigate life, by means of lessons you wouldn't have survived. So before you speak, consider if *any* aspect of your existence resembles the experiences of normal women, much less one like me, who earns her bread by submitting to men's vilest desires?'

Henrietta almost retorted that she'd had her share of tribulations, but she thought the better of it. After all, what *did* she know of Miss du Pont's life – and who was she to pass judgement, anyway?

'Forgive my presumption, Miss du Pont,' she said instead. 'You are quite correct. I spoke out of ignorance.' Faint surprise crossed the opera dancer's face. 'But, please, let us return to the matter at hand. You never answered my question about why you didn't receive the necklace until this month.'

'True, I didn't,' Miss du Pont replied, in a milder tone. 'After I sucked Perceval off in January, he was furious. Vowed it would be his last transgression. Even mentioned confessing all to Miss Babcock.' She snorted. 'I never thought he really would until I first saw them together. That prim piece gave me such a *pitying* look, I hated her on sight. I can endure a lot, but I don't want *pity*. So, I devised a plan to teach her a lesson and benefit myself, as well. I wrote to Perceval, demanding he purchase this necklace from Rundell and Bridge's or I'd tell *The Hawke's Eye* what had happened in January. Perceval agreed by return post, but I chose the time and place, and invited Hawke along, by which means I cleverly achieved both purposes: I got diamonds and now Miss Babcock knows what it's like to have pitying glances cast her way – or she *would* have, had your husband not been so stupid as to die the very day Hawke's column was published. Sadly, no one pities a woman affianced to a duke, even if the duke sticks his prick in opera dancers' mouths.'

'Where did Perceval get the money for your necklace?' Henrietta asked, thinking of a perplexing problem with Miss du Pont's story. 'He had no allowance from my husband and he isn't skilled enough at gambling to win it.'

'That I can't say.' Miss du Pont picked up her handkerchief and twisted it absent-mindedly. 'Perhaps you should ask him yourself.'

Yes, and Henrietta possessed the perfect leverage to get the truth from Perceval...

As she rubbed her fake pregnancy belly, gathering her courage, her attention shifted to the handkerchief in Miss du Pont's hand. A jolt of recognition shot through her. Not only was it the exact shade of the handkerchief Theo had purchased at the Millford apothecary that very morning, but it also bore embroidered bilberries, though in a different design.

'Miss du Pont, have you ever visited a village in Surrey called Millford?'

A fierce flame ignited in those obsidian eyes. 'I've divulged all I know concerning matters relevant to you. I see no reason why I must be subjected to questions unrelated to Perceval. Since I have been nothing but cooperative, perhaps Your Highness might allow me to finish my breakfast in peace?'

Henrietta was taken aback by the response, but Miss du Pont *had* been helpful and for no personal gain. 'In that case, thank you,' she said, resigned. 'If you ever have need of assistance, you may call upon my help.'

'You are hardly in a position to make such an offer,' the dancer said. 'Have a care, Your Grace. With people as angry as they are now, who knows but this might be just the time for Old Bailey to show that nobs aren't above the law. I can imagine a duchess swinging would go a long way towards quelling revolution.' Her black eyes gleamed. 'A very long way indeed.'

CHAPTER 22

Confessions

An imaginary noose was tightening around Henrietta's neck, yet she refused to capitulate to fear. As she walked with Theo towards Severn House, her veil again covering her face, she told him *almost* everything Désirée du Pont had said. She didn't mention the opera dancer's idle threat.

She and Theo did discuss the price on her head, however. To verify Miss du Pont's claim, he purchased a selection of newspapers, which they read at a dark coffee house on Piccadilly. Indeed, it seemed that although Libby Forman had been charged with the murder, the magistrate still sought to question everyone who had been near Edmund that day – and of them, the only person who had not cooperated with the investigation was Her Grace, the Duchess of Severn. Furthermore, the articles claimed, it appeared the duchess had vanished. There was an offer for information on her whereabouts and anyone caught harbouring Her Grace might face criminal charges.

'It seems as if the magistrate suspects me,' Henrietta said. 'Why then has he charged Libby with the murder?'

'Perhaps he's hedging his bets.' Theo scanned a page of *The Times*. 'Giving himself two options to take to trial. One, whereby you and your maid collaborated, which circumstantial evidence might support. But if public opinion resists the hanging of a duchess – or your father exerts his influence successfully – he can change his tale. Say you were always innocent and then condemn your maid. Above all else, he will want to appear competent and prevent rioting.'

Henrietta pressed her roiling stomach. 'He doesn't care if an innocent woman dies?'

'The poor are expendable.' Theo looked up from the paper, a shadow of sadness crossing his face. 'Did you know your maid well?'

'Not particularly.' She picked at the edge of the scarred tabletop with her thumbnail. 'She had only been in my employ for a month before Edmund's death.'

Theo settled back in his chair, coffee in hand. 'Would you be sad if she hanged in your stead, this woman you barely know?'

'Of course!' Henrietta was appalled that he would even ask. 'Although I take offence to "in my stead", for I am innocent as well. I don't want *anyone* to die for a crime they didn't commit.'

He stretched out his legs, crossing his ankles. 'Yet it happens frequently enough.'

'Are you thinking of your mother?' she asked gently.

He sipped his coffee. 'In truth, I don't know for absolute certain my mother wasn't guilty, though she pleaded innocent at her trial. In the interest of fairness, I suppose it's possible she might have felt forced to steal to provide for herself and for me. I suspect, however, that the mistress contrived the supposed theft to destroy her.'

'Why, though?' Henrietta asked, aghast. 'What could possibly motivate such a depraved action?'

He lifted a hand. 'Jealousy? Revenge?'

Henrietta's eyes widened. 'Oh!' She caught her breath and leant closer, speaking even lower than before. 'The master of the house was your father, was he not?'

'Yes,' he said quietly.

'Oh, Theo!' Henrietta clasped her hands to her heart. 'Your poor dear mother's tale is the most dreadful I've ever heard. Surely, *surely* your father tried to protect her? What prevented his success?'

'He was dead by the time his wife brought forward the complaint. He drowned, in fact, not far from Millford – that was the investigation to which I alluded yesterday. But perhaps he wouldn't have saved her, even if he'd lived.'

'No, no, that cannot be.' Henrietta covered Theo's hand with one of hers. 'I know he would have saved her. Your father must have been a good man.'

His straight brows lifted. 'Why on earth do you assume such a thing?'

'Because *you* are good,' she said ardently, though she was revealing sentiments perhaps more wisely left hidden. 'You have been so kind to me these last two days.'

A flicker of emotion crossed his face, but it disappeared swiftly, replaced by a hardened edge. 'I'm embroiled in your mess now, so what choice do I have?'

'A great deal of choice.' She wasn't put off by his manner. They were both under considerable strain and he must feel the threat of criminal repercussions for aiding her, as she felt that phantom noose. 'You could take me to Bow Street and collect your reward. Instead, you're helping me.'

His face was a mask. 'Well, as for my *father's* goodness, I doubt it. While I have never heard him described as a cruel man, he was most certainly an infamous womaniser – and do you not feel that any man who seduces an innocent maid, barely eighteen years of age, in his employ, under his protection, cannot be a good man?'

'It is sadly not uncommon.' Henrietta traced the rim of her coffee cup, a suspicion forming. Enberry Abbey was near Millford, and Edmund had once told her Marlow's father – *his* godfather – had drowned in a river accident. 'Theo, I realise your father died before I was born, but do I know the family?'

His eyes cut to hers. 'Yes.'

Ah, so it was as she'd thought. Neither good nor bad, but certainly interesting to contemplate. 'Your father was the previous Lord Marlow.'

He tightened his jaw, looking off into the distance, but gave a curt nod.

'You're Edmund's cousin,' she said quietly.

Theo gave her an incredulous stare. '*That* is the relation you mention, when there is a nearer, dreadful one?'

She reached for his hand again. 'Dear Theo. The present viscount being your half-brother doesn't alter who *you* are. You are good, kind and brilliant, as different to him as the sun is to the darkest night.'

'I despise him,' Theo hissed. 'He is vicious and vindictive, and cares for no one but himself. Yet the same man's blood runs in my veins as in his.'

Henrietta leant closer. 'Is that why my tryst with Marlow affected you so?'

Theo gripped her hand tightly. 'He would have hurt you. I don't know how, whether in heart, mind, or body, but he would have hurt you had you taken him as your lover. Far more than a mention in a gossip column that almost everyone treats as rubbish.'

'But I didn't need your interference. I had already come to that conclusion myself. That's why I sent him away.'

'I know,' he said heavily. 'Rather, I know *now*.'

He was the picture of misery. Henrietta let the matter go,

turning instead to something gnawing at her curiosity. 'Do you think Edmund knew of your connection to Marlow when he saw you in the workhouse?'

'I doubt it,' Theo answered. 'Neither Marlow nor your husband ever gave me reason to believe they suspected a connection. Or anyone else, for that matter.'

She tapped her fingers on the table. 'He couldn't have known. If he had, he would have taken a greater interest in you. You see, though of course I never knew the late Viscount Marlow – your father, I mean – he was Edmund's godfather, and dear to my husband's heart. Edmund spoke nothing but good about him. Yes, your father was known to have a weakness for women, but he was also a brilliant politician, a great Whig leader and well regarded in society. It was Marlow's *mother* whom Edmund disliked profoundly. He described her as vicious to servants, savage to her horses, even degrading to her own son. She's the reason Edmund always strove to be at peace with Marlow, even when Marlow would attack him ruthlessly in Parliament. He said Marlow hadn't stood a chance to learn kindness with such a mother.'

'Well, naturally, I despise her also. She murdered my mother – though I've always assumed my *father's* unfaithfulness drove her to some of her cruelty.' Theo spat out the word 'father', as if it were distasteful. 'No matter if he possessed some leadership qualities, I shall never think well of him.'

'In the end,' Henrietta said gently, 'his character is irrelevant. *You* are a good and kind man, and that is all that matters.'

Her words did not seem to soothe him. 'Why all this profession of my goodness?' he asked, his tone sceptical. 'I thought you hated me?'

'I don't hate you.' She looked at her folded hands. 'In fact, at the current moment, I'm inclined to think very well of you indeed.'

'Now that you know I'm half blue-blooded?' he asked cuttingly.

She grew angry. 'Stop it, Theodore! Such a comment is

unworthy of you and demeans me. I think well of you because you have been exceptionally generous and good to me, and I am extremely grateful.'

Theo's shoulders slouched. His small flare of temper melted away, leaving only quiet sadness in its wake. His frank but never frightening displays of emotion – quickly tempered – were something Henrietta appreciated, after living so long with someone who kept nearly all emotion hidden.

'Forgive me, Henrietta.' He raked a hand through his hair before dropping his arm heavily on the tabletop. 'This subject doesn't bring out the best of me.'

They fell silent, finishing their coffees and perusing the periodicals, but Henrietta struggled to concentrate and soon suggested they walk to Severn House.

'We'll have to wait for Perceval to emerge, for my servants won't permit us access unless I reveal myself,' she said as they strolled briskly along Park Lane. 'Let us sit in the park and watch the door.'

Henrietta led Theo through the Chesterfield Gate to a bench with a clear view of Severn House through Hyde Park's wrought-iron railing.

As they sat, his nearness brought the pleasant scent of shaving soap. 'So what's the plan?' he asked. 'How do you intend to confront Perceval?'

Henrietta considered. 'I must approach him when there are no servants about. Perceval isn't a brave man. If we can catch him alone, we have a chance of frightening him into damning himself.' She frowned, glancing behind her shoulder. The park was dotted with pedestrians strolling the lanes and equestrians on the bridle paths. 'The trouble is, every moment in Mayfair increases my chances of being recognised.'

'If you are spotted, we will run,' Theo said. 'I know the back ways, the concealed lanes, the hidden places. We'll flee to the horses and out of London, where we'll disappear into the country to continue the investigation.'

Henrietta blinked, impressed by his forethought. 'That's all well but for our lack of money.'

'I am strong and a hard worker. I'll provide for you.' Theo's voice was steady, his gaze unwavering, and Henrietta felt a flutter in her chest. 'Not in the manner to which you are accustomed, but I will keep you clothed and well fed, with a roof protecting you, a fire in your hearth and a comfortable bed to sleep upon. Anything you need, I shall earn, so you may work towards proving your innocence in safety.'

Her heart swelled as if it would burst; it was the most romantic declaration she'd ever received. For a moment, she allowed herself to imagine a simple country life with him, extending far beyond their investigation. She pushed aside thoughts of the inevitable hardships – including her lack of housewifery knowledge like baking or sewing – and instead bathed her vision in a golden wash. A quaint cottage with roses and chickens, with Theo stacking wood while blurry-featured poppets ran about his legs. And, for a moment, it was all she wanted. But reality soon intruded. She could not live in hiding, in obscurity, cut off from her family for ever. Neither did she want to abandon her dreams of aiding reforms and supporting Theo's journalism.

Still, Henrietta keenly felt the generosity of his offer – and with that, she knew two things: Theo would make an excellent husband and father, and the future Mrs Theodore Hawke would be a fortunate woman indeed.

'Thank you.' She slipped her hand in his, lacing their fingers together. The weight of her previous deception tugged upon her conscience and she wanted nothing but honesty between them. 'Theo, I wish to make a confession.'

*

Theo's last defences against loving Henrietta crumbled when she explained the terms of her husband's will and confessed she'd considered using him to get her with child.

'I always had reservations, Theo.' Her eyes glistened with unshed tears. 'I don't think it was quite fair of Edmund to ask me to take a lover – not when I was so innocent and didn't understand what it would entail – though he was as trapped by circumstances as I was. But the fact that I had reservations doesn't excuse that if you had ... *you-know-what* with me last night, I would have let you complete the act in whatever manner you chose, without telling you first about the will. I am heartily ashamed of myself, Theo.'

He embraced her, gently pressing her head against his shoulder. 'I forgive you.'

She blinked up at him. 'How can you so quickly?'

'Because I know you were acting out of a misguided sense of duty.'

'You understand!' she said, as if it were a marvel. 'Duty and individuality have clashed within me all my life – and that conflict made me miserable during my marriage. As a child, I was told to sit when I wanted to run, to be silent when I wanted to question, to conform to the values of others when I wanted to be true to myself. I was nothing beyond my pedigree, my face, my body. A tool of advancement for my family, a vessel for my husband's heir. But there are some things I cannot do, even for duty. To be dishonest is to betray myself.'

He smiled tenderly and she reached for his hand. 'Theo, please know that even when I gave myself other reasons, I wanted you for *you*. More than simply to fulfil a duty. Whatever our differences, I've always recognised you as a man of integrity, albeit sometimes misguided, and the more time we spent together, the more I found to admire. Your kindness and generosity. Your cheerfulness through every stage of our journey. I admire how you express your emotions openly, even anger, and yet forgive quickly. Though,' she added, her brow furrowing slightly, 'I'm not certain why you were angry with me both times before we were intimate.'

'I was angry because I knew you were withholding the truth,' he said. 'Perceval revealed these terms of the will when he called upon me two days ago.'

She drew back to meet his gaze, but he pulled her close again, unwilling to release their embrace yet. 'That's why you didn't . . . complete it.'

He rubbed soothing circles on her back. 'No, love, that's not why I didn't take your virginity last night.' He'd refrained because he'd known he'd fall in love if he did. Now, he found himself in the same hopeless situation, even *without* the coupling.

'I wouldn't have thought you would have gone through with it if you had known,' she said.

'I wouldn't have finished inside you without protection, no. But there are ways to couple and yet avoid pregnancy.'

A pause followed. Then, her voice muffled by his coat, she said, 'I knew that, but . . . what are they?'

He explained about withdrawal, sheaths and sponges. 'Or there's what we did last night, which brings pleasure without penetration.'

Henrietta nestled closer, snuggling deep into his embrace, and so they sat, their breath rising and falling in tandem.

Suddenly she stiffened, her body tense.

'Perceval.' Her chin tilted subtly towards Severn House. 'With Jane Babcock but no servants. This is our chance.'

She sprang to her feet and strode purposefully towards her quarry while Percy and Miss Babcock strolled through the gate, both clad in black, their arms intertwined.

They gazed intensely into each other's eyes. Like two people who shared a deep love.

Or possibly a dark secret.

Theo rose to follow Henrietta, his senses on alert. He'd do anything to protect her.

CHAPTER 23

Perceval in the Park

Henrietta wished Perceval were alone, not accompanied by Jane Babcock. Nor was busy Hyde Park ideal for a confrontation. Stepping onto the path some twenty paces behind her husband's cousin, she reminded herself, 'Needs must when the devil drives.'

'Indeed,' Theo agreed quietly at her side.

'Keep trailing them,' she told him. 'Meanwhile, I shall cross the lawn and attempt to draw them off the path near the Ring, so we can speak to them away from prying eyes and ears.'

The Ring, a racetrack surrounded by a dense band of elms, lay a short distance from the main public road. Henrietta hitched her skirts to arrive ahead of Perceval and Jane. At the northern edge, the trees grew the thickest. There she waited. When Perceval neared, trailed by Theo, she let out a sharp scream and collapsed to the ground, clutching her ankle.

Perceval and Jane turned towards her cry, but so did several other people, including Theo, who sprinted towards her, concern etched on his face. Perceval and Jane proceeded on their way.

Henrietta called loudly to Theo. 'Sir, 'tis my ankle I injured, but I fear I may lose my baby as well. Please fetch a lady to assist me.'

Realisation dawned on Theo's face. He pulled his hat brim low, shading his features, and called towards Jane Babcock, hiding all trace of his faint Cockney accent. 'Madam, this lady requires the assistance of another lady. May I presume to trouble you for a moment of your time?'

Jane didn't hesitate to step forward, despite discontented rumbles from Perceval. 'Nonsense, Perceval,' she said over her shoulder. 'One should never turn one's back on someone in need.'

Guilt twisted Henrietta's gut, but the deception was for Edmund's sake. She *had* to discover the real killer and catching Perceval unawares was her best chance to assess his guilt or innocence.

She let Jane assist her up, still pretending to have a sore ankle until Perceval approached. Then she whispered a quick apology in Jane's ear, grabbed both of her wrists and pulled them behind her back, and stepped deep into the cover of the elm trees.

Perceval's eyes widened in genuine terror. He leapt to the rescue, but Theo intercepted him and mimicked Henrietta's stance. Perceval barely thrashed as Theo restrained him, but he did sputter with anger. 'What is the meaning of this? If you seek to rob us, this is stupidly done, in sight of many bystanders. Unhand us at once or we shall call for help, and the two of you will rot in Newgate.'

Jane remained calm, peering keenly at Theo. 'You're that journalist. Theodore Hawke.'

Perceval twisted to view his captor. 'And so he is, my love! Hawke, you blasted fool, I sent you to find my cousin's widow. What do you mean by—' He jerked his head towards Henrietta and squinted at her veiled face before turning as red as a pickled beet. 'You *witch*. So you cast your lusty lures and caught Hawke, did you?'

Theo's jaw clenched. 'That's enough, Percy. I won't hear you talk to her that way, any more than you'd let me disparage Miss Babcock.'

'Ah, so it *is* like that,' Perceval said spitefully. 'I thought you didn't stoop to that level, Hawke. I thought you were vehemently opposed to the idea.'

Henrietta's stomach churned. 'The idea of what?'

'Nothing but Percy's foul suggestion that I purposely seduce you in order to expose you as an "adulterous thief", as he said. You know I would never have done such a thing.'

'I do indeed,' she replied, acquitting Theo, but growing furious at her husband's cousin. 'Perceval, you are a vicious snake.'

'Whore.' Perceval spat the insult back and Henrietta thought Theo would explode in anger. He must've increased his grip because Perceval began to squirm.

'Percy, this is your last warning.' Theo's voice was as tight as a bowstring. 'Do not insult Her Grace's honour.'

'Taking on the airs of a gentleman now, are you, Hawke?' Perceval said, his voice a fraction of an octave higher as he wriggled. 'Speaking of honour? Do you intend to *challenge* me?'

'Perceval.' Jane's tone was reprimanding. 'That's exactly the sort of attitude I've told you to curtail. Mr Hawke is correct to defend the duchess's honour, just as any man is correct to defend the honour of any woman.'

'But do you see her stomach, Jane?' Perceval simmered with anger. 'She has something stuffed up her petticoats, pretending she's with child. It is just as I said. She will find a foundling and steal my inheritance.'

'Is that so, ma'am?' Jane asked. Though she was a slip of a thing and only nineteen years of age, her gaze didn't waver.

Admirable.

Henrietta gentled her voice. 'The succession of the dukedom is very much on my mind, but my first concern is to discover who murdered my husband, so no innocent dies for the crime. Perceval is the most likely suspect.'

Perceval scoffed. '*You* are the likeliest suspect, if it wasn't the maid. You were alone with him at the time of his death.'

'I worked that out long ago – you framed me as the murderess by using a poison that doesn't act instantly. It's a perfect crime, Perceval – if you get away with it, both Edmund and I will be dead, with no impediment to your becoming duke and with no expensive widow to support. But I shall ensure you don't elude justice.'

'Pretty theory, but a figment of your imagination that certainly won't hold up against the evidence of your guilt.'

'But I had no motive, Perceval. Think on that. Why would I have killed him? Even if I were that depraved, why do it without having first secured my fortune through the birth of a male heir?'

'Perhaps you are in love with one of the men you cavort with,' Perceval replied.

'With what men do I cavort?' she asked, exasperated. 'Name a single lover ever linked to me, other than Marlow, thanks to Mr Hawke misinterpreting an interaction.'

Perceval sneered. 'There's only one way to interpret Marlow ploughing you up a garden wall.'

'Oh?' she said. 'Just as there is only one way to interpret your placing diamonds around Désirée du Pont's neck while engaged to Jane?' Perceval narrowed his eyes, but Jane registered no surprise or concern. Clearly, Perceval *had* spoken to her about the matter. 'Of course there are always multiple sides to a story. Mr Hawke, tell Perceval whether you misinterpreted my interaction with Marlow.'

Theo cleared his throat. 'Her Grace is innocent of adultery. She was always faithful to her husband in mind, body and spirit.'

'Ha!' Perceval laughed. 'She's convinced *you*, but you've fallen for her wiles. She could feed you any story and you'd believe it.'

'No,' Theo said. 'I speak the truth.'

'Ah, she provided proof, then, did she? No doubt you checked if she's intact—'

Theo snarled as he tightened his grip on Perceval, who wriggled again like the worm he was.

'Please soften your hold, Mr Hawke,' Jane said, and Theo did so immediately. Perceval fell limp and panting against his body. 'This is descending into unpleasant squabbling when we ought to have a rational conversation.' Jane's words held a note of finality; she would make an effective duchess. 'I believe you had no motive to kill your husband, Your Grace. But Perceval also had no motive.'

'Is not his inheritance of a title, influence and wealth motive enough?' Henrietta asked.

'Motive enough to abandon all human decency and kill my own cousin?' Perceval sputtered. 'People don't kill for titles, Henrietta. Not in modern times at least. Besides, why would I risk everything *now*, when I had just been fortunate enough to win the heart and hand of the most wonderful lady in the world? Why *now*, when I was about to stand for Parliament in the upcoming Wendington by-election? Where I was nearly certain to win, with both Edmund and the bishop's backing?'

Henrietta frowned. 'The borough where Bishop Babcock resides?'

'Yes, the MP died. And lest you think me responsible for *that* death as well, I'll have you know he was four-and-ninety years of age and suffered from a lung infection. He died in bed surrounded by his family.'

Henrietta glanced at Jane. 'Is this true, about the by-election?'

'The solemn truth,' she said. 'When Perceval, the duke and my father presented me with this idea in early March, I felt I could finally accept Perceval as a husband. Although I already loved him dearly despite his faults, I couldn't marry a man without purpose. When he first proposed, at Christmas, I insisted he change his lifestyle if he hoped to win my hand. To my great surprise, he began at once and has never wavered.'

Henrietta decided to tell what she knew. It was worth having to buy Miss du Pont a new necklace to save Jane from an unhappy marriage. 'He wavered when he visited his mistress in January.'

'Strictly speaking, yes,' Jane said calmly. 'But he confessed all to me at once, and, while you may think me naïve, I am inclined to believe him the victim in that case. Miss du Pont and her manservant bound him to a chair.'

Henrietta raised her eyebrows. 'I think you *very* naïve if Perceval told you so and you believed him.'

'He also showed me the rope burns,' Jane said firmly. 'And his story was collaborated by Miss du Pont herself, who is *not* a kind woman. After Perceval gave her the necklace, which I watched from afar, I caught up with her near the gate. She admitted she forced the … interaction and acted as if she had every right to treat a man however she wished.'

'Men haven't been kind to her,' Henrietta said. 'You and I cannot judge a life so different from our own, I think.'

'No matter what one has suffered, it is not right to inflict suffering on others in retribution,' Jane said sensibly, and Henrietta felt that truth as well. 'Furthermore, by Miss du Pont's own admission, Perceval was always fair to her. She was simply angry about the dissolution of the arrangement and wanted revenge. Were the tables turned and a man had treated a woman as she treated Perceval on that occasion, you would be appalled. You'd blame the man, not the woman. Why not afford Perceval the same consideration?'

With a heavy sigh, Henrietta admitted she might have been mistaken. A weight descended on her shoulders. When there were always multiple sides to a story, how was she ever to determine what happened to Edmund?

Jane's expression softened. 'Truly, Your Grace, Perceval is striving to be a better man.'

'Yet he physically attacked me,' Henrietta said. 'After the will reading. Did you know?'

Jane's questioning gaze turned to Perceval.

Perceval pursed his lips. 'Only to prevent her leaving. Your parents and I agreed it was best if she stay with them, since we all knew her to be lying about being with child.'

'I never said I was with child,' Henrietta said. 'I simply didn't say I *wasn't*.'

Jane looked upon her fiancé severely. 'Perceval, you owe Her Grace an apology.'

Perceval started to whine. 'I never hurt her. She fought back and *I* was the one who ended injured.'

'Perceval!' the small lady admonished, and that was the final word.

Perceval looked sheepish. 'Forgive me, Henrietta, for the way I treated you in the weeks after Edmund's death.'

'I don't,' Henrietta replied. 'Not yet, anyway. And I have many questions still, for much about your story doesn't make sense. Why give Miss du Pont the diamond necklace to silence her blackmail if Jane already knew about the . . . encounter you had in January?'

'Because Désirée threatened to go to the gossip gleaners, just as I was preparing for the by-election. I couldn't have that in the papers or I'd risk losing. In a district that loves Bishop Babcock, voters wouldn't have taken kindly to my slighting his daughter.'

Henrietta considered. 'When did Edmund learn of the necklace?'

'The evening before he died, when we dined at Severn House. Earlier that day, Désirée had viciously informed me that she'd fed Hawke our meeting location to ensure he observed the interaction.

Désirée was intent on destroying my happiness with Jane – and I feared she might succeed, for the parliamentary seat was vital to demonstrate my commitment to self-improvement.' He glanced at Theo. 'Losing that seat due to Hawke's exposé would not only jeopardise my political aspiration but also risk losing Jane. I wanted to disclose the situation to Edmund before it became public.'

'Or you wanted to kill Edmund, because Jane would surely marry a duke.' Henrietta was still reluctant to believe his tales. 'Explain this: if you had that discussion the night *before* Edmund's death, why did you wish to speak to him so urgently *after* the article's publication?'

'Because Désirée *still* wasn't satisfied, even after my public humiliation. She is intent upon either destroying me or extracting all she can for her financial gain. That day, I received a new threat from her and I went immediately to Edmund for advice, for I didn't know how to weather the storm without aid.'

Jane was nodding. 'Miss du Pont is *not* a kind woman,' she said again.

Henrietta recalled something Edmund had said, just before his death: 'It remains to be seen if Perceval's newfound maturity can weather this storm.' He'd cautioned Henrietta against optimism.

'What did Edmund reply that afternoon in the library?' she asked, hoping Perceval's answer might go some way towards proving or disproving the veracity of his story.

'That I should seize the opportunity to prove my newfound maturity, to Jane and all. That I should shoulder duty and not balk at challenges, but rise above them.'

Yes, that sounded exactly like something Edmund would say.

Perceval pouted a little. 'I could tell he doubted my ability to succeed ...'

That matched what Edmund had told her, Henrietta realised.

'But I was determined,' Perceval continued. 'Immediately after the interaction in the library, I went to Jane and her father. We spoke for hours, and at last I realised honesty was my best path forward. We were drafting an address I meant to publish prior to the election, in which I laid bare the facts of my association with Désirée, when my manservant arrived with word of Edmund's death.'

'My father and I witnessed his shock, Your Grace,' Jane added. 'I have no doubt he felt true grief.'

'Of course I did.' Tears pooled in Perceval's eyes. 'You may not believe this, Henrietta, but as a fatherless boy I looked up to Edmund. The occasions he made time for me became my happiest childhood memories...'

'Yet you blackmailed him, once you learnt of a certain matter?' Henrietta snapped.

Perceval flinched, but he held her gaze. 'I made *many* poor choices in my youth. As the only child of a bereaved mother, I was frequently overindulged. I fell to bad influences at Eton and maintained those acquaintances into adulthood. Some might say Edmund, as the head of the family, should have taken a hand in my upbringing. But I blame no one but myself; recognising this has been crucial to my self-improvement. The only proof I can offer of my underlying good intentions is that even *before* meeting Jane, I cut all ties with the Scourers.'

Henrietta met Theo's eyes. She read a quiet acceptance in the slight raise of his shoulder and the tilt of one brow. 'Why then were you so cruel to *me* after Edmund's death?'

'It always struck me as mighty hypocritical of my cousin to lecture me on duty and responsibility, when he married you only to cheat me.' Perceval scowled. 'Neither of you were friends to me, Henrietta.'

Henrietta's head began to throb. The relationship between the cousins had always been complex and bad behaviour had occurred on both sides. Did this make Perceval a murderer, though? It was beginning to seem unlikely, especially given Jane's steadfast, practical support.

But one thing still didn't make sense. 'Perceval, Edmund had cut off your allowance. How did you get the money for the necklace?'

'I bought the necklace,' Jane said. 'No doubt Rundell and Bridge's has an account of the sale, should you not believe me.'

'I have proof of everything I've told you, Henrietta,' Perceval added. 'Letters from Edmund regarding the election. Bishop Babcock has some as well. You know Edmund's hand, his voice. You'll know them to be genuine at once.'

Henrietta rubbed her temples. If only Edmund had been more upfront about his life and dealings, solving this mystery mightn't be so challenging.

As if his thoughts aligned, Theo asked, 'Would not your husband have spoken to you about this, Your Grace?'

'No,' Henrietta said. 'Edmund disliked my talking about politics.' Or Perceval. Or James, or estates, or many other things. Edmund had spoken to her of horses and sailing, of dinner menus and social duties. Of men she might consider taking as lovers on his gentle but endless quest for an heir. But never of important matters.

She loosened her hold on Jane's wrists. 'I'm sorry,' she said softly. 'I hope I didn't hurt you?'

'Not at all.' Jane rubbed her wrists as she observed Henrietta closely. 'I rather hope we haven't hurt *you*, ma'am. I know you loved the duke.'

'Thank you.' Henrietta blinked back tears. She was impossibly emotional lately. Yes, there was a great deal of strain in her life, but she prided herself on her self-control. Lest she succumb to sobbing now, she turned to Perceval with another question. 'Why then did Edmund change his will the night before he died?'

Perceval shook his head. 'How should I know? I had hoped

Edmund trusted me. It was a bitter blow to receive that final confirmation that he had no faith in me at all.'

'I have a theory on that matter,' Theo said. 'Could the rewriting of the will relate to His Grace's encounter with Mr Beaucastle the day before his death?'

Henrietta reflected. Yes, Edmund had intended to will Grenham to James. She'd known that – that's why she'd been so surprised when it had been willed to her. What if Edmund's personal fortune had also been willed elsewhere? Perhaps Edmund had always intended a widowed Henrietta to live on her dower's share of the dukedom's income. Perhaps his favouring of her in the will rewriting was bitterness towards *James*?

'But why then make such a fuss over my having a year to deliver a child?'

'Recall what Mr Beaucastle said on that matter as well,' Theo said.

Henrietta thought back. Edmund had told James that the end of their love affair had made him view his marriage differently. That she was loyal to a fault – and that fault, of course, was her refusal to take a lover to give him an heir – and he needed to act. So, as best she could conclude, Edmund truly *had* intended to conceive his own son by her. The kiss the night before his death had been a first tentative step in that direction, as she suspected when she'd spoken with James.

She mused aloud. 'I suppose he specified a year because he was an eleven-month baby himself. Given the rumours about me, he wrote his will to ensure that if he got me with child and died while I was pregnant, there would be no speculation regarding the parentage of our baby. After all, he hadn't expected to die the next day.'

The thought of what she had lost – a family with Edmund – was enough to break her heart all over again. She closed her eyes until the stinging prickle of tears passed and she'd regained control over her emotions. 'He intended to father a son on me.'

Jane encased her in delicate arms. 'You lost that too, when he died. Your grief is great and there is little I can do to ease it. But know that I am your friend, and you are in my prayers daily.'

Henrietta returned the embrace. Jane was wise beyond her years. No wonder Edmund had admired her. Henrietta herself had not been so sensible at the age of nineteen. She'd been lovelorn and headstrong, determined to have Edmund or nothing, unwilling to relinquish an impossible dream.

'I shall help him, ma'am,' Jane was whispering in her ear. 'I shall help him make good use of his seat in the Upper House. We shall continue to strive for the reforms to which your husband dedicated his life. Under my tutelage, Perceval will learn. Just now, we were talking over this excellent treatise.' She released the embrace, reached into her reticule and withdrew a copy of the same treatise Henrietta had been reading the afternoon Edmund had died – the one she now realised was written by Theo. 'It advises the revision of voting restrictions, to allow everyone the right to vote, as well as the—'

'The revision of property rights, so married women can own their property in their own right.' Henrietta finished for her. 'It's a very good treatise and as I personally know the author, I can attest to his excellent political thinking.'

She smiled at Theo, who recoiled in surprise before rather sheepishly grinning in return.

Jane observed, once again not missing a thing. 'Ah, you wrote this, Mr Hawke? I commend you – I have followed your anonymous treatises for some time. I can always tell your writing—'

'By his rational approach to seeking truth?' Henrietta said.

Jane smiled, showing a dimple in her left cheek. 'Yes, and by the way he uses his very understanding of opposing arguments to support his thesis.'

Theo muttered a rather embarrassed thanks and released Perceval.

Perceval rolled his shoulders. 'Henrietta, if it is any comfort, I expressed to the magistrate on the day of Edmund's death my sincere doubts that you killed him. Although I admit the evidence is condemning, I shall support you, should this come to trial. I was the one who suggested they bring in your maid; in my mind, she is the most likely culprit as she poured the wine.'

'Edmund poured the wine,' Henrietta replied. 'And I do wish you had left Libby out of this – she couldn't say boo to a goose. No, if it wasn't you, me, or James Beaucastle, it was Marlow, by simple process of elimination. I merely need proof.'

'Perhaps that's best left to the authorities?' Perceval said.

'No,' she replied, smoothing her skirts over the swell of her pretend pregnancy. 'The people will demand that *someone* hang for Edmund's murder and it would be much easier to hang a maid or a duchess over a viscount, who would be tried by his peers and no doubt found innocent. A nobleman hasn't hanged in this country for sixty years.'

'You are a noblewoman. You could expect the same,' Jane said.

'I can't. Too much evidence stands against me and public opinion has long questioned my faithfulness. The prosecution could easily resurrect old rumours. Moreover, I won't be tried by a jury of noblemen, as I am not a peer in my own right. And I must protect Libby. It is essential I uncover irrefutable proof of Marlow's guilt. Something his peers cannot deny without incensing the populace, which they cannot afford to do.'

Jane extended her hand to Henrietta. 'Then I wish you the best of luck, Your Grace.'

Henrietta pulled her into an embrace instead. 'Oh, I *do* like you,' she whispered into Jane's ear. 'I am happy for you to take my place. You will be the duchess I wanted to be, and may God bless your work.'

She released her and found that Jane's eyes swam with tears. 'That means the world, coming from Your Grace.'

Henrietta smiled, feeling like a duchess herself for the first time in days. 'I must be Henrietta to you from now on.' She turned to Perceval, lifting her chin and speaking with the authority ingrained since childhood. Even as a fugitive fighting for her life, she could still be a great lady. 'Perceval, I am not with child,' she said. There was a brief twinge of grief, for she was relinquishing the dream of a family with or for Edmund, but it soon passed. The same reason that had prevented her from fulfilling that request while Edmund had lived still stood – deceit went against her nature. 'I will inform Mr Quigley that you are the undisputed Duke of Severn as soon as I have cleared my name.'

Jane kissed her hand. 'That is very good of you.'

'No, it is the right thing to do.' Henrietta released a deep breath. 'Of course, if I am hanged, then you will achieve the same.'

Perceval shook his head. 'We shall do everything in our power to ensure you aren't hanged.'

She appreciated the support but doubted his ability to help. 'For now, just conceal both my presence in London and my association with Mr Hawke.'

Perceval reached into his pocket. 'D'ye need money?'

Henrietta did, but hesitated to ask and in the interim, Theo answered. 'I have money, Your Grace.'

Perceval's eyes lit at Theo's use of the honorific.

'Remember, Perceval,' Henrietta said firmly, 'what "Your Grace" signifies. Not wealth or power, but favour granted by the Crown, which rules by divine right. A favour that comes with solemn responsibility and duty to this country, its king, and its people. As Duke of Severn, duty must always, always come before your own needs and wishes. Never forget that or you forget yourself before God.'

Jane clasped a hand to her heart. 'I couldn't have said it better.'

Perceval and his fiancée were on their way soon after, walking arm in arm through Hyde Park, and Henrietta leant against an elm tree for support. Emotions washed over her – fear and exhaustion, grief and yet tenuous hope.

Theo laid a gentle hand on her shoulder. 'That was well done, but I imagine it wasn't easy. Need a drink?'

'Only an embrace,' she said, turning into his arms. She rested her head against his broad shoulder. '*This* is nice.'

'It is.' He rubbed his palm over her tight back, easing her tension. 'What's our next step?'

'There's only one suspect left, so we have our killer, don't we?' she asked glumly. 'I suppose Marlow wasn't as pleased as Edmund thought about their meeting that afternoon.'

'To Marlow House, then?'

'To Marlow House.'

Joining hands, they walked from the park.

CHAPTER 24

A Companionable Evening

A maid beating a rug in the mews behind Marlow House was easily bribed for information for a shilling, but she said Marlow wasn't home. 'He's not like to return 'til the morrow – then he's off to his manor in Surrey.'

'He's travelling to Enberry Abbey tomorrow?' Henrietta asked.

'Aye, but it won't do you no good to seek him out anyway,' the girl added, with a desolate glance at Henrietta's stomach. 'Even if that's his lordship's babe, you won't get nothing from him.'

A loitering groom added his bit free of charge. 'Aye, his lordship won't help you, miss. He's already got a new mistress and he's with her tonight.' He nodded towards Theo. 'You let that fellow do right by you, eh?'

Henrietta opened her mouth to protest the misunderstanding, but, before any words emerged, Theo assured the groom he would.

Then he hired a hackney to return them to the city.

A wave of exhaustion washed over her as she collapsed onto the bench seat inside.

Theo took her hand. 'You're tired.'

'I am,' she said. 'But I think it best if we confront Marlow in Surrey. We have several more hours of daylight. Shall we return to the Pickled Dog? It's no more than two hours on the road.'

'I propose we stay here tonight,' Theo said. 'My rooms are more comfortable than the Pickled Dog, and Mrs Ford's dinner far better. You take the bed, I'll sleep on a pallet and we'll leave at daybreak.'

His plan sounded *nearly* perfect.

But Henrietta had no intention of letting Theo sleep on the floor.

Theo practically licked his plate clean of the hearty dinner Mrs Ford supplied at a moment's notice, as if she'd been cooking all afternoon. Henrietta ate with equal enthusiasm, which delighted the landlady no end. Mrs Ford fluttered and fanned herself as they devoured fried beef in morel sauce, spinach with cream and poached eggs, cold jellied eels, and plum cake, stuffed with currants and topped with custard.

Afterwards, the landlady left them with a tea tray. Theo's gaze lingered on Henrietta as she nestled into his armchair, her hand curled around Mrs Ford's prized floral cup, wisps of steam playing before her heavy lids. Never had he wished more fervently that no class distinctions lay between them, for he loved the sight of her wearing clothes he'd purchased, in lodgings he'd provided.

This stolen moment was precious, seated together in companionable silence, a breeze dancing through the room, the late afternoon sun mellowing to golden hues.

Theo ran his fingers through his hair.

Lord, but he was in a fine mess. Caught up in a star-crossed love if ever there was one.

'Dinner left me delightfully drowsy,' Henrietta said, yawning.

He glanced at his small mantel clock. 'Not yet six, but we might as well sleep. It'll be easier to rise early.'

Henrietta drained her tea and rose. 'May I wash in your basin?'

He leapt to his feet. 'I'll fetch hot water.'

Ten minutes later, he'd taken the tea tray to the kitchen and returned with a steaming pitcher, leaving her to wash in his bedroom.

Then he paced, unable to settle.

Concern after concern raced through his mind. His half-brother was a dangerous man. What was worse, he was dangerous and clever. If Marlow was indeed the killer of the Duke of Severn, they'd be hard-pressed to find evidence or obtain a confession. Yet everything from Henrietta's safety to the wellbeing of Mr Scripp's employees depended upon their success.

And what if the success came? Yes, Henrietta would be saved, and that was *nearly* everything, but it wasn't *quite* everything, because he'd still lose her. She would return to her world and he to his, and though they might see each other on occasion – he amongst the sight-seeing crowds and she amongst the glittering beau monde – their lives would no longer intersect meaningfully.

Because even in the unlikely circumstance of Henrietta falling in love with a Newgate-born gossip-gleaner, she'd never marry someone so beneath her in status and fortune. Nor would her family – her father, her brothers – permit it.

Theo poured two fingers of gin and tossed it back in one biting swallow. Then he cradled his head on the mantel.

His bedchamber door creaked; he needed to oil the hinge. He looked up and Henrietta stood before him, one hand on the door jamb, wearing the chemise he'd bought her earlier that day. Soft cotton, blue ribbon ties, the prettiest in the shop. Worth every extra shilling.

'I left some water for you,' she said, smoothing her freshly combed blonde waves. 'Come in when you wish.'

She was more beautiful than the sun.

He wanted her to know.

'Henrietta...' The words of love stuck in his throat. As did the enquiry if their second partnership still stood.

She took a step in his direction. 'Yes, Theo?'

'Er, thank you,' he said. 'I'll be in soon.' If she asked for him, he wouldn't bungle matters as he'd done the night before, but he would not initiate the encounter. She knew her own mind now, of that he was confident. If she wanted him, he'd know. Eventually.

She held his gaze and then lifted a shoulder. 'Whenever you're ready.'

She glided back into the room, and Theo poured himself another gin as she pulled back the bedcovers and fluffed his pillow. The sunlight streaming through her cotton chemise silhouetted her body. Breasts, hips, bottom.

Theo squeezed his eyes shut and swallowed his gin, controlling his lust lest he develop a ragingly obvious cockstand. Only when the rustles and sighs of her settling on the mattress ceased did he open his eyes again, enter the room with single-minded focus and ready himself for bed.

After completing his ablutions, he met her gaze in the looking glass. Her head was propped against a pillow and his quilt was tucked under her chin.

'Good night, then,' Theo said stiffly.

'Good night? I doubt it will be, if you sleep on a pallet on the floor, for then I shall be cold in this bed.'

His pulse raced. 'And is there a way I could ensure your warmth, Your Grace?'

Slowly, she slid the covers down, revealing bare shoulders and the tops of her breasts. 'I foolishly removed my chemise and now I'm shivering. The only way you could warm me is to sleep with me.'

Theo had never undressed so quickly in his life.

CHAPTER 25

A Different Sort of Tussle

Theo was glorious nude. All taut muscle and hardness, the shaft of his manhood erect, and Henrietta wasn't the least bit cold.

A fire raged inside her.

This time, she wasn't frightened. This time, she had no doubts. She knew exactly what she wanted.

'Will you do *everything* with me tonight?' she asked as he slid under the covers beside her, bringing a rush of cool air and then the radiating warmth of his skin.

He lay on his side, propping himself on one elbow, and ran the backs of his fingers down her arm. She shivered deliciously in response. 'Are you certain you want that?'

'Absolutely certain. My conflicting feelings about what I thought Edmund wanted gave rise to my fear yesterday. Please, show me how to please you?'

He smiled tenderly. 'You're pleasing me now, just by lying next to me.'

She lifted a quizzical brow. 'But lying next to each other isn't *everything* I want to do and I'm not certain how to proceed.'

'Do whatever feels good or exciting, and I will follow your lead.'

She nibbled her bottom lip. 'And if you don't like it?'

'That's a slim chance, but if I don't, I'll tell you.' He threaded his fingers through a thick strand of her hair and brought it to his lips. 'You do the same with me, and then trust and honesty will be at the centre of our union.'

She pressed her hand to the curls on his chest, over his heart. 'Trust and honesty?'

He grinned. 'The two most powerful aphrodisiacs.'

Her heart swelled. 'I like that.'

She slid the flat of her palms over his forearms, which were veined and muscled, and lightly covered in dark hair, while he grazed the curve of her hip. Sensation rippled where he touched. Her inner muscles involuntarily contracted and a first surge of pleasure made her arch her back to press herself against his chest. Her nipples ached when they touched his skin. Another throb of pleasure shot between her legs and she brought her lips to his. He tightened his hold on her waist, pressing their hips together so his erection lay between them, iron hard against her unyielding pubic bone. He cupped her neck and their lips brushed together, soft, sensuous.

She held back her kiss. The anticipation was a bliss of its own. Her heart skipped beats every time his breath swelled his chest against her. She could make out each golden fleck in his heavy-lidded eyes, hazed with desire.

'Sweet Jesus, Henrietta.' His lips moved against hers. 'Kiss me, love.'

She captured his mouth and their bodies melded together. Her hips above his, her breasts against his chest, the area between her legs soft, wet and wanting to yield, and his shaft rigid and hot on her abdomen.

She slid her thumb over its slick tip. He gasped sharply, breaking their kiss, and she hesitated. 'You don't like it? Or you do?'

'I do.' He kissed her forehead, her nose, her cheeks. 'There is nowhere you could touch me that I wouldn't like, but *there*? That's like this for me.' He stroked the throbbing nub between her legs.

A wave of pleasure hit and she squirmed in his arms. 'I want to kiss you. Down there. Like you did to me, last night? May I?'

His eyes grew dark, his breath fast and pained. 'Fucking hell, yes.'

She pushed the covers to his calves, bathing his body in the evening light. Clear liquid beaded on the tip of his erection, and she slid her tongue over the velvet-smooth curve. Salty. The fluid was salty. She liked it. She liked Theo's taste, as he'd seemed to like hers. She slid her mouth down his shaft.

A moan ripped from his throat.

She sucked, as he had done to her the night before. His body stilled, but his sounds of pleasure thrilled her. She loved having him in her mouth. Loved running her tongue around his tip while she sucked. Loved how he panted for her. He was so solid, so rigid. So thick her mouth stretched to encase him.

He suddenly pulled back his hips. 'Stop, love.'

She disengaged. 'Did I hurt you?'

'No,' he said after a moment. 'You did the opposite. I've never felt anything that good in all my life, but I was about to spend and we have other business first.'

He brought her towards him, laying her back upon the crumpled mass of pillows, blankets and sheets. Then he leant over her, his hardness at the apex of her legs. She spread herself eagerly, thinking that the moment had arrived when he would take her, make her no longer a virgin.

But he didn't. He let his shaft rest between her thighs and lowered himself onto his elbows. 'Another kiss, love. I want to taste me in your mouth.'

That was so deliciously dirty, she wriggled beneath him, which evidently drove him feral. His mouth clamped over hers, his tongue thrusting her lips open. His passion was fiery, lusty, virile, and yet it was a caress as well. Even as he feasted on her mouth, he was making love to her, making her feel safe and cherished. She moaned, curved her legs around his thighs, lifted her hips to meet him, and her heart opened like a blossom, with feelings so powerful they brought tears to her eyes. She released a single sob then, and that broke their kiss, but he captured her bottom lip as he disengaged, his tongue brushing against its plump curve. After a gentle tug, he released her, only to growl against the corner of her mouth. 'I've wanted you for so long.'

She covered his jaw with kisses, wanting to imprint herself all over him. 'How long?'

'Since the first time I saw you,' he replied, which was so startling she stopped kissing him. 'Dressed in ivory lace with the bells of St George's pealing. You were a goddess walking amongst mortals. I fell in love with you, in a way.'

'You felt so much?' she asked, amazed, and he nodded sheepishly. 'And so you reacted all the more strongly when you saw me in the arms of a man you despise?'

'Yes, though I'm ashamed to admit it.' He traced her collarbone. 'That night, your behaviour seemed at odds with the woman I'd sensed you were. Instead of giving you the benefit of the doubt, I convinced myself I'd been foolish to idealise you, silly to tuck you into my heart. I started observing you, seeking evidence of flaws to excise you from my thoughts. But it didn't quite work that way. The more I saw, the more you perplexed me. Were you loving and generous? Were you cold and calculating? Were you shy? Misunderstood? Were you aloof? Or were you instead truly as lonely as you sometimes seemed, even at parties with five hundred guests? Lord, it sounds perverse now, but it is how I earn a living... and the fact of the matter is, the more I watched, the more I wanted to believe in your goodness and recapture the admiration I'd felt in Hanover Square.'

'Why? Why did it matter?'

'It was the way you looked at me on your wedding day.' He brushed an errant curl from her forehead. 'I caught your attention – I knew I did – and perhaps I imagined it, but you looked at me with genuine interest. As if you *saw* me. Truly saw *me*, as something more than another face in the crowd. Later, I doubted myself, but, then, when you saw me again in the garden niche, you *recognised* me, and I realised ... or I think I realised ... I hadn't imagined it after all.'

'You didn't imagine it.'

His brow furrowed. 'What then were you thinking when you gazed at me on your wedding day?'

Her cheeks warmed. 'I'm rather embarrassed to say.'

'You thought me attractive?'

'It wasn't that.' And lest she offend him, she quickly added, 'Of course I noticed you were handsome, but that wasn't why you caught my attention. That day was the happiest of my life. I was wholly and completely in love with Edmund. I still believed he would desire me. Being attracted to another man was the furthest thing from my mind. Even one as handsome as you.' She bit her lip. 'Theo, you may not like this, but you caught my attention because your expression reminded me of Edmund. The resemblance between you still strikes me occasionally. That's why I wasn't particularly surprised to learn you were cousins.'

'*Second* cousins. A rather distant connection.' He lifted a sceptical brow. 'I'm uncertain how I feel about your liking my looks because they remind you of your husband.'

'Please don't make something sweet into something perverse,' she said earnestly. 'I loved Edmund dearly. The reason I failed him is because I'm not able to love someone with my heart and be disloyal to him with my mind or my body. And while it's true that if he were alive, I wouldn't be here with you, now that I give myself to you in this way, there is only you, Theo. You that I'm attracted to, for *you*, not because you look like Edmund. But because I admire you.'

'That means more than you could know.' He gazed down at her tenderly. 'When you offered me a kiss that night in the garden, I was hurt. I was angry, even. Unhappy with myself, because I wanted to accept, when your husband had once given me the means to create a new life…'

'He gave you a half-crown.' She threaded her fingers through his hair and brushed the waves from his forehead. 'Edmund *was* a wonderful man, but I can attest that was by no means his greatest act of charity.'

'He gave me what I asked for, which was all I needed. I wouldn't have accepted more. But it wasn't just that that made me dislike your offer of a kiss… I hated that you offered me a *meaningless* kiss. A kiss of bribery. Of payment. If you were offering a kiss, then I wanted you to *want* to kiss me. To like me, to approve of my honour and goals, and be *moved* to kiss me. If you had, I would've instantly forgotten my respect for your husband – which I'm not proud of admitting, but it's the truth.'

Henrietta's heart melted. 'You wanted a kiss that meant something, or no kiss at all?'

He furrowed his brow. 'Pathetic, but yes, I did.'

'And in the pond when you claimed that kiss at last? Why did you accept it when you thought me only interested in using you?'

'Well, you weren't married any more.' He moved his hips, his erection rubbing between her thighs. 'And because in the end, I am only a man and you are a goddess.'

'Oh, then I am glad you stopped matters yesterday,' she said, with a new rush of warm sentiments. 'I am glad we waited. Because now we come together in honesty and with nothing and no one between us. Only us. Wanting to join our bodies.'

His eyes glistened; he closed them quickly, so quickly, and dipped his face to her neck. He trailed kisses over shoulder, murmuring words like 'perfect woman' and 'my goddess'. His attentions were hot ambrosia, driving her to madness, making her swollen folds throb.

'My Theo,' she gasped when he began lavishing kisses upon her bosom. She nudged his head towards one tight, sore nipple, and when he circled his tongue around its aching peak, a groan wrenched from her throat.

Then he suckled her, and electric jolts of pleasure shot through her body.

She manipulated her other breast, trying to ease its torture. When he slipped his fingers between her legs to rub her to pleasure, Henrietta had to turn her head to smother her sobs into the pillow. Peaks built, ebbed, then peaked higher, and she begged for all of him.

His expression grew serious. 'Are you certain you still want this?'

'Yes,' she said. 'Thank you for asking, but yes, yes and yes.'

'Then I'll make love to you with my cock now,' he told her. 'And after you have your release, I'll withdraw to have mine, so as not to get you with child. Is that what you want?'

Her hands gripped her pillow. 'Please.'

'I will be gentle, but, when I stretch you, it may hurt.' His consideration was endearing, especially as Henrietta knew he burned with lust as great as hers. 'Your body is made for it, but if it is ever more than you can bear, or if you change your mind, tell me and I will stop – and we can both have a different kind of release, like we did last night. Yes?'

Henrietta nodded, but she knew she wouldn't stop him. She *needed* that stretching now – only he could ease the tightness coiled inside her. Soon Theo would brand her as his in this rite of passage she'd longed for. He'd be her first, the man to whom she'd made herself the most vulnerable, and who had been gentle and beautiful through it all. 'I want this, Theo. I want *you*. So very much.'

He smoothed her hair from her face. 'Let's put you in a position where you can easily move away, should you need a moment.'

He aligned her body in front of his, both on their sides, so she slipped into the shape of him like one spoon beside another. 'Look into my eyes,' he said, propping himself on his elbow so she could turn her head and meet his gaze. 'Keep watching me.' His voice was throaty and thick. Heavy with desire. 'I want to see your pleasure.'

He placed one leg over hers and positioned his shaft at her opening, and she gasped at the feel of him there, hard and jutting. Already a sharp pain shot from where he nudged, but it was tempered, for the pressure soothed the throbbing. His jaw softened. His eyes grew hazy. 'I am so hot for you, woman.' Henrietta felt the strength of his passion. He was holding back so as not to hurt her, when she wanted a thorough mounting.

'I'm hot for *you*.' She tilted her bottom into his pelvis, driving him deeper, uncomfortable, and yet heavenly. She rocked her hips until pleasure originated *inside* her and her muscles clenched around him.

He half yelled, muffled into her hair. 'You feel so good around my cock I want to bury myself in you.'

'Please do, Theo. I expect it'll be like swimming in cold water: one swift plunge and the shock will be over for me, and there'll be nothing but the pleasure.'

'I have to slow down for a moment or I'll finish in you accidentally.' His breath grew heavier and he reached around her hip. 'So first let's bring you back to the edge.' He rubbed through her folds in his expert way, with his finger and the calloused pad of his thumb, and the pleasure began to peak at once, and when it reached heights that made her cry out, he thrust – not all the way, she knew, but enough to make her no longer a virgin. He crossed the point of ache, his shaft stroked her inside while his fingers rubbed her faster, and Henrietta drove her bottom deeper towards his pelvis until she reached a peak hitherto never found.

Then she clasped his forearms and let herself fall over the edge.

Into an intensely shattering release.

She cried out – she cried out *his* name – she wanted to cry it out for ever, be with him like this for ever, letting these waves wash over her forever, suspended in pleasure with him.

With her Theo.

'My Theo,' she cried again, digging her nails into his skin, and he moaned his answer against her shoulder. As the pulses of her inner muscles ebbed, she melted and he cradled her.

'What a release, woman.' His voice was rough, and his London accent strong. 'Your cunt wants to milk me dry.'

She didn't feel like a duchess now and she loved it. She was a woman, a hot, sweaty, lusty woman in bed with a gorgeous man, exuberant in their shared passion.

Henrietta squeezed herself on Theo's delicious erection until her toes curled. He withdrew, crying out, straining against her as hot liquid coated her lower back. 'Oh, my sweet, beautiful darling.' He panted into her ear, his seed dripping between them. 'Whatever shall I do now?'

'What do you mean?' she murmured, relaxed and satiated. So pleased with the experience, and so pleased with herself for the pleasure she'd given, that her eyelids were already heavy with sleep. 'You will sleep beside me and when we awaken, we shall do that again.'

As Henrietta fell asleep in his arms, Theo grew uneasy. A hair-raising, skin-crawling hunch told him trouble was brewing. Not here, not between *them*, where honesty and trust and respect reigned, but somewhere else. A malevolent force, rearing up against the woman he loved.

He should rise. Venture out to investigate. Ensure Henrietta's safety before returning to bed and sleeping beside her.

But he couldn't. Not when she slept so deeply, her head resting on his arm, her legs entwined with his, her hand tucked under her chin. She'd endured so much in the past fortnight. She *needed* this peaceful, healing rest.

His chest swelled with a profound warmth of sentiment. 'Whatever shall I do when I must part with you, my love?' he whispered into her hair. 'You've spoilt me for other women, for my heart is wholly yours.'

Even more so now than at Hyde Park when she'd confessed everything to him. With all the beauty of what they'd just shared, both in conversation and in physical love, she had embedded herself into his very soul.

There was no recovery from a love like this.

He tucked her closer, so that she might sense how he would protect her with his life, and achieve an even better rest for it. His desire for her flared again, but she needed rest now, not more lovemaking. At least, rest first and more lovemaking later, as she'd said.

That's what he would do, Theo decided. Let her sleep in his arms for now. He'd awaken her in a few hours. They'd take pleasure in each other's bodies again and then they'd leave the city, seeking Marlow.

Or seeking obscurity, with Theo's protection, if his sense was correct and trouble brewed.

His eyes closed and he let himself fall asleep.

He'd soon regret that choice.

CHAPTER 26

Flight in the Night

Henrietta was dreaming of being cradled in an embrace as sweet as when her French nursemaid used to wrap her in warm towels. But it wasn't Marie-Jeanne holding her. Nor was it Mama, for the strong arms cradling her smelled not of flowers, but of ink and soap. She was marvellously safe and comfortable, and everything would have been perfect except that there was a distant banging, growing louder and louder…

The cradling arms vanished, though the comforting scents lingered.

Henrietta opened her eyes. Theo. He had been cradling her; now he sat alert on the mattress, his chest gleaming like marble. Silver moonlight bathed his bedchamber. The banging was an incessant knocking.

'What—'

Theo's hand gently covered her mouth.

A deep voice yelled from outside the house, accompanied by louder banging. 'Open upon orders of the chief magistrate!'

She jolted upright, heart pounding. 'They're here for me. Perceval betrayed us.'

Theo jumped to his feet, pulled on his shirt and yanked on breeches. As Henrietta searched under the counterpane for her chemise, the banging stopped.

'Surround the house, men,' the deep voice said. 'Block the exit in the court. Eyes on every window and door.'

The knocking recommenced. 'Open at once, or everyone within this house will be charged with aiding and abetting a suspected murderess.'

Henrietta threw on her chemise, truly frightened. She prided herself on bravery, but if caught, she'd face trial. And likely the gallows. Her hand flew to her throat as she sought Theo's eyes in the dark. Her terror was mirrored there and the imaginary hemp tightened.

She *couldn't* die. Not now. Not when she and Theo had just begun to explore their wondrous connection.

But then the terror vanished from Theo's eyes and he grabbed her shoulders firmly. 'Darling, climb down the downspout, as you did as a child. Once we are in the court, I'll lead you to safety. It will take them two or three minutes to make their way round the market and through the lanes.'

Henrietta's breath came short and fast. 'But they'll corner us once they arrive. Is it not better to hide in the house?'

He drew her close, folding her into his arms – the comfort of her dream all over again. Theo was safe. Theo would care for her.

'Trust me,' he said, and Henrietta knew she could.

Her strength surged. 'Leave your boots,' she said as he reached for his footwear. 'It's easier with bare feet.' She grasped the iron downspout beside the bedroom window, throwing one leg out and bracing her feet on the bricks. 'Use your toes to grip the wall and trust the pipe.'

Seconds later, her feet touched the cold stone of the court. She looked up; Theo was descending. He jumped from slightly higher than she had, seized her hand and led her across the court. He threw open the door to a shed and closed it quickly behind them. Windowless dark enveloped them, but there was hay under Henrietta's feet. The stench of ammonia pierced her nose. Soft coos surrounded her.

'A chicken coop?' she asked. 'But they will check this door, surely?'

Outside, booted feet echoed in the court.

It was over. They were here.

Theo drew her close with a protective arm. 'Mrs Ford's cold storage larder is under this coop. We reach it through a door hidden by shelving. Hold on to me. Be silent so as not to wake the hens or the rooster.'

She clutched his shirt, shuffling behind him. Something creaked open in the darkness and Theo's arm slipped about her waist.

'Spiral steps down. Watch your head. 'Tis a very low ceiling.'

Henrietta slid her foot forward, finding the edge. She descended tentatively, her head brushing the ceiling even as she hunched. Several steps later, at a twist, Theo secured the door behind them. Henrietta held one hand against the damp, rough-hewn stone wall to guide her descent. The ammonia smell dissipated, replaced by musty cellar air.

'How are you not falling?' she asked Theo. 'I'm on the wide edge of the stairs and I can barely keep my balance.'

He chuckled. 'I've been climbing these steps for a decade, sometimes lugging a side of beef for Mrs Ford. She trails me, praising my strength, but I suspect she's eyeing my arse as I bend over.'

A giggle escaped Henrietta. 'I cannot blame her. You have a very nice bottom. I've admired it myself several times of late.'

They were at the foot of the stairs by then, the dank air chilling her bare legs. Theo swooped her close and nuzzled his face into the curve of her neck. The new growth of his whiskers rasped against her tender skin like a cat's tongue. 'We're safe now, but talk like that'll soon have me hard.'

Henrietta's pulse raced. 'I love it when you speak dirty to me,' she said, borrowing a phrase she'd heard her brothers use when they thought her nowhere nearby. 'Especially in your Cockney accent. It makes me want you to carry me away and ravish me.'

He growled against her neck. 'You like a bit of rough, Your Grace. And God help me, but I like a bit of fine.'

Though still sore from their lovemaking, she pressed her pelvis against his. Expert fingers slipped between her legs. 'Bloody hell, woman.' He groaned. 'You're wet for me and now I *am* hard.'

She bit at his shoulder, where his unfastened shirt exposed his skin. 'Can we again?'

"Tis one way to pass the time.' He pressed her against the wall, hefting her to his waist. 'Wrap your legs around my hips.' She complied as he freed himself from his breeches. His erection nudged her tender opening. 'Lord, I want you more than ever.' He panted as he began to enter her. 'I'll try to go slowly—'

'No. All the way, all at once.'

'If you tell me to, I shan't hold back, love ...'

'Please, Theo.'

He plunged, filling her more completely than she could've imagined, smothering another groan into her hair. They rocked in unison, waves of pleasure built rapidly – until loud footsteps above instantly stilled them both.

'Tear apart every shed and crevice in this court,' the deep voice ordered.

Henrietta's heart jumped to her throat, but then Theo's lips caught hers and he kissed her worries away. 'That's Haggett leading the search,' he murmured into her ear, softer than a butterfly's wings. 'No doubt chosen because he never takes a bribe, but he's as stupid as a post. Any man with half a brain would've secured the court before knocking at the door. He won't find us.' He started to move within her again, gentler now. 'You're safe, darling.'

Above them, many boots now stomped, accompanied by a great ruckus. Flapping of wings, squawking, a rooster's crow, and over all that, Mrs Ford's furious scolding. 'Have a care! If you release my chickens to roam the streets, they'll be stolen quick as lightning. Then how will I feed my lodgers, I ask you?'

Through it all, Henrietta's pleasure rose, so she listened with substantially more curiosity than fear.

Another man's voice called out. 'Nothing here anyway. Just a chicken coop.'

'And so I told you.' Mrs Ford screeched at the men. 'I watched Hawke and his doxy leave hours ago. At quarter past noon, they headed across the market with her in a purple dress.'

'And I told *you*, the bed was still warm from their fucking,' Haggett's deep voice replied. 'And she ain't a common doxy, she's the Duchess of Severn, murderess and whore. What's more, and what should have you quaking in your boots, is that I know you are a bloody liar, woman, and so I shall tell the magistrate. Our informant's story is that the duchess called upon her at one this afternoon and she was wearing a *blue* dress and a bonnet with a veil. The same blue dress and bonnet with a veil currently in Hawke's rooms. So, if you value your neck, you might want to start telling the bloody truth…'

'Miss du Pont informed on us,' Henrietta whispered. 'I should have told you she threatened me…'

'Shh,' Theo murmured, still moving in her. 'What's done is done and I will protect you.'

He cupped her breast, flicking his thumb over her nipple, and Henrietta's head fell back against the wall. She squeezed and released him, her inner muscles matching his rhythm. His breathing deepened each time, hot against her cheek.

Mrs Ford continued to yell. 'And so one person's blue might be another person's purple, and a woman might own more than one gown and bonnet, especially if she's a duchess, as you say. That's the trouble with trusting one witness over the other, isn't it?'

'No, the trouble is, you're protecting Hawke.'

'Why would I risk my life for him?'

'I've shared a pint or two with the scoundrel over the years, and heard him speak of you ...' The conversation descended into vicious bickering and Henrietta let it recede from her thoughts. Theo was thrusting faster and the pleasure inside her swelled. She tightened her hold around his shoulders.

'That's it, darling,' he murmured. 'Come for me, but don't make a sound.'

The thrill of the forbidden, the naughty, the daring, excited her. Without the sense of sight, every touch was all the more tantalising. Squeezing her legs around his hips, she let him push her into bliss. She bit his shoulder hard to avoid screaming as stars burst behind her tightly squeezed lids. *This*, she thought as the waves coursed through her – *this* was everything she'd ever imagined from romantic love. No – this was *more* than she'd ever imagined.

And so, in a dank cellar below a chicken coop with the Bow Street Runners eager to destroy her, Henrietta Percy's wild, romantic heart soared at last.

Theo eased Henrietta to the floor once they'd both found their release.

Then he kissed away her worries while Mrs Ford and Haggett argued above their heads. Theo's touch distracted her. Eased her. He would do it all night, if it helped.

Besides, it might be his last chance to hold the woman he loved. When he'd awoken to the Runners banging on the door, he hadn't abandoned hope, but realising there was a slim chance of escape, he'd formed a secondary plan. One that gave him immeasurable peace.

In the event of their capture, he'd shoulder the blame. For everything. He'd confess to the murder. He'd claim he then abducted the innocent duchess as she sought her country estate to grieve in peace. He would attribute his actions to an obsessive, unrequited passion. He could spin a believable tale. After all, everyone said he was infatuated. His behaviour over the last five years, staring at her intently in public, grasping any excuse to write about her, would support his claim. Lord, he *had* been obsessed with her, after all.

That was nothing to how he felt now.

He loved her.

Loved her so much he would die for her.

Hadn't many people said the gallows loomed in his future? Had not the hangman's noose shadowed his entire existence? Well, let his life conclude as it had begun. With a hanging. There was always a pleasing symmetry to an ending that mirrored a beginning.

Then Henrietta would live.

He was tempted to turn himself in immediately, so that her struggles would end at once. But an arsehole like Haggett would insist on taking her as well, no matter what Theo said, and she'd faced enough indignities already. Almost any other Runner would take a bribe and turn aside as she fled to the safety of her father's house, but not Haggett. The magistrate had chosen tonight's hound dog well. He knew several of the others liked Theo.

Besides, Henrietta *wouldn't* flee to her father's. She'd undoubtedly continue to search for her husband's killer – except with Theo imprisoned, she'd be alone.

In the coop above, Mrs Ford seemingly gained the upper hand and demanded Haggett and his men either leave or assist in gathering her chickens. Which action he chose, if either, remained a mystery, but the footfalls left the shed.

Theo tucked Henrietta's arm around his to lead her to a more comfortable spot. Even he couldn't see in total darkness, but he knew the lay of the cellar enough to guide her to a bench seat. 'Come, darling. Hold tight to me and I will make you more comfortable. We may be here a while.'

He sat her upon his lap and she leant into his embrace. She was wearing only her thin chemise and she shivered in the damp air. Theo cradled her as best he could, rubbing her limbs to warm them.

'Do you think they are gone?' she asked after about a half an hour of silent kisses. 'Could we try to escape? Get to our horses?'

Theo shifted slightly, still holding her. His bottom had grown numb on the bench. 'Barefoot and unclothed, we'd attract too much attention both in London and on the road. And without my purse, we can't change our condition. For now, we must wait. Mrs Ford will help us.'

He hoped.

'She knows we are here?'

'Likely so, darling.' That or eventually Mrs Ford would come to her cellar for food and find them then. 'Try to rest against my shoulder for now.'

They didn't have to wait long. Henrietta stiffened at the sound of footsteps but relaxed when Mrs Ford's voice murmured to her chickens above. Soon, the door creaked open and the light of a single candle pierced the cellar. Then the door closed.

'Theo?' Mrs Ford called down the stairs, her face illuminated by the flame, eyes squinting to see beyond its reach.

'We're here.' He rose, helping Henrietta to her feet. 'Thank you, Mrs Ford.'

His landlady inched down the stairs, a sack in one hand. At

the bottom, she took in their state of dishabille and pressed her lips into a disapproving line. 'I thought the better of both of you.'

Henrietta hung her head – the first time Theo had ever seen her appear ashamed. He jumped to her defence. 'It's not quite what it seems, Mrs Ford.'

'I don't care if it's only a quarter what it seems, it's a sketchy business. She's not three weeks a widow to one of the greatest men what ever lived, whom she ought to be grieving like the rest of the nation is, and yet the way the two of you are going at each other would put a brothel madam to the blush.'

'No matter how this looks, we are not being disrespectful to Severn in the way you think.' Theo paused, recognising he echoed Henrietta's words from five years before. He glanced at her. She met his gaze, chin lifted, a knowing gleam in her eyes. No trace of shame remained. 'As much as I've tried over the last few days, I don't think I completely understood how much I hurt you until this moment, Henrietta, when I find myself misjudged in the same way.'

She smiled. 'You've redeemed yourself a few times over.'

Mrs Ford grunted. 'I'm sure I don't know what you're talking about. Any way you look at it, it ain't as it should be, and I don't see as how it will lead to anything but more tragedy. It may well be the undoing of me, but, Theo, I've loved you like the son I never had, so my heart won't let me do nothing but help you.'

'Thank you,' he said again.

'Yes, thank you, Mrs Ford,' Henrietta added. 'And when I clear my name, I shan't forget what you've done for me.'

'And if you don't clear your name,' Mrs Ford said, unappeased, 'it will be my neck breaking along with yours. If indeed they *would* hang a duchess, even if she be a murderer.'

But with that final spurt of vitriol, Mrs Ford's anger seemed to dissipate. 'Here, loves, like as you can't help it. You've been at each other's throats for years and now you find yourself thrown together and passions rise, and if I were as young as the pair of you, I daresay I'd do the same. Let's get you dressed. It's nigh on midnight now; before the night progresses much further, you should be well out of London. Come daybreak, the news will spread and you won't be safe here. Now, Your Grace, they filched your clothes, so I brought some of Theo's things, as well as my sturdiest boots what I use for mucking out the chicken coop. No one will mistake you for a man up close, but maybe from a way's off the disguise will work.'

As they dressed, Mrs Ford filled them in on what she'd learnt from the Runners. Someone had informed Bow Street that the Duchess of Severn was in the company of Theodore Hawke, who was helping her avoid the authorities. Separately, the maid, Libby, was missing from Newgate.

Henrietta froze in the process of buttoning one of Theo's waistcoats over her shapely bosom. 'She escaped?'

Mrs Ford lifted her hands. 'The Runners didn't share the particulars. But they seem convinced you and your maid worked together to kill the duke.'

Henrietta's shoulders slumped. 'How anyone can suspect Libby is beyond me. I'm glad she escaped. Her situation was even more precarious than mine. I'm relieved her life no longer weighs in this balance. Unless they find her ...' Her face clouded with worry.

'Let us hope not,' Theo said.

'Yes, let us hope she stays hidden. I don't want to die and I don't deserve to die, for I am innocent – but I also couldn't live knowing someone was killed to spare me.'

Theo murmured soothing assurances, but her statement didn't alter his resolve. He'd still die in her stead, if needed. Oh, she might grieve for a time – his heart ached at the thought – but one day, she'd be glad he'd made the sacrifice. She'd think back on him kindly.

What a salacious story it would make, he mused, his lips

twisting with bitter amusement. *Obsessive Reporter Stalked Duchess of Severn for Years* would sell thousands of papers. Scripp would be delighted. And Theo deserved it, for how he'd harmed her and others with his gossip columns. He would give his life in retribution.

Henrietta pulled on one of his tailcoats, too long in the arm and loose at the shoulders. She looked so damned good, standing in the candlelight in his clothes, with her hair a tousled mess. His ravishing adventuress. Theo imprinted the image in his mind. Upon the gallows, he decided, he would close his eyes and conjure it. He would die with a smile upon his face.

'Lud, Theo.' Mrs Ford huffed. 'You can't do nothing but gape at her like Romeo at Juliet.'

What an apt comparison.

Five minutes later, Theo led Henrietta out of the court. The moon was nearly full and the night cloudless, potentially laying them bare to prying eyes, but they slunk through the shadows of the mews as best they could on the way to the inn where they'd stabled their horses.

Henrietta tried to tuck her arm into his, but Theo gently removed it.

'You and I are both *men*,' he said. 'So we must walk as such. We mustn't do *anything* to draw attention or rouse suspicions.'

'I admit,' she said shakily, 'the danger hasn't quite felt real until tonight. I'm frightened, Theo. If we do not find sufficient evidence against Marlow within hours, all may be over for me.' She took a deep breath. 'I do not want to die, but I shall be brave throughout.'

Secure in the knowledge that *he* would hang in her stead, Theo marvelled at the hands fate dealt. It was that symmetry of life again, was it not? For it was both odd and right that his last hours of freedom would be spent travelling in reverse the final journey of condemned Deborah Hawke, as he ventured to the home of his late father to confront the son of his mother's killer.

CHAPTER 27

Black Eyes

A brilliant moon and clear skies allowed them to travel at a steady trot. Henrietta estimated the time at one thirty or two in the morning when they arrived at the court of the Pickled Dog. As Theo helped her dismount, a group of men poured out of the tavern, reeking of ale and sweat.

She was attempting to pass unnoticed to the stable to board her horse, but one man took an aggressive interest in two strangers in the inn court. The scar on his face identified him as Sam Walker, who'd tried to pick a fight with Theo the day before. As he lumbered closer, his disfigured lips curled into a wicked grin. Henrietta's stomach sank. He recognised them and crowed.

'Look, men! It's the London boy and his gentry mort, now trying to dress like a man. As if her bubbies don't give her away.'

Theo stepped forward with a clenched fist, which led Sam to attempt to spit in his face, but the spittle was thick with mucus and dripped to Sam's chin instead. He cursed and smeared a purple handkerchief over his mouth. 'I disliked you yesterday, London boy,' he said with a snarl. 'But I hate you tonight.'

Henrietta had set her mind to bravery and this was her first test. She stepped boldly between the men, still holding her horse's reins. 'My companion and I caused you no trouble yesterday, so please let us go about our business tonight.'

'We only tolerated you yesterday because of the rain,' Sam replied. 'We don't hold with gentry here and you didn't fool us by pretending to be a maid. Seek your own kind at Enberry Abbey.'

'Nay, don't send her up there,' another man said. His sorrowful voice was kinder than Sam's, and only then did Henrietta recognise him as Jim King, who had seemed to be the leader the night before. Tonight, however, he stood slump-shouldered, his hands in his pockets, as if the weight of the world rested upon him. 'She won't come to any good there, no matter who gets to her first.'

'You have a softness for this lady nob, Jim,' Sam said. 'Take care or we might question where your loyalties lie.'

'I've proven where my loyalties lie.' Jim stared at the moon and spoke quietly, as if to himself. 'Else, I wouldn't have done what I did tonight. God have mercy on my soul.' He jolted, turning frantically to Henrietta. 'Flee. Flee now, while you still can.'

The mad look in his eyes startled her, but she refused to be frightened. 'I cannot. I have business here, which I must begin before Lord Marlow arrives in a few hours' time. If I succeed, I may rid you of his oppression, therefore if everyone would step aside and allow us to board our horses—'

Sam snorted. 'We'll be rid of his oppression soon, but it won't be you what does it for us. Venture up to the big house and you venture to your death, as ill-prepared as you are. He's there already and you didn't even know.'

'*Already?*' Henrietta's plan had been to sneak into the house and attempt to gather any evidence she could find – letters, diaries, *anything* that might incriminate him. She hadn't planned for the confrontation yet. Sam was correct – she was ill-prepared.

'Aye, came in tonight, he did, in his thundering carriage.' Still holding his purple handkerchief – the same as hers and Miss du Pont's – Sam pointed in the general direction of the road that ran by the mill and then waved the handkerchief in front of her nose, as if it held some significance. 'Death,' he said dramatically. '*Death* has gone to greet him.'

Henrietta took a step back, not wanting the wad of spittle to hit her if it flew off the handkerchief. 'Why do you thrust that in my face?'

All the men – save Jim King – laughed uproariously. 'Nightshade,' said Sam, as if it were all a delightful joke. He spoke over his shoulder to his companions. 'She don't know it when it stares her in the face. How does she think she'll survive?'

Henrietta recoiled against Theo. 'Nightshade?' she asked. 'Millford Blue is dyed with *nightshade*?' But even as she said it, she knew it to be true. Hadn't Edward's nightshade monsters faded to a pale purple over the years? And the embroidered berries ... not bilberries at all, but something deadly ...

'Aye, in that mill there,' one of the men said, with a note of pride.

Henrietta grimaced, thinking of how she'd held her handkerchief to her nose and to her mouth. 'Is the cloth poisonous?'

'Not with the way we treat it here,' another man said. 'We wash it with gin, which draws the poison out but leaves the colour as pretty as can be.'

Gin ... the drink Jim King had given her. 'Is the gin poisonous?' Henrietta asked, her voice rising in panic. Had Jim King tried to poison *her* yesterday afternoon, and then she'd given the drink to Theo? She put her hand to Theo's chest, frantically hoping he was unharmed.

Jim spoke. 'Aye, the gin is poisonous ...'

Henrietta's heart stopped.

'But it wasn't the gin I gave you yesterday.'

Breath gushed from her lungs; she was dizzy with relief. Lord, but Theo meant so much to her. How desperately she wanted to extract them both from danger, so that they might forge a life together.

Sam progressed towards them. 'Now, get out of here. We've had enough trouble of late without more from you.'

The loitering men grumbled their agreement, and one amongst their numbers began singing the ballad of 'Bess the Black-Eyed Beauty' from the night before. He sang it pointedly, as if it should have meaning to Henrietta.

Henrietta tilted her head. 'The black-eyed beauty. Who is she?'

'*A treasury is our common land, united all we make our stand,*' Sam said, quoting Eliza King's march, as if in answer to her question.

'The black-eyed beauty is Eliza King, then.' Henrietta had suspected as much the first time she'd heard the ballad, when she'd also wondered if the radical leader might be related to Jim King. She glanced at Jim now, but he was looking at the sky again, as if he hadn't heard.

Sam's cruel grin made another appearance. 'She knows who you are, though she didn't tell us, did she? Says you're not in service, though. Said you lied to us, but you're not our enemy so we shouldn't put you away. *She's* the mistress of disguise, but you ain't. We knew you weren't what you said you were.' Sam's eyes shone. 'Up at the big house, she is.'

'She's *here*? At Enberry Abbey?'

Sam nodded his answer.

'Why has she gone to Lord Marlow's estate?' Henrietta asked.

Sam released a cold, braying laugh. 'Revenge.'

Bits and pieces were trying to slip into place in Henrietta's mind. These men were radicals; Eliza King was their leader; they had respected the Duke of Severn; Marlow had murdered

Edmund. 'Revenge for the murder of Severn?' she asked. 'She has gone to kill Marlow, because Marlow killed Severn?'

Sam gave her a non-answer. 'You'd best ask her.'

Henrietta was beginning to feel both frustrated and frantic. If Eliza King killed Marlow before she got a chance to extract a confession from him or discover irrefutable proof of his guilt, *she'd never be able to prove that she hadn't murdered Edmund*. Marlow's death would be cold comfort, for she would still hang. She'd still lose everything. Her life. Her future. Her family.

And *Theo*.

'Where at the big house?' she asked, her panic mounting. She *had* to find Eliza King before the radical succeeded in her goal. Henrietta had to stop her, convince her to let Marlow face a jury of his peers. 'How will I find her? How will I know her?'

Jim King answered, his voice sad but steady. 'You'll know her by her eyes. As black as death they are – unless they ain't. But you don't know what I'm talking about, nor will you learn from me, 'cause there was a time when she was different and until I can forget that, I won't betray her.' He paused, then inclined his head in a slight bow. 'Your Grace.'

Henrietta inhaled sharply, but she didn't deny her identity.

The significance of the exchange was not lost on the other men. '*She's* the cuckolding duchess?' Sam's face was more purple than his handkerchief. He lunged for Henrietta, but Jim stayed Sam with a firm arm across his chest.

'Calm yourself, Sam. Mayhap she is what the papers said, never a loyal wife, but I've learnt enough in life to know an outsider should never judge a marriage.'

'Not much left to speculation, the way she carries on with London boy,' Sam said.

Henrietta's first impulse was to defend herself and Theo, but she'd barely opened her lips before she realised her feelings were pure and loving and good, and she oughtn't *have* to defend them.

So she clenched her jaw and seriously considered planting Sam a facer instead.

As if he understood, Jim nodded. 'The truth is a complicated thing, Sam. A complicated thing indeed. Rarely black and white. Rarely so simple as that.'

'That is perhaps the greatest truth of all,' Theo said, and Henrietta fell for him all over again.

Then it occurred to her that those were the first words he'd spoken during her questioning of Sam and Jim. Like with James, and with Miss du Pont, and with Perceval, Theo had let her conduct the interrogation, never once attempting to assume control, or tell her he'd manage for her. She met his gaze and hoped hers spoke volumes, because though she couldn't utter her feelings before this hostile crowd, she loved him.

Oh, how she loved him.

Jim was watching. 'Your Grace, let me warn you and your friend against venturing to Enberry Abbey.'

'I have to,' Henrietta replied, and her anxiety left her. She was strong now. Strong in love, strong in purpose, strong in body, strong in determination. 'Now more than ever, I must. I cannot let her kill Marlow.'

Jim shook his head. 'You're not the fight she plans to fight, but she won't let you stand in her way either. One more dead aristocrat is nothing to her. Nothing at all. She don't feel remorse. Not any more. Not the black-eyed beauty. She don't have a kind heart any more.'

An ice-cold chill ran down Henrietta's back.

Because she suddenly knew exactly who Eliza King was.

CHAPTER 28

Two Hearts, One Hand and a Key

'Miss du Pont is Eliza King, Theo,' Henrietta said as they cantered along the lane leading to Enberry. Sam, who seemed gleefully keen on their deaths, had told them the estate gates were a mile up the river road and that the manor house was a half mile beyond that. With time being of the essence, Henrietta had decided not to stable their horses. 'Not only does she have black eyes, like the song, but she's been to Millford before. The purple handkerchief was proof and she became cagey when I asked about it. Then she refused to answer my question.'

'But you said she was the daughter of aristocratic refugees?' Theo asked. 'With the way Jim King spoke, I assume she's a relation and he's no Frenchman. I wager his ancestors were working this land long before the Conquest.'

'Recall what he said about outsiders not judging a marriage? Perhaps he is her husband. Clearly, he loves her dearly – or he once did. Maybe he married a much younger woman he thought to be sweet and mouldable who turned out to be much more trouble than he'd expected, like I was to Edmund.' A lump rose in her throat. Oh, how she missed her husband, even while loving Theo. Her sentiments weren't contradictory; both men belonged in her heart, her love for them different but boundless. 'I suspect,' she continued, 'Miss du Pont deduced during our conversation that Marlow is Edmund's killer, since she knew of Perceval's innocence. She informed on me to the Runners, perhaps for the reward money, and then headed to Surrey to deal with Marlow.'

'If she intends to kill him, perhaps we had better leave her to it, rather than risk our lives to save him?' Theo said. 'The world won't mourn *his* death.'

'No, we cannot. If Marlow dies before I irrefutably prove his guilt, I will hang for this crime. If Miss du Pont succeeds in killing Marlow, she won't afterwards come forward in my defence with what she knows – both because it will incriminate her and because she doesn't like me. If I hang, I will just be one more dead aristocrat, as Jim King said. In fact, it might even aid her goal – it will show the people that even the nobility can hang.'

'You won't hang,' Theo said.

'The odds are against me.'

'You won't hang. Henrietta, let us turn around before we risk our lives with whatever awaits us at Enberry.'

His confidence was beginning to annoy her. 'Your advice is shockingly ill-considered, Theo. My danger is very real. You yourself have said so numerous times.'

'You won't hang,' he said again, with a note of finality. 'I promise.'

Henrietta pulled up her horse's reins, stopping to scowl at Theo, who likewise halted his mount. 'How can you be so complacent? Until now, you've shared my concerns. What has changed your mind? Because in case you hadn't noticed, I appear guiltier than ever after fleeing the Runners!'

He lifted his chin and shifted his gaze towards the moon, his mouth set in firm lines, his expression full of high-minded determination. Henrietta knew that look. It was the same look Edmund would get when he was set upon doing something he deemed noble and sacrificial, and Henrietta suddenly knew *exactly* why Theo was so confident she wouldn't hang.

Fury consumed her and she tightened her fists over her reins until her knuckles ached. 'Damn you, Theodore Hawke. You intend to do something thoroughly stupid, don't you? You plan to confess to Edmund's murder to clear my name. No doubt your sordid imagination has already cooked up a salacious tale of murder, scandal and abduction, all designed to make you look like a heinous villain and me like a persecuted, wronged angel.'

His brows lifted. Clearly, she was correct and he hadn't expected her to guess. 'If it comes to that,' he said, adopting his expression of martyrdom again, 'of course I shall give my life to save yours.'

'You stupid, stupid man!' Fury hazed her vision. 'And this great falsehood is to be told by the truth-seeker of Mayfair. What happened to your steadfast devotion to *truth*?'

'It was supplanted by an even greater devotion,' he said, so nobly Henrietta wanted to scream.

The confession of his feelings only angered her more. If they loved each other, they must fight for a life *together*. 'If you dare to attempt such a thing, you won't make it to the gallows, because I shall kill you myself first. Damn you for even thinking it, Theo. Damn you for making that plan. Damn you for imagining you can leave me.' Her voice cracked. 'Did you even consider how I would feel about the matter? Do you think I lost Edmund, only to find you and then have *you* torn from me as well? Do you think my heart could handle that, you beast? Are you so cruel?'

His expression softened, almost pleading. 'My darling Henrietta, you cannot die. You have so much to share with this world.'

'You're damned right I do!' She blinked back hot tears. 'And so do you. I don't want either of us to die. Not me, when I've only just begun to live, and not you, when you are on the cusp of the brilliant article that will change your life. No, Theodore, you're not allowed to die for me. We *both* must live. We may have made mistakes in the past, but we have attempted within our confines to do the best we can – and we bloody well have done nothing to deserve the gallows. Therefore, we are going to ride up to Enberry Abbey and we are going to stop Miss du Pont from killing Marlow, so we can have the answers we need to prove my innocence. And we are doing it now.'

With that, she spurred her horse, leaning forward into the uphill canter – but with an aching heart, she realised the chances of them both surviving the night were slim and she couldn't let her last words to Theo be words of anger.

She turned her horse. He was still at the bottom of the hill, alone in the moonlight. Their gazes locked and he wore his heart on his sleeve as much as she must be wearing hers. She hurled herself out of the saddle as he did the same, and they ran to each other, their arms outstretched.

They collided in a fury of passion. He drew her up to him; she threw her legs around his waist. Then they kissed. Oh, how they kissed. The kiss to end all kisses, full of all they felt but hadn't yet expressed to each other. When they broke away, she pressed her cheek to his.

'Thank you,' she whispered into his ear. 'Thank you for being beside me every step of this dangerous path. Thank you for holding me, and for protecting me, and for comforting me, and thank you for your wisdom, and thank you for letting me lead this investigation, and thank you for … for sharing your body with me. Thank you for being my dear, my *dearest* friend.'

She didn't meet his gaze as she broke the embrace and returned to her horse. Her emotions were so close to the surface they might boil over at any point, and for now she must be brave and focus.

Her life depended upon it.

Not only her life, but her hopes and dreams as well.

And the life of the man she loved.

Adoration surged inside Theo as he followed Henrietta through the Enberry Abbey gates and into a wooded area where they could shelter their horses.

She was her own woman in a way she never had been before. No submitting to a father or a mother or a brother or a husband or a lover. Henrietta Percy knew exactly what she wanted and she wasn't going to accept failure.

And she'd spoken as if he had a place in her heart. She'd kissed him in a way that felt ... if not like love, then something very close indeed. She'd called him her dearest friend. Whatever happened at the end of this investigation, when they parted ways to live in their separate spheres, the Duchess of Severn would carry tender sentiments for Theo into her future. And if he could make something of himself, he might, one day, win her heart fully. It was an *almost* impossible dream, but it was real enough to give his life new purpose.

No lights shone from within Enberry Abbey as they approached. The huge Gothic towers, relics of the medieval church, rose silhouetted against the silvery sky. The entrance faced the west, with the vast, arched double doors locked and ominous. The moon provided sufficient illumination to edge their way to the south side, looking for other doors or open windows, but nothing presented itself until they rounded to the east. The river side. There, a Palladian wing faced the tiered back gardens, with a row of French windows glinting in the moonlight on the ground floor. One door was open; thin white drapes covered the entry on the inside and fluttered in the breeze, breathing in and out of the house.

Henrietta stopped him by placing a hand on his chest. 'Eliza King must have entered through that door. We are searching for two dangerous quarries, so I think it best if we divide our efforts. That way, if one of us lands in trouble, the other can come to the rescue. Whichever of us finds Eliza King first must convince her to stay her hand until we can gather proof of Marlow's guilt. Whichever of us finds Marlow first, keep him alive and try to get him talking. I shall enter here. For now, please hold back or look for another entrance into the house.'

Theo agreed with reluctance. The plan was sound, though he disliked the idea of her being out of his protective sight. 'I insist you carry the pistol,' he said, reaching into his coat pocket where he'd put the weapon after extracting it from his saddle bags.

She took it, checked its ammunition and cocked the hammer. 'I have one shot.'

'Use it well.'

She nodded, glanced to the house and made ready to move, but Theo placed a hand on her shoulder. 'Wait, Henrietta.'

Her beautiful eyes met his. 'Yes?'

He couldn't let her go yet. Not without expressing the senti-ment in his heart. So he drew her closer and pressed his lips to her forehead, and he said words he'd never uttered to any person, ever before, because, as a street orphan with no family and few friends, there had never been anyone for whom he'd felt the sentiment. 'I love you.'

She pulled back slightly, her gaze locked with his, perfectly solemn. 'I know.' She pressed his hand between her breasts. 'I can feel your love, *here*, and after this is over I have something to say to you as well. But first, I must find justice for Edmund and prove my innocence.'

'Say it now?' he asked, hoping against hope.

She shook her head. 'Not yet. I want to be a free woman when I say it, but you know what I feel.' And she kissed the palm of his hand and kept it held to her lips, her eyes tightly closed until he could be in no doubt that she returned his love, as fantastical as the notion was.

There were so many things he wanted to ask, to share, and to marvel at with her, but now was not the time, and then she was gone, releasing his hand, dashing towards the house and disappearing into the curtained door as Theo watched.

He held his breath, intent on catching any glimmer of movement from the house interior or from the gardens. He counted the seconds. One. Two. Three ...

A gust of wind swept up from the river. The French door slammed shut.

He stiffened. Watching. Waiting. *Had* the wind closed the door? Or a person?

When the answer came, it stilled his heart. Stealthier than a shadow – and almost as hard to discern in the nighttime, even with his eyesight – a hand reached between the drapes from inside the house. It was the slim hand of a woman, but it wasn't Henrietta, for the arm attached to it was bare and Henrietta had been wearing his wool coat.

Then the hand turned a key, locking his love inside.

CHAPTER 29

A Ballroom Confrontation

Enough moonlight filtered through the thin curtains for Henrietta to ascertain she'd entered a large ballroom. Smooth parquet floors and a ceiling so high it was lost to darkness. The wall across from her displayed full-length portraits of previous Marlows in court robes, with the present viscount in the centre, his arrogant features murky with shadow. Below the portraits, busts stood on pedestals, perhaps counterparts to the painted faces above. Along the two sides, floor-to-ceiling mirrors lined the walls, with chairs sitting primly below. Behind her, marble statues stood between the French windows, like ghostly soldiers.

She tightened her grip on her pistol and prepared to cross the room. There were mirrored doors to the right. Through them, she'd likely enter either the formal dining room or a drawing room; from there, she could find her way into the main part of the house. She suspected Eliza King would be aiming for Marlow's bedchamber.

She took more steps forward, as silently as she could in Mrs Ford's heavy boots.

Then the door behind her slammed shut, so that she nearly jumped out of her skin.

She began to turn, to see if wind or human had closed it, but the cold laughter of Viscount Marlow filled the space from the *other* direction. With her heart pummelling her chest, she turned her attention back to the wall of portraits and busts.

One pale visage, almost consumed by shadows, wasn't a bust at all. It was the viscount, his skin and blonde hair nearly as white as the marble in the moonlight.

She lifted her pistol, aiming it carefully at his upper thigh. If she had to shoot, she couldn't kill him. Not when she needed proof of his guilt. 'Don't move, Marlow. I can shoot the spade off an ace at twenty paces. My brothers taught me that.'

The laughter stopped abruptly. 'Well, well,' he said, his slurred voice echoing in the emptiness. 'I mistook the identity of my guest. *You* are not who I was expecting, my lovely duchess. The Runners are inept fools, but I assumed they'd be capable of catching two people as bumbling as you and your lover. Where is Hawke, by the by? Lurking in the shadows, ready to swoop to your rescue if you find yourself in a spot of bother?'

Marlow's accurate guesses threatened to unnerve Henrietta, and the realisation that it was Marlow, rather than Désirée du Pont (a.k.a Eliza King) who had informed on them added to her confusion. But more pressing matters demanded her attention. She stepped closer, keeping her aim.

'By now, Hawke is no doubt in a holding cell on Bow Street,' she said, the lie inspired by her interaction with Theo on the way to the manor. 'He confessed to Edmund's murder to allow me freedom. First thing in the morning, he will be dragged into the magistrate's court and he'll be at Newgate soon after. His lovesick obsession proved useful, but I'd rather Edmund's true killer hang.'

Marlow snorted. 'My dear, you are either a liar as well as a tease, or you are more devious than I realised. Either way, I find my old attraction resurging, especially with you dressed like a streetwalker who has stolen her lover's clothes.' He took a swig from a bottle she hadn't seen he was holding and wiped his mouth with the back of his hand. 'Which might be closer to the truth than not. Tell me, do you enjoy my half-brother's fucks?'

Ah, so then Marlow knew of his relation to Theo. His manner caused her stomach to roil, but she couldn't give in to her revulsion. Facing down a murderer required focus. Engaging him in conversation when he was at least half drunk might be the best way to extract a confession.

'Immensely.' She inched across the parquet. 'But why such an intimate query?'

He didn't answer at once. Instead, he studied her from the corner of his eye and took another drink. 'Given your affinity for broom-boys and nancys, I suppose it's no wonder I didn't get up your skirts years ago.'

'Don't insult what you can't understand, Marlow,' she replied, defending Edmund.

'What do you imagine I can't understand? Buggery?'

'No,' she said. 'You can't understand love.' She hadn't realised Marlow knew Edmund's secret, but she found herself unsurprised. After all, her father, her brother, Bishop Babcock – all members of Parliament, in either the Upper House or the Commons – had seemed to understand when Perceval hinted at the will reading that Edmund had never consummated their marriage. 'You used that against him, didn't you? You whispered it in other politicians' ears, over the years.'

Marlow lifted his shoulders. 'A raised eyebrow here or there at opportune moments. I can't be blamed if people understood subtleties, for I certainly didn't *say* anything. It's not the sort of thing a gentleman speaks aloud, as I advised Perceval Percy years ago when he told me.'

Henrietta saw red. 'I knew you were a thorn in Edmund's side, I just didn't know the extent.'

'I wasn't half the thorn in Edmund's side that he was in mine.'

'How so? He was never cruel to you. In fact, he cautioned people to be considerate, since you grew up with such a vicious mother.'

'My mother was a saint for what she put up with,' he said. 'It was my father who was the vicious one, unable to keep his prick out of any fanny he could find.'

'As if you are any different, Marlow?'

'But I am different.' He put a hand, splay-fingered, to his chest. '*I* recognise that I could never be faithful to one woman and that is why there's no current Lady Marlow. My father did not show my mother the same consideration.'

'Edmund always said your father was a good man.'

Marlow glanced at the bust to his right, running his hand over it like Hamlet with the skull of Yorick, and Henrietta supposed it to be the late Lord Marlow's likeness. Perhaps it bore a resemblance to her Theo.

'Yes,' the viscount said at last. 'Edmund would say that. My father and his father were the same man.'

Henrietta stepped back. Her grip on her pistol loosened and her arm fell slack to her side. At first, she wanted to protest... Edmund's father was the sixth Duke of Severn, the round-faced, pink-cheeked nobleman whose portraits hung throughout the homes where she'd been mistress for half a decade. But then she thought again. *Perceval* resembled the sixth Duke, whereas Edmund had looked nothing like him. Meanwhile, Edmund and Marlow had always looked more like brothers than cousins. And then there was Edmund's mother's oddly insistent claim, that

Edmund had been eleven months in the womb … Had that been a lie to cover an indiscretion?

She cocked her head at Marlow. 'Your father and Edmund's mother?'

He drank from his bottle. 'Were first cousins, as you know. Evidently in love with each other since childhood. But she was a great beauty with little fortune, and, at the time, he was a third son, years from his majority, so their fathers withheld consent. Then the old Duke of Severn cast his eye upon her for a second wife after his first had died childless, and, well, no sensible parent allows an impoverished daughter to reject a duke for a third son, who is her first cousin to boot. So off she went, a girl of seventeen with her almost sixty-year-old husband. When she gave birth to Edmund nearly a year after her husband's departure on a diplomatic voyage, she claimed she'd carried the babe overly long in the womb and upon the old man's return, he celebrated the birth of his son and heir, rather than throwing his cuckolding bride and her bastard out on the street.'

Ah, a noble action on the duke's part and for all one knew, perhaps a sixty-year-old, childless aristocrat *was* thrilled at the birth of a healthy son to bear his name and give joy in his twilight years, no matter who had sired the boy.

'If the sixth duke accepted Edmund as his own son, then so he was,' Henrietta said firmly. 'Anyway, why should you care? It's not as if Edmund stole anything from you. He inherited the title and lands of the Duke of Severn, to which you have no claim by birth or by blood. *You* inherited your mutual father's name and wealth.'

'Ah, but he *did* steal from me. He stole our father's love. By the time I came along ten years later, our father already had his golden son, seemingly perfect in every way. What did I matter, then? How could any child, even a legitimate heir, compare to the brilliant, beautiful Edmund Meredith Percy, future seventh Duke of Severn? Yet why did Edmund need *my* father's love, when his legal father was devoted as well? That bastard spent his childhood basking in the adoration of a gentle mother and not one but *two* fathers—'

Marlow stopped abruptly.

'While you had none of that?' Henrietta said. 'And so you hated him?'

Marlow waved a dismissive hand. 'Bah, that matters not. I was not the first unloved child in this world and I shan't be the last, either. I hated Edmund for many reasons. I hated him for his smug perfectionism. I hated that he could make people adore him so effortlessly. I hated him for that noble mien he always displayed, while in truth he was nothing but a criminal, doing utterly unnatural things with men.'

'And so you killed him?' She lifted her pistol again. Marlow's motive was even greater than she'd assumed. Forty years of venomous jealousy had festered in his veins and when Edmund had seemed on the cusp of his greatest achievement yet – party leadership – Marlow's hate had consumed him until he'd enacted the ultimate revenge. 'You pretended to come to an arrangement with him to put him off guard, but then you murdered him.'

Marlow chuckled. 'Is that the conclusion you've come to, my pretty one?'

'It's what happened,' she said.

'No, I assure you I was quite pleased with the arrangement your husband and I came to – for it involved *you*, my dear. I was to get you in my bed at last, if I simply promoted him as the next Whig leader to my dear friend, the King.'

Henrietta's blood ran cold. 'That's not true. Edmund never agreed to that.'

'He *suggested* it and I agreed readily. He said he needed an heir, as Perceval simply wouldn't do, and as he and I were ... *cousins*, and he himself appeared ... *infertile*, would I do the deed with his comely wife?'

Henrietta faltered. Marlow could not have chosen any method of attack that would disarm or hurt her more. But fortunately, that thought saved her from despair – because that might very well be *exactly* what Marlow was doing…

'Tell me,' he said, interrupting her thoughts. 'Would you have welcomed me into your bed, had your husband insisted upon it? Would you have *obeyed* him, as you vowed before God?'

She considered, and the answer was devastating when it came to her. Yes, she would have. She might have cried all the way through but had Edmund absolutely and with finality insisted that she take a certain man to her bed, even Marlow, she wouldn't have refused.

Because all her life, she'd been a pawn to powerful men. Her father, her brothers, her husband. They had meant well, but they had dictated her choices, controlled her actions and concealed truths from her.

But she *wouldn't* be a pawn any more.

She was taking charge of her life. And she *would* survive.

She narrowed her eyes as she gazed at Marlow over her pistol. 'It doesn't matter what I would have done. That life and those choices are as dead as Edmund.'

'I never intended to promote him *for ever*.' Marlow continued after a pause, still attempting to hurt her. 'Only until I tired of you, which would have been well before the next election.'

Then and there, Henrietta made the choice not to believe Marlow's tale. Likely, he was trying to poison her thoughts, knock her off-kilter. And even if it were true, what did it matter? Why should one lapse of judgement on Edmund's part cloud the many wonderful memories she had of her husband? Had not she herself made an error of judgement when she encouraged the proposal and agreed to the marriage? Edmund had forgiven her, because he was a good and kind man. He would never have made such a deal with Marlow – but *if* he had, Henrietta loved him enough to forgive him.

She only fell in love with good men.

Two good men, specifically. Who happened to be half-brothers.

And though the third brother seemed eaten up with hatred and malice, Henrietta cherished the close relation between Edmund and Theo. It explained why they fitted so companionably into her heart, her feelings for one never at odds with her feelings for the other. Theo and Edmund were different men, yes, but at the core they shared the attributes she valued most highly. Kindness, honour and a deep concern for the affairs of all people.

But those were thoughts to ponder and cherish another time.

Now, she must deal with a murderer.

She aimed her pistol more carefully at Marlow's thigh. 'I know you're lying. You disliked whatever deal Edmund offered and so you poisoned him.'

He chuckled. 'Silly child, I am not Edmund's killer. I would never kill in such a gauche manner. When *I've* killed . . .' He paused, staring at her intently. 'Pardon, I mean if I *were* to kill, you would find no traceable evidence. There are many ways to make a murder look like a suicide.' He observed his bottle. 'Or an accident,' he said, taking a swig. 'A drowning accident, for example, such as ended my poor father's life when I was only twelve.'

'You killed your father?' Henrietta asked, horrified.

Marlow's smile was vicious. 'My, how sordid your imagination is. Did you not hear me say his death was an accident? It happened here – in the River Enberry, at the foot of the tiered gardens – about five months after your broom-boy was conceived.'

Marlow was as evil as the very devil. 'You are hinting at it without saying it, wanting me to know you killed your father. And so, I know you killed Edmund as well.'

He shook his head. 'Not Edmund. With Edmund, I merely

engaged in self-preservation. If he died as a consequence, I am not to blame.'

The hair rose on Henrietta's arms. 'What do you mean?'

He nodded at her pistol. 'I'm tired of staring at that toy of yours. Put it down and we can talk more.'

'Not a chance.'

He watched her steadily as he swigged from his bottle. 'Then I suppose you must be made to obey.'

'Go ahead and try.' She was a skilled markswoman, confident of her aim, her willingness to shoot to maim, if it came to that, and of her physical strength against a drunk Marlow. 'I have five elder brothers, so I learnt long ago how to best any man in a fight.'

He licked his lips slowly. 'I didn't say anything about a *man*.'

And before she could absorb his meaning, a looped rope fell over her head and down to her extended arms, and then was yanked so hard she had to drop her pistol to the floor to keep the noose from strangling her. With not a split second to spare, she managed to pull it past her shoulders, but then it tightened so securely around her torso she could barely breathe.

She turned to face her attacker.

And stared straight into the black, black eyes of Désirée du Pont.

'You *are* Eliza King!' But the moment she said it, she knew it couldn't be. Eliza King would never attack her *before* Marlow, who was the enemy of her causes and the killer of their champion.

Yet if Désirée du Pont wasn't the radical leader, why was she at Enberry Abbey?

And where *was* Eliza King?

CHAPTER 30

The Nightshade

Eliza King had locked Henrietta inside Enberry Abbey and Theo must save her without revealing his presence. With that purpose in mind, he dashed past the row of French windows and around to the north side of the mansion, frantically testing for unlocked windows or doors. When his search proved unsuccessful, he removed his coat, wrapped it around his fist and readied his arm to strike out the pane of a French door that led from the house to a garden of ornamental trees and flowering bushes.

A woman spoke from behind his shoulder. "'Tis best to enter silently.'

Startled, Theo turned to face the speaker, but for once his eyesight failed him. No human form was discernible amongst the thick cluster of lilac trees from which the voice had emanated.

Until she glided forward.

Slim, cloaked and hooded, her features in shadow, she approached soundlessly and stopped a yard away. A slight tilt of her head, and then, 'Why are you here, Mr Hawke?' Her voice was measured and intelligent, her accent working-class. Yet her recognition of Theo meant she was no servant or local villager. If she was Eliza King, as Theo suspected, then *who had locked Henrietta in the house?*

He forced himself to speak calmly. 'I am here to catch the Duke of Severn's killer. If your purpose is the same, we are not adversaries.'

She chuckled, light as rustling leaves. 'I'm not here to catch him. I am here to *kill* him. If you attempt to impede me, we are indeed adversaries.'

'I'll gladly help you apprehend him, but I urge you to let the law judge and sentence him.'

'The law is more renegade than I, Mr Hawke,' she replied coldly. 'The law is vacillating and biased. I am neither.'

'But the lady I love is inside this house, in great danger, and if you kill Marlow without first garnering irrefutable proof of her innocence, she will be condemned.'

'Do you love Henrietta Percy?' Surprise tinged her tone. 'Perhaps there is an interesting story there – how a gossip journalist came to love a duchess. If I cared a fig for matters of the heart, I might wish to hear. But I don't believe in romantic love. Not when men are so often cruel liars.'

'I am no liar,' Theo said. 'I seek the truth, in all its nuances.'

She lifted her shoulders lightly. 'While I am indifferent to Her Grace's survival, Marlow won't be. If he finds her first, she'll join the other women who have entered these grounds on their own two feet, only to exit by way of the Enberry.' She pointed to the river, a shining silver ribbon flowing past the terraced gardens.

Theo's skin crawled. 'Is he so evil as that? The killing of women?'

'Whores, barmaids, scullery wenches – and now, an unfaithful, troublesome duchess. What matter such lives to a lord? Nay, what matter lives like that to the *law*? And lords and law are often one and the same. Marlow is the local magistrate, but even were he not, what magistrate bothers to investigate one more sinful female who evidently took her own life? My own sister lies buried at the crossroads, not in the churchyard, which is why I learnt long ago to take the law into my own hands. Until the law sees all men as equal, and all women as equal to men, there can be no true justice.'

'Are you Eliza King herself, or her supporter?' Theo asked.

The woman pulled back her hood, revealing a pale face framed by brown hair pulled into a severe chignon. Her large eyes were an indeterminable pale colour – at odds with the description of a black-eyed beauty. 'Elizabeth, Eliza, Betsy and Bess. Are you familiar with that children's rhyme, Mr Hawke?'

'I've heard it,' he replied.

'My followers sometimes call me the mistress of disguise. My very name lends itself to disguise and I enjoy the challenge of concealing even my most unique feature, so that no one will recognise me unless I choose. Before the sun rises, I shall be Eliza King again. But now, I am the Nightshade, because nightshade brings death. Do you dare enter with death, Mr Hawke?'

Theo kept his voice steady. 'I'll do anything to save Henrietta.'

Her slow smile sent chills down his spine. 'Come then, Mr Hawke. We shall see if your duchess yet lives.'

She withdrew a long, thin instrument. As she worked it into the glass door's keyhole, Theo's mind raced.

'Since *you* are Eliza King,' he said, 'who is the woman inside? Your assistant?'

'Someone else in grave danger, though she may be unaware.' The lock clicked. She turned the knob, then paused. 'Are you armed?'

'No, but I am strong,' he replied, determined to find his half-brother, prove the villain's guilt and save all three women in danger. Thank God Henrietta had her pistol. Since he'd heard no shot, she must not have had cause to use it. That or she was incapacitated. 'Are *you* armed?' he asked, pushing into the house, eager to reach his love.

'Twice over.' A wicked dagger glinted in the dim light as Eliza withdrew it from the recesses of her cloak. She also lifted a vial dangling from a chain about her neck.

'Poison?' he asked, confused. Why was Eliza King showing him the murder weapon Marlow had used against Severn? Did her style of justice involve killing a murderer by the same means with which he had killed?

She opened the vial, sipped, and then grinned, her lips slick with clear fluid. 'Depends upon who's drinking it.' Suddenly, she grabbed Theo's head and pressed her lips to his mouth.

Theo pushed her away, sputtering.

Chuckling lightly, she capped her vial. 'Such a small amount won't kill you.'

'I object to the assault.' He scowled, wiping his wet lips. She'd left a sticky residue and the putridly sweet taste lingered, like overripe berries spiked with cheap gin.

She watched him intently. 'You'll face worse assaults, soon. Be more alert.'

That's when Theo noticed her eyes were no longer pale.

They were as black as a moonless night.

'I'm *not* Eliza King. What a stupid thing to think.' Miss du Pont had managed to yank Henrietta to the floor with the rope and now straddled her middle as she secured her arms to her side. The opera dancer was lean but *strong*, and Henrietta found herself powerless to resist. 'I am the mistress of Lord Marlow, who took me into his keeping shortly after Perceval the worm left me for his bluestocking. He helped me plan Perceval's destruction.' She smirked at Henrietta. 'I *knew* you hadn't any notion of my new lover. You don't know anything, do you? And that is why you find yourself in a very bad situation, is it not, Madame Duchess?'

Marlow stood nearby, looking down at them both. He'd found Henrietta's pistol and was stroking the barrel with one pale finger. 'Secure her arms to her torso, Désirée, but tie her legs spread between two of those pedestals. I shall have my way with her later, after I've taken care of my business. And *then*, Duchess, you will take a long swim. Should your corpse happen to wash ashore before it's completely consumed by the fish, everyone will think you drowned yourself rather than face the gallows.'

Henrietta's defiance surged despite the chill in her veins. 'I'm an excellent swimmer. My family will never believe I drowned.'

Marlow tapped the pistol against his palm. 'Such valuable information, my dear. How convenient when the victim assists in planning her own murder. You'll shoot yourself instead, with this pretty pistol engraved with your arms. We'll take a little journey first – later, after I've dealt with my business – so your body isn't found near here.'

'I'll fight you every step of the way, Marlow.'

His smile mocked her. 'Like you're fighting now?'

Fury coursed through Henrietta, but he was correct. She lay wriggling as helplessly as a fish out of water.

But she didn't resign herself to death *yet*. Yes, her chance of escape had become frighteningly slim, but Theo hadn't been captured. And Eliza King might yet have a part to play, if there was indeed a *second* black-eyed woman on the Enberry grounds, as the Millford men claimed.

And on top of that, Henrietta herself was no sapskull. If she managed to win Miss du Pont to her side, she stood a chance of overpowering Marlow. She bent her mind to this purpose... what could she say? What could she promise? The opera dancer hated men, did she not? And if Henrietta could just prove her innocence and gain her freedom, she would once again be one of the wealthiest people in the kingdom. Perhaps *Henrietta* could provide for Miss du Pont, so that the opera dancer need never take a lover again, unless she wished to do so...

Just then the mirrored door opened and Theo stepped into the ballroom.

Almost before Henrietta could register his presence, Marlow raised his arm and metal glinted in the moonlight.

Henrietta shrieked a warning. 'Flee, Theo! He has my—'

Marlow pulled the trigger.

Henrietta opened her mouth to scream...

But no explosion of gunpowder sounded. The hammer clicked against the ball. Then silence. A wave of overpowering relief swept over her and a sob of gratitude tore from her mouth. The cap must've fallen off when the weapon had crashed to the parquet floor earlier.

Cursing, Marlow threw the pistol across the room. It hit a bust and fell into the shadows. 'No matter.' He shrugged. 'It was the impulse of the moment and would have been an untidy way to dispose of you, although I do like the thought of Henrietta scrubbing your blood off my floors.' He laughed. 'Good evening, *brother*.'

Theo glided sideways from the doorway, lingering in the shadows of the mirrored wall. The room was growing darker, the moon likely close to setting, but a couple of hours must remain until the first light of dawn.

'You are no brother to me, Marlow.' Clever Theo was by now completely hidden in shadow, whereas Marlow stood in the brighter section of the ballroom. 'Now, release the duchess and I might let you live.'

'You fancy yourself her saviour, don't you, Hawke?' Marlow said. 'Do you love her, in fact? Hilarious to think this is where my prank five years ago would end.'

Henrietta frowned, uncertain of Marlow's meaning.

'What prank?' Theo's voice asked from the darkness.

Marlow paced languidly back towards Henrietta. 'Don't say I never did anything good for you, brother. I saw you lurking in the garden at that soirée, scouting for salacious stories. Meanwhile, the duchess was fluttering about me, such a foolish, inept flirt, willing to prostitute herself to please her husband. I knew Edmund would have told her to be discreet. I knew she was as green a virgin as ever there was.' He spoke to Theo but looked directly at Henrietta, a glint in his eye. 'And I could never resist an opportunity to hurt Edmund – he's my half-brother, as well, like you, as I've explained to Henrietta – and so I took her to the niche where you lurked, and gave you a show, simply because it amused me for the kingdom to think I'd cuckolded—'

'Release her *now*.' Theo's voice was laced with hate. 'Or I'll—'

'You'll what?' Marlow's boot hovered above Henrietta's throat, the stitches on his leather sole clear even in the dim light. 'Just give me reason, Hawke, and I shall crush her neck.'

There was no reply from Theo.

Marlow laughed, but thankfully moved his foot, brushing it along Henrietta's jaw as he withdrew.

Miss du Pont's absence suddenly struck Henrietta. 'Be careful, Theo. Miss du Pont is lurking in these shadows and she's an expert with a rope. And you were correct, she's *not* Eliza King—'

'Miss du Pont is keeping me company,' said a feminine voice. 'And quite right, she's not Eliza King.'

Into the dimly lit middle of the room, a shadowy form stepped. No, *two* shadowy forms: Miss du Pont, with a knife to her throat, held tightly in front of another woman.

'Libby!' Henrietta said in astonishment. Although the straight-backed young woman with dark eyes bore only slight resemblance to the mousy, clumsy maid, Henrietta recognised her.

'Ah,' Marlow said, with a clap. 'Our guest of honour arrives at last. The very reason I travelled to Enberry tonight rather than upon the morrow. My dear Miss King, I knew you'd surface here when Désirée relayed the Runners' information that Libby the clumsy, stupid maid was missing from Newgate. *Missing*, they said! As if you'd been mislaid by the warden, rather than rescued in a plan meticulously orchestrated by radicals and traitors.' He spread his arms theatrically. 'And so all the players are finally present, those I expected and those I did not. Now I wonder, with such an intricate web of lies and deceit before us, how shall we unravel this convoluted tale?'

Puzzle pieces fell into place in Henrietta's mind. The maid who was so fascinated by Edmund and the fugitive radical leader, known as a mistress of disguise, were one and the same. 'Libby, if you are Eliza King, why come to me as a maid?'

'A reconnaissance mission,' Libby, who was now Eliza, replied calmly, quite as if they were having an afternoon chat. 'After Cato Street, it was imperative I disappear for a time, but I can never be idle in my mission. A position in your household allowed me access to your husband's private papers. I was able to study his habits, learn his daily schedule, identify his closest companions, whose counsel he valued and whose he did not ... all information I intended to employ—'

'Oh, *do* tell the truth, Eliza,' Marlow interrupted, sounding bored. 'You intended to fuck him, of course. To make him want you, to go to his bed, to become his mistress. Work him over until you had the reforming People's Duke in your radical pocket. A clever plan, perhaps – *had Severn fucked women.*'

'I employ what means I must to achieve my ends,' Eliza said, a note of pride in her voice. 'Exploiting male weakness *can* sometime prove useful, yet, unlike you, my imagination can extend beyond fucking and murdering. But tonight, there *will* be murder. The question is, who amongst us will die, and who – if any – will live to tell the tale?' She dug her knife into Miss du Pont's skin until a bead of dark liquid dripped down the dancer's white, swanlike neck. Miss du Pont's eyes flashed with defiance and her lips pressed into a line.

Marlow rubbed his hands. 'Do kill *her*, if you want. You'll save me taking the trouble myself, for naturally I must dispose of all witnesses after I kill you, Eliza.'

Henrietta recoiled against the cold floor, sick with horror. Marlow was as mad as he was evil... he seemed positively *gleeful* at the prospect of watching his mistress die.

Eliza didn't bat an eyelid, however. 'Exactly what I would have expected of you, my lord.' She smiled at her captive. 'But you, Miss du Pont? Did you realise your lover holds your life so cheap? If not, how does the knowledge that he intends to kill you make you feel?'

Miss du Pont's silence spoke volumes. Marlow had turned his only ally present against him. Foolish, foolish man.

This shift would work to their advantage. If only Henrietta's ropes would give way, she'd help Eliza take control and organise Miss du Pont and Theo. Together, they could subdue Marlow and extract a confession, witnessed by all. Surely even a jury of Marlow's peers couldn't dismiss the testimony of *four* people, when one was a duchess and another the most popular radical leader in Britain.

Feeling renewed hope, she flexed and stretched her legs, testing the ropes for weakness, but her efforts only succeeded in drawing Marlow's attention.

He nudged her jaw with his boot. 'Do you imagine Eliza is going to help you, Henrietta?' he asked, as if he read her thoughts. 'Do you think she will assist you in turning me over to the law? Well, she won't. Because she *can't*. Because she's not your ally. She is the true murderer of Severn and she carries the murder weapon in that vial about her neck.'

'The duchess isn't a fool,' Eliza said. 'She knows I'd never kill the nobleman most likely to one day champion my cause. No, I'd kill the person who stood in Severn's way, if the chance were to present itself. I poisoned *your* wine, Lord Marlow.'

Henrietta gasped. It was as she'd always known. No one would have wanted to murder someone as gentle and kind as Edmund. No one except ...

'You knew.' She looked at Marlow. Tears stung her eyes and her throat clogged. 'That day in the library, you stared at Libby so intently ... I thought it lechery, but, no ... you recognised her ... you knew her to be the radical leader so lauded in the village beside your manor ... you knew your wine to be poisoned ... you *did* kill Edmund.'

'Not in the least,' Marlow said. 'I merely handed the glass your maid gave me to Edmund out of courtesy, so he might drink first.'

Eliza shook her head. 'How I cursed my stupidity later for not watching you closely. You knew the wine I gave you was poisoned, and you knowingly handed it to Severn. *You* killed him.'

'I didn't know the wine was poisoned, I merely suspected it when I recognised you as a child of bloody Jim King, the man I'd long suspected to be the father of Eliza King. As far as I could tell, the whole pack of you King mongrels had differently coloured eyes ...'

'Certainly, my elder sister, Nelly, did. You took her to your bed when she was but fifteen, and shortly after you got her with child, her body was found in the Enberry, swollen and bloated, her skirts tangled in the mill wheel. Frightened the locals, it did. Suicide, they called it. Even respect for my father didn't stop a pack of superstitious fools from fishing out her body and burying it at the crossroads, lest her condemned soul take to wandering.'

'I had nothing to do with your sister's suicide, Eliza. I told her to take care she didn't get with child; unlike my father, I don't care to populate Britain with my bastards. When she chose to disregard my warning, evidently because she'd imagined I'd marry her if she carried my brat, I told her she could go hang for all I cared. Apparently, she chose to drown herself instead.'

'Lies, of course,' Eliza said. 'I have longed for your death, Marlow. For years, I've dreamt of it. So much so that my eagerness made me careless that afternoon, I admit. I never expected such a perfect chance... the duke, calling for his wine... that fool footman so easily distracted... just the right amount of nightshade upon me to ensure you wouldn't die in Severn's home, but later, when none would suspect a member of the duke's household... a mere moment to decide if I should strike, all while knowing I couldn't let the opportunity pass, though I had too little time to disguise myself properly... Damn that I failed then, but I shall succeed in bringing about justice for Severn and for Nelly tonight, and all will be well...'

Henrietta grew increasingly horrified as Eliza spoke. 'All will be well?' she asked, unable to believe her own ears. '*You* brought the poison that killed my husband into the library! How can you think another death will make all well? Nothing can bring back what was lost and you had a hand in that terrible end.'

Eliza raised her shoulders. 'Innocents die on the path to justice.'

'Callous, unfeeling woman!' Henrietta strained her neck to see the radical more clearly. 'You killed a great man in the prime of his life and you show no remorse.'

For the first time since her capture, Miss du Pont spoke. 'Ah, and so now you begin to understand, Madame *Naïveté*. Just as your class is callous about the lives of the likes of us, so too can we be about your lives. That is what the French aristocracy learnt, nearly thirty years ago. But while my grandparents' necks were sliced, *I* shall not die in such a way.'

She was a dancer and a skilled one at that – Henrietta's eyes widened in amazement, for Désirée executed the most exquisite pirouette within Eliza King's arms. More fluid than the ocean, she performed a *plié*, slipping out of the radical leader's grasp and grabbing the knife. *Jetés* and *chassés* brought her across the ballroom floor towards Marlow.

But there her luck ended.

Marlow swiped a bust from the wall of pedestals, pulled back his arm, and, just as Désirée extended hers with the cruel blade glistening, he smashed the marble head into her elbow.

There was a sickly crack, the breaking of bones. Désirée didn't scream; the sound she made as she crumpled to the floor was low, guttural and far more anguished. Her skirts billowed about her and the knife clanged against the parquet.

Theo emerged as Marlow reached for the knife. He rushed towards Henrietta, seeking to put himself between her and Marlow's blade.

But Henrietta wasn't the woman Marlow attacked. *His* sights were set on Eliza.

Eliza was as unmoving as a statue, almost as if she were waiting. Theo altered course to intervene, but Marlow was upon Eliza too quickly. Once, the knife struck. Deep into the woman's chest. Out it came, its blade no longer glistening but covered in a dark substance. Down it struck again and this time Eliza fell. Soundlessly, until she hit the floor. Then there was a whoosh, like wind through trees.

Theo was upon Marlow and *this* fight was an equal match. Two men, no weapons. Fists to the jaw, the nose, the face. Kicks to the stomach, the legs, the groin. Grunts and raw violence. No quarter given by either.

And Henrietta strained against her ropes, gritting her teeth to employ every ounce of strength she possessed. All to no avail, for she was as trussed as a Christmas goose. She cried out in desperation, but cries didn't release restraints. She was the last woman remaining who had the physical strength to assist in the fight, but she needed help.

'Désirée.' She called out to the crumpled form nearest her.

'Eliza,' she said to the other woman, who was more towards the centre of the ballroom. Neither moved, but someone made a sound. 'The knife,' she said. 'Where is the knife? Cut my bonds and let me fight for us. We are no longer adversaries, but allies against a monster. For the sake of Nelly, for the sake of Severn, for the sake of all Marlow's innocent victims, for your own sake, *cut my bonds.*'

Because if one of them didn't, all hope was lost...

CHAPTER 31

Death Comes to Enberry Abbey

Moments ticked past. Neither wounded woman moved and Henrietta's hope slipped away. Eliza must be dead, she reasoned, and Désirée unconscious from pain.

Theo and Marlow's fight filled the ballroom. They were locked in a desperate struggle for survival and though Marlow was older, he struck with ruthless brutality, for he sought to kill Theo by any means necessary, and Theo was hindered by his humanity.

Through it all, Henrietta repeated the names of Désirée, Eliza. She called them to stay with her, to stay alive, not to give up the will to live.

A feminine exhalation brought the first spark of hope. Then a rustle. A movement. Eliza's cloaked form was sliding across the floor and Henrietta's heart leapt. 'You're alive,' she whispered as the radical leader pulled herself closer, extending her right arm, sliding her body on its side along the parquet, extending the arm again. Repeating the process. A trail of black liquid smeared the floor where she'd been.

Eliza paused beside Désirée. Touched the dancer's face. 'I cannot go on,' she murmured, two dark heads side by side. 'Take the knife. Cut her bonds. If she is not released, four people die tonight rather than only one.'

Désirée moaned, but the words and touch roused her. 'I will be sick,' she said, with a strangled cry, and she made good her prediction.

'It is the pain,' Eliza said as Désirée retched. 'Your arm is broken, but your spirit is not. Gather your strength. Pull this knife from me, cut the duchess's bonds and you will live to dance again.'

Désirée sat up, the men too locked in battle to notice. She pulled back Eliza's cloak, revealing a blood-soaked torso. Eliza's hands were clasped around the hilt of the knife, the blade entirely sunk into her body.

'The blade staunches the flow,' Henrietta whispered urgently. 'Eliza, if Désirée removes the knife, you may die.'

The corner of Eliza's lips quirked. 'I am the great Eliza King, and, as such, I am immortal. In death, I shall be more powerful even than in life. The people will avenge me. My causes will succeed at last. Besides,' she looked at Henrietta keenly, 'I've allowed innocents to die merely because their lives stood in the way of victory. I close my eyes at night and though I think of them, I cannot bring myself to mourn. In a way, I am already dead inside.'

Henrietta understood. Eliza was not without any conscience. 'If I survive tonight,' she told her former maid, 'I shall avenge your sister. Officially, Marlow will hang for your death and for Edmund's, but, at the same time, Nelly will receive her justice. Nelly and the other restless souls, whomever they may be.' She transferred her gaze to Désirée, who sat watching them. 'And your testimony will help bring this about.'

Désirée snorted. 'Who'll believe what I say?'

'The people will.'

'But it is not the people who will try Marlow,' Désirée said. 'It's the House of Lords. What do *they* care about the people?'

'In a large enough group, the people have a voice louder than that of all the aristocrats, and they will thirst for vengeance for the killer of both the Duke of Severn and Eliza King. If Marlow's peers don't hold him accountable to the full extent of the law, with the state of this country what it is, there could be a revolution. That's not the answer any of us want, not even you, Désirée, after what the last revolution took from your family. There are innocents and the guilty on both sides; let us take action so no more innocent blood is shed.'

Désirée visibly paled as she studied Eliza's blood-soaked front. She made to move her uninjured hand towards the knife hilt but then she recoiled, covering her mouth instead. 'I cannot do this thing. I shall feel I've killed you ...'

Eliza acted swiftly. A weak but curt nod. A movement of her arms. A slurp as the blade withdrew. A gush of blood in its wake. An offering of a blood-soaked weapon.

Désirée didn't hesitate then. As if her will to live suddenly possessed her in force, she began to saw at Henrietta's ankles. One foot was freed. The bloody blade slipped, hit the floor. Désirée wiped her hand, smearing dark liquid across her skirts, and picked the knife up again. Another foot freed.

The pool of blood around Eliza was growing. Seeping, spreading across the ballroom. The radical leader clutched her cloak to her stomach as Désirée began to hack at the ropes binding Henrietta's torso.

'What voice and influence and fortune I have,' Henrietta said to Eliza, 'I shall use to amplify the honourable causes of the people.'

'I believe you.' Eliza's voice was barely a whisper. 'I watched you. I watched you save journal articles. I watched you observe the radicals. I heard you encourage your husband to think more extensively than he already did, and I believe you mean it. You'll do it for your husband, whom you loved—'

'Yes,' Henrietta said. 'But even more than that, I'll do it for the people.'

And she'd do it for herself. Because she believed in the cause. Because she was not a pawn. Not powerless and weak and reliant on the advice of men. She was a woman of independent means and independent thought. She would use her life to make a difference.

'*A treas'ry is our common land*,' Eliza said.

Henrietta nodded. '*United all we make our stand.*'

The last rope slipped free and Désirée placed the knife in Henrietta's hand.

'Staunch Eliza's wound, Désirée.' Henrietta rose to her feet, ready to aid Theo in his fight.

Désirée moved towards the radical. Then she stopped. 'She's already dead, Your Grace.'

Henrietta looked down. Eliza's ghostly white face was motionless, her black eyes staring but forever sightless to this world. And it was up to the next world, whatever that might be, to judge Eliza King. The good and the bad of her, tangled so tightly together.

Henrietta's heart ached for Jim King, deprived of two daughters by the same vicious man. He was yet another reason Henrietta must see justice done.

Resolved, she rushed forward, knife in hand. She did this for the people of Britain. She did this for Edmund. For Theo. For the King sisters, for Désirée du Pont, for Deborah Hawke, Theo's innocent child-mother. For Mrs Ford, so she would come to no harm. And she did it for her brothers, who had ensured she knew how to fight.

She couldn't possibly let them down.

She wasn't going to let anyone down.

Least of all herself.

CHAPTER 32

The Promised Scoop

'You must go to London,' Henrietta said to Theo.

Bruised, battered and bloody, they stood holding hands, looking down on Marlow's limp body, bound with the ropes that had restrained Henrietta. Henrietta had struck his temple with the hilt of the knife one time more than was *technically* necessary, and that, combined with the effects of the alcohol the viscount had consumed, had rendered him not *quite* unconscious, but *extremely* mellow.

'I shall stay here and ensure Marlow remains secure while you fetch the authorities,' she continued. 'Marlow must be the local magistrate, so seek Sir Robert Baker in London. But go first to Perceval and obtain his assistance.' She put into his bruised hand her engagement ring, still attached to its ribbon necklace, and Marlow's signet ring, which she'd yanked from his finger. The damn thing was no doubt responsible for splitting Theo's beautiful lips, and for the sharp cuts on his cheeks and forehead. 'Then go

A LADY'S GUIDE TO MURDER [307]

next to my father. Show him these rings and he will believe you. Once you have their support, all of you must visit the magistrate together. Sir Robert will listen, then.'

The household staff – who numbered only five, and were housed in an outbuilding near the kitchens – roused soon after Theo had left, and while the housekeeper and the maids wept from the ballroom doors at the sight of Eliza King's bloodied body, nary a servant was the least bit concerned for their master.

'A doctor for Miss du Pont,' Henrietta said, when the only manservant asked what she needed. 'And a pot of tea, please. But no one else must enter this room and no one can touch Miss King's body until the magistrate and his Runners arrive.'

'Should we close her eyes?' Désirée asked after the servants had left them with a tea tray. The opera dancer shuddered as she looked at Eliza's sightless stare.

'We must leave them for now,' Henrietta replied, adding several sugar lumps to the tea she'd poured for Désirée, who needed strength. 'We mustn't touch a thing and we mustn't conceal a fact. The magistrate must know it all, even the part Eliza played in my husband's death.'

Désirée took the offered teacup. 'But we want Marlow to hang for that crime, do we not?'

Henrietta poured her own tea. 'We want justice to be served rightly.'

'But who then killed your husband?'

Henrietta dropped a sugar lump into her cup. 'I am no judge or barrister, yet it seems to me Marlow and Eliza share the guilt.'

'But what if he's declared innocent and walks free?' Désirée asked, her black eyes peering over her steaming cup. 'He'll come for us both then, you know.'

Henrietta stirred her tea and delicately tapped the spoon against the cup's rim. 'He is the undisputed murderer of the most popular reformer in Britain, and the co-murderer of the People's Duke. He will not be declared innocent, Désirée.'

After that, they drank their tea in companionable silence.

It was a few hours past dawn before the London company arrived. Theo, whose bruises had darkened so dreadfully that Henrietta longed to smother him in gentle kisses and cool compresses, stood against the pedestal and portrait wall. Beside his father's bust, as it happened, whether or not he realised. Henrietta's father and George, who had come as well, sat on either side of her, in three of the prim chairs along the mirrored wall. In the centre of the room, Eliza's body lay in a pool of congealed blood. Marlow was slumped against a chair on the far side of the room, his bruised face ghastly, his blonde hair and his shirt slick with his sweat. Désirée had been made more comfortable by the doctor – rather, the Millford apothecary – and lay on a pallet with her arm reset and bandaged, but she'd bravely and sacrificially refused all pain relief until after she could give her testimony to the magistrate.

Sir Robert and his Runners examined Eliza. They interviewed Désirée. Their questions for Henrietta were mercifully few, and delivered with respect and humility.

Then the magistrate knelt before Marlow. 'My Lord Marlow, witnesses have given testimony that you boasted of giving the Duke of Severn a poisoned glass of wine, and that you were solely responsible for the cold-blooded murder of Miss Eliza King, whose mutilated body lies before us now. Do you deny these allegations?'

'Fuck you,' Marlow said, his speech still slurred. 'Fuck you and fuck them.'

'Do you deny these allegations of murder, sir?'

Marlow spat a wad of bloodied saliva directly onto Sir Robert's bulbous nose. 'Not in the least. I'm goddamned proud of it.'

Those were the last words Henrietta ever heard the viscount

speak, for Marlow's head then lolled back and he appeared to slip into unconsciousness.

'Well, and so we have that answer.' Sir Robert wiped his nose and then pulled himself to his feet. 'Your lordships heard the confession?' he asked Henrietta's father and brother.

Papa and George gave curt nods, accompanied by severe scowls.

Quaking, Sir Robert inclined his head at Henrietta. 'I owe Your Grace an apology.'

'You will exonerate the duchess today in a public statement,' Papa said, his blue eyes flashing, while George bobbed his head enthusiastically. 'Before the sun sets, I want your statement released to every press in the kingdom. Otherwise, I shall take legal action against you for slander and defamation of character and putting my daughter to harm.'

Sir Robert hastily agreed. 'I shall write the statement at once and send it to London with two of my best men on the fastest horses in his lordship's stable.'

'They will also deliver an article written by Mr Hawke,' Henrietta added, looking towards Theo, who still stood alone by the bust of his father. 'He will write the full account, and it will be published today, in a special edition of *The Hawke's Eye*.'

'*What?*' George exclaimed. 'You cannot be serious, Hen!'

'I'm perfectly serious.' Henrietta's heart swelled as she smiled at her love. 'I couldn't have done this without Mr Hawke. He was my partner every step of the way, saving me repeatedly—'

'You saved yourself, Your Grace.' Theo sounded so loving, and so proud.

Tears sprang to Henrietta's eyes, causing his handsome, bruised face to waver. 'I promised you the scoop,' she said. 'That was our deal.'

'I didn't do this for the scoop, Henrietta.'

'I know. But I want you to have it anyway.'

For a moment, silence reigned, and it was as if they were alone. Just them, and the bond of love stretching between them.

But some rather frantic head movements from Henrietta's father and brother drew her back to reality. They were *not* alone – and George had gone exceedingly red in the face.

'Now, see here, man,' her brother said. 'If you have been taking liberties with my sister—'

Henrietta laughed outright. 'Oh, stop, George. And, Papa, don't you begin. I'm quite capable of deciding who may and may not take liberties with me. It's time you realise I am my own woman.' She stood, mustering what dignity she could wearing Theo's too-big clothes, now bloodied and muddied. 'And now I shall take my leave in order to help Mr Hawke find paper and a pen. He has an article to write.'

They sought the library. As they walked through the soaring medieval-abbey-turned-grand-hall, early morning sunlight streamed through the eastern rose window, spilling red, blue, and gold over the flagstone floors.

Henrietta leant her head against Theo's shoulder. 'When you have finished your article, return with me to London in my father's carriage. I intend to spend a few days recovering at Lockington House. We shall both have peace there.'

'Oh, no, Henrietta,' he said. 'I cannot travel in your father's carriage, nor would I presume to stay in his home. Your family despises me and with good reason.'

'That is soon to be forgotten.'

Theo tugged at his bloodied shirt collar sheepishly. 'Perhaps once my article is published and they have acclimatised themselves to our friendship, I *might* have a chance of redemption.'

'Redemption has nothing to do with it. My parents will like you – no, they'll love you – the moment they realise how dearly, how deeply, and how completely *I* love you.'

He halted, his eyes searching hers, hope flickering in their gold-brown depths. 'Do you truly? *Can* you truly love me?'

Her cheeks warmed as she cupped his chin gently. 'I love you so very, very much.' The tension melted from his features, joy shining despite his bruises. Smiling, she nudged him towards the library door. 'But now you must write, sweetheart.'

'Not *quite* yet, my love.'

Theo swept her into his arms. As his lips found hers, the beams of light from the stained glass seemed to brighten, surrounding them in the most glorious colours, and the love in Henrietta's heart filled her chest to bursting.

In Theo's embrace, she was home.

And though they didn't need fireworks, Henrietta imagined them anyway.

EPILOGUE

Grenham Park, Berkshire

After Michaelmas, 1820

Butterflies danced in a gentle breeze as Henrietta tended to her flower garden, snipping early autumn blooms with her maid.

The sun was warm through her black silk mourning gown. Though the ache of Edmund's absence was lessening, there was sorrow in her grief diminishing as well, and so she had resolved to wear black and grey for a year, to weave Edmund's memory into the fabric of her life. A part of her would forever lament what might have been if he had lived. The prime minister he might have become; the child they might have raised; the ways their marriage might have matured and deepened over the years, like one of the fine wines he'd loved.

But another man resided in her heart now as well, and his place there didn't feel like disloyalty. Edmund would have been happy for her. How he would have laughed at the joke, his grey eyes twinkling in delight, that she'd unknowingly fallen in love with his half-brother. A man who embodied the same admirable traits of honour and kindness.

The clip of hooves on the gravel drive turned her head, and once she convinced herself the vision before her was real, and no figment of her imagination, her heart leapt.

It was Theo, arriving on the black gelding Perceval had gifted in gratitude for services rendered to the Percy family.

Her body tingling with excited anticipation, Henrietta placed the scissors and blooms in her maid's basket. Though they'd exchanged letters, she hadn't seen Theo in almost three months and it was all she could do not to hike up her skirts and fly to him in a most undignified manner. After a week spent recovering at her parents' house, they'd parted ways, so she could retire discreetly to the country for her mourning, and so that Theo could address the offers of employment he'd received after his article.

'D'ye want me to take the flowers inside, Your Grace?' her maid asked, her unusual eyes sparkling – one light green and the other pale blue.

Henrietta smiled at the girl. When she'd offered to provide an education for Jim King's remaining daughter, who wished to be a clerk, he'd agreed only if thirteen-year-old Maisy served as Henrietta's maid while pursuing her education. 'Yes, Maisy, please do. Put them in water and I will arrange the vases later. Then you may attend to your lessons with Mrs Aldworth.' The local vicar's wife, who had once been a governess, taught Maisy penmanship, composition and bookkeeping in the parsonage just down the lane.

As Maisy walked away, Theo dismounted, handed his horse to a groom and approached, hat in hand, the autumnal sunlight highlighting the golden tones in his brown hair.

He bowed deeply. 'Your Grace.'

She laughed. 'Goodness, do stop. You still manage to make it sound sarcastic.'

'I assure you, that is your imagination,' he replied, hand over heart. 'You are the embodiment of grace.'

'Silly man.' She scolded him to disguise how madly her heart fluttered. 'Now tell me how you managed to arrive so swiftly, when I sent my reply to your query only this morning? Does your horse fly?'

'I confess I didn't wait for your letter. I realised I needed to see you, even if you turned me from your door.'

'You knew perfectly well I'd welcome you with open arms. In fact, come into the walled garden so I can greet you properly after an absence of nearly three months.'

He grinned and she took his arm.

There were two walled gardens at Grenham: the kitchen garden, with its produce protected from rabbits and roes, and the smaller medicinal garden, less often entered and fragrant with the scent of herbs and wildflowers. Rosemary, thyme, sage. Horseradish and garlic. Lavender, marigold, and yarrow.

She guided Theo to the medicinal garden and latched the wooden door behind them. Then she wrapped her arms about his neck and kissed him deeply.

The sensation was instantly familiar – that of dissolving into his embrace, craving nothing but his companionship, his presence, his love.

The feeling of being home.

When they at last broke their kiss, she laid her cheek against his shoulder. He smelt of ink and warmth and Theo. 'I've missed you terribly.'

'Same, my darling.' He kissed her forehead tenderly. 'How have you been?'

'Well enough. And you?'

'Lovesick, but busy.'

'Congratulations again on your post with the *Westminster Morning Journal*,' she said, referring to Theo's new employer, one of Britain's leading political newspapers. 'Does it bring you satisfaction?'

'As much as I look to work for personal satisfaction, yes. Since I can't vote or stand for Parliament, I never expected to have real opportunity to influence political agendas, so in that sense, it's a dream come true. It's simply that my work is no longer the dream of my life.'

Her heart skipped, for she strongly suspected *she* was the dream of his life. 'I love you,' she whispered into his neckcloth, hoping the declaration would encourage any question he might wish to ask her. For surely he had a *reason* for this unexpected visit?

'I love you, too.' But he sounded sad and he disengaged from their embrace after kissing her once more. 'I'm here for a reason, other than wanting to see you.'

She knew from his tone of voice he hadn't come for the reason she'd hoped. But she tucked her disappointment away. That beautiful, longed-for time would come when it was meant to be.

Her gaze fell to the folded broadsheet Theo pulled from an inner pocket of his tailcoat.

Unlike other newspapers, the *Westminster* printed headlining news rather than advertisements on its front page, and so she immediately saw *The Death of Marlow* in bold print and under that, the name of the author. *Theodore Hawke.*

'Ah, the deed is done.' She felt oddly flat. There was no serenity, no additional peace with the news that Marlow had hanged. The world would not miss the vile viscount, but his death didn't bring back Edmund.

'I wanted to bring you this in person before your copy arrives with the London post later.'

'Thank you,' she said, but she didn't move to take the paper.

'Do you want me to read it to you?' he asked.

'No. You are kind to bring it, but this is the first thing you have written that I shan't read – not for some time, at least. But you may tell me about it, briefly.'

Theo returned the newspaper to his coat pocket and gestured to a stone bench. 'Perhaps we should sit?'

She agreed, for her legs had gone wobbly and her stomach churned.

Once seated, Theo cuddled her against him, which helped restore her equilibrium. 'It happened yesterday morning,' he said. 'Since the weather was fine and Marlow was despised, it attracted the largest crowd I have ever seen. No doubt the novelty of a peer hanging was an additional draw. I watched from a rooftop, so I had an unobstructed view and avoided the crush. The crowd was festive, as is so often the case with executions. That always saddens me. No matter how evil the person or the deeds done, there is a perversity, I think, in taking pleasure in a death.'

'Did you write that in your article?' Henrietta asked.

'No, for now I'm sharing that thought only with you. This article was not the place to protest capital punishment. Feelings were too strong around Marlow's death and his crime was too grievous. The murders of both the People's Duke and of Eliza King left too many thirsting for his blood. He had to hang, as his fellow lords knew when they proclaimed him guilty.'

Henrietta nodded against Theo's shoulder. 'Did Marlow go bravely to his death?'

'He didn't weep or resist or beg, so he was brave enough, I suppose. But he was belligerent and scornful. Spat at the jeering crowds before his head was covered. They repaid him by singing Eliza King's song as the noose was tightened and the drop fell, so those were the last words he heard in this life.'

'Poor Libby.' Henrietta sighed. 'Her death will always sadden me. Had life been kinder to her, she might have channelled her talents solely to greatness.'

'Indeed, my love.'

Henrietta sat up and folded her hands in her lap. On the far side of the garden, a robin hopped about industriously. As she watched it peck at the rich soil, a single tear trailed down her cheek. 'Did Marlow die immediately, or did he suffer?'

'An instant death, it seemed. Does that disappoint you?'

'No, no,' she said. 'I am not so cold-hearted, though I still have terrible dreams of poor Edmund's suffering.'

As Theo patted her folded hands, the robin stretched his wings and took flight over the garden wall. Gratitude swelled inside Henrietta. She gave thanks for her home, her estate and all she could provide for the comfort of others, from her tenants to the villagers to the vicar's wife to Maisy – and even the soaring robin, his red breast round over his full stomach.

Henrietta would not dwell in darkness.

Onwards and upwards, like the robin.

'Ah, well, so there it is, and both the people and the peers are satisfied,' she said primly. 'Thank you for telling me, but I don't think I shall want to talk about this again for a long time, if ever.'

'How are you, truly?' he asked, squeezing her hands. Her wedding ring dug into the sides of her fingers. It was one Percy jewel she had no intention of relinquishing during her lifetime, and Perceval hadn't asked for it when she returned the other items so they would be ready for his bride. Jane Babcock was soon to be the new Duchess of Severn, upon which time Henrietta would be known by the dreadful-sounding title of 'Dowager Duchess of Severn'. She was far too young to be a dowager.

'Truly, I'm managing, Theo. All is not quite as I want, but I love Grenham and I love having a home of my own. I received great satisfaction in watching the harvest come in. Though the late summer was wet, the crops fared better than they have in many years, so there was real cause for joy amongst the tenants.' She smiled. 'James Beaucastle has taught me a great deal. Indeed, he calls upon me nearly every week and he's become a lovely friend.

His companion comes as well – a Mr Herridge, who is a perfect dear. Oh, and Mr Herridge has a little boy! His nephew, you see, adopted from a sister with ever so many children. The boy's name is Oliver, and he's six years old and such a darling – but the poor love was dreadfully frightened of me at first, until I took him to watch the harvest one afternoon and then we decided there was a haystack simply begging to be jumped in. Afterwards, he told me duchesses aren't so terrifying, after all.'

Theo grinned. 'The duchess farmer and her young protégé.'

'There's something wholesome and healing about steward-ing the land, and simply being a part of a country community,' Henrietta said, looking at her hands. 'It won't fulfil me for ever, but it works for now.'

'And then?'

'Well, I hope you aren't too happy with your current employ-ment.'

Surprise flickered in his eyes. 'Why?'

She smiled. Recently, she'd begun to dream of ways to support the causes dear to her heart and she'd decided that founding a periodical dedicated to discussing peaceful progress towards much-needed reforms was a perfect place to begin. 'Because I intend to start a newspaper and I shall need an editor.'

A shadow of something crossed Theo's face, but then he returned her smile. 'Henrietta, you should be the editor.'

'I know nothing about it.'

'You know more than you think you do, but I would be happy to assist for a time until you feel confident.'

He looked at her and Henrietta could see the depth of his admiration in his eyes, and her heart flipped again. He truly believed in her. The real her, not the lady in a gilded cage, but the woman who sought to free herself from those constraints. To carve out her own place in the world and set an example for other women to follow, should they wish to fly against convention as well.

She threw her arms around him again. 'Dearest Theo, I have missed you so much I could hardly bear it.'

'As have I, Henrietta.' His lips found hers and there was nothing but that feeling of wholeness, of completion, of home.

When they parted for a breath, he spoke against her cheek. 'Henrietta, I have no right to ask, though I love you as much as any man ever loved any woman. I have nothing, and no one would look kindly on our union. Everyone will think me a treasure-hunter when it's not your money I want in the least. In truth, I wish you were penniless and in need of a protector and a provider, for then I could come to you—'

'Oh, stop, Theo, stop!'

He drew in a sharp breath and buried his head on her shoulder. 'You're correct. I must stop – even I would advise you against accepting me. If you marry again, it should be to a lord, someone from your class, someone who can match your wealth and station—'

'For heaven's sake, you really must stop.' She smiled as she broke their embrace. 'Just ask me, Theo. Just ask.'

Slowly, amazement overtook his face, but there was caution in his voice when he spoke. 'You can't be serious, my love? You would not give up being the Dowager Duchess of Severn to become plain Mrs Hawke?'

'Well, I would, if it came to that,' she said, laughing. 'But it won't. I'm still the daughter of a marquess, so I could never be plain missus anything. I shall be Lady Henrietta Hawke and I happen to think that sounds very well indeed. Now, I do wish you'd ask me.'

Then Theo rapidly went into action, rising from the bench only to kneel at her feet and take her hand. 'Henrietta, I love you with every breath I take and I shall love you for the rest of my life.

Since the first day I beheld you, there has been no other who could compete with you in my heart. Though I can bring nothing to our marriage but my adoration, my mind and my determination, I shall endeavour to be worthy of your love, and I ask for nothing in return. Keep your properties and your money in trust against me. I want you to—'

'Oh, my heavens,' Henrietta said in exasperation. 'I know you are a man of words, but this really is too much. Just ask.'

He gazed up at her with such intense love it took her breath away. 'Henrietta, will you marry me?'

'Yes, Theodore, yes!' She pulled him beside her on the bench so she could throw herself into his arms. 'Yes, yes and yes.'

For a time, their embrace was enough, for there was nothing to do but bask in their joy. Then, after sharing the most perfect of kisses, she placed a hand on his cheek.

'But there are two stipulations.'

His expression grew serious. 'Anything.'

'I want you to be the owner of Grenham, in the usual manner of a wife's property becoming the husband's upon marriage.'

He protested, but Henrietta stopped him by placing her hand over his lips.

'No, don't argue. I will safeguard my dowry as well as the fortune and Welsh estate I inherited from Edmund, because I do wish to keep my autonomy, but I want to share Grenham with you. I want to make you a man of property, so you can vote, and so you can stand for Parliament one day.'

His face clouded with gratitude. He closed his eyes briefly, and when he spoke again, his voice shook. 'Thank you, my love.'

Her heart swelled. 'You see, a lady also can feel pleasure in being a provider. It needn't all be one-sided.'

'Yes, we shall both provide, for we will each have times of need and times of strength. But you spoke of two stipulations and you have given only one so far.'

'The second is that we must wait until July to marry. I want to give Edmund the respectful period of mourning he deserves.'

Theo drew in another breath, but he nodded. 'I understand. Of course. We must do what is right. Nine more months is nothing – I'd wait decades if you asked it of me. I agree it is for the best, for you might meet someone else in the interim, in which case I shall of course release you—'

Henrietta laughed, shaking her head. 'You really are talking far too much today, Theodore. I shan't change my mind. You and I shall wed next summer. In London, for all to see, and think what they will, for that is how I intend to live now. I shall be proud of you, proud of us, proud of our love for each other, and the work we embark on together.'

'As will I, though proud doesn't even begin to cover my feelings.' He kissed her again and then rose. 'I should return to London. I'll make myself scarce in the upcoming months, so you may have all the space you need to mourn, but if I might continue to write to you?'

Henrietta waved her fingers. 'Naturally you must write me beautiful love letters, but don't spend many hours upon the task. I shall require frequent visits, for as long as you can spare from town. You know I dislike a cold bed.'

'But the wait?' he asked, clearly confused.

'Nine months until we wed, but certainly not nine months apart. These last three have been unbearable. We must be together as often as possible – so you can teach me newspaper editing and I can show you the ways of a country squire. There's no time to waste, so you must stay tonight.'

His brow furrowed. 'Are you not concerned about the potential scandal?'

'Don't tell me Theodore Hawke is afraid of a little gossip,' she said teasingly. 'Just … no children yet, sweetheart. Only after we marry.'

He agreed readily. 'And then how many, love?'

'Dozens.' She laughed. 'Half of them boys, and the other half girls every bit as strong and wild as their brothers – but now I think that's enough conversation, Mr Hawke.'

'What do you want instead, Your Grace?' he asked with a smile.

She nodded to a secluded niche filled with potted herbs. 'Five years ago, I invited you to take liberties with me in a garden, and you refused. I hope you won't refuse again?'

His smile broadened and he picked her up, throwing her legs over his forearm and holding her as securely as a babe against his chest. 'I always regretted that decision, so I shall relish the opportunity to make amends.'

'You regretted the decision not to kiss me that day?' she asked as he made his way to the niche. She knew the answer, but she wanted to hear him say it again. And maybe a thousand more times, over the course of the many, many happy years to come.

He hefted her more securely against him. 'Every time I closed my eyes and tried to sleep, every day after that, your face came to my mind, with your lips pursed, offering me that delicious kiss. So, yes, I regretted it daily. Or nightly, rather.'

Henrietta nestled against his shoulder. 'I knew you were obsessed with me.'

'And I always will be, darling.'

HISTORICAL NOTE
and
ACKNOWLEDGEMENTS

The year 1820 was a dark time for many Britons. The joy and relief of Waterloo and the end of the Napoleonic wars was over, replaced by high unemployment, poor social services, and weariness with the Tories, who had been the dominant political party for an exhausting thirty-seven years. As Regency enthusiasts, we might look back with some amusement on the figure of 'Prinny', the Prince Regent during George III's final, decade-long bout of 'madness', but he was not amusing then. He was an extravagant, narcissistic buffoon who cared nothing for duty, was cruel to his wife, and didn't concern himself in the least with easing the plight of others. He spent lavishly on his pet architecture projects, his mistresses, his dinner table, his horses, and the like. Starting in 1820, Prinny became King George IV to the disappointment of nearly everyone, and Britons did not even have a popular heir to the crown to give them hope. Beloved Princess Charlotte (hailed by the people as 'Europe's Hope and Britain's Glory') and her infant son had been dead for just over two years, and Victoria was an infant in her crib, not yet considered likely ever to be queen.

When my editor suggested I write a romance-murder mystery based on an off-page character in *A Debutante's Desire*, in which a fugitive duchess is suspected of murdering her husband, I knew I wanted to set the story in this turbulent year, and I knew I wanted the duke's death to be related to the political situation.

Dukes of the Georgian era were powerful politicians, heavily involved with the day-to-day workings of the government. I chose for my duke to be a reformer. At this time, the Whig party was fractured, with some members promoting reform, some more conservative, and a very few calling themselves 'radicals'. At the risk of oversimplifying, it was in the 1820s that the Whigs began to unite around a reformist mindset, but the more radical members formed their own Radical Party. In time, the Radicals and the Whigs would unite under a new name: the Liberals.

While I did not delve deeply into politics in this novel, I strove to place the death of the fictional Duke of Severn in a time and place and under circumstances in which a political assassination could happen, and I attempted to recreate the mood of the era with some realism. As hard as life must've been in the 1820s, the seeds of change were being sown during this decade. Beginning in 1832, several reform acts eased corruption in Parliament, and it became increasingly fashionable for the affluent to turn their attention to the plight of the poor, of children and of animals. Victorian restraint and morality would rise from the extravagance of the Georgian era.

The pendulum of history is constantly in motion. I reflect on this often while writing and reading historical fiction. Dickens set *A Tale of Two Cities* in 'the best of times, … the worst of times', but I believe that quote describes any time. Good and bad, lightness and darkness, will always coexist, weave together. There is rarely one without the other. But, as Theo would say, there's nothing for it but to embrace every day we get, and to try to leave the world a better place.

*

As always, I extend heartfelt thanks to my editor Sanah Ahmed, my agent Kate Nash, and to everyone at Orion, especially Suzy and Sally. My thanks as well to the two dear Jessicas and to Suzy Vadori. Massive thanks to Chris McKay for patiently answering my questions on historical firearms; I hope I got it right. Thanks to Stephen for his assistance with a plot hole. And shout out to *Bookaholic Bex*, best-ever travel companion to Madeira!

One personal note – a bit grim but I think it must be said – is that this was by far my hardest book to write. When I was a teenager, my father was murdered. That single, horrific, violent act has affected my entire life. There is nothing 'cosy' about an actual murder, but I thought I was emotionally ready to tackle a light-hearted murder mystery; as it turned out, it was intensely difficult, but I'm glad I persevered – and I even managed to weave a few threads of hard-learned lessons into the narrative. So, my thanks to family and friends for their understanding and love as I struggled.

My biggest thanks of all goes to you, my readers. I hope Henrietta and Theo's story sparked a little joy in your life, whether you're facing the best of times or the worst of times – or a mixture of both.

CREDITS

Felicity George and Orion Fiction would like to thank everyone at Orion who worked on the publication of *A Lady's Guide to Murder*.

Editorial
Sanah Ahmed

Copy-editor
Suzanne Clarke

Proofreader
Sally Partington

Contracts
Dan Herron
Ellie Bowker
Oliver Chacón

Audio
Paul Stark
Louise Richardson

Design
Dawn Cooper
Charlotte Abrams-Simpson
Loveday May

Editorial Management
Charlie Panayiotou
Jane Hughes
Bartley Shaw

Finance
Jasdip Nandra
Nick Gibson
Sue Baker

Marketing
Corinne Jean-Jacques

Production
Ruth Sharvell

Sales
Dave Murphy
Esther Waters
Victoria Laws

Rachael Hum
Ellie Kyrke-Smith
Frances Doyle
Georgina Cutler

Operations
Jo Jacobs

Don't miss Felicity George's 'The Gentleman of London' series . .

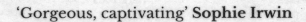

'Gorgeous, captivating' **Sophie Irwin**

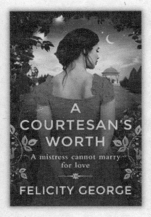

'Evocative romance' **Virginia Heath**